BURDEN OF THE CROWN

BOOK 3 IN THE LAND OF MAGADHA SERIES

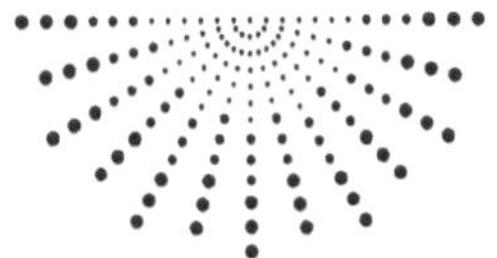

ANNA BUSHI

Library of Congress Control Number: 2022902643

ISBN 978-1-7364103-4-9 (paperback) — ISBN 978-1-7364103-5-6 (hardback)

When you live in the hearts
Of those you love
Remember then
You never die.
- by Rabindranath Tagore

To RJ, who created the beautiful map of Magadha, you will travel in my heart and live in my books.

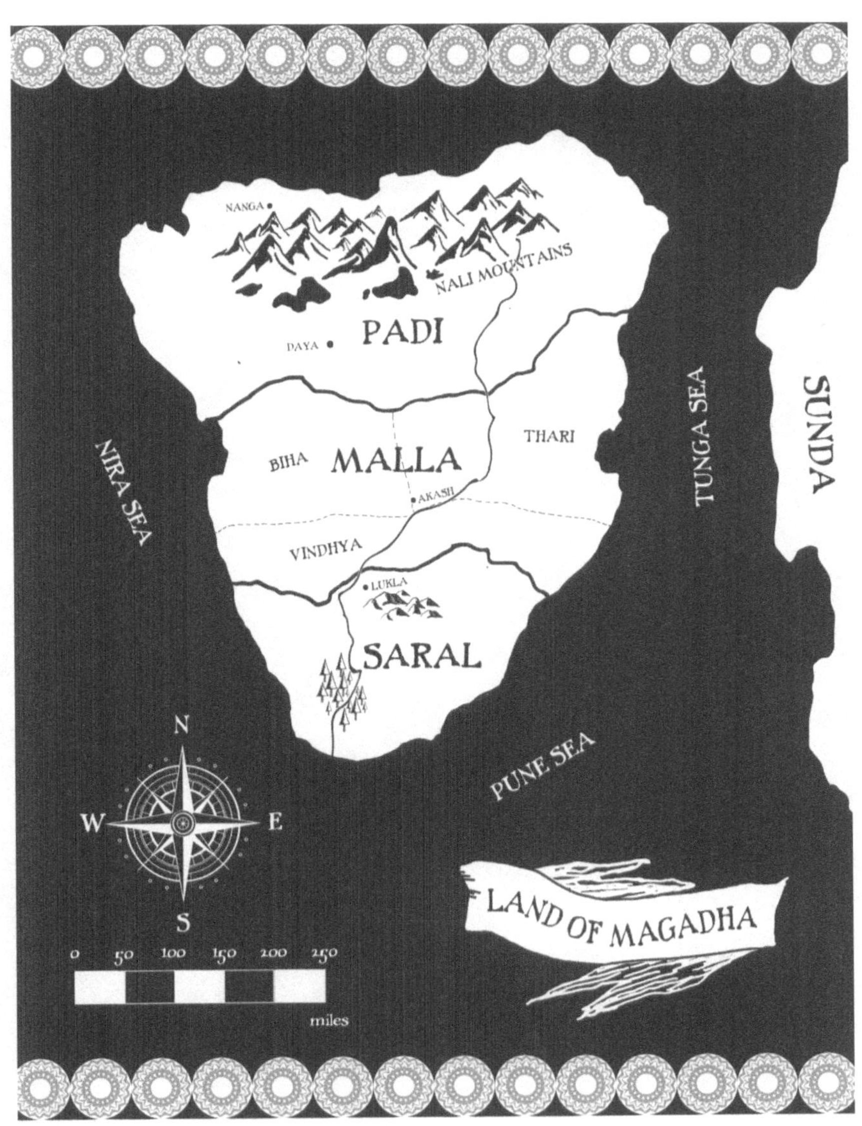

NANGA
NALI MOUNTAINS
PADI
DAYA
BIHA
MALLA
THARI
TUNGA SEA
SUNDA
NIRA SEA
AKASH
VINDHYA
LUKLA
SARAL
PUNE SEA
N
W
E
S
0 50 100 150 200 250
miles
LAND OF MAGADHA

CHARACTERS

MALLA KINGDOM

- King Jay
- Queen Aranya, wife of Jay, princess of Saral
- Sudha, wife of Jay, daughter of Chief Mani Vindhya
- Queen Mother Meera, sister of Jay, mother of King Nala of Padi
- Queen Kayal, daughter of Aranya and Jay, wife of King Nala of Padi
- Princess Heera, daughter of Aranya and Jay
- Prince Vikram, son of Sudha and Jay

Vindhya House

- Chief Mani
- Sudha, daughter of Mani, wife of King Jay
- Darsh, son of Mani, general of Malla northern command
- Dayan, son of Mani, brother of Darsh

- Hasan, cousin of Mani
- Rish, brother of Hasan, cousin of Mani

Biha House

- Chief Navin
- Chief Guard Kapil, cousin of Navin

Thari House

- Chief Giri, general of Malla southern command

* * *

SARAL KINGDOM

- King Vasant
- Queen Priya, wife of Vasant, daughter of Meera
- Prince Chandra, son of Vasant

* * *

PADI KINGDOM

- King Nala
- Queen Kayal, wife of Nala, princess of Malla
- Princess Yamini, daughter of Nala
- Queen Mother Meera, mother of Nala
- Queen Priya, sister of Nala, wife of King Vasant of Padi
- Prince Amar, brother of Nala
- Prince Atul, brother of Nala
- Prince Kanishka, cousin of Nala
- Princess Mala, second cousin of Nala
- Prince Naren, second cousin of Nala

* * *

SUNDA KINGDOM

- King Kanva
- Prince Uday, son of Kanva
- Princess Ratnavali, daughter of Kanva

1

JAY

$\mathcal{S}$alty air wafted through the tiny window and touched my skin like a coarse fabric. The sea crashed against the ship, drowning the faint noise of sailors shouting on the deck above me. Picking up a scroll, I noticed the swirls in the honey-colored table revealed by the morning light. I traced the markings on the wood with my finger, marveling at the craftsmanship of Malla carpenters.

From outside my door came a thud of footsteps and a knock. I glanced up as my son strode in with my nephew on his heels. My son, Vikram, resembled my younger self, captured in a portrait in Akash.

"Father, there are beautiful coral reefs around here, and Atul and I want to take a boat to explore," he said. The waves rocked the vessel gently like I had rocked these boys when they fit in my palm. Vikram swayed on his feet, brimming with energy. He exuded easy confidence that I had not possessed at sixteen.

"Uncle Jay, the Sunda siblings want to join us too," my nephew, Atul, added. Meera had asked me to foster her son seventeen years ago, and I had raised him ever since. Born just a few months apart, my son and my nephew had grown inseparable and caused a lot of trouble with their boyish antics.

I raised my eyebrows. "Atul, Princess Ratnavali is betrothed to your brother. I don't want any mischief before the wedding," I warned them. King of Sunda had also agreed to a marriage alliance between his son, Prince Uday, and my daughter. We were on our way back to Malla with the Sunda royals. I had planned to hold the two weddings in Akash and unite the Magadha and Sunda kingdoms for another generation.

Vikram grinned, assured of his ability to convince me. "Father, we would not dream of it. And her brother will be coming along." His curly hair bounced as his gaze darted between his cousin and me.

Before I could reply, Rish marched in. Water glistened on his short gray hair as his alert eyes scanned the room.

"They want to take a boat to the reef," I told him.

"It is drizzling now. A preamble to a storm headed our way, King Jay. Getting caught in it would not be wise."

Vikram continued to smile while Atul crossed his arms and turned away from Rish. I wondered what caused this hostility I sensed in my nephew toward Rish. Born out of wedlock, we had kept their father-son relationship hidden from Atul. The world only knew him as a Padi prince, though his birth father could never bestow such a title on him. Rish watched his son guardedly, keeping his emotions in check.

"Uncle Rish, we will be back in a short while before the storm crosses our path," Vikram answered readily. Rish glanced at me, signaling his deferral to me on this matter.

"Does Ratnavali know how to swim?" I asked.

"She swims like a fish," said Vikram.

"Or so she claims," Atul added with a wide grin.

The boys were good swimmers, and the storm might yet miss us. I could not deny them this harmless excursion. "Use your head and stay safe," I waved them away, and they departed, talking excitedly.

"I indulge them too much, Meera will say. Not reining them in or disciplining them," I said.

Rish's lips curled up a tiny grain. "I am no expert, my Majesty. Queen Meera raised my daughter along with hers."

"Do you have any matters to discuss with me?" I asked.

Rish pushed his hair back out of habit. He must have cut it short to avoid any likeness to Atul. Though Atul resembled his mother, the boy had grown tall like him, unlike his half-brothers.

"Yes, my Majesty. King Nala wanted to discuss trading Padi wool," he answered. We spent an hour going over them.

"Nala is a tough negotiator," I remarked on his astute demands for using Malla seas to sell Padi carpets. Rish had served as his regent till my nephew came of age.

"He has inherited his mother's qualities and rules with a wisdom beyond his age," he answered. His eyes shone with pride. For Nala or his mother, I couldn't tell.

"I am eating my midday meal with Kanva. Why don't you join us?" I invited him. Rish acquiesced.

Kanva ambled in. The Sunda King, the youngest of us, had aged the most in the past two decades. He took a seat, pushing his chair farther from the table to allow room for his sedentary potbelly. His laborious breathing from his walk to my room matched the sound of the wind outside.

"Uday and Ratnavali have left with the princes on some expedition," he stated. My servant fetched our food, and the aroma of sesame rice filled the air. Our conversation then focused on the weddings set to take place in Akash.

"Vasant has departed Saral to attend the wedding," I said. As my older brother's son, the Malla throne rightfully belonged to Vasant. However, my brother grew up as the Saral prince and never learned the truth about his birth. After his death, Vasant ascended the Saral throne. And I harbored hopes of seeing my son on the Malla throne.

"Queen Meera and her sons are making their way to Akash as well," added Rish. It would be good to see my family gathered in one place. And talk to Meera about my inner turmoil. I wanted to let the past stay buried and crown my only son as the Heir to Malla, a desire that had grown like a wild forest.

"After their marriage, I will head back to Sunda. Uday wanted to spend some time traveling around Malla. He will come back later with his bride," said Kanva.

Later that day, many matters demanded my attention. I had been away for more than a moon month from Akash, and I read Kapil Biha's last scroll to me. Kapil, a childhood friend, and sworn guard, now served as the Chief Guard of Akash. He had cautioned me about an uprising in the kingdom to our west. Rebels appeared to have overthrown the royal family ruling Kashgar. Kapil mentioned that half a dozen boats had landed on Malla shores with Buddhist monks who'd fled this upheaval. The head monk wanted to meet with me to seek refuge in Malla.

The wind blew through the window facing the sea, causing my scrolls to flutter.

"It is picking up," observed Rish, walking in.

Looking up from the parchment, I remarked, "Kings are not faring well."

Rish looked puzzled. "Here in Magadha?"

"No, to our west in Kashgar," I replied.

My guard strode in. "My Majesty, the boats are not back yet," he exclaimed, and our eyes turned toward him.

"The one with the princes?" I asked.

"And Princess Ratnavali," he replied.

A large wave rocked our boat, and thunder pierced the sky. "Find them and haul them in," I ordered.

The guard ran out.

"I will check on them as well," Rish said and left. I lasted in the room till the next big wave.

Dark clouds gathered, and the sea tossed our ships like leaves on a flowing river. Rain pounded the wooden deck. Feet rushed on the slippery floor to furl the sails, faces a blur in the wind and deluge. Men raised their voices to be heard above the din of the roaring waves and thundering skies. I joined Rish on the deck, my wet clothes sticking to my skin.

"Any news?" I asked, peering at the water.

"No, my Majesty," Rish said, not taking his eyes off the sea.

The captain approached us and said, "Three other boats left with them, my Majesty. The sea is turbulent, but my men are good sailors. They would ensure the safety of the princes."

Still, dread filled my heart as I clutched the boat. They were mere boys out on the water in the midst of a storm. A twenty-foot wave rose to pound us. Would their tiny boat handle these peaks and valleys? Lightning struck the sky, splitting it apart. In the blaze, I saw the huge waves rocking our ships.

Rish cursed under his breath as he squinted into the darkness. I stood beside him, two fathers anxious for the safe return of their sons. Why had I agreed to their idiotic expedition?

Deep in my thoughts, I was startled to hear Rish speak. "I have been part of King Nala and Prince Amar's lives since their births, and they welcome me readily. I had hoped to find similar acceptance with Prince Atul." Meera wished for it too. She had felt guilty depriving the boy of his father, though it best served Atul's interest.

Suddenly, men yelled and pointed. Hands lifted lanterns and tried to shed some light into the darkness. A cloud departed, and moonlight shone through. I caught a brief glimpse of a boat.

"Do you see it?" I yelled, running along the deck for a better view. Other footsteps followed, and I arrived at the bow.

"Two boats," someone shouted, and my knuckles clutching the boat turned pale. Four vessels had left earlier. I heard Rish's sharp intake.

"Fools," I heard the captain swear. "It is too choppy for the boats to approach the ships. The waves will smash them. I hope they stay away till the storm passes."

I had fought in many battles with little consideration for my life. My heart had never pounded then as it did on that deck.

"The boats are coming closer," a sailor remarked.

"Maybe someone is hurt," Rish ventured.

The captain heard him. "Drop the ladder, boys," he ordered. He pointed to four men and barked, "Take long ropes with you, swim to the boats, and bring them in slowly."

A man appeared behind me, gasping for breath. Kanva.

"Are they back?" he asked.

"No," I replied.

"Uday and Ratnavali are poor swimmers. They cannot handle

these waves," he wailed, and the cold crept into my limbs. I had raised two imbeciles who believed the Sunda siblings' lies. And I claimed the title of the biggest idiot among them for letting them go before a storm.

"Three boats filled with experienced sailors escorted them, Kanva. They will be safe," I muttered. I wanted to believe it as well.

We waited for what seemed an eternity in the rain that changed from a waterfall to a trickle. A faint light appeared on the horizon, and the wind slowed to a breeze. I caught sight of two boats drawing near with wet rags of bodies. *Vikram and Atul,* my heart whispered.

A commotion erupted as men crowded around the ladder to pull them up. In a haze, I heard the words "hurt" and "missing." Without awareness, I walked toward the noise.

A sailor handed over a body, and Rish rushed forward.

"Atul," he exclaimed and took the limp body into his arms. A faint moaning arose from the boy. He was alive.

Rish staggered, and I steadied him. "Take him to the physician," I ordered, and he clutched his son to his chest and left. My eyes turned to the ladder as Ratnavali appeared in the arms of a sailor. Her father shuffled to her as the sailor gently lowered her. "Father," she exclaimed and hugged Kanva. Sobbing, she said, "Uday is missing." I heard those words as if I stood in a deep well, and she was at the surface.

I eyed the men who rescued Atul and Ratnavali and asked, "Where is Vikram?"

They shook their heads. "His boat capsized, and Prince Vikram and Prince Uday got caught in a current."

"Send men to search for them," I commanded, trying hard to keep the desperation out of my voice. *Find my son.*

2

MEERA

I sat in the chariot, holding my grandchild, Yamini, on my lap. Her long lashes framed her eyes, and she clutched a straw doll dressed in bright clothes in her hands. I told the two-year-old a story about the doll, one I had narrated many times before.

"The doll floated on a cloud looking for a girl to play with. The wind went swish, carrying the doll. A girl spotted the doll with her big bright eyes and called out to it. Upon hearing her, the doll landed with a plop on her lap. They wore matching skirts and swirled around the room." It felt like yesterday when her father, Nala, had sat on my lap. My son had worn the Padi crown for seventeen years, a burden he bore well.

She twirled the figure in her hands and mouthed some of the words she had memorized.

Today, I added a new line to the story.

"The doll and the girl rode on a horse which trotted clip-clop on a road that dipped and rose."

"Clib clob, gamma," she squealed in delight.

A mare appeared alongside us, and Queen Kayal, my niece and daughter-in-law, waved to her daughter. That elicited another squeal.

"Ma, clib clob." The child extended her arms to her mother, wanting to be carried off on the horse.

With a smile that lit her eyes, Kayal gazed at her daughter. She had inherited my brother Jay's eyes. "Stay with grandma," she sang. "I will play with you soon."

"Aunt Meera, there is a storm heading our way. Nala wants us to reach some shelter before we get caught in it. So we will not stop for a while," she said, tucking the end of her lotus-colored sari into her waist.

"We will be fine," I answered. "I have a banana here to feed her if she gets hungry."

Kayal nodded and galloped away. I watched her join Nala in the front. As was tradition, my brother and I had strengthened our blood ties with the marriage of his daughter and my son. Nala had now ruled Padi for longer than his father. He talked to me about the affairs of the kingdom out of habit. He had no real reason to consult me anymore. With his capable queen and a dutiful brother, he governed the land with grit and generosity. I had passed my burden to an able younger generation. A mother's pride surged in my heart at the thought of my children.

We expected to be in Akash in a few days. After Amar's wedding, I looked forward to spending some time in Malla with my youngest son. At the thought of Atul, guilt rose in me like smoke from a block of wet burning wood. Guilt for letting him grow up without his mother and father. Guilt that had caused me to ask Rish to join Jay on his journey to Sunda. Rish was reluctant to go. What did I hope to accomplish by getting them together? Unlike Nala and Amar, who grew up with Rish as a surrogate father, Atul barely knew him because I had kept them apart purposefully all these years. I exhaled slowly.

Rish had been my tree to shelter under in rain, wind, and heat. He had helped raise my boys and trained them in court intrigue and warfare. Like a scorched earth drinking rainwater, I took all he had to offer—his love, loyalty, and protection. He had asked for nothing in return. I knew why I sent him to Sunda. I wanted to bestow on him the love of his son. As if I could make that happen just by getting them together.

Guilt ate at my heart because I had nothing else to offer the man I loved. Rish captured my heart nearly three decades ago. However, I had married another for duty. My kind-hearted husband had cherished me. But fate intervened in the form of my brother-in-law, who murdered his brother.

Yamini sought my attention by pulling my ear, and I returned to the present.

While my mind had wandered, the wind picked up, and the trees swayed side to side. A gentle spring rain reached the earth, and the air burst forth with the fresh smell of soil brimming with life. A faint ancient scent also wafted in the wind, evoking images of the men and animals who had lived and died on this soil.

I reached my hand out in the rain to feel the droplets on my skin. My thin golden bangles slid down my wrist.

"Me too," yelled Yamini, and she stood on my lap to reach out. Her contagious joy spilled over. I loved the rain as a child as well, especially the first one after a dry spell. The parched earth would welcome the downpour, and I would run along the small creeks singing songs. My mother, a wild spirit, had not tamed me. Her death did.

I hoped to travel soon to Saral to visit my daughter, Priya, and my three-year-old grandson, Chandra. Priya had married King Vasant and ruled as his queen. At the thought of touring my mother's lands, anticipation filled my mind with images of coconut trees and paddy fields. I had heard of warm ocean water in Kadal that stretched as far as the eye could see. I was the master of my time now, with no father, brother, husband, or son dependent on me.

A horse turned back and approached us. Amar rode his stallion with ease and turned around just past the chariot.

"Mother, did you notice we have crossed into Malla?" he asked with a wide grin. I stopped wiping my granddaughter's hands and craned my neck, surveying the surroundings. My heart quickened even though the trees around me had not changed much from a mile ago. *Home*, the wind whispered in my ears.

I glanced at my middle son with a matching grin. "I almost missed it," I said. While Nala took after his father and Atul took after me, my middle son blended the two of us. We were headed to Akash for his marriage to Princess Ratnavali of Sunda. A princess he had never met, but he bowed to his brother's and king's wishes.

"Me too. Our queen remarked on it," he said sheepishly. Kayal called this land home as well. The rain dripped down his forehead and alongside his nose.

"What is your brother's plan?" I inquired.

"There is a temple a mile south on this road. We will take shelter there," he said. I nodded.

He continued, "Do you need anything, Mother?"

I shook my head. "No, my son. Don't wait for my chariot. Take shelter from the rain."

"A little rain never hurt me, Mother," he smirked, his lean, boyish frame bending forward as he galloped away.

In a little while, a granite temple loomed to my left. The chariot entered the temple courtyard and halted in front of the main hall. Water rolled down a dozen steps leading inside. Pillars carved with various deities lined the outside of the hall. Nala took his daughter from me and handed the child to her mother. Kayal covered the child in blankets and ran up the steps to take shelter.

Nala extended his hand to me. I had not yet reached the age of needing help to climb down, but I took my son's hand as a gesture of kindness. I smiled at the thought of someone helping Jay off a carriage. At forty-five, my brother still eclipsed many younger men in strength.

"What is it, mother?" Nala asked as we quickened our steps. Raindrops made wet patches on my indigo-colored sari.

"Nothing. Just foolish musing. I imagined someone helping your uncle Jay off a carriage."

He gazed at me with his father's eyes, and his lips curled up a tiny grain. "Or Uncle Rish. You don't need my help either, Mother. I like offering it, though," he said, gently squeezing my hand. My dear boy had grown into a considerate man like his father. A young man handed us some dry cloths, and we wiped our hands and faces. A sudden thought occurred to me. "The storm appears to be headed east. I hope the ships sailing from Sunda escape the eye of the storm."

"Malla has some of the best sailors and shipbuilders. They will be fine," said Amar approaching us.

"Your hair is still wet," I admonished him.

Nala grinned at his younger brother. "Listening to your mother is good training for listening to your future wife."

Amar rolled his eyes and waved for a servant to fetch him a towel.

A commotion outside caught our attention. Nala and Amar strode to the front, and I followed them. One of our supply wagons had rolled on its side.

"I will go help," Amar said, and he ran down the steps.

Nala ordered, "Have everyone take shelter, away from the trees."

I drifted back inside, looking at the sculptures on the pillars and walls. A carving of Goddess Durga seated on a lion caught my attention. The sculptor had chiseled the fine details of the mane remarkably lifelike. I reached my hand up to trace the serene face of the goddess. Her calm face, instead of the usual battle fury, piqued my interest. I strolled to the next pillar when a bright light illuminated my surroundings. Before I could perceive the source, I heard Nala's yell. With my heart dropping to my stomach, I ran to the front. A wagon had caught fire, and chaos ensued.

My eyes searched and found Nala running toward it. Slowly, my gaze traveled to the burning cart, and I found a figure on fire. My heart stopped as I observed Amar staggering back. Someone covered him in a rug and rolled him on the ground, putting out the flames.

My son! A wail left my throat as my feet descended the steps and hastened toward him. Nala reached him first. He scooped his brother up in his arms like a child and carried him to the temple. A tremor ran through my limbs, and I struggled to breathe. As he came closer, color faded from my face when I noticed my son's charred skin. The wind howled, and the world around me disappeared as I ran to my boy.

3

JAY

A turquoise-blue sea glittered in the sun with barely a whisper of wind. The calm Tunga Sea mocked me while a storm raged in my mind. I watched several boats search for Vikram and Uday with increasing despair. The ships stood still with the sails rolled and oars idling. The anchors held them in place, preventing them from moving with the currents. In the stillness, I could hear my heart pounding like a war drum. Men's voices in the boat carried over to me, but I could not decipher them. Seagulls took flight and circled the ships. Scavengers! I wanted to shoot them down with arrows. With effort, I controlled my anger.

My mind wandered into the past. It felt like yesterday when I had taught the three boys how to hold their swords. Vasant, Atul, and Vikram grew up as brothers. In the blink of an eye, the babies crawling under my legs had turned into young men. The four of us riding our horses around Akash was a familiar sight to the city residents. I took them with me to visit noblemen and soldiers. They listened while I held court. I asked for their advice in council meetings.

Vikram, the youngest, ruled the hearts of the court. As prince of Malla, his mother and grandparents granted all his wishes. While I tried to remain impartial, my son tugged my heart in ways the other two did not because I could see myself in him. When I embraced him, I forgot my promise to Meera to consider making Vasant the heir of Malla. A father's heart had refused to deny his son the throne.

A lump formed in my throat as I imagined my son drowning in the storm last night. I uttered a prayer, a new act for me. *Please, gods. Take me if you need royal blood. Spare the boy. Let him live.*

I heard a noise, and Rish materialized beside me.

"How is Atul?" I asked, glancing at him.

He rubbed his eyes. "He is fine. Just minor scrapes and bumps."

We stood silently watching the men dive into the ocean, looking for the other princes.

"Prince Atul wants to talk to you. I will keep watch and come get you if there is any news," he said softly. Rish made sure he used the title of prince for Atul, even in private conversations. It must be his way of erecting a barrier around his heart. A barrier to keep his love for the mother and the truth of the child's parentage hidden from others.

With reluctance, I went to find Atul. Vikram's room stood adjacent to Atul's. I opened the door to peek in. A silk board for a game of dice had been laid out on his table. A silver bowl held long stick dice and several seashells. Atul, Vikram, and Uday spent many hours playing the game where the winner was the first to bring their four men home. I could picture them seated around the table, laughing as they rolled the dice. Exhaling the breath I held, I shut his door quietly.

I knocked on Atul's door and entered. He hauled himself up on his bed when he saw me.

"Any news of Vikram?" he asked, his lips trembling. I pulled a stool close to his bed and sat down.

"They are still looking," I answered. My eyes scanned his face and bare chest. Apart from a few bruises, he appeared fine.

"How are you feeling?"

"Fine, Uncle Jay," he muttered with his eyes downcast.

He drew circles on his thigh with his finger. "It all started brilliantly. The sea beckoned us like a young maiden. She rolled out her emerald carpet and paraded strange sea creatures. We saw a pod of dolphins, and Vikram and I swam to them. They looked very similar to the river dolphins in our Chambal River," he chattered.

As I listened, a bitter thought flashed in my head. Why was he unhurt while my son was missing? I clenched my fist to suppress this vile view. I had raised my nephew from birth, and my blood flowed in him. I should be happy he'd survived.

The boy saw the emotions playing on my face and mistook them for disapproval.

He flinched and took a few shallow breaths. He gazed at me with my sister's eyes. "Uncle Jay, a large wave overturned our boat. Vikram and I surfaced immediately, but we found no sign of Princess Ratnavali and Prince Uday. We swam around in the dark waters. When a flash of lightning struck, I saw the princess erupt, gasping for breath. I swam to her and caught hold of her braid. I held her from behind and yelled to Vikram. He shouted at me to get to a boat while he searched for Uday. With the princess in tow, I swam to the nearest boat. The last thing I remember is helping her onto the craft. Then my head must have struck something because I lost consciousness. When I came to, men were pulling me up the ladder. I left Vikram behind." His hand clutched the blanket tightly, and his chest rose and fell rapidly.

His pain caused a tightening in my stomach. I reached out and squeezed his arm and whispered gently, "This is not your fault, Nephew. You did the right thing by rescuing Ratnavali. And I have not given up hope for Vikram. I taught you both how to swim and rescue others in the water. He will have remembered at least some of my words."

A knock sounded on the door, and I said, "Come in."

The door opened to reveal Ratnavali and her father.

"Princess," Atul exclaimed and reached for his shawl draped on a chair. I stood and passed it to him. He draped it around his shoulders and swung his feet to the ground.

"How are you, Ratnavali?" I asked. She sniffled and wiped her red-rimmed eyes.

Continuing to gaze at Atul, she murmured, "I am fine, thanks to your nephew."

Color rose in the boy's cheek as he stammered, "I j-just did my duty, my lady."

"Any news?" Kanva queried, and I moved toward him.

Shaking my head, I replied, "Nothing yet."

"I wanted to thank you," said the princess as she approached Atul.

"No need, my lady. You are betrothed to my brother, and I am charged with protecting you," he answered clearly. The boy had sense.

"Kanva, I am headed back to the deck. Do you want to join me?"

He nodded, and we strolled together. "Ratnavali and Uday are close. She is blaming herself for her brother's loss," said Kanva.

"Atul and Vikram are closer than most brothers," I answered. "He is distraught as well. I hope Vikram kept his senses and swam to safety with Uday."

"He is my heir," Kanva murmured. I wanted to make Vikram mine. Was I being punished for courting the throne for my son?

"We will find them," I assured him while burying my anguish.

I jolted my head at the sound of approaching footsteps. Rish spotted me and said, "They found something." I broke into a run and emerged onto the deck.

"This way," Rish guided me, and I followed him. Kanva fell behind, and I did not bother waiting for him. He would catch up soon enough.

Men parted the way for Rish and me. We skidded to a halt near the captain. He barked orders at his men, and my eyes swept the water. I saw three boats clustered together. In one, two sailors were hauling a fishing net. A thousand knives plunged into my heart as I held my breath. Questions swirled in my head, but I did not want answers for them. My wife, Sudha's face swam into focus, and her words rang in my head. "Keep our son safe, my lord."

I gripped the hilt of my sword tightly. Resisting the urge to shut my eyes, I watched the net holding a large dark object rise out of the water. Men around me spoke, but nothing penetrated my fog. After an eternity, the boats rowed toward the ship. Wordless noises reached my ears as ladders dropped.

One of the boats was attached to a harness, and two large men pulled it up. When the boat reached the top, they grabbed it and lowered it onto the deck. A boulder crushed my chest as I watched two men take a covered object from inside and lay it gently on the deck floor. Kanva gasped as we approached the human-shaped body. Someone had hastily covered the corpse in a cloth from the boat, and I ordered, "Reveal the face."

Rish dropped to his knees and gently unraveled the sheet. Sweat trickled down my back as I waited in misery. A bloated face with many abrasions came into view. The smell of seaweed and dead fish rose into the air. Despite the wrinkled skin, I recognized the boy.

"My son," screamed Kanva and tumbled next to him. I staggered back a few steps, breathing in large gulps of air.

Kanva cradled the head on his lap, and tears rolled down his cheek. A loud howl preceded Ratnavali as she flew in. Slumping beside her father, she sobbed.

My eyes sought the men who recovered his body. Beckoning them, I walked a few paces away. Atul and Rish joined me as I questioned them.

"What happened? Tell me all."

One spoke solemnly. "We had several boats search the area, and one of the divers found him. His body was facing the bottom with his back to us. We used a fishing net to haul him up."

"Any sign of Prince Vikram?" asked Atul.

The man shook his head. I glanced at the grieving father and said, "Continue the search for him."

Later that evening, I went to find Kanva. In a tiny room with no windows, the embalmed remains of Prince Uday rested on a dark wooden bench, and Kanva sat next to it, muttering. A lone lantern flickered in a corner.

"Kanva, I am sorry," I said and squeezed his shoulder.

He looked up at me with red eyes. "Did they find Vikram?"

"No," I said, my breath caught in my throat. "Not yet."

"My first wife was a lovely girl. She was weak after bearing Uday.

My physician advised against her carrying more babies. She still relented to my needs and died giving birth to Ratnavali."

I listened to his tale, understanding his guilt. After Vikram was born, our physician warned us any more childbirths would be fatal to Sudha. I had reluctantly refrained from our marriage bed since.

"I have two boys from my second marriage. Mere babies still. Uday was an ideal prince and loved by our people. I don't know if I have it in me to groom another prince," he wailed, his shoulders rocking in grief.

"You are the king, Kanva. You will find a way to carry on," I said. *Would I have the strength to follow my own advice if they find Vikram in the same condition?*

"I have no heart to travel to Malla. I want to board my ship and sail back to Sunda," he said, taking a deep breath.

"Kanva, we are closer to Malla. The wedding of Ratnavali and Amar must go on." I left unsaid that it would be better to cremate his son in Malla rather than take a rotting corpse back to Sunda. No father had the heart to hear that.

"This is an ill omen, Jay," he remarked. "It is better to halt the wedding."

Superstition roiled the royal families. Because of Heera's engagement to Uday, some would blame my daughter's ill luck for Uday's death. My late stepmother would have combed Heera's horoscope to find remedies to fix her misfortune.

"Kanva, we prepare ourselves and our sons for both life and death from the day of their births. I see no reason to stop the wedding." I clung to these words like a shield.

The next day, I sent for the captain.

"My king, our men have searched every foot of the sea for Prince Vikram. There is no sign of him."

I clenched my fist and asked, "Do you have any hope of finding him?"

"My Majesty," he said softly, "if he were alive, we would have found him by now."

"If he drowned?" I whispered, a lump blocking my throat.

"If he drowned, currents might carry his body for miles. He may wash up on Magadha shores eventually. If a fisherman recovers him, they can identify him by his jewels." I wanted to throttle his throat, but I resisted. He spoke the truth and did not deserve punishment for that.

I dismissed him and wandered to the deck. Boats still crisscrossed the sea, divers plunging in to search for Vikram. As the sun sank, all hope of finding him alive drained.

I made my way to the captain. "Set sail for Malla," I ordered and went to my room. The ship came alive, and I heard the anchors heaving up. Free at last, she rocked gently in the wind. I shut the door and collapsed on the floor. Sobs shook me as I mourned the loss of my only son.

4

MEERA

ala carried his brother in his arms while ordering the men to create a makeshift room. Two stretched a faded cotton fabric across the pillars, and another spread a thick cotton blanket on the floor. Amar moaned in pain, and my heart squeezed tighter with each lament. Nala set him down gently on the blanket, and our physician and his apprentices removed his charred clothes and blackened jewels.

Nala appeared next to me and took my elbow. "Mother—"

I interrupted him, "I am not leaving my son."

A servant brought a pot of boiling water, and the physician dipped a cloth in it and gently rubbed the withered skin and tissue. As Amar grunted in agony, I began singing his favorite song as a child, of a boy flying beside an eagle. Tears brimmed in my eyes, and Nala wrapped his arm around my shoulders.

Cold water replaced the warm water treatment. The burnt smell had dissipated, and instead, the odor of human sweat permeated. As darkness descended around us, Nala directed his men to place lanterns on the floor. In the flickering light, Amar's skin looked like a boiling stew with erupting bubbles.

After many hours, the healer wrapped him in an ointment of

beeswax, sandalwood, and herbs. He gave him a drink of herbs that lulled him to sleep.

The doctor stood up, wiping his hands. He approached us and said, "No danger to his life."

A sob escaped me, and I collapsed against Nala. My son held me tightly and thanked the man for saving his brother.

The physician continued, "No damage to any vital organs. Most of his scars will fade, but some will remain forever." My beautiful boy was scarred for life. My heart tore into pieces on hearing that. I straightened slowly and wiped my eyes with my fist.

The physician paused and rubbed his forehead before adding, "The fire struck close to him and burnt his right upper side, especially his face. His eyes are swollen now. I have wrapped them in an herb mixture to reduce the inflammation."

My throat constricted like a hot iron held in a vice. We were headed to his wedding, and the groom lay disfigured on the floor. I cursed the cruelty of fate. A voice whispered in my mind that I deserved this for having murdered the man who bore my son's name. *No,* I pleaded with any listening god. *Please don't punish my children for my past mistakes.*

Others dispersed, leaving me alone with Amar. I sat down on the floor beside him and clasped his left hand. I shut my eyes and prayed to Goddess Durga to restore him to full health. A faint smell of sandalwood from the ointment hung in the room.

I sensed footsteps coming near and opened my eyes. Nala stared at his brother and swallowed a few times.

"What caused the wagon fire?" I asked my son. With the rain, it seemed strange for it to start.

"I had the same question, Mother. I have tasked my men to find out. The cart held a few barrels of our cooking oil, causing it to spread quickly."

He then whispered, "I will watch him, Mother. Please go and eat something. Kayal is waiting for you."

A sigh escaped me. I stood up slowly, grasping the hand Nala held out. I wandered into the temple and found Kayal sitting on some stone steps. Two carved lions on either side of the steps guarded the deity hidden behind closed doors. She handed me a leaf plate with some rice. I collapsed beside her and took the food.

"How is he?"

"He will live," I said with no joy. I had sent my father, brother, and husband to war, not knowing if they would return. But this was no battlefield. Did nature cause this cruel act when all he'd wanted to do was help?

We were supposed to be heading to my son's wedding. Rage at my son's trauma coursed through me like a colony of bats flying into the night. My hands kneaded the rice into balls to subside my fury. As the anger seeped out, anguish surged like floodwaters.

My niece reached out and squeezed my arm. "Amar will be back on his horse soon."

"Princess Ratnavali is coming to wed an unsullied young man. What will she say when faced with his scalded skin?" I worried.

"What is there to say, Aunt Meera? She is betrothed to him. If this had occurred after the wedding, what would she have done?" argued Kayal. In the faint light emanating from an oil lamp hung from the ceiling, her eyes sparkled with intensity. My brother Jay had trained my niece in warfare. She had inherited his courage and her mother's forthrightness. "Besides, a scar or two adds to the beauty of a man's face, Aunt Meera."

I mulled over what she said. A part of me wanted to make sure my boy's betrothed did not resent the match. We ate in silence. I did not taste the morsel I put in my mouth. After a few swallows, I gave up and headed to wash my hands in the courtyard. Moonlight cascaded around us, and I saw the temple elephant swaying gently. His huge body merged with the dark shadows surrounding him while his tusks glowed like slivers of the moon. I held my leaf plate to him, and he reached with his trunk to grab it. I rubbed his side and then rinsed my hands in the water drawn from a well.

On a night like this, almost three decades ago, I plotted with Madhavi to get rid of my fiancé, Prince Amar. During the act, she died, releasing me from Amar's chains. Her death weighed on my mind as I ambled back to my son, named after his uncle. I spent the rest of the night watching over him, my mind dwelling on the past. Just as the roosters got ready to welcome the dawn, I fell asleep dreaming of her.

Madhavi, clad in a sari the color of an elephant, approached me with her hips swaying side to side to the sound of her anklet bells. "You forgot me all these years, Princess Meera," she accused me as her dangling earrings swung in agreement. "No, I never did. I took care of your family and the other dancers," I said, defending my deeds.

"Mother," a voice reached my mind, still suspended in a dream. A gentle tap on my shoulder followed. I opened my eyes and shut them immediately in the bright light flooding the room. I rubbed my face and sat up slowly.

"Are you okay, Mother?" Nala inquired. He kneeled beside me on one leg. I gazed at him and nodded.

"You were muttering about Madhavi," he persisted with a frown. "Who is she?"

"A ghost from my childhood," I mumbled and turned toward Amar. The boy slept with his hand curled into a fist. His raw skin looked grisly in the morning light. My throat constricted at this sight.

"The physician was here earlier to check on him," Nala said. He searched my face with the astute eyes of his father. "I read a poem in one of Father's books. About a man unable to let go of the ghosts of his past. Even though it slowly turned him mad."

I smiled at my son. "At my age, the ghosts have deep roots that reach all corners of my mind. It is impossible to uproot them. Though, some might affirm they have already turned me mad."

He chuckled. "Not anyone that knows you well."

A soldier approached us hurriedly. "My Majesty, we found an arrow tip in the ashes."

Nala stood up. "In the wagon that burned yesterday?"

"Yes, my Majesty. It is not one of our weapons."

Nala and I exchanged glances. Did someone set the fire deliberately? Why?

Another man rushed in with a mangled object. "This is the wheel hub from the wagon," he said, holding it up. There was a metal arrowhead embedded in it. I rose to my feet to view it better.

Nala reached in and pulled it out. "Secure the perimeter. Search the surroundings for any signs of men hiding," he ordered, his brows furrowed in concentration.

Once we were alone, I voiced my fear. "Two arrows. One to overturn the wagon. Second to set it on fire. Like a hunter waiting for its prey, someone waited for the right moment." I did not understand the motivation for this.

Nala nodded, still inspecting the object in his hand. "Why did they want to hurt Amar?"

"I don't know," I said, dread gripping me. "Your brother cannot travel for many days. What do you plan to do?"

He looked up and touched my arm. "Mother, I will send a messenger to Akash asking for an escort. I will stay here with Amar. I intend to send some of our men with Kayal and Yamini to Akash. Please go with them."

"No, my son. My place is beside your brother. As our king, your safety is of utmost importance. Accompany your family to Akash."

He relented, "I will leave men to protect you, Mother." He left to set the plan in motion.

I wandered to the courtyard. My maid tumbled next to me.

"Kantha," I gasped and grasped her hand.

"My lady, I arrived late last night in the supply wagon. While he fed us rice, the cook told me what had happened. My heart nearly stopped on hearing his tale. I have been anxiously waiting to see you and Prince Amar," she rushed on, her emotions playing on her lined face.

She had helped me raise my children, and now I clung to her like a child myself.

She squeezed my arm gently as her eyes welled up. "Queen Meera, please take me to the prince."

When we approached the boy, I halted, my heart stuck in my throat. She moved toward him and sat on the floor. Her fingers hovered in the air, looking for an unburnt part of my son to touch.

They landed on his wrist, and she stroked it lightly. Slowly, I trudged forward and dropped beside her. I leaned my head on her aging shoulder and her arm wrapped around me.

"He will be fine, my lady," she whispered, rubbing my back. Tears slid down her chin and landed on her lap. "He will be fine."

Apart from brief rests that day, I remained with Amar. The physician had given him an herb mixture to sleep through the pain. I eyed his chest as it rose and fell and considered who plotted this fire. Did someone not want him to marry Princess Ratnavali?

Around midday, my granddaughter pulled me away to show me a deer with her fawn. While we watched the baby following its mother on unsteady legs, I heard approaching steps.

"Amar is awake, Aunt Meera," Kayal said urgently. I followed her rapidly, my granddaughter in tow.

I paused at the threshold of the makeshift room. My son rested flat on the blanket with his eyes still wrapped tightly. On hearing our footsteps, he turned his head toward us. I moved forward and sat beside him.

"Mother," he whispered.

I took his hand in mine. "I am here, Son," I said. Tears glistened in my eyes.

"Amar," said Nala as he charged in. He dropped to the floor beside me. He'd brought the physician with him.

"How are you feeling?" he asked his brother.

"Like I am on fire," Amar grunted.

"As your body heals, the pain will disappear," the physician said while he checked his patient.

"Why are my eyes covered?" asked Amar.

"They were swollen from the heat. I have applied a preparation to reduce the inflammation. I will remove the bandage soon," the healer answered. After completing his examination, he stated, "Prince Amar is making good progress. I will be back in the evening to change his wrapping."

Sometime later, Nala took me aside. "We have secured the area. I will leave sufficient guards to protect you and Amar. Once I reach Akash, I will send additional men to travel with you."

I touched his arm lightly. "Once you arrive, talk to Kapil Biha, Jay's Chief Guard. He is also the Malla spymaster and can help us find the men behind this."

The next day, I watched Nala depart from the temple steps. The horses led the way at the front, and the supply carts pulled by oxen followed. Soon the temple emptied, leaving only a few of us behind.

My days merged as I watched my son heal. Some parts of him appeared almost normal, like sunburnt skin. On other regions, scabs had formed. His reddish blistered skin peeled away, and new skin grew in its place. One morning, as the sun's rays swept in, the physician finally removed the cloth around his face. His singed eyebrows came into view first. Then his scalded eyelids appeared. My stomach tightened in fear as I gazed at the reddish scars around the uncovered area.

Amar opened his eyes slowly. The swelling had rendered his eyes as only slits. He wailed, "I cannot see."

5

JAY

I sighted the light emitting from the top of a Shiva temple as we approached the Malla shore. A shallow basin atop the shrine held the fire. A family, who lived nearby, lit it every night to warn the ships off the rocks. This beam, though, appeared to beckon me closer. Her long bright fingers faintly illuminated the slippery rocks. *I am hungry*, she called out to me. *Come satiate me*, she courted me. I imagined the ship heading to the sharp rocks and crashing into them—breaking into pieces—dissolving my hurt and pain.

"King Jay," my guard whispered and pulled me back. I realized I had leaned over the railing on my toes. I muttered something to him and wandered to my room. Like sweat coating my skin, pain coated my mind. What deeds in my past lives had caused me to lose my son? I had held his hand when he took his first steps. He had sat on my lap while I told him tales of the great Malla kings. His face swam into my mind and drowned me in a current of torment. Far above me, there was a world filled with happiness, laughter, and warmth. But where I lived, anguish thundered against me like the ocean surf hitting the rocks. I had nowhere to hide from it.

I clenched my fist and called my servant. "Find me some arrack to drink," I said.

He stared at me with his mouth open. "Arrack, my Majesty?"

"Yes," I whispered and dropped onto my bed. I closed my eyes shut. As if that would prevent images of my boy from scouring my heart.

My servant walked in with a pot. "Our cook had a stash. Made from sugarcane. My Majesty, this is unusual—"

I interrupted him. "Leave it here, and don't disturb me." He slunk away.

I poured a cup and stared at the liquid. My father had advised against drinking because it caused many to lose control of their actions. While I partook on occasion with my men to celebrate our battle victories, I otherwise had followed his advice.

I gulped the entire cup and set it down. Today, I wanted to lose control. Today, I wanted to forget.

In a distant world, a voice called out in dismay. I swung between darkness and nightmare. A cold hand touched my shoulder. I shuddered and threw up the contents of my stomach. I was aware of murmuring around me. A rough hand wiped my face, and I longed for the gentle touch of Aranya. As awareness crept in, so did the raw emotional pain. I tried to pull my mind away from it, but my head throbbed from the effort. I heaved once more, and someone held my head. Like waves crashing on the shore, hurt pummeled me. I allowed my body to be cleaned and focused on steadying my breath. A cup touched my lips, and I drank deeply. My thirst quenched, I opened my eyes and cringed at the flood of light. Slowly shapes took the form of men. My servant cleaned the floor while Rish frowned at me.

Noises on the deck above penetrated my haze. Following my gaze, Rish said, "We have made landfall."

I nodded and stopped abruptly when the action caused a sharp stinging behind my eyes. Rish murmured something to my servant. He departed and came back with a hot liquid. He handed it to me carefully. A strong smell of ginger and black pepper floated on the steam. I grasped the cup with both my hands and took a few sips. The liquid burned my throat on its passage down. Then it dulled my throbbing head.

Suddenly, I realized I was alone with Rish. I sighed and looked at him. His eyes reflected empathy and understanding. "Did you ever get drunk?" I asked.

He looked through my window and answered, "Not in many decades, my Majesty. Not since I joined Queen Meera's guard." A drunken guard would be useless. A drunken king, more so. "I understand the desire to obliterate some memories," he added, glancing at me.

Foolish errand, I thought. Vikram's young face remained etched in my memory, haunting me. "Mount a search for my son," I ordered and dismissed him. I wanted to return at least the boy's remains to his mother.

As the sun shone overhead, I stood on a small seacliff watching the boats sailing along the shoreline. From my vantage, they appeared like lanterns floating on temple ponds. This port had a natural deep harbor, and the shale covered the tiny beach. Against the dark background of these rocks, a body would be easy to spot from a vessel. My insides twisted, imagining the half-decomposed body of Vikram. I scanned the ground below, my heart thudding like the sound of hooves. Two fishermen repaired their nets, and another covered a hole in his boat. A few of my men surveyed the land on foot.

A shout erupted from one of the boats. I leaned forward to watch the crafts row toward a small bay. One boat reached the shore first. A man jumped from it and walked purposefully. After a few feet, he stooped down and picked up something. Frustration mounted in me at being too far to see the object. Then fear replaced it.

I heard a noise and saw my nephew, Atul, climbing up. "Uncle Jay," he greeted me. A gentle wind rustled his hair. The boy had made a full recovery since the storm.

I pointed to the bay. "They found something," I said, fighting to keep my tremors down.

He gasped and leaned forward. "Bones," he choked out as he stretched his neck to view them.

The tiny hope I held was extinguished at his word. Anger and terror churned my insides. Rage surged like an arrow looking for its mark. My gaze fell on the young man beside me. He left my son to drown in the cold dark sea. A sudden urge to push him down the cliffs took hold of me. I stepped back in fear. The boy was my sister's son and my blood. However, the monster unleashed in me did not listen to reason. It thirsted for vengeance. I shut my eyes and mind to it and howled, "Go find out."

I heard his footsteps as he leaped over the rocks. I clenched my fist to control my trembling. Gradually, I opened my eyes. A crowd had clustered below. Taking a deep breath, I climbed down. A mist of saltwater hung in the air. Rish stood at the bottom.

When he saw me, he shook his head. "That is not him. The bones were old." Did he mean they belonged to an old man? Or had they been on the shores for a long time? It did not matter. Nothing mattered anymore.

His eyes, full of pity, pierced me. I did not want his pity. Fury unfurled in me like a serpent. His son lived while mine had perished. I spun away to avoid lashing out at him.

"My Majesty," he began sympathetically.

I cut him off. "Take Atul, King Kanva, and Princess Ratnavali, and head to Akash."

He cleared his throat. Then, I heard no sound from him for a long moment. Whatever he wanted to say remained unsaid. He strode away to carry out my command.

I strolled along the water. The sound of the waves matched the waves of despair pounding my heart. My steps faltered as I came upon a large dead fish nestled among the rocks with flies buzzing around it. A stinking rotten smell assaulted my nostrils. My stomach heaved as I imagined my son washed up along the shore.

"Uncle Jay," Atul interrupted my crushing thoughts. A sigh escaped me. I had imagined Rish and Atul far away from me to elude my wrath. He continued, "Rish can take King Kanva and Princess Ratnavali to Akash. I want to help with the search." Even in my muddled state, I observed the lack of any title for Rish. I had no time or patience for this.

"No," I said coldly.

"Uncle Jay," he persisted. "I don't want to travel—"

"No," I snapped. "Is it too much to ask you to obey a direct command? Leave with Rish to Akash. Ensure the safety of the Sunda royals."

His face reddened at my words. My eyes softened at his distress. The poor boy had grown up with Vikram. He was likely suffering a loss as devastating as mine.

"Atul, I have lost my son. I want no harm to come to you," I said quietly. *Especially not from me.*

Tears glistened in his eyes, and he blinked them away. He nodded rapidly and departed.

For the next few days, I haunted the coast like a ghost while my men scoured the sea. A noise caught my attention, and I turned toward the sound. The sky and the sea had merged into one gray mass. The air hung heavy with mist, and two boats rowed toward the shore with the men on them waving frantically. I hurried toward them as the vessels slid on the coarse sand. One of the sailors hopped from the boat and held out something in his palm. It glinted faintly in the light that escaped the clouds. My feet slowed down with my breath stuck in my throat. I had faced death callously over the years, but this scared me.

"We found this jewel on the seafloor," the man said to his audience. I reached him and stretched my palm. He dropped the gold chain with a pendant into it. As my heart thudded, I brought it closer to my face to inspect.

"Did you find anything else?" someone asked.

"No. We dived in the water and swam several yards in circles but found nothing else."

The Vindhya pendant sparkled in my palm. I remembered when Sudha clasped the chain around our son's neck. I traced the gold jewel absently. Gulls were making a big racket above me. "It is his," I whispered. Silence descended around me, even the birds growing quiet. "Where is my son?" I asked, hiding my gloom.

"My Majesty, the ocean is vast—" started one, but he withered under my glance.

"A sea creature could have brought the necklace to our shores. We can continue the search at dawn," said my captain.

As I clutched the ornament to my chest, the truth stared at me, waiting for acceptance. "No need. Tomorrow we head to Akash," I said. I felt as if I could hear the ocean calling out to me. It said, *Your son is dead*. Grief settled in my stomach. I wandered away from the crowd toward my tent. A hole the size of my fist gaped open in my heart. Tomorrow I would become the king again. Today I wanted to remain a father and mourn my son. I roughly wiped the tears that ran down my cheeks.

6

MEERA

I watched as Amar weaved his way to the chariot, his guard
hovering nearby. His exposed skin appeared raw and
tender. A sharp pain spread in my chest at the disfigurement of my
handsome boy. I observed his clenched fists hanging by his sides and
knew the effort it took him to keep an erect posture. He needed more
time to recover, but we decided to head to Akash instead of lingering
here. He would receive better care there. And I hoped the company of
his brothers might cheer him up. My presence just irritated him. I
could not help but rejoice in his recovery while he mourned what he
had lost forever.

When he reached the chariot, he hesitated a moment and then
climbed in. He had regained limited use of his vision. He could see
about a foot in front of him. *Death would be better than this*, he had
lamented. *No*, my mother's heart had screamed.

I waited for him to settle in, then approached the carriage. A light
wind rustled my sari. The smell of the honey and sandalwood used to
treat his burns emanated from my son. I ascended to my seat, and our
small procession snaked its way through the fields. Amar shifted restlessly, trying to find a place of comfort. The sun crept in, warming our
legs.

He sighed suddenly. "I cannot marry Princess Ratnavali."

I gazed at his face marred by the fire. "You cannot be the one to break off your betrothal."

He uttered a curse.

"Amar," I admonished him.

"You want to place her in the awkward position of rejecting me. And what about me? Do I bear the humiliation of her rejection with a smile?" he growled.

"She will not reject you. You are still a Padi prince and brother to the king," I argued. My mind oscillated between giving the girl a chance to refuse his hands and compelling her to marry him. My thoughts wandered to my own engagement to the prince of Padi, the man my son was named after. Amar turned out to be a monster, and I had him murdered to escape his clutch. I shuddered to imagine Ratnavali poisoning my son if she resented him for a forced marriage.

"The king of Sunda agreed to the union because he wanted me to lead his armies in battle. Help him fend off invaders. How do I do that being blind?" he said, raising his voice. "I am of no use to Nala either."

"There is more to being a prince than fighting in battles," I muttered. I had ruled Padi for many years without ever setting foot on a battlefield.

He scoffed at my words.

"Amar, someone set you on fire. They wanted to kill you. You cannot allow them to win by losing hope."

"Sometimes, I wish they had succeeded in assassinating me."

I remained silent, my stomach in knots at his hurt feelings. I wished I had lost my sight instead of him. What use had I for it beyond gazing at my children and grandchildren?

Time passed slowly in the confines of the carriage, and I drifted off to sleep. A bump on the road rattled the chariot and woke me from my slumber. I stretched my arms and scanned the surroundings. The limestone wall of the Akash city forts gleamed in the sun, and a lump rose in my throat at the familiar sight of my childhood home. Palaces and temples came into view as we neared the gates.

"We are here," I said, touching my son's shoulder. He turned toward the light outside and stared for a moment. He then kicked the carriage vehemently. As the chariot vibrated, I wound an end of my sari around my finger. *Time would heal his wound*, I consoled myself.

The horses stopped at the entrance to the king's palace. Nala and Atul ran down the steps to greet us. I glanced at my youngest son with emotions surging through me like a flash flood. I had not seen the boy in almost a year, and he had grown taller than his brothers.

He reached us first. "Amar," he exclaimed and grasped his brother's hand.

"Atul," my son said and stepped down. The brothers embraced while tears stung my eyes.

"Careful," muttered Amar as he disentangled from Atul's clasp.

Nala touched the back of his brother's head gently. The one unharmed part of him. "You look better than when I last saw you."

Amar grunted in response.

"Can you see me?" Nala persisted.

"If your nose touches mine," Amar said.

"You will be able to glimpse Ratnavali when you kiss her then," Nala teased his brother.

Amar drew his lips into a thin line to express his displeasure.

I descended, and the brothers spun to face me. My youngest, named after my husband, who had claimed him as his son, approached me and touched my feet. I folded the boy into my arms and held him tightly. The top of my head only reached his chin now. He took after his birth father in height. After a few moments, I let him go, and my eyes scanned the entrance for Rish. He did not appear among the few gathered. Neither did my brother or nephew, Vikram. I found this strange, as Atul and Vikram had grown inseparable.

"Where is Vikram? Is your Uncle Jay in the city?" I asked. I noticed the dark circles under Atul's eyes as he flinched at my questions.

"Mother, let us retire to your chamber, and we can discuss it there," said Nala. A knot of worry formed in my throat on hearing his grave tone. I allowed him to guide me inside.

Sunlight streamed in through two large windows and illuminated the entirety of the sitting room. Atul shut the door as I walked to an ornately carved bench. Once seated, I watched my sons nervously. Nala stood near me, and Amar wobbled in slowly. Atul strode to the window and glanced outside. My scalp prickled with dread.

"Atul," Nala prompted.

Atul turned inside, and his eyes darted between us. A dark cloud hung over his face, and my heart lurched.

"A storm charged us in the middle of the Tunga Sea. Vikram and I were on a small boat with the Sunda royal siblings. Our sailors rescued Ratnavali and me. But Prince Uday perished, and we suspect Vikram met the same fate," he moaned.

I did not register his words.

"Vikram is dead?" Amar asked in disbelief, forgetting his own misfortune.

Atul covered his face with his hands, his shoulders rocking. I flew to his side and embraced him. He sobbed into my shoulders as I rubbed his back. Slowly, as his words sunk in, my heart despaired for my brother. How was Jay coping with this loss? I needed to see him and provide what comfort I could.

"Where is Uncle Jay?" I asked.

"He is on his way home after a futile search effort along the Malla shores," Nala answered.

"Is Rish with him?" I asked. It had been two months since I last saw him. I missed his steady presence by my side, especially in light of these tragedies. I felt Atul tense at the mention of his name. I wondered why.

"Uncle Rish left to see his daughter," Nala replied. It seemed strange that Rish would leave without seeing me. Especially if he knew about Amar's accident, but I could not worry about that now. I had bigger things to take care of.

"It is good Rish left before you arrived," stated Atul.

"W-why?" I stammered. I noticed he had called him Rish in a sign of disrespect. While Rish was a father figure to my older two sons, he had remained a stranger to his offspring. My hopes of seeing them grow closer on their trip to Sunda crumbled.

Color crept up Atul's face. "Mother, you must have heard the rumors about you and Rish. He should not be seen with you."

I gasped. Rumors had swirled about Rish and me for decades. I had gone to Padi as a young bride of nineteen. He had accompanied me as my guard. I loved Rish, but I had not married him. Instead, I married the then king-in-waiting, Prince Atul. I had come to love my husband and did my queenly duties faithfully. Except for the boy standing in front of me, my behavior was beyond blemish. And none dared to mention rumors in front of Jay or me. This foolish child had listened to tales without crushing them. Did he believe them? My skin crawled at the thought.

Nala admonished his brother, "Atul, are you forgetting you are addressing our mother?"

"No. I am not blind either," he said quietly.

"Unlike your brother," Amar muttered.

"Enough," said Nala. "Our father appointed Uncle Rish as my regent before his death, and he has served me well. I will not hear you speak ill of him or our mother. Apologize," he ordered.

Atul stared at the ground and pressed his lips together. Without looking at me, he said, "There is nothing to apologize for. I only spoke the truth." I noticed the hard edge to his voice. And the cold anger emanating from him hit me like waves on a shore.

Without waiting for my response, he stormed from the room. Tears gathered in my eyes as I felt like an elephant's trunk squeezed my insides. Rish had tried to do the right thing even when I made it hard for him or led him on a path strewn with trouble. To hear my son disparage our relationship tormented me.

7

JAY

The palaces, towers, and temples loomed on the horizon, and the sight of Akash gave me no pleasure. I brought the news of my son's death to his mother. A strange feeling spread throughout my limbs. Dread. I dreaded seeing my wife and witnessing her despair. I had faced enemies on a battlefield with more courage than now. Hope had fled me too.

In the distance, a dust cloud loomed. It slowly moved toward us. In the front, Kapil Biha appeared on a brown mare. He served as my Chief Guard now, but he was a childhood friend who grew up with me. He had served as my shield in many battles, protecting my life from enemy swords and arrows. He pulled his horse to a stop in front of me.

"King Jay," he said solemnly. We rode forward alone, with others falling behind at a sign from Kapil.

"King Kanva and Princess Ratnavali arrived safely," he stated while his eyes scanned my face.

"Hmm," I said, my mind far away.

"You look haunted," he murmured. I glanced at him. He swallowed and said, "I am sorry, Jay. Sorry I was not with you—"

"It would not have made any difference," I interrupted him. Nothing mattered anymore. Didn't he understand that?

"I may not have helped with the search. I might have helped you," Kapil said softly.

"What? Would you have held my hands while I cried?" I mocked him. I did not want his pity or his help.

"If that is what you needed, yes. Or hold your head while you throw up. Or stop you from getting drunk—"

"My only son is dead," I erupted. I clenched the hilt of my sword. "He is dead, and holding my head or hand will not bring him back." As head of my guards and my spies, Kapil knew almost everything that happened in Malla. It was no surprise that the tale of my drunken stupor reached him before I did.

"I know how that feels, my Majesty," he said, his eyes piercing me like a dagger. Curse it. I had forgotten he had lost his son in a skirmish with bandits two years ago.

We did not speak for some time. As we neared the palace gates, I asked, "How do you fill the vast emptiness in your heart?" The hole in mine had grown into a mountain.

"You can only shrink it gradually. It never goes away. I spent hours in the training yard, letting physical fatigue mask my pain. You helped me too."

"I did? How?"

A smile spread on his face. "A month after my son had perished, you came to me. You said you needed me. Those simple words spurned me out of my slump. You gave me a purpose. I don't need to tell you that Malla needs you now."

I remembered his anguished face then. I could not bear it at the time and told him selfishly that I needed his help to rule the kingdom.

We stopped at the front of my palace. The sun shining overhead brightened the entire city, contrasting my dismal mood. Golden temple domes glittered, and marble towers gleamed. No lamps or flowers to welcome me home, though. Instead, two kings stood on the palace steps. My nephews. As I dismounted, they approached me and touched my feet. For a moment, an urge to strangle their exposed necks coursed through me. In horror, I stepped back, my heart beating like a drum. Unaware of my turmoil, they rose and looked at me. Had I turned into a monster? Where had this urge to kill my nephews come from? I was afraid to find the answer.

Vasant spoke first. "Uncle Jay, tell me the news is false. I cannot imagine young Vikram perishing at sea. He swims like a fish." A tightness appeared around his lips. I had raised him along with my son. He gazed at me with tenderness, and his pity pierced me like arrows.

Unable to form any words, I nodded.

"Let us go in," said Nala and led the way.

After offering his condolence, Nala stared at his folded arms, lines appearing on his forehead. Something bothered my nephew. "What is it, Nala?"

He cleared his throat. "Uncle Jay, someone deliberately set fire to my wagon."

"Fire? Here in Malla?" I asked, shocked. Who would dare to commit such an offense here in my kingdom?

He nodded. "An arrow was fired at my wagon, causing it to overturn. While Amar helped to straighten it, a second arrow caused a fire. The blaze burnt him." His voice shook at the end.

"How is he?" I asked. I felt ashamed of my wish to strangle my nephews earlier.

"He lost his sight." Nala winced as he shared this detail.

I observed the news with a grimace. "Do you know who is behind it?" I asked, glancing at Kapil.

Kapil shook his head. "I have no leads, my Majesty. With your nephews ruling Saral and Padi, Magadha has been at peace for seventeen years."

"Nala, do you suspect anyone?"

"I cannot imagine who would want to hurt my little brother," he answered.

I rubbed my chin. "You look alike. Especially from a distance. What if the fire was meant for you?"

"Me?" he asked with a frown.

"You are the king. You are likely to have more enemies than your brother."

Vasant asked, "If Nala dies, Amar ascends the Padi throne. What would be achieved by this?"

Nala replied, "A new king is easier to influence."

"Yes," I agreed. "Nala, while Kapil investigates the matter here, seek answers in Padi." They dispersed, leaving me to ponder this. Who could be this hidden enemy?

I spent the rest of the day avoiding Sudha. I had no answers to the questions I expected from my wife. With my prolonged absence from Akash, I had many matters to attend to. That kept my body busy while my mind dwelled on that fateful day at sea. Sudha's maid came looking for me, and I hid from her. Like a boy of five.

As the sun disappeared, I reluctantly made my way to her chambers. My feet felt like they were stuck to the floor, and I moved as if I were wading through the mud. Outside her closed door, I stood for some moments, breathing deeply. Guards fidgeted around me, not helping me calm down. With a sigh, I knocked on her door.

The door flung open, and there she stood. With uncombed hair and red-rimmed eyes, Sudha stared at me. She grabbed my shoulders, and I stepped in, allowing the door to close behind me.

"Jay, where is my son?" she sobbed into my chest. Her tears wet my skin, and I hesitated to touch her.

"I lost him at sea," I whispered.

Her fists pounded against me. "No, no, that cannot be true," she wailed.

I held out the Vindhya pendant. "I brought a piece of him back."

She took the pendant in her hand and glanced at it for a moment. Then she flung it away and collapsed at my feet. The chain landed on a lit lamp, and the swinging pendant mocked me. I gathered her in my arms and carried her to her bedroom. Daylight had faded, and in the dark, I collided with a table and stumbled. She moaned in my arms, and I tightened my grip. I made my way to her bed and laid her down gently. A faded moon hung above the palace.

"For ten years, many shunned me because I was childless. Then,

Vikram was born, and my life changed," she said, looking up at me. "You have protected all of Magadha. How could you fail your son?" she asked.

I sat beside her and buried my head in my palm. Vikram's face floated in my mind.

"He wanted to explore the sea corals. I never learned to say no to him. I let him go even though a storm was approaching us," I narrated the story, and fresh pain prickled my skin.

"I have seen him swim, Jay. How could he drown?"

"He was trying to save the Sunda prince."

"I have not breathed or eaten or slept since—," she said, tears streaming down her eyes. I reached to wipe them, and she turned away from me. I pulled my arm back in anger. Did she think only she felt his loss?

"Aranya and I are too old to bear another heir for you. What do you plan to do? Discard us and marry a younger woman to carry your child?" she asked, each word stabbing me.

I hauled myself up. Without another word, I marched out. I wandered the palace halls aimlessly, pain and fury burning my insides.

"King Jay," a voice hailed me. I emerged from my fog and glanced in the direction of the sound. King Kanva of Sunda waved at me from inside his chamber. "Join me for my meal."

When had I last eaten? I entered his room and dropped onto a chair. A servant placed a plate filled with tamarind rice, long beans cooked with coconut, and sweet rice pudding. Exhaustion overwhelmed me, and my stomach growled in hunger. I ate the food without savoring any taste. Kanva directed the servants to leave us alone.

When the door closed, he said, "I cannot have my daughter marry that blind boy."

I paused with my hand in midair. "What blind boy?"

"Your nephew."

Did I lose my mind as well as my appetite? Slowly, my conversation with Nala drifted into my memory.

Kanva continued, "Amar turned up burnt and blind. He looks like a skinned boar. One of the reasons I consented to the match was because of his prowess on the battlefield. With my son gone, I cannot take on a sightless son-in-law. Sunda would be defenseless. We have to cancel their engagement. What use is a blind prince?"

A blind prince was better than a dead prince. "You cannot break the alliance," I said.

"Only to form a new one," he whispered.

His tone caused me to look up from my plate.

"You have lost your only son. You need an heir. Ratnavali is young and will give birth to many children. I would rather her wed a king than marry a prince who will rot in his palace."

I sat dumbfounded by his words.

8

MEERA

My daughter, Priya, descended from the chariot holding her son, Chandra, in her arms. I enclosed them both in a hug, and the boy squirmed to get away. Releasing them, I took in her glowing cheeks and her rounded hips. My daughter followed my gaze and leaned in to whisper, "Four months."

I kissed her forehead and whispered a prayer for her and her unborn baby's safety.

"How is my favorite sister?" asked Nala.

As the siblings greeted each other, Vasant approached me and touched my feet. I embraced my son-in-law. "Is all well in Saral?"

"It is, Aunt Meera. We are excited about your visit. Priya has been making arrangements to welcome you."

I observed the rightful heir to Malla. If I looked for the signs, I could see his resemblance to my father, King Vikram. My brother, Nakul, had perished before learning the truth of his birth. His son, Vasant, remained in the dark as well and ruled as king of Saral. Did Jay's and my actions cause our recent ills? If Jay's son had perished, should I push Jay to name Vasant as the crown prince? Would that cause chaos in Malla and Saral? Should we let the past remain buried? I wish I knew the answers to these questions.

43

"Mother," Priya called, pulling me out of my spiraling thoughts.

With the palace in mourning for the lost prince, Aranya had arranged a small family gathering to welcome the visitors.

Sitting beside me, Aranya whispered, "Fools are already placing the blame for Prince Uday's death on my daughter, Heera. Her luck and horoscope did not cause the storm to rise."

As I nodded, I saw Heera seated next to my son, Amar. The cousins talked with their heads touching. Marrying Crown Prince Uday would have made her queen of Sunda one day. Such a match might be out of her reach now. Royal families drowned in superstitions. Still, Uday's death before the wedding would allow my niece to marry again. If he had died after their matrimony, she would have been a widow for life, as per our customs.

My eyes sought my youngest son. Atul had avoided me since his outburst the other day. Now, he sat between his sister Priya and the Sunda princess, Ratnavali. The princess seemed to hang on to his every word. The boy appeared not to notice the attention lavished on him. A worry sprouted in my mind. Atul had saved Ratnavali from drowning. Gratitude could form a powerful basis for an attachment. But the girl was betrothed to his older brother. His blind older brother. I decided to consult Nala on this matter. As king of Padi, he had more say in his brothers' lives than I did.

Following my gaze, Aranya said, "With one wedding canceled, I hope the other can still proceed. Have you spoken with King Kanva?"

I shook my head and searched for Kanva. He was not among the gathered.

"I heard you plan to visit Saral after the wedding, my lady."

"Yes, I am. Padi rests in the good hands of my son and your daughter. They don't need me anymore. I want to spend some time with my daughter, Priya, and my grandson."

She smiled. "I would not assume they don't need you anymore. Yesterday, while I was with Kayal, she mentioned her beloved Aunt Meera a dozen times."

I returned her smile. "Old habits. Maybe, you can visit Kayal in Padi while I am gone. If Jay can spare you." Aranya had ruled Malla beside my brother, and Jay had relied on her to run the kingdom during his prolonged absences.

Later that day, I made my way to see Sudha. As her maid announced me, she rose to greet me.

"I am sorry about Amar, my lady. I wanted to come and see you myself."

I noticed the lines on her forehead. Her usually immaculate hair was bundled into a haphazard bun. Her necklace and earrings did not match. What effort did it take her to get out of bed in the morning?

I clasped her hand. "Any news from Jay?"

Tears spilled down her face at the mention of my brother's name. "He is on his way home. Without my son, Vikram."

I hugged her tightly as she sobbed into my shoulders.

After a few moments, she regained her composure and guided me to a seat.

I struggled to form words. Her world had revolved around her only child. What could I say to bring her peace? I squeezed her hand. "I am here to listen if you want to talk."

She gazed out the window, saying nothing for a while. "You know how boys are at that age. They no longer want to spend any time with their mothers. But before he left for Sunda, he came to see me one evening. He did not stay for long. He handed me some white Champa flowers he had picked. He'd seen the flowers while riding around Akash and thought of me. I have always loved being a mother and never wished for anything else."

My heart wept for her.

In a few days, Jay arrived in Akash. He did not come to see me, so I went looking for him. I found him in the small council room with Kapil Biha and Giri Thari. The three men were in earnest conversation when the guard announced me.

Jay glanced up and saw me. "Meera," he exclaimed and approached me. Up close, I regarded his sunken eyes and unshaven face. Others left the room as he bent to touch my feet. After, I pulled him into an embrace. His chin rested on my head, and he held me tightly for several moments.

"Meera, I heard about Amar. How is he?" he asked, releasing me.

"He is coming around slowly." My grief had shrunk in size compared to his. "I heard you did not recover—"

He rubbed his forehead. "No, we only found a pendant of his."

"Is there no hope of him being alive?"

Tears glistened in his eyes as he clenched his fist. "Hope?" he hissed and paced the room.

I wandered to a bench and sat down. I did not know how to comfort my brother.

He halted suddenly and said, "Meera, I spoke to Kanva yesterday." I waited for him to continue. My brother dropped down beside me and leaned forward.

"He wants to break the engagement between Amar and Ratnavali." He stared at the ground, avoiding my eyes.

I sighed. "I expected this."

"He is offering her hand in marriage to me instead," he whispered.

"You?" I exclaimed. I could understand why Kanva would prefer Jay to my son. Jay ruled Malla. Ratnavali's future son could become his heir. But did Jay want to marry a girl young enough to be his daughter? His wives, Aranya and Sudha, would surely resent such a match.

Another thought crept in like smoke entering a closed room through the gaps in the door. While my brother contemplated his third marriage, I remained a widow for seventeen years. Tradition dictated I mourn my husband my entire life as if I could only honor his memory by suffering. My chance of happiness perished with his death.

My brother's eyes darted to my face. Pain, grief, and confusion poured out of him. I reached out to place my hand on top of his.

"I have no heir, Meera."

"What about Vasant?" I asked. He was the rightful heir to the throne.

"He sits on the Saral throne. Uprooting him from that position would serve no purpose. The rest of his past stays buried with us," Jay said, with an edge to his voice.

"Jay, what happened to Vikram and Amar seems like a warning. To correct the mistakes of the past." Madhavi's face hovered before me, accusing me of causing her demise.

"What was my mistake in this chaos, Meera? Ruling Magadha till my nephews came of age? Why did I deserve to lose my son?" he snarled. The wrinkle of his brows and the firm set of his mouth spoke to me of the weight of the kingdom on his shoulders.

I had no answer to his questions.

"Revealing Vasant's tie to Malla will jeopardize two kingdoms. And the Thari and Vindhya houses would then revolt against him and me." I sensed the wisdom of his words. However, my guilt guided me in a different direction.

He pulled his hand from mine and stood up. "I have decided to marry her. She is young and can bear me a son." He had usually put his desires beneath the needs of the kingdom, so I could not doubt him now. Yet, a wave of worry gripped me and caused me to question the path we had taken.

9

JAY

eera stared at me as if I had suggested murdering the Sunda princess instead of marrying her. I thought my sister would be the easiest to persuade. Now, I felt like the connection between us had severed. Anger clawed through my skin. What did she know of the sacrifices I had made?

"Meera, the crown does not rest on your head like an anchor pulling you down. You are free to leave Padi. You can decide never to set foot there again. I am tied to this throne until my death, or I can find someone foolish enough to wear the crown," I ranted, my rage growing like a kindled fire.

Her eyes softened as they locked onto mine. Her compassion grated me. She had three sons. Very much alive. For a moment, I felt like I was losing my son all over again.

"Have you talked to Ratnavali?" she asked.

"Not yet," I said, puzzled by her question.

"She has been clinging to Atul since they arrived," she said.

"Atul?" I asked. *My nephew?*

She nodded.

That boy had saved her from drowning. But, my sister should know Kanva would not accept a union with him. Not if he ever learned the truth about him. My father had made the mistake of keeping my brother's true identity a secret. That concealment caused Nakul's death and burdened me with kingship. Meera and I had continued this tradition by camouflaging Atul's parentage. It was one thing to lie to protect Meera's honor. But to ensnarl Ratnavali in it would be a fallacy. "Any marriage alliance between Ratnavali and Atul is out of the question. You should know this, Meera."

Hurt flashed in her eyes. It caused a raw and painful burn in my stomach. My sister had been on my side since my birth. Comforting and guiding me. I could not be mad at her for my misfortunes.

"I am sorry, Meera. I did not mean to dredge up—"

"No, you are right. It is folly to think of it, and it would perpetuate another falsehood. Still, talk to the girl first before you announce your decision."

Later that afternoon, Ratnavali, with her father, Kanva, moving slowly next to her, arrived in the garden. She wore a simple sari in the color of a lotus petal and minimal jewels.

She walked over to join me while her father followed a few feet behind.

Sunlight dappled through the trees, and a pleasant wind brought us the fragrance of the flowers.

"Ratnavali, do you have any objections to marrying me?" I plowed right ahead.

She startled at my directness and then shook her head slowly.

"You would be my third wife," I continued.

She surprised me by answering, "My Majesty, my father said he needed your help to defend Sunda. I am happy to do my part to protect my kingdom."

Duty. I let out my breath slowly. "You will be afforded the comforts of this palace. Your needs will be met. And I expect you to bear my children." I had a duty to my kingdom as well. To further my bloodline. A bitterness spread through my throat.

Her face reddened, and she gazed at the ground. "I understand," she whispered. I knew I chained her with my burdens. But I had no choice.

I looked at her and her eyes caught mine. It transported me to the middle of the sea on a rocky boat. Pain stabbed my chest. I wanted to choke her for surviving the storm. I felt the same way when I looked at Atul. I had decided to send him away from Akash. *This panic would pass*, I consoled myself. I would not be afraid of gazing at my soon-to-be bride.

That evening, I invited my family to share their meal with me. My wives, Sudha and Aranya, sat side by side on two ornate chairs. Aranya held our granddaughter on her lap, both women playing with her. My youngest daughter, Heera, stood by the window with her back turned toward the room. Nala and Kayal arrived together. He inclined his head in my direction and stood behind his wife while my daughter sat next to her mother.

My eyes ran over them. I had tried to do the right thing, never questioning the path laid out before me. Recently, the route climbed uphill, and I was exhausted. A desire to simply walk away swept through me. To be free of these obligations. I quelled it.

"Vikram perished at sea, leaving Malla without an heir," I started. All eyes bored into me.

"Kanva offered his daughter's hand in marriage to me," I continued, and I sensed Aranya's shoulders stiffening in disapproval. She knew the history behind Nakul's birth. However, what I had worried about never materialized. Though she had no blood tie to Vasant, she continued to care for her nephew as if Nakul was her brother. That part did make sense. He was more her brother than mine, despite our blood relation. I only hoped she would not reveal the secret today.

Heera spun around. "Ratnavali wants to marry you?" she asked in disbelief. They were of the same age. A sudden embarrassment filled me at her questioning. Did she think I desired this marriage?

"Want has nothing to do with royal marriages," Kayal said sagely. She continued, "There is no grandson for our father to foster. He has no other choice."

A warmth spread through me at my eldest daughter's generosity.

"She is betrothed to Amar," Heera continued. Sudha appeared far away, not paying any attention to this conversation. Others remained silent.

"Her father wants to break off their engagement," I answered, glancing at Nala. His brows furrowed at my remark. But he knew we could not force the alliance with the recent mishap.

I turned toward Heera. "We will find him a suitable match," I said to placate her.

"I will marry him," she answered, shocking me. "My betrothed is dead, and Ratnavali no longer wants to marry him." Her head held high, she gazed at me, almost defiantly. *Marry a blind prince?*

My eyes darted to her mother. Aranya looked at her daughter too. Then her eyes met mine with acceptance.

Suddenly, Sudha spoke. "You could not even wait to cremate your son before deciding to marry again." Every word pierced like a dagger in my chest.

10

MEERA

My loneliness hit me the hardest at night. When I tossed and turned, trying hard to grasp the ever-elusive sleep, I missed my husband the most. Alone in a large four-poster bed. It had been seventeen years since his passing. I had managed to get through the days. For a while, I had a kingdom to run and children to raise. Now, I filled the days with things of my choosing. Time spent singing or with my grandchildren. However, nights stretched forever, cold and desolate.

I threw my blanket off and rose from my bed. Losing my husband had been like losing a limb. I had struggled initially and learned to live without it. But a constant ache persisted like a splinter in my foot. I stopped suddenly, realization dawning upon me. How could I disregard my own child's struggles after losing his sight? In my gratitude for Amar's recovery, I had dismissed his pain.

Amar came to visit me as the dawn finally arrived. I watched the birds taking flight when he entered my room.

"Mother," he said and wandered to my side.

I looked at him. "Are you ready for the big day?"

"I am not sure," he said, peering at me. "I feel like I am trapping Heera in my misery."

I pulled his head down and kissed his forehead. "No, Son. She is choosing to share her life with you. It is a rare gift. Cherish her."

"I worry that she will regret it."

"Amar, your uncle is marrying his third wife today. If Heera married Crown Prince Uday, do you think her life would have been easier?"

He seemed to mull over what I said. "Do I have your blessing, Mother?"

"And my love," I added and squeezed his arm. "Find happiness, my child."

Given a choice, my brother would have preferred a simple exchange of garlands with his bride. Her father insisted on a traditional ceremony, and he'd gone along with it. Sudha, a grieving mother, had left Akash to visit her father, wanting no part in the wedding. Aranya, my brother's queen, had helped with the arrangements and took part in it graciously. Only the tightness around her lips revealed any misgivings.

My heart held no resentment against Jay. I knew he grieved for his son. And he carried the burden for the kingdom like a mule carrying a heavy load. A load he could not set aside.

When he sought my blessing after the wedding, I hugged my brother tightly. The strain of the past few weeks showed up as tiny lines around his eyes. When I let go, he seemed moved. "Meera, every year, I think I have finally grown out of relying on you. Then something happens to show me how much I still do."

After Jay's somber wedding, Heera and Amar's ceremony sparkled with joy. Heera radiated contagious happiness and showered us all with it. Her delight rubbed off on Amar, and he smiled for the first time since his accident. When they exchanged their flower garlands, I showered them with rice coated in turmeric. Their union ushered in the summer season, and I hoped their life together would be filled with warmth and an abundance of bliss.

As I wiped the wetness in my eyes, Nala wrapped his arm around my shoulder. "Mother, I am glad we celebrated two weddings today, despite all that happened."

I nodded. "Heera will be good for your brother. She is going to drag him out of his melancholy. Help him heal," I said, my voice wavering with emotion. He squeezed my shoulder gently.

"Mother, they are planning to spend some time here in Akash before heading to Padi. Aunt Aranya is accompanying them." I hoped Jay's wedding had not created a rift between him and Aranya. She had been his able partner in ruling Malla.

"Kayal and I will join you as you head south to Lukla. Just for a fortnight or two," he added.

I smiled at him. "I would love the company."

My eyes swept the large hall. "Where is your brother, Atul?"

"Is he still avoiding you?" Nala asked, exasperated.

"He is young." I defended him.

"Mother, at his age, I ruled Padi."

"And did it with wisdom beyond your years," I agreed and glanced up at him. He bore the burden of the crown remarkably well—like his father. Tears welled in my eyes with pride. He kissed my head, his hand anchoring and steadying me.

"Atul will be joining us in Saral. Uncle Jay wants him out of Akash for some period. Maybe it is time I took a more active role in his life. With Amar hurt, it will be useful to have him in Padi, helping me."

"Yes, that will be good for him. He is hurting deeply after his cousin's death," I added. My son had also become restless after Vikram's demise, with no roots to tie him down.

Kayal joined us then, her face flushed with happiness. "Beautiful ceremony. Weddings make me happy."

"I will store that in my memory," Nala teased her.

Standing beside me, she looked across at her husband. "If I don't bear you an heir in the next decade, I will give you my blessing to remarry," she said with a smile on her lips.

"That will not be necessary," Nala said, gazing at his wife like only she mattered in the universe. I felt a pang when I remembered his father looking at me similarly. "I have two brothers," he continued.

Watching their playful banter, tenderness welled up in my heart.

Then I noticed Kayal touch her stomach tenderly. "You have news to share?" I asked.

"Yes, Aunt Meera. I am expecting another child," she said, her eyes crinkling in joy. Melodious notes from a veena reached me as I hugged them both tightly, my love spilling over.

11

JAY

"Aranya," I called her name earlier that morning as I walked into her chambers.

She waved her maid away and sat still on her chair.

"You think I am making a mistake," I said, gazing at the reflection in her mirror. She had been my voice of reason for over twenty-five years. I very much wanted her on my side for the union about to take place.

She sighed softly and looked up. Her eyes were not unkind.

"You lost your son. So did Kanva. Grief coats your decisions."

I pulled her into my arms, and she leaned her head on my chest.

"I cannot make Vasant my heir. That will rip both kingdoms apart. Rivals will sprout. Calling him a usurper, they will vie for both thrones," I reasoned.

She straightened slowly, one hand against my chest, her eyes locked with mine.

"You have two daughters. Either of them could have given us a grandson to foster," she said.

"You want me to rest the fate of the kingdom on unborn grandsons?" I asked.

She put some distance between us. "As opposed to unborn sons?"

56

she argued. "If not grandsons, your sister has three sons. She was a Malla princess. One of her sons could be your heir. No one will call them usurpers."

Rage raised its head in me. Did she think I had not contemplated this possibility?

"Before Amar's accident, I might have considered making him my heir," I grunted.

"Amar? You raised Atul since he was a baby. He worships you and emulates you. It would have made sense to make him your heir and offer his hand to Ratnavali." Secrets. I kept too many of them. I accepted my sister's indiscretion out of my love for her. What if the truth about his birth came out? But he had more Malla blood than either of his brothers. He was the son of a Malla princess and a Vindhya man. No, that would not do.

She watched my struggle, and something heavy settled in my chest. I took her hand. "I have to do this, Aranya. I am asking you to support me." I barely breathed, afraid that she would pull away.

Instead, she slipped her arms around my neck and nodded. Our foreheads touching, we stood together, like we had done when we were younger, when everything had seemed easy.

I found my daughter, Heera, seated on the floor with Yamini, playing with wooden dolls. I joined them on the rug, and my granddaughter handed me a carved elephant.

"You want to play with us, Grampa?"

"Yes. Tell me how."

"You move the elephant behind the horse," she said, pointing to her line of dolls. Heera lifted her horse to guide me. We followed the directions of the child, laughing and singing.

Kayal strode into the room quietly and leaned on a chair to watch us. "You used to tell us these outrageous stories, Father."

"We would act them out, crawling on our bellies," Heera added.

"Making ridiculous noises."

My eyes darted between them, wondering where the years had vanished. As Kayal came closer, I squeezed her hand. She had grown into a wise queen, just like her mother. "I miss those days," I whispered.

She dropped to her knees and kissed my head. Then, she gathered her child. "I will let the two of you talk," she said and left me alone with her sister.

Heera moved closer to me, and I put my arm around her.

"My child, your mother and I raised you to be a queen." If she had married Uday, she would have been one.

She nestled against my shoulder. "Father, Uday is dead." Had she read my mind?

"I can find you another prince," I said, pressing my lips to her forehead.

She gazed at me. "Amar is a prince."

"A blind prince. Life with him will not be easy." *Marrying any prince is never easy.*

"Like it has been easy for my mother?" she asked, her eyes sparkling with emotion.

"In trying to be a good king, I have not always been a good husband or father," I replied, regret in my voice.

"I like him, Father," she said.

I observed her. "Are you sure, Heera? A girl only gets to marry once."

She nodded. Then, she added, "And, you are not a bad father."

I put both arms around her and held her tightly.

As I entered my chamber, a familiar face greeted me. "Somu!" He had raised me as a child and been by my side until recently.

I hugged the thin man tightly while he patted my back. I guided him to a seat and dropped down beside him.

"My king, I heard about the prince," he said and looked at me with kind eyes. I swallowed.

"You have borne the weight of the crown remarkably well. Don't judge yourself harshly," Somu said, touching my arm gently. He knew me well.

"I am named after a great king. I have been falling short since that day," I said and smiled ruefully.

"King Jay, your great-grandfather would be proud of you. I mingle with the common folks more often these days. They lead prosperous and peaceful lives under your reign." His eyes shone, filling me with warmth.

"My great-grandfather ensured the continuation of the Malla line. I am still struggling," I said, sharing my doubts with him.

"You are young, my Majesty. And you are marrying a princess who can bear you children. And you have nephews," he said. He knew the story of my parents and their firstborn, Nakul. My father concealed the truth and set in motion actions that resulted in my brother's death. The echo of my father's actions reverberated into the next generation. My nephew ruled Saral instead of Malla.

"Enough about me. How are you doing?" I asked.

"You have been generous with me. I lack for no comfort. My only trouble is keeping my two servants occupied. I make them sweep the floors twice daily," he said, smiling.

I laughed. "How is the pain in your legs? Is the physician treating you for it?" Despite his thinning hair and gaps in the rows of his teeth, he seemed healthy.

"That pain has sprouted a few siblings. But the physician is tireless in helping me. He comes to see me often with new balms to apply to my old body. Whether they help or not, I do like the company."

That brought forth my guilt. I did not visit him often enough. "I should come to see you more often," I said. I could never repay him for all he had done for me.

"My Majesty, when you are in Akash, you make time to share at least one monthly meal with me. I cannot ask for more. Queen Aranya invites me to the palace concerts and feasts. And Queen Kayal visited me with her daughter, Yamini."

I brightened at the mention of Kayal. "It seems like yesterday she was Yamini's age. Now she is Queen of Padi."

"A magnificent queen, from what I observed," Somu beamed.

"Somu, I am glad you came to see me," I said as he got ready to leave.

He touched my head and departed.

The wedding day arrived just like any other day. I had married Aranya for love and Sudha to keep the peace. Did I now marry Ratnavali because a grieving father asked me? Or because I, a grieving father too, needed a male heir? I barely saw my bride, though she sat beside me for most of the day. The ceremony, the feast, the music—all exhausted me.

I made my way over to her chambers now, with no pleasure or anticipation. I just wanted to do my duty as a husband. Ratnavali sat on the edge of her bed, twisting her braid. Her red sari shone vibrantly against her skin. Her eyes leaped to my face before casting them down.

I averted mine quickly. I had avoided looking at my bride today. She reminded me of things I wanted to forget. Or else I would drown in sorrow.

I marched to the window and stood for a moment, my arms folded across my chest. I could not kiss my bride or look into her eyes or— the list felt long. Images of my dead son barreled in my head each time. I let out a deep breath. I had prepared for battle, knowing I might perish. This felt worse. But I had to get it over.

"Take off your clothes," I ordered, clenching my fist.

12

MEERA

A young priest walked out of the inner sanctum and offered us the lighted wick lamp on a silver tray. I cupped my hand around the light to accept the blessings of God.

"Queen Meera, I had heard you sing when I was a young boy helping my father. Would you please—if it is not inappropriate to ask you to sing..."

"It would be an honor," I said and glanced at my daughter. Priya nodded her head. We sang a song about God Krishna's playful antics as a young child. Surprisingly, my sons Nala and Amar joined us.

When the song ended, my daughter hugged me. "I miss singing with you, Mother." I stroked her back. It would be lovely to spend a few months with her in Saral.

Amar's fingertips hovered near Heera's, and the newlyweds' faces lit up as they leaned into each other and whispered. Was I ever so happy? *Yes*, a voice whispered back. A long time ago, Rish and I had stolen glances at each other across a crowded room, naively believing our love was possible. Then I sacrificed my attachment for duty. A sharp pain rose in my stomach. I missed his near-constant presence by my side.

I sought my youngest. I found Atul holding his nephew, Chandra, and they rang the temple bell together. As the room vibrated under the sound, I stilled my heart. I had many things to be thankful for, I observed, my eyes sweeping over my children and grandchildren. Maybe it was time to let the past go.

A lone figure came into my view, and I saw Ratnavali praying intently, her palms clasped and head bowed. I had asked Jay to join us. He sent his bride instead. A gray cloud hung over her head. Did she still mourn her brother, or did something new cause this gloom?

When we returned to the palace, I went to find my brother. I located him in his chambers, talking to Kapil. He sat at the large rosewood table with carvings of a tiger family on it. Jay and I had sat with my father for many meals in this very room. My fingers traced the edge of the table as memories came flooding in. Jay had not changed much in here, and I could still picture my father seated at the head of the table, regaling us with stories.

"Our sea captain has searched all the waters that the current could have carried him to. No sign of Prince Vikram. The search around the shores was futile too," Kapil said.

Jay sat like a statue, apparently drained of feelings. Then, slowly he seemed to emerge from a void. "Should I abandon the search?" he asked, a slight tremor in his voice. My heart went out to him. Without knowing for sure, this uncertainty most likely wore him down.

"I will ask the men to continue combing the land for another week. And have them talk to the fishermen," Kapil said, without much conviction about finding my nephew.

"Find me a body, a bone, something," Jay said, a wrenching appeal in his voice. "I need to cremate my son."

Kapil dipped his head and limped out. He was injured in a battle a few years ago. Jay had made him the Chief Guard of Akash and then sent him home to heal. In his new role, Kapil had remained in the city while Jay had continued his travels.

I patted my brother's shoulder and wandered to the smaller sitting room to look at the portrait of my father. The painting of a young man just crowned after his brother's death stared back at me. Of his five grandsons, it shocked me that Atul resembled his grandfather the most. My son had inherited the stubborn jaw and the determined eyes of my father. My child had refused to talk to me since he'd flung his accusations at me. Allegations that had merit in them because I had kept the truth hidden from him—for his sake and mine.

Jay came and stood beside me. "I ask myself what our father would do."

"When you went missing, he shared the story of Nakul with me. Hoping to claim him." It had come as a shock to learn that I had an older brother growing up as the Saral prince. My father never revealed the truth to Nakul, and Jay and I had followed the same path.

"I have no other sons," Jay said bitterly.

He had married Ratnavali to produce an heir. "Not yet," I corrected him.

He glanced at me and looked away. But I saw the pain and guilt in his eyes.

"Jay, try not to hurt Ratnavali," I said carefully, trying not to accuse him.

He laughed and shook his head. "Like you tried not to hurt your husband."

His words drove a thorn into my skin.

"Meera, we were raised to put Malla ahead of everything else. And we do. And we end up hurting the people who love us. Our father hurt our stepmother. I have hurt Aranya, Sudha, and now Ratnavali. You have hurt Atul and—" He left Rish's name unsaid. But his meaning sunk clearly into my heart. I had wounded both of them.

He put his arm around me and kissed my head. "We are monsters in a way. Relentless and cold. That makes us good rulers. Not necessarily good people." Madhavi's face drifted into my vision, accompanied by a swell of remorse. I could not change what happened to her or my husband. But I still had time to make amends to Rish, if I knew how. And Jay felt guilty too. I could see it in the lines around his eyes.

"Jay, you have been a good brother to me. And I know you will step in front of a sword aimed at your daughters' or wives' throats. Your faults don't make you a monster. It makes you a human."

His eyes misted. "Since I lost Vikram, I have felt unmoored. At times, I have wanted to punish Ratnavali for living while my only son drowned."

I squeezed his arm. "Jay, your feelings are natural. At times, I have felt jealous of you too."

"Jealous?"

"Yes," I whispered. "Especially the fact that you can marry multiple times."

"Meera," he said softly. "I wish I could do something to ease your pain."

I smiled without joy. "You are a powerful king, but even you cannot change fate."

"I know that," he sighed.

* * *

PREPARATIONS for our journey south took days, and finally, the leaving neared. We gathered in a large hall, saying our farewells.

Amar needed more time to heal before he could travel. So he and Heera had decided to remain in Akash and then travel north to Padi.

I hugged my son, glad to see the smile on his face.

"Don't worry about me, Mother," he whispered in my ear. I felt a load lift off my chest.

Jay wandered over. "Go to Kadal and see our mother's portrait," he said.

"Jay, I am looking forward to it. And to visit our uncle."

He squeezed my shoulder. "I cannot believe you have never been to Saral. Coconuts taste so much better there."

"And jackfruit, I hear." I smiled.

Nala approached us.

"Nephew, remember what we discussed. Use the precautions you would normally use in enemy territory. Till we identify who was behind the fire attack, I want us to be cautious," Jay said.

"Yes, Uncle Jay. Vasant and I will be vigilant." It worried me that the culprit was still at large. We had no indication of their identity.

A mild day welcomed me as we made our way outside. A parade of horses, chariots, and supply carts lined the road, ready to take us south.

Vasant, Nala, and Atul mounted their horses, an easy friendship between them. Vasant and Atul had grown up together in Akash with Vikram and remained close. With Vikram gone, they reminisced about old times. Nala and Vasant found a different kind of kinship. The cousins belonged to the rare society of kings and maintained a steady stream of conversation, asking and giving advice.

I climbed into the chariot with my daughter and my niece. My grandchildren, Yamini and Chandra, were delighted in the procession of vehicles and filled the space with their musical voices. I adored how their eyes sparkled with wonder and their need to share that feeling with us.

Over the heads of their children, the two queens gossiped about all that had recently happened.

"I love Uncle Jay. But why did he have to marry that girl? Poor thing looked lost today," said Priya.

Kayal defended her father. "He did not desire this. He is the king of Malla. With my brother's death, he lost his only heir."

As their exchange veered into their pregnancies and impending births, I let my mind wander to my conversation with Jay. And the men I had hurt. Had I ever considered what Rish would want from me? Or had I always placed Malla and Padi ahead of him? The answer came without hesitation. My duty had led me down the path of sacrificing him. A part of me whispered he would be better off without me. In Vindhya, he would be near his daughter and family, who loved him. And they would not expect him to suspend his needs.

I set aside my musings and viewed the changing scenery outside. The land turned greener as we headed south. I savored visiting my mother's land. A warmth spread through my chest at the thought of seeing her childhood castle.

On either side of our road, I saw a row of Moringa trees. The fragrant white flowers swayed in the wind. A female sunbird with a matching white underbelly constructed a nest on one of the trunks, while the male covered in golden feathers twittered nearby. I noticed several foot-long pods hanging from the branches. The three-sided pod held a delicate flesh that absorbed the flavors in spicy stews. My children loved scraping the soft pulp with their teeth while the gravy dripped down their chins.

One afternoon, Nala approached our chariot. "All the important women in my life assembled in one place," he said, grinning mostly at his wife. Her face blossomed like a sunflower at dawn. His daughter, Yamini, stretched out her tiny hands, and he leaned over to pick her up. "Especially you, little one," he said, wrapping her in his arms.

"Brother, we all know how much you love Kayal and how greatly you respect our mother. Me? I cannot be on any of your favorite lists," my daughter teased her brother.

"Little sister, the day I married you off, and you became Vasant's problem, I added you to my list." With a laugh, he continued, "At the bottom, naturally."

"Nala, are we stopping?" Kayal asked.

"Yes, there is a stream close by. If we halt early, we can bathe in the river while there is still daylight."

Soon we camped on a grassy meadow dotted with tiny blue flowers. Like ants carrying out their tasks with cooperation, men and women helped pitch tents, feed the animals, and unload the supplies. The creek ran nearby, and the water glittered like diamonds. Once our food preparation got underway, we headed to the stream to wash off the grime. I dropped onto the wet sand and plunged my hands into the cold water, splashing it on my face. My daughter and niece stood in knee-deep water, each holding their child in one hand and their sari in the other. The men bathed downriver from us, around a rocky cliff hidden from our view. I moved back a few feet and sat on dry land, letting the sound of the flowing water soothe me.

A piercing howl reached me, disturbing my peace. I opened my eyes and scanned the area. Priya and Kayal stood alert, facing the direction of the sound.

"Go, find out what is happening," Priya ordered a Saral guard.

I stood and walked toward them as they got out of the stream. I helped dry the children, listening to the voices floating toward us.

Only garbled sounds reached me and then another ear-splitting cry. Without waiting, I rushed toward the sound, my heart pounding.

I saw Atul, bare-chested and with a hastily draped dhoti around his waist, run into the small forest with a few men. I saw no sign of Nala or Vasant in the water.

"We found him," someone yelled, and I spun around. Birds took flight from their tree nests, adding to the commotion. Out of breath, I pondered what to do next when Kayal arrived next to me, a dagger in her hand.

"Aunt Meera," she gasped. "What is going on?"

"I don't know, my child. I just saw Atul run into the forest."

A wail rose close to us and the clang of metal. I peered into the trees, the vanishing light painting everything in shadows.

Atul strode out, holding—

"Vikram," I shrieked. My nephew. Alive.

He kept repeating the phrase, "I did not mean to."

Atul spoke gently in his ears, his arm wrapped around his shoulder, comforting the weeping boy. Both appeared unhurt.

I ran to meet them when I saw a sight behind them that stopped my heart.

Vasant and a guard supported a man between them, half carrying him. Blood oozed out of his chest, staining his clothes.

Nala? The word left my lips, but no sound came out. The world stopped, and all thoughts emptied out of my head. A deadly cold cloaked my body.

Kayal saw them too. "Nala!" she screamed and ran to my son. My heart exploded into pieces.

13

JAY

a delicate light caressed the small council room, mirroring the cloudy day outside. Kapil Biha, Chief Guard of Akash, a position previously held by his father, talked about the Buddhist monks seeking refuge in Malla. Kapil wanted me to grant an audience to their head.

Giri Thari, my southern commander, disagreed. "The king has already granted them shelter in Malla. What is the need for them to meet with him?"

"The head monk wants to thank the king personally. And he wants a land grant to build a temple."

My brows furrowed. "Land grant? We have many Buddhist temples here in Malla. What is the need for another one?"

"My Majesty, these monks belong to a different sect than the ones common in Malla," Kapil answered.

I shook my head. "I have offered them asylum in Malla. They are free to practice their religion here. And I will protect them like the rest of my people. If they want land, they have to talk to my chiefs, like Giri Thari here."

Giri Thari, also the chief of the Thari house, grimaced. "If I offer land to one group, I will be besieged by requests from the others. They can collect coins from their followers and buy some land."

"They don't have many followers in Malla," Kapil reasoned. "My Majesty, please spend a few moments with the head monk. That is all he is requesting. And the unrest in Kashgar could spread here. It is best to be prepared. These monks would be more willing to help us if you allow him to call on you."

Kapil had served me well, and I trusted my lifelong friend. I nodded. "Arrange for a meeting then. And find out more about the revolt in Kashgar. I want to know if that poses a threat to us."

He dipped his head.

"Any news on who attacked my nephews?"

Kapil shook his head. "All my usual sources have come up dry."

I clenched my fist in frustration. "Kapil, if I cannot protect my family, how can I protect my people? Offer a reward for information. I want the offender brought to light soon."

That night, I sat in my room mulling over what Meera had said about hurting Ratnavali. Whenever I gazed at her, my wife's face transported me to that fateful day on our ship. Images of my son ran through my head, and rage at his death buried me. That anger coursing through me about her survival usually left no room for any affection. It ruled out a chariot ride in public with her or any activity in daylight.

Tonight, I noticed no moon rose over the castle. I could not abandon my duties as a husband completely. And the darkness offered a path. I made my way to her chambers.

"My lord, I was not expecting you. Let me ask the maid to light some lamps," she said. Her tone indicated surprise or maybe shock. I had ignored her for days now.

Light would hamper what I needed to do. "No need for light. I prefer this darkness," I whispered. I could only see an outline of her face, her features shrouded in blackness.

I reached out and clasped her hand. She trembled at my touch. From fear, no doubt. I pulled her closer. Her heart thudded as if a hunter chased her. I did not blame her for her reaction. I had acted like a beast the last time I'd approached her physically.

I traced the lines on her palm gently. "I have not been myself lately," I said.

She made no reply. After a while, her breathing steadied. I emptied my mind of thoughts. Suddenly, I noticed a faint flowery smell waft from her. A flower I could not place. My fingers traveled to her throat. Her skin warmed under my touch, and a different kind of shudder passed through her. I stepped closer and brushed her full lips with my thumb. Her mouth parted, and she leaned into me. Did she forgive me? Though I had treated her no worse than many married men, guilt cloaked me. She deserved better.

"Ratna," I said softly, my face hovering near hers. Her breath mingled with mine. My eyes closed, and I waited for her to make the next move. After an eternity, she kissed me. Salty tears mingled with longing.

The following morning while Kapil and I discussed a few matters, I heard the rustle of silk. My throat tightened, and my tongue froze.

"My lord," Ratnavali said breathlessly and stood at the threshold. *Idiot*, I thought. Why had she come to me in daylight? Did she have no sense of self-preservation?

I clenched my fist for a moment, knuckles turning white. Under Kapil's watchful eyes, I waved her in.

"Have you arranged a meeting?" I barked at Kapil.

His eyebrows rose a tiny grain. He knew me too well to miss my anguish. "Yes, my Majesty. I will bring him to you tomorrow," he said while his eyes searched my face.

I cast mine down, avoiding his scrutiny. "Meet me in the training yard," I said and dismissed him.

Ratnavali viewed the portraits in the room, her back to me. As I approached her, she turned. Her eyes sparkled, and a light blush colored her cheeks. But a venomous snake raised its head in my mind, ready to strike her. I wanted to strangle the long slender neck I had kissed tenderly. Last night. In the dark.

I halted and tore my eyes away from her. I pointed to one of the paintings and rambled something. She replied. But no words penetrated my fog. A heavy silence fell. I wandered to the window, my arms crossed over my chest.

"Did I do something wrong?" she whispered. She had moved closer to me. I reached and took her hand in mine without looking at her.

"No, the mistake is mine." In marrying and ruining her life. "I need time to mourn my son," I muttered. The urge to choke her soared in me. To punish her for living while my son had perished. I dropped her hand as if her fingers burned me. "Don't come to me," I reproached her. She sank back from me. "Allow me to visit you," I added in gentler tones.

When I arrived in the training yard, I had enough rage to crush a boulder. Kapil walked around the young recruits, offering suggestions and showing them different moves. When he saw me, he signaled to one of his men to take over.

We walked to a quiet corner, away from the others.

"What do you want to do today?" Kapil asked, his tone masking the concern in his eyes.

"Wrestle," I said, my anger spilling over. Kapil found a soldier to wrestle with me. A young man I had not met before.

I was flat on my back in no time. Another opponent would have their knee pressed to my throat. Not with Kapil around, though. Kapil pushed him away and stretched his hand to me. I grasped it, and he pulled me up. He had sworn to protect my life when he and I were sixteen. Almost three decades ago.

"Jay," Kapil said under his breath, calling me by name. A sign that he spoke as my friend. "I can listen if you want to talk," he whispered.

I trusted him with my life. The temptation to open up to him engulfed me. About the monster in me that wanted to destroy my wife Ratna for just being alive. A beast that chased my other wives away. Sudha had fled to her father's palace. Aranya made plans to leave for Padi with Heera. But I could not express my fears to him. I needed him to respect me, not pity me.

"There is nothing to talk about," I answered with a shrug. Then, I closed my eyes and cleared my mind.

"I am ready," I said.

Kapil stared at me intently and then signaled to the young man.

We fought, sweat dripping, our arms around each other, neither giving an inch. That was not true. My opponent could have thrown me down a few times. He ignored those opportunities and fought at my level.

Before we parted, I remarked, "I have not trained with such a good wrestler in a long while."

His eyes lit up, and he bowed to me. "My Majesty, the honor is mine."

After he left, Kapil remarked, "He is a king's man."

"You know how to find the best of them. And I knew how to choose good friends."

He grinned at me. "I found you hiding under a table. That means I did the choosing."

"Unfortunately, you were terrible at picking a playmate," I said, a lightness in my chest.

"My father warned me about being friends with the prince," he said and paused.

I waited for him to carry on.

He cleared his throat and continued, "He was right. It is not easy. It does test us. But I would not change anything about it."

I touched his shoulder. "Me neither."

I joined Aranya, Heera, and Amar for our evening meal. The boy had transformed since his wedding to my daughter. Her face dazzled like a gem glittering from the sunlight.

We sat in Aranya's chambers, and my eyes swept the room. Aranya's walls were bare. When my stepmother reigned as queen, portraits of fierce goddesses adorned the walls. My sister, Meera, never liked those paintings depicting brutality and mayhem. She had not been on a real battlefield with bodies slaughtered, lying in piles.

I observed the wooden sculptures that stood on the floor or tables. These life-like sculptures showcased ordinary life: fishermen on a boat, a boy on top of an elephant, a dancer in her swirling sari.

We sat on a mango wood table, polished to a gleam. The young couple stole glances and held their hands under the table. My eyes caught Aranya's. Our minds traveled back in unison to a past when we were that young couple, filled with love and an abundance of hope.

Heera giggled and brought us back to the present.

"Amar, I see you are healing well."

"Yes, Uncle Jay. Some of these scars will remain with me till death. Otherwise, I am feeling fine. I am planning to start training again."

"Your sight?" I asked.

He knitted his brows. "No change. I can only see about a foot in front of me."

"Stay here in Akash. Our healers are well known for their miracles. There is no need for you to rush to Padi."

"Father, you were ready to send me across the sea to Sunda," Heera teased me.

"I was a fool. With you gone, this palace would be empty." Children had filled this palace. My daughters, nephews, and son played and sang and danced in these halls. Then, my nephew, Vasant, left first to rule Saral. Next, Kayal married Nala and reigned as his queen of Padi. I had imagined my son, Vikram, and my nephew, Atul remaining in Akash. I had pictured grandchildren. Now, I could not even look at my nephew without my chest constricting in pain.

Heera put her arms around me. "Maybe, we can stay a few fortnights."

A few fortnights. Like a child abandoned at a village fair, a feeling of being lost rose in my throat. I questioned this practice of sending daughters away with their husbands. I exhaled slowly and kissed her forehead.

The next day, a man of my age stood in front of me in saffron robes.

"Head Monk Yonten," Kapil said, introducing him.

He radiated a serene calmness. I bowed my head to him and guided him to a seat.

"Monk Yonten, Kapil has briefed me about your troubles in Kashgar. I offer you and your disciples asylum in Malla."

"King Jay, may Buddha shower his blessing on you. For centuries, our monastery existed in Kashgar. The royal families there had served as our benefactors. Recently, a severe drought caused hunger and famine in the kingdom. And our ruler forgot his duty to aid those in need. People revolted against the lavish spending of the monarch while they starved. Angry men ransacked my monastery. Our weak king could offer us no protection. We left with only the clothes on our backs and our religious texts," he narrated, without anger or bitterness.

I watched him, astonished. Anger bubbled up in me at even the slightest provocation. How could he remain calm in the face of these atrocities?

"You are probably wondering why I am here," he paused and shut his eyes briefly. I watched him intently, preparing to say no to any request for temple lands.

He opened his eyes and gazed at me. "I preach non-violence and peace, so this is hard for me to say. Kashgar is suffering. With no strong ruler, some corrupt men have taken over. King Jay, I need your help to fight them and recover Kashgar."

I viewed Kapil, and he raised his brows.

"Monk Yonten," I said, "the fighting in Kashgar is wholly unrelated to me. Unless your king requests my help, my involvement will look like a conquest."

He lowered his voice. "He did. He sent his young son with me, fearing for his life. Our king may very well be dead. I brought the boy disguised as my student. Your battle prowess is well known even among us monks. Please help us defeat the usurpers and set our prince on the throne. We will tutor the young prince in the ways of a righteous ruler to ensure he does not repeat the mistakes of his father."

Before I could answer, a knock sounded on our door. Kapil opened the door, and Giri spilled in. "My Majesty, your son is alive."

I bolted from my seat.

14

MEERA

asant carried Nala into the tent and laid him down on his stomach. A knife with a silver handle protruded from his back. Kayal nearly collapsed at the sight of the blood oozing out of the wound. I held her tightly while squashing my fear.

"Priya," Vasant called out to his wife. She wobbled in, stricken by her brother's injury.

"Take care of Aunt Meera and Kayal while I fetch the physician," he said and hastened out.

"I don't need any care, my child. But Kayal does," I said to my daughter. "Kayal, go with her. I will come to get you when he awakens," I added.

Immediately, Kayal wiped her eyes and tightened her lips. "I will stay with you, Aunt Meera. Priya, take care of my daughter."

Priya squeezed her arm and left as the physician came in. Time came to a stand-still. Kayal and I remained in the tent while others flowed in and out.

Nala's skin had turned gray and pale. The knife was out, and the healer had wrapped his chest tightly with a balm made of neem leaves. Kayal sat beside him and wiped his skin with a cloth dipped in warm water.

I held his cold hand and prayed silently. *Let him live.*

Atul came in, looking like a ghost. "How is he?" he whispered.

I glanced at him, unable to voice my thoughts. Leaving Nala to his wife, I grabbed Atul's elbow. "Let us find a quiet spot."

He draped his arm around my shoulders, supporting me, as we walked outside. In the predawn darkness, only a sliver of a moon guided our path.

"How is Vikram?" I asked about my nephew.

"He is sleeping now. But it took a while to calm him down," he said, with a slight tremor in his voice.

"We should send a messenger to your uncle," I added, reality seeping in.

We halted under a tree. "Vasant already dispatched two messengers, one to Uncle Jay and another to Aunt Sudha."

I wound my sari around my finger. "What happened? How did Nala get hurt? Start at the beginning."

A cloud passed over his face. "Mother, we heard a scream while we were bathing. Nala ordered me to get our guards while he and Vasant went to check out the noise. When I returned, they had already slaughtered the two men holding Vikram and freed him. I was shocked to see Vikram. The last time I saw him was in the Tunga Sea, swimming against storm currents." He paused and rubbed his eyes. I reached up to tousle his hair, wanting to take all his hurt away.

"Vikram recognized Vasant and me immediately. We grew up as brothers, so that made sense. But, he seemed frightened of Nala. I reassured him, and then Nala spoke to him. Vikram listened to us quietly. We thought the matter settled and made our way back. The two of us walked behind Nala. Suddenly, he grabbed my dagger and plunged it into Nala. Before I could even react." He buried his face in his palm, a shudder passing through him. I wrapped my arms around him and rubbed his back. Tall like his father, he bent to rest his head on my shoulder.

"I failed to save Vikram then and Nala now," he howled, with a horrible cry tearing out of him.

"Son, neither was your fault," I said, patting the back of his neck.

With Nala wounded, Amar blinded and Atul broken, worry for my sons caused unbearable pain in my chest.

In one corner of my mind, other questions bubbled up. How had Vikram come to Vindhya lands? Why would he fear Nala? The coast was miles away. His arrival here appeared to be a deliberate act.

Atul straightened and wiped his eyes with the back of his palm. "Mother, get some rest. I will watch Nala."

I shook my head. "Let us go relieve Kayal."

Later that day, I found Vasant in his tent huddled with a few of his men. When he saw me, he said, "Aunt Meera, I will join you shortly."

While I waited, my mind traveled to the past. His mother, Riya, a childhood friend of mine, had jumped out of a window to end her life. Her unhappy marriage to Nakul drove her to this fateful decision. When Jay had told me what happened, guilt tore at me for neglecting her. I had indirectly caused her death by proposing her marriage to my brother, and my role in her demise still haunted me. And Vasant's father, my unclaimed brother, was killed before I could reveal the truth of his birth to him. I pushed those old thoughts aside to focus on my new worries.

Vasant dismissed his men and came to stand beside me. "Aunt Meera, I was going to come and find you myself. To talk about these strange happenings."

I plunged right in. "Vasant, Vikram was lost at sea. Every time I think about it, I have more questions than answers. Who brought him here? Why here, instead of Akash, the Malla capital? Why would he stab Nala?"

My nephew's eyes widened, and for a moment, he looked like his father. "Priya was not exaggerating about you, Aunt Meera. When I discussed these matters with her, she asked me to talk to you."

Despite my troubles, my lips curled up. "My daughter might have magnified my capabilities."

"Not merely her. Uncle Jay would often wish for your wisdom when stumped by a challenge." My brother. I had almost forgotten him in the chaos. What relief would flood his mind on hearing about his son?

Vasant continued, "Here is what I know so far. The two men with Vikram appeared to be Thari men. They did not put up much of a fight. I asked my guards to search the forest, but they found no one else."

"Did you talk to Vikram?" I asked.

He hesitated for the beat of a drum. "Not yet. Vikram does not seem like himself. I wanted to wait for Uncle Jay to arrive before I questioned him."

Before I could respond, Atul burst in. "Nala is asking for you."

The air around us changed in an instant. We rushed to him. What thoughts my head held, I could not tell, beyond my prayers. Please, save my son, I pleaded to all the gods.

His wife, Kayal, knelt beside him, holding his hand. Tears poured from her eyes and dripped down her chin. Priya hovered near his foot, sniffing. I took his other hand, and the coldness shocked me. I pushed his hair out of his pallid face.

"Mother, Vasant," he whispered, and Vasant moved closer to him.

"Kayal is carrying my child. If it is a boy, crown him—"

"No," I wailed. "I need you. Kayal needs you. You will live to raise your son." Kayal sat frozen on the other side, speechless with anxiety.

"Mother, I do not have much longer. Listen to me carefully. If it is a boy, crown him and make Amar his regent. If it is a girl, crown my brother as the king of Padi. Take care of Kayal and the children," he said, out of breath.

"We will take care of them and Padi," Vasant said in a reassuring tone.

Nala glanced at me. "Mother, please guide Amar, as you did with me."

I wept with uncontrollable grief. "I am too old for this. Don't leave me like your father."

He glanced at his youngest brother. Atul stepped forward. "Listen to our mother," Nala whispered. Atul nodded, his face gone gray.

"Mother?"

His bravery and purpose gave me strength. I buried my emotions deep inside to give my son what he needed. "I will look after them all.

Padi, Kayal, your brothers, my grandchildren," I promised, kissing his forehead. He shut his eyes, a calmness settling on his face.

With tears blinding my eyes, I stumbled out. A soft hand supported me and led me to my tent. My daughter. Days merged into one vast emptiness, and Nala passed away peacefully, handing his burden to me. Nala's death crushed my heart like a boulder and drowned me in sorrow. I had no strength left in me to lift my head, let alone help my son rule. I curled up like a child, struggling to breathe.

"My queen," a voice called, and I raised my head. A deep yearning filled me as I gazed at Rish's silhouette outside my tent.

15

JAY

chariot and a few horses rode in front of me. I overtook them on my mare. Sudha peeked out of the chariot.

"Jay," she exclaimed, a mix of emotions playing on her face. "Our son is alive," she gasped as if she needed to steel her heart against her longing. Or maybe that was how I felt, reluctant to let hope in.

"I can take you to him faster," I said and held out my hand. My wife's gaze penetrated my heart, and she grasped my wrist. Bending down, I put my arm around her waist and lifted her onto the front of my horse. She clasped her fingers around my neck and buried her face in my chest.

Someone cleared their throat, and I glanced up at Rish. I had forgotten he'd gone to visit his Vindhya family. He dipped his head. It surprised me it took him this long to rejoin Meera. I tugged my reins and took off; the others followed.

Among wisps of clouds in the distance, I spotted a flock of birds with a leader in the front and others behind it, forming an arrow shape. The lone bird at the head might be their king or queen. The others trusted it to keep them safe and take them home. Like my citizens trusted me. When my son disappeared, that faith felt like an enormous burden—like a boulder pressing on my chest, trapping me.

80

I had wished to be free of it as if that was a possibility. Sudha murmured something, bringing me back to the present.

When we arrived at the campsite, an eerie stillness greeted us. My heart pounding, I dismounted and helped Sudha down. Vasant walked out of his tent and wordlessly pointed toward another. With our fingers twined, Sudha and I entered this tent. She tightened her grip, and I squeezed her hand gently. As my eyes adjusted to the dim light, I spotted two figures huddled together. When Vikram and Atul looked up, Sudha left my side and ran to her son.

"Mother," he choked, and she hugged Vikram to her chest. Atul inclined his head and departed. I walked over to my family and ruffled my son's hair. Then, I embraced both of them, taking in deep breaths of air.

Vikram broke out of our clasp and stepped back, his eyes haunted. "I hurt Cousin Nala," he wailed like a little child and sat on the floor, burying his head between his knees.

Sudha dropped to the floor beside him and stroked his back. "Your father will take care of him."

"He cannot. No one can. He is dead," he cried in anguish.

Nala? I couldn't make sense of his words. As the initial elation of finding my son faded, questions pelted my mind. It had been more than a month since he'd disappeared. Where had he been all that time?

I left the mother and son alone and went to find my nephew, Vasant. I did not have to go far. He stood outside a nearby tent, hopping from foot to foot, an old habit from the past. Something continued to be amiss.

"What is going on?" I asked, my tone impatient.

Without answering me, my nephew led me inside. Then, he launched into a strange tale, starting with him finding my son and ending with Vikram stabbing Nala. A fearful unease spread through my limbs.

"How is Nala?" I asked, afraid of the answer.

"He died this morning, Uncle Jay," Vasant said, swallowing a few times.

"Kayal," I blurted. "Where is my daughter?" I had prayed for my son's safe return. Had the cruel gods taken my son-in-law away in exchange for my son's life?

Kayal was rocking her child in a dimly lit tent. When she saw me, her lips trembled. I crossed the room in a moment and swept them both into my arms.

"Father," she cried. "Nothing makes any sense. How could he die? He was full of life."

I took Yamini from her and swayed side to side, watching her eyes droop shut. Soon, she grew limp in my arms. I set my sleeping grandchild on a small cot, and Kayal covered her with a thin cotton blanket.

I guided my daughter to a bench. "Kayal," I started and floundered. How should I comfort her? No words came to my mind. She leaned her head on my shoulder, and I wrapped my arm around her.

I remembered all the darkness that took hold of me when I thought my son had perished. "Kayal, I wish I could ease your pain and make it vanish. Even a king does not have that power. Only time can heal your wound. In the meantime, I want to keep you safe. I will send a message and order Giri Thari to come and take command here. He can lead the search effort to find Vikram's captors. And a contingent of soldiers will escort you to Akash."

"Nala wanted his ashes spread over the Nali mountains in Padi," she whispered, her mind far away.

"After your child is born, you can make the pilgrimage yourself," I said, pressing my cheek against her head. I should have kept them all in Akash. Why did I let them out of my sight?

"Vikram stabbed my husband," she said, fiery light in her eyes as she gazed at me. "Why would my brother do that?"

"I intend to find out," I said, many unanswered queries swirling in my head.

She looked at me doubtfully. "Father, he is your son and heir. Do you want the truth to come out?"

I pondered her question. "My child, I may not like the answer," I whispered, a chill spreading through my limbs. "But, as king and father, I will seek it." Vikram must be innocent of murdering his brother-in-law, even if he had held the blade. I could not imagine my son committing such a horrendous act of his own violation. Someone must have coerced him. Who?

I held her chin. "I will find out who is responsible for Nala's murder, and I will punish them," I promised her.

16

MEERA

ish entered the room, and instantly the tent appeared too small for us. I wanted to collapse into his arms and unburden all my worries. Instead, we stood at a respectable distance, and he scanned my face. His eyes pierced my heart, intent on learning all my sorrow.

"Nala is dead, and a fire burned Amar," I cried, my voice wobbling. My mind had stopped functioning beyond the grief I held.

He tousled his short hair, more gray than black. "I cannot fathom —I am sorry—I should have been here." He took a step toward me and then stopped. "I am sorry," he whispered as he clutched his hands behind his back.

Tormented by his presence, I moved away. I had no right to expect anything from him, yet I didn't want him to leave.

"After we landed in Malla, things got tense with Prince Atul," he muttered and rubbed his eyes. Prince Atul. My son. One he could not claim as his. "I thought it best to—"

I remembered what Jay had said about me hurting the ones who loved me. Rish's hurt reflected in the emotions flashing on his face. Inflicted by my actions.

I stuffed my feelings into a trunk and locked it. "Rish, I am sorry too," I mumbled. *For using you and hurting you.*

"How can I help, my queen?" His stiff chest and tight shoulders told me of his tremendous effort to control himself while his eyes blazed with fierce emotions.

I swallowed a few times, trying not to think about his arms around me. I longed to be held and comforted. I pushed such thoughts away to get my head to focus on his question.

"Nala wanted me to crown his yet-to-be-born son or his brother Amar. I would be starting over with a new king. If you want to stay in Vindhya, I understand. But I could use your h-help," I stammered, my emotions choking me.

"My queen," he said softly. "I am still sworn to protect and obey you."

"No," I said harshly. Rish's eyes narrowed as if inspecting me for the first time and wondering what had come over me. "I release you from all the oaths. I don't—Rish, you are free to choose." I had never given him a choice in the matter before.

"Free to choose?" he repeated, his brows furrowed.

"To spend your days with your daughter and your family. You have already given me more than I can ever repay in this life or the next."

"After all these years, are you questioning my loyalty?" he asked, heat coating his words.

"What? No." I sounded confused even to my own ears. "Rish, I don't doubt your loyalty."

"What do you want from me then?" He sounded resigned.

I wanted him to choose me. Not because my father or brother had ordered him. My desire sounded foolish. Did I question his love? Or did I fear his rejection? "I don't know if I have the strength to start over. To help my second son rule."

"Meera," he said in a strange voice, causing me to look at him.

I pressed my fist into my sides. "I need you—your help," I stuttered.

His fingers that stood still previously now danced on his thighs. "How can I say no to you? But, putting some distance between us seemed prudent in light of what Prince Atul said."

"Rish?" I struggled to utter what I wanted. I did not care about rumors. If they had not hurt me thirty years ago, they could not hurt me now. However, I had nothing to offer him in return. Beyond more pain and hurt.

"Mother, Uncle Jay is here," said Atul as he strode in. He paused when he saw Rish, his gaze darting between us.

"Atul, I asked Rish to come to Padi with us. To help Amar and me." Though, he had not agreed yet.

Atul's thinly drawn lips expressed his displeasure. "I will likely remain in Akash with Uncle Jay and Vikram, Mother. Unless you need my help as well."

Rish remained frozen, but his flared nostrils betrayed his emotions.

What had happened between these two for them to take on a fighting posture? Before I could find out, my brother marched in. And the already small tent seemed overcrowded.

"Meera," Jay said while he observed the other two. Then his gaze rested on me, and his face softened. Without saying another word, he embraced me tightly. My anguish at Nala's death threatened to drown me. I wanted to beat my chest and tear my heart out. But that would have to wait till I was alone. A lone tear dripped down my chin onto his chest.

He released me and stepped back. "I have asked Vasant to join us," he said as Vasant entered the room.

"Meera, Vasant mentioned your suspicions. They mirror mine. We don't know where Vikram was for the past 45 days or who saved him. We don't know how he came to be here. I will talk to him, but he may not have the answers." We listened intently to him and made no sound apart from our breath.

"I have asked my Southern Commander Giri Thari to come here and scour the area. Kapil will activate our spies." Jay looked at me as if to check if I approved. I inclined my head.

"Vasant wants to continue his journey south. Meera, I assume you are no longer going to Saral?" He paused and waited for me.

Saral, my mother's land, still seemed out of my reach. Not trusting myself to speak, I shook my head.

"Then, my men will escort you and Kayal to Akash. And we can decide the next steps there."

He turned to Atul and Rish. "Atul, I need your help with Vikram, so join us." The boy dipped his head.

"Rish, do you have any urgent matters in Vindhya?" Jay asked.

"No, my Majesty."

"Then, Meera's safety is your responsibility," he ordered. Without looking at me, Rish bowed to his king. So much for my attempt to give him a choice.

Atul cleared his throat. "I am not sure that is wise, Uncle Jay," he said.

"What is not wise?"

"Asking Rish to guard my mother," he muttered. I noticed Rish flinch before he rearranged his face. It irked me to hear Atul call his father by name. Though Atul remained in the dark about the relationship, this blatant sign of disrespect troubled me. No wonder Rish seemed upset at him earlier.

"Why? He has done it incredibly well for close to three decades." Jay said, brushing away any concern.

"There are rumors…" Atul started. My heart pounded in my ears, deafening me. How could he bring this up in front of all of us?

"Rumors? If you mention any rumors about Rish or your mother, I will throw you in a dungeon till you learn better," Jay snapped. Atul gulped back the rest of his words.

"Leave, all of you. I have more things to discuss with my sister," Jay ordered, and the room cleared.

17

JAY

*R*umors. That idiot would cause his own downfall.

"Jay," Meera said. I looked at her drawn face and creased lines around her mouth. This tragedy had aged her.

"I cannot stop for long in Akash. I have to take Nala—cremate my son in Daya," she gasped and covered her mouth.

I squeezed her arm as she clasped her hands tightly in front of her chest. I guided her to a mat and sat beside her. She sat immobile as if moving might open her flood gates of despair. We were no strangers to death. While the distance of time had faded, the images of my past and memories of one day remained etched in my mind. On the day of our mother's death, Meera and I had huddled together in her room. I had not completely understood the loss of our mother and what that meant for us. But my sister did, and she had protected me from the conniving royals around us.

After a long pause, she added, "I have to take Amar, Heera, and Kayal with me to Padi."

"Kayal? She is expecting a child. All this travel cannot be good for her," I protested.

"She is carrying a royal child of Padi. One who should be born in Padi. Like me, your daughters are no longer Malla princesses. They

88

are Padi's daughters now. Send whatever men you want to protect them. Amar will act as the regent till the child is born," she said, her voice growing stronger.

"Her child will be in danger then," I worried. I wanted to keep my children near me, though what Meera said made sense.

"Jay, both Amar's injury and Nala's death happened on Malla soil. The danger is no less here," she said. We still did not know who was behind Amar's incident. It must be somebody new to Malla. Otherwise, Kapil's net would have snagged them already.

"Jay, do you think both events are linked? Is someone eliminating Padi royalty?" she asked, her finger winding her sari end.

I rubbed my nose. "They maybe. But we cannot be sure. Vikram is not himself. We don't know why he acted the way he did." Another long pause followed while our minds traveled roads long forgotten.

"Will you investigate the murder of my son?" she implored, looking at me.

My throat tightened at her words.

"I don't blame Vikram," she added. "He is a pawn in someone else's game."

I nodded. "They will not go unpunished."

She sat still for a moment. I remembered my despair when I thought I had lost Vikram. I knew what she was going through. "Nala was a wonderful king. All the mistakes I made as a new monarch, he avoided them easily," I said.

"He was a thoughtful son, caring and considerate," she whispered, her voice trembling.

"You raised him well, Meera," I said. She had succeeded where I might fail. That notion troubled me deeply.

"He takes after his father," she replied, winding her sari end.

That gave me the opening to ask her what I had in mind. "Meera, I don't know how to comfort Kayal." I hesitated to add more. My sister was a widow herself. She would be able to help my grieving daughter walk the arduous path ahead. Suddenly, I considered if my wives would grieve at my death. A sinking feeling settled in my stomach.

My sister patted my shoulder. "I will look after her. I promised my son that. I cannot bring her husband back, but she will not lack for a mother's love."

She viewed me kindly. "Nala was a good husband, and life for Kayal will not be easy. But she has her father's heart. She will survive." As if she read my mind, she added, "Don't be too hard on yourself, Jay. You have been a good father to your children. And a great king."

* * *

Vasant departed to Saral with both of us pledging to send the other messages. Giri Thari arrived shortly after. Rish, Giri, and I discussed what to do next.

"Start in the neighboring villages. Trace Vikram's path. Someone must have seen him arrive," I said.

Giri nodded. "We will comb the area, my Majesty. And Kapil has spies scouring the seaside villages for any news."

Rish gazed at me. "Have you talked to the prince, King Jay? Does he remember anything of his journey?"

I had broached the topic with him briefly. He became agitated when he tried to recollect what had happened to him. I decided to give him time to heal and dropped the subject.

"Not yet. My son needs time to mend," I replied without elaborating.

Leaving Giri to continue the investigation, the rest of us made our way back to Akash. Kapil had sent additional city guards, so we marched like a conquering army coming to lay siege to the capital. Under a cloudless sky, I gazed at my beloved city gleaming in the distance.

The gates were thrown open, and the army snaked its way in.

Aranya found me in my chambers soon after my arrival.

"Jay, what happened to Nala? Is it true that Vikram stabbed him?"

I sighed. "I don't believe Vikram knew what he was doing," I said, worried about my son. The boy looked frightened of his horse, so he'd traveled in a covered chariot with Atul. "And I don't want rumors about him spreading," I cautioned my wife.

90

I had ordered the royal physician to inspect him. In his present state, it would be impossible to crown Vikram as my heir.

"I don't like this at all, Jay. First Amar and now Nala. Someone is targeting the Padi clan. Our daughters' lives might be at stake next. I don't want to send Kayal and Heera to Daya. Let them stay here." Aranya rubbed her elbow as she spoke, betraying her nervousness.

I tried to reason with her. "Aranya, a married daughter is part of her husband's family. And Kayal may be carrying the future heir to the Padi throne."

She knew all that. She had left Saral to start a new life with me in Malla. But reasoning with a mother's heart was futile. "Jay, talk to your sister. She will listen to you."

"My sister is also the queen of Padi," I added more sternly than I intended.

"You both put Magadha ahead of everything and everyone," she said, her eyes narrow slits. Without waiting for my reply, she stormed out.

The news I learned later that night revealed the arguments with my wife to be in vain.

Kapil brought the physician to me. "My Majesty, I have examined the prince. He is physically healthy but appears to be addicted to poppy milk. Someone must have given it to him to treat his pain."

"Poppy?" I asked.

"Yes, King Jay. I don't use it, but many healers in Kashgar utilize it to suppress pain. Whoever treated the prince had let him grow dependent on it. He is struggling without this indulgence. I would avoid any mention of the recent trauma or any other upsetting matter in front of him. With proper care, I expect him to make a full recovery in time."

"Would the addiction make him delusional? Exhibit irrational fears?" I asked.

"It might, my Majesty. While under its influence, the reality could become twisted." Did someone who knew its effects bend his perception? Point him as an arrow at Nala's chest?

We talked more about my son's treatment, and I thanked the man.

Throughout this conversation, Kapil oscillated as if he held a lighted charcoal piece in his hand. After the healer left, I said, "I cannot imagine you brought me good news."

"I heard from our Padi spy chief. Prince Kanishka is attempting to seize the throne."

"Kanishka? Parth's son?" I asked. Seventeen years ago, Parth had murdered his brother, King Atul. At the time, I could not save my brother-in-law from his clutches. But I had punished Parth for his acts. I had him banished to Kashgar and then killed him many years ago.

Kapil nodded. "Some Padi royalty appear to be supporting the usurper."

18

MEERA

ayal and I cleaned Nala's body, my mind empty of
feeling like a parched desert. We left his face to the
end. When we lifted the cloth covering, a sob escaped Kayal. She
dropped to her knees, covering her eyes with the crook of her elbow,
another cry erupting from deep inside.

Even to attempt to comfort her seemed futile. "Kayal, get some
rest. I will finish here," I said gently.

With moist eyes, she gazed at me. "There is a hole in my chest
where my heart used to be. How did you find the will to wake up each
day?"

The lonely nights of the past flashed through my mind. "I lived for
my children. And to protect the kingdom entrusted to my
safekeeping."

"On his death bed, Nala admonished me to live. To attend a feast,
watch a dance drama, get wet in the rain." She straightened her
slumped shoulders. "His love for me warms my insides and lights my
path."

His father had loved and cherished me, too, though I had trampled
it in my weakness. "He was devoted to you, my child. Few queens can

93

depend on such fidelity from their husbands. Still, your path will be riddled with bumps," I said.

"Aunt Meera, with you as my guide, I can overcome these obstacles." She wiped her eyes and stood up, tenderly resuming the cleaning of my son's face. "Nala told me to listen to you. He worshipped you."

I had been a fool. I went looking for help in the wrong place. Kayal would be my partner in ruling Padi. She and I would have to strive to live up to my son's lofty ideals.

My daughter, Priya, came to my tent to bid me farewell.

"I cannot bear to see you suffer," she cried and wiped her damp eyes with the back of her hand. For a long while, we just held each other tightly. My heart ached for the child I had lost, not wanting to let the one beside me leave my side. But when you raise a daughter, you harden your heart at her first breath. She would always belong to another through marriage as I belonged to Padi.

"I am still holding on to hope you will visit me in Saral one day," she said with a deep longing in her voice.

"My child, my life has been like a river brimming with rain, finding new paths to cut through. Maybe one of these paths will bring me to Saral," I added with equal yearning. I had imagined days filled with silence and solitude in my twilight years. Now, I faced the task of grooming a new ruler.

We hugged again, tears filling our eyes.

* * *

Jay had completed our travel arrangements, and we started our journey under a gray sky. We transported Nala in a special cart decorated with flowers. My mind still refused to acknowledge that my firstborn had died before me.

We proceeded on the same path we had traversed just days ago. The same row of Moringa trees now stood brown and faded. Our animals and wheels crushed the wilted white flowers on the ground.

The hot sun blazed as I arrived in Akash in an emotionally suspended state.

Amar entered my chambers behind me.

"Mother," he cried out.

Looking at his stricken face, I stretched my arms and hugged him tightly.

"What do we do now, Mother?" he asked, his brows furrowed.

"Your brother appointed you as regent to his unborn child," I told him, and his lower lip trembled. "If Kayal gives birth to a princess, then you will be crowned as Padi's next king."

He covered his face with both his palms. "I am nearly blind. I can barely take care of myself. I cannot do this. You have a third son. Let Atul wear the crown."

Atul could not sit on Padi's throne. He had no Padi bloodline. I owed that much to my late husband. "What foolishness is this? I am not going to crown my youngest in place of his older brother."

"Why not, Mother? In the Mahabharatha tale you used to tell us, the older blind brother was set aside, and they crowned his younger brother Pandu instead." His injuries had mostly healed, but ridges and bumps replaced his prior smooth skin. As he talked earnestly, the dark reddish scars seemed to reflect his mood.

"The Mahabharatha epic is a tale of caution. The sons of the two brothers fought over the kingdom and destroyed it in the process," I said, exasperated.

"Atul and I are not those brothers. Mother, it is difficult for me to refuse you, but I will not sit on the throne," he said, jutting his chin forward.

"Amar, do you think it was easy on me when your father died? Nala was nine years old."

"Nala grew stronger and wiser every day, and your burden eased. What do I have to look forward to? A lifetime of pity?" He moved away from me and crossed his arms, then bent his head, so his chin touched his chest.

Instead of understanding, anger surged through me. "Easy? Do you think my life has been easy? You are a coward. Kayal has more strength than you," I ranted.

At my outburst, he turned to face me, his narrow eye slits even smaller. Color rose in his cheeks. "Queen Kayal? I could never compete with Nala or her. Crown her then."

Fool. I would if a woman could sit on the throne.

Amar marched out of the room, banging my door shut. My anger ebbed away. I collapsed on the floor. I had nursed Nala at my breast, wiped his tears as a child, and held him in my lap as he'd slept. In turn, he had honored me by becoming a great king and an even better man. And now, my son was gone forever. I wept from some deep part of my heart, and my tears stained my sari like raindrops during a monsoon. *Gone forever.*

My brother found me curled up on the floor, limp and lifeless.

"Meera!" He rushed to my side and knelt on the floor. My eyes were swollen shut from all my crying, but I could still hear him. He lifted me gently and carried me to my bed.

"Have you eaten? Where is your maid, Kantha?" he rattled, worried about me.

"Jay?" My voice sounded hoarse. "What do you want?"

"Nothing. It can wait," my brother said.

"It cannot be worse than losing my child. Go ahead and tell me," I mumbled. I tried to sit up, and Jay rearranged my pillows to help me. He handed me a cup of water, and I gulped it down.

Then he took a deep breath. "Prince Kanishka is claiming the Padi throne."

For a moment, I did not understand my brother.

"Parth's son," Jay added.

Parth, my brother-in-law, had murdered my late husband. Though Parth had been dead for many years, the mere mention of his name provoked my anger. Nala and I had been kind to his son, Kanishka, affording him all the comforts of a prince.

"He cannot claim the throne with Amar alive," I said.

"He is asserting that he is older than Amar and not blind. Some Padi elders are supporting his claim."

"Prince Naren?" I asked, and Jay nodded. Naren was my husband's cousin.

"I will gather Amar, Atul, and Rish in my chambers. Join me after you have cleaned up and eaten something," he added. His eyes swept my face with his brows furrowed.

"Don't worry about me. I am still alive," I muttered. Unfortunately. While my loved ones departed.

He kissed my head and turned to leave. "Ask Kayal and Heera to join us too," I called to him. He paused and gazed at me. With another nod, he strode out.

I washed my face in the nearby basin and let the cold water wipe my tears away. Nothing could wipe the anguish from my spirit. I draped a clean white sari around me to mourn my son. Kantha brought me hot broth, and I took a few sips. The liquid burned my throat and eased my hunger. But it offered no solace to my heart.

Jay had sent my youngest to fetch me. Whatever his misgivings about Rish, Atul's face softened when I glanced at him.

"Mother, the others are gathered and waiting for you," he said. With the emotions swirling on his face, he appeared vulnerable. His body had barely caught up with his height, and he looked lean and hungry. How had I forgotten how young he was?

"I am ready, Son," I said.

He hooked his arm through the crook of my elbow, and we walked through the dark halls. Even though he slowed down to match my pace, I could sense his restlessness in the swinging of his free arm.

"Is all well with Vikram?" I asked.

"No," he said and paused. "He is afraid of his own shadow. I have been sharing his bed, so he does not have to sleep alone."

Mired in my misery, I forgot to ask Jay about his son. I sighed. Then I warned Atul. "Make sure you don't let word of his illness spread."

"I know, Mother. That is why only Uncle Jay, Aunt Sudha, or I take care of him."

Voices floated from Jay's room as we neared it. Rish would be there. I should ask Atul to refrain from hurling insults at him. But I had no strength left in me to argue with another of my sons.

As I walked in, the voices quieted. Atul led me to a seat beside Kayal. She reached and squeezed my arm as I lowered myself down.

"Kapil, tell us what you know so far," Jay directed.

Kapil stood at an angle, favoring his injured leg. "Queen Meera, when the news of King Nala's death reached Daya, Prince Kanishka gathered other royal members together. He is older than your sons, Prince Amar and Prince Atul. He is staking a claim to the throne and has gained supporters," he addressed me.

I replied, "If Naren is supporting him, General Gambhir will side with him too. I understand him plotting in secret, but I don't comprehend why he would go public with this. Jay, by himself, commands a larger army than Padi. Combined with the Saral army under Vasant, this battle would end before it started. There is something else we don't know. And it is emboldening Kanishka."

Jay nodded. But, before he could say anything, Amar spoke. "Mother, here is the perfect solution to our dilemma. I don't want the crown, and you don't want Atul wearing it. Let us crown Kanishka. That fool is actively seeking it," he said with a laugh that did not bring any warmth to his face. Instead, it made his scars appear menacing.

Heera moved to the edge of her seat, her face flushed in agitation. As she prepared to calm her husband, her sister, Kayal, touched her knee and shook her head subtly.

I returned my gaze to my son. "His father murdered yours," I said in a clipped tone. Atul regarded the scene unfolding with his mouth open.

"We cannot burden the son for his father's crimes," Amar said.

"Amar, I am not having this conversation with you now," I said sharply, my voice raising.

"We are discussing Padi succession. And you want me to accept your choice without having a say in the matter? Do you care about Atul or me? Or only about the throne?" Like a king cobra strike, he spewed venom with his words, and I recoiled from it.

"Amar," Jay said, clenching the hilt of his sword. His lips stretched thin. "Your mother is the elder of our family, and I will not allow you or anyone else to disparage her," he said, his eyes sweeping the room.

Amar hauled himself up, his face awash in crimson. "Sit down," Jay commanded in a quiet voice. "I have no time for your temper tantrums."

Rish stepped forward and touched Amar's shoulder. The boy jumped out of his skin.

"I did not mean to startle you, Prince Amar."

"Uncle Rish!" Amar peered at the man beside him. I realized now what he had been trying to tell me all along. With his sight gone, he did not know who had gathered here.

Amar almost leaped into Rish's arms, like he had done many times as a young child. Rish hugged him tightly, patting his back. Amar had never known his father. And Rish had helped me raise him.

Atul's face reflected his revulsion at the sight. With a deep frown, he turned aside. My heart shriveled at my youngest's contempt, but I focused on the bigger problem at hand.

"We are here among family. Do I have your permission to speak my mind, my Majesty?" Rish asked.

Jay inclined his head.

"Prince Amar, a conspiracy stole your sight. For a young man, this is devastating." Rish paused and stole a glance in my direction. My heart stood still.

Rish continued. "Like Sanjaya acted as King Dhritarashtra's eyes in the Mahabharata epic, we can find a loyal guard who can serve as yours." I remembered this story. Sanjaya even possessed divine sight and narrated the Kurukshetra war to the blind king.

"Your mother and all of us here," Rish concluded, "have confidence you can overcome this physical obstacle to rule Padi wisely. Someone attacked you from behind instead of facing you on a battlefield. You giving in will let them win." Memories came rushing like rainwater flooding a dry creek. Rish had aided me similarly countless times when I had become frustrated with the boys. Especially Amar, who had rebelled against my rules. Rish had an incredible ability to calm him down and make him listen to reason. I never realized until this moment how heavily I had relied on him while the boys were young. Rish had even helped Amar learn to ride his horse, fight with his sword, and had taught him battle strategies and more.

Amar rubbed his chin. "Will you help me, Uncle Rish?" That was a common phrase my children had uttered growing up.

"It would be my honor," Rish said. A range of emotions coursed through me, and I did not have time to decipher them.

"We need to send an envoy to Daya on Amar's behalf. Rish would be an excellent candidate. He knows Padi royal dynamics well. What do you think, Meera?" Jay asked.

I sensed Kayal shifting in her seat. "Let us ask our present queen first," I deferred to Kayal.

Kayal's eyes shone at my gesture, and her father's lips curled up. "Kayal?" he prompted.

"I cannot think of anyone better," she answered.

"Any objections?" All were quiet. "Rish, head to Daya. Make Kanishka see reason. I am ready to go to war to see my grandson or nephew seated on the throne. I hope it does not come to that," Jay stated.

Rish caught my eye as if to ascertain my wishes. I dipped my head slightly, a sudden warmth spreading throughout my chest.

19

JAY

ifeless, Nala's corpse rested on top of stacked sandalwood planks along the Chambal Riverbank. Meera had reluctantly agreed to cremate her son here in Malla. Amar lighted the pyre of his brother, reciting hymns to release his soul to the next life. My nephews and I circled the burning fire. A fortnight ago, I had worried about not finding my son's body to cremate him. Now, in a twist of fate, my sister had outlived her oldest son. As I watched the embers from the flame, her tormented face drifted into my mind. I worried a part of her had died with her son. The smell of burning flesh mingled with sandalwood assaulted my nostrils.

I shifted to escape the odor, and my glance fell on Rish. He stood farther away from us, but he had played a colossal role in Nala's life. As our eyes met, I noticed the dampness in his. I had wed women I did not love while he could not marry the one he wanted. But I had enough worries of my own without taking on another man's concerns.

We washed our bodies in the flowing river water, cleansing ourselves. Cold ash from the pyre would be collected later today and placed in a clay urn to be spread on the Nali mountains.

The brothers walked in front with their arms around each other's shoulders. A subtle way for Atul to guide his sightless brother while Amar remained sensitive about his injury. Rish and I followed a few feet behind. Rish's glance darted to his son's back frequently. Their rift had thrown them apart, probably breaking the father's heart. However, Atul had been my anchor these past few days. Vikram was at ease with his cousin. His mother and my fragile emotional states made things more difficult for the boy. Sudha broke into tears in his presence which frightened him more. And my frustrations with his fear played on my face. While we created a vicious cycle with our actions, Atul showed remarkable patience and compassion for my son.

Rish and I headed to my chamber to discuss his trip to Padi. He stood quietly, staring out of my window. The sun had begun its descent, and noises from the garden below carried over.

"Rish, I want to avoid a war," I said, and he spun to face me. "But we have to be prepared for one. Talk to our northern commander, Darsh Vindhya, and ask him to prepare for a conflict. Take some of his men with you to Daya," I ordered, and he acquiesced. My brother-in-law, Darsh Vindhya, now commanded the northern troops.

"My Majesty, I am bothered by Prince Kanishka's action. Prince Naren and General Gambhir are seasoned warriors. They must have a plan to capture the throne. Otherwise, this makes no sense," he said, rubbing his chin.

Yes, I worried about that too. Some key element eluded me.

"Rish, use stealth to find out what their plans are while publicly sharing with Kanishka and others the wishes of my nephew, Nala. Their king wanted his son or brother to sit on the throne. If Kanishka persists in his foolishness, I am willing to defend their birthright with my sword."

"I will deliver your message, King Jay. I will also try to find out who else is aiding him," Rish said. He stood tall, with age enhancing rather than diminishing his stature.

I sat down and wrote two brief messages, one for my northern commander and another for Kanishka. I handed them to Rish.

"I have made preparations to leave tomorrow at dawn," he added and departed.

I organized a feast that night to celebrate Nala's life. As I accepted the condolences of my minister, my daughter walked in. The sight of Kayal in a widow's white sari with her bare forehead and lack of jewels stopped my heart. Aranya, who stood near me, grabbed my arm, and her fingernails dug into my skin.

"She is too young for this, Jay," she cried, and I agreed with my wife. "You were supposed to protect her," she accused me. I had no answer to that.

Kayal approached us with a serene face. Aranya hugged our daughter tightly. "You are carrying the heir to Padi. Allow me to pamper you, my child."

"Yes, Mother. I promised Nala I would take care of myself," she answered with a determination that made me proud.

I embraced her next. "My grandmother and my sister abandoned the white sari after the initial eleven days mourning period," I said. It tore my heart to see her in clothes with no color.

She looked at me and said, "I intend to wear this till I give birth, Father." While doubts plagued me, she seemed clear on what she needed to do.

My sister found me afterward. Her attire matched my daughter's except for the bangles on my sister's arms. "When did you switch to wearing white?" I asked. And why? I wanted to see them in a saffron silk sari with gold threads. Not in this grief-stricken cotton.

"I intend to wear it as long as my daughter-in-law," she answered. I could not argue with that.

"Jay, let us walk to a secluded spot. I have something important to discuss," she added.

She wound her sari around her index finger. Something troubled her. I took her elbow, and we walked to the palace garden. Darkness shrouded us with lit torches dimly lighting our path. I found a bench by the pond, and we sat side by side.

"First Vikram and then Nala. This is an ominous sign, Jay," she started.

"Sign for what?" I asked with my brows furrowed.

"Us failing to rectify our mistake. This throne belongs to Vasant by birthright," she hissed.

"Do you think he would have made a better king for Malla?" I asked, puzzled.

She hesitated for a moment and appeared like the sister from my youth, about to tease me. "No, I don't think that at all."

"Then, I am the only one injured by the decision to wear the crown. Why am I being punished?"

She sighed. "I have made many mistakes. Dancer Madhavi died for me. I don't want my children to pay for my transgressions." I assumed she counted Rish as one of her transgressions.

"Meera, that is not how any of this works. If you commit any mistakes in this life, you will be reborn, and you will pay for them then. But these are not wrongdoings. You and I, as rulers, require people to fight for us. You know how many lives my sword tip has claimed?"

"Vasant—"

"What about him? He sits on the Saral throne and looks after his people. Meera, we talked about this already. We need to bury that past. If we claim Vasant as our father's grandson, who wears the Saral crown then?"

"I cannot lose another child, Jay," she quivered.

I reached to squeeze her arm. "Meera, remember what you told me seventeen years ago. When I expressed my doubts before my coronation? You said this was Father's wish. If it is his wish, then I cannot be a usurper."

"Nala is dead, and Amar and Atul are angry at me," she said, her hands trembling.

"Tell Atul the truth, Meera," I said.

She glared at me. "No. I told the truth to the one person that needed to know. My husband."

"I guessed it, and so did Rish. From his hostility to Rish, I can tell Atul suspects too," I said softly.

She shook her head. "No, Jay. I cannot."

"I cannot tell Vasant either," I said.

We were quiet for some time. "I will consult your royal astrologer and fix a day to perform a *pooja* to please the gods," she mused.

"Sudha wants to perform a *yagna*, a fire ritual to thank the same gods for bringing her son back. Join her," I said. *If gods were real, the world would not need kings*, I thought. But I kept it to myself.

I escorted her to her chambers and then proceeded to Vikram's.

Vikram and Atul were playing a game of dice. My son rolled the long wooden rods and moved his shells around the board.

"I am winning, my dear cousin," he said, tapping the table with his fingers.

"Wait for me to roll before you claim victory, Vikram," Atul said. He then threw the twin sticks.

Vikram shook his head while laughing. "Bad, bad throw." My lips curled up at seeing him exhibit confidence and joy.

Atul shrugged his shoulder and moved his pieces. I almost stopped my nephew from making the wrong move. But he caught my eyes, and I realized he was deliberately losing to my son.

"Uncle Jay," he greeted.

Vikram looked up, and a shadow passed over his face. My poor child. The past few days, I had let my disappointment in his condition be visible on my face.

I stepped closer and tousled his hair. He made a move to end the game.

"No, finish it. I will wait." I assured him and wandered around my old chambers. His grandfather had taken him hunting in the Vindhya forests. He had hung the head of a male spotted deer on the wall, its antlers two feet wide. A large stuffed crocodile rested on the floor, its mouth propped open. I had never enjoyed hunting animals for pleasure. I had killed too many on the battlefields. My father-in-law, Mani Vindhya, who'd never fought, hunted for amusement.

I heard chairs scraping on the floor as the game wrapped up.

"You always win, you rascal," Atul said and bumped his cousin's shoulder. A grin covered my son's face. They talked about their game strategies, and I watched my boy with an insatiable yearning. Almost losing him had made me want to capture every one of his gestures and words.

Atul cleaned up the board while Vikram wandered toward me.

"Atul told me about Prince Uday perishing at sea."

"Yes, we recovered his body after the storm," I said. A sharp pain stabbed my chest at that memory.

"He also said you married his sister, Princess Ratnavali," he asked with his eyes cast down. I scanned his face. Was he angry at me? Had his mother said something?

"I d-did," I stammered.

"Why? She was betrothed to Cousin Amar," he asked, glancing at me for a beat of my heart. Then he stared at the floor again. How would I explain the madness that took over me?

"Her father did not want to continue the engagement after Amar's accident," I said.

"You could have forced him to honor it," he said, a faint color spreading on his cheeks. He still refused to look at me.

"Why would I? I have daughters too," I said, clenching my fist—a lie. I had not thought of my daughters. Only about the son I thought I'd lost. And I had convinced myself I needed another heir.

"Why is marrying an old man better than a blind one?" he asked sharply. Old? I wanted to slap him across his face. I clenched my fist tighter.

"I am still your father," I said coldly. "Did you forget that?"

"No, Father. You remind me of that constantly. Since your new wife is about my age, can I call her by name, or do I address her as Mother?" he asked, glaring at me.

I did strike him then. His head swung from side to side. "I will not tolerate such insolence from you," I snarled and strode out.

Wave after wave of fury and despair pounded my chest. I marched through the dark halls breathing hard. I heard hurried footsteps follow me. Had that boy forgotten some insults?

"Uncle Jay," called Atul. He came to a halt beside me, still breathing normally.

"Vikram regrets his words," he said.

His comment only made me angrier. "Since when do I need a messenger from my son? He can come and apologize to me himself," I barked and left him. Atul did not follow me.

My steps took me to Ratnavali's chambers. Her guard opened the door and let me in. My son's barbs rang in my head. *Old!* I entered her bedroom, still seething.

As I took off my sheath and dropped it on the floor, she woke from the noise.

Like a startled horse, she looked around. "My lord?" I had not visited her in many days. I should not be here now. Not with anger coursing through me.

I bent to pick up my sword, and she stood up at the same time. Her body collided with mine, and I grasped her waist to steady her.

"Are you leaving already?" she asked.

I was about to say yes. Then my wife placed her palm on my chest and gazed into my eyes. Her face glowed in the half moonlight, her hair unrestrained and tumbling down to her waist.

"Will you stay?"

I hesitated for a moment. She leaned closer, our hearts touching. Instead of replying, I crushed her lips with mine. She trembled under my arms. Had I hurt her? As I pulled apart, her fingers wound through my hair and tugged me closer.

"Don't leave yet," she whispered against my throat. I gathered her in my arms as my kisses left a trail of warmth on her neck.

20

MEERA

In the predawn hours, I made my way to the stables. Rish and his men saddled their horses, talking in a low voice.

Rish saw me as I stood at the threshold. With raised eyebrows, he approached me. "Queen Meera, I would have come to you if you had sent for me," he said and bowed his head. The conversation stopped, and all eyes observed us.

I adopted his formal tone. "Commander Rish, I wanted to discuss your plans. Would you mind walking with me?"

I waited till he joined me, and we strolled to a spot a few yards away. We stopped under a ficus tree with an arm's length distance between us. His men could still see us, but they could not hear us anymore.

"My lady, King Jay wants to avoid any conflict." He then proceeded to narrate what he had discussed with my brother. I only paid partial attention. I trusted my brother and Rish to handle this delicate situation. Instead, my gaze swept over him from head to toe. I had fallen in love with him over twenty-five years ago, and he still caused flutters in my stomach. The passing years had been more than kind to him. His short hair enhanced his chiseled cheekbones and chin. His broad shoulders—

"My lady," he whispered, his eyes gleaming like deep wells with the crow's feet at the corners resembling streams feeding them. I could fall into them and never climb out. Warmth spread in my cheeks when I realized I had been gaping at him.

"I apologize for Atul—"

"Apologize?" he asked.

"For his b-behavior," I stuttered.

He ran his fingers through his hair. "Why? Because things did not work out according to your plan?"

"Plan? I did not plan for his hostility," I said with rising anger.

"He called me names that no—" He stopped short of calling himself a father. Even in his fury, he knew he would cross a line if he did so without my sanction. But our culture valued filial respect and affection. I had denied him that. Rish pushed his fist into his hip and took a deep breath.

"What do you want from me, Meera?" he asked, all formality gone. His face became a mask.

What did I want? To throw my arms around him and weep on his shoulders. To wipe the sorrow in his eyes. To wake up next to him every morning. "I do not have any claim on you to expect anything," I said.

"You are mistaken, my queen. I had laid my heart at your feet. But you rejected it. More than once." With no backward glance, he marched away. It hit me with a pang. Every time I had a choice, I rejected him. But what did he expect me to do? Marry an untitled warrior when enemies threatened my kingdom? I had hurt him, choosing duty above love. What was the use of lamenting choices already made?

I made my way back slowly, with my heart broken into pieces. Even through my heartbreak, I could not bring myself to hate him. I could not fault him. I had taken him for granted and pushed him far beyond the limits a man would tolerate.

A cold breeze swept through, causing me to shiver.

Rish approached me, walking his horse. His men had already mounted their rides.

"If you allow me, I can escort you to the palace gates, my lady." I scanned his face, but any feelings he had for me remained buried or gone. Except for his eyes. They seemed to reflect some concern for me. Did he retain some tenderness for me? Or was it worry for a lone woman shivering in the cold? It did not matter.

I was as adept at hiding my true emotions as he. We had years of practice.

"That will not be necessary, Commander," I said stiffly.

"I will not fail Prince Amar, my lady," he said as he mounted his stallion. He had never failed me. The same could not be said about me.

He rode away, leaving me alone.

The next day, Queen Aranya came to see me. She had put her gray-streaked hair in a bun. A simple crown embedded with glittering rubies rested on her head. With age, she had gained a natural elegance. Jay often left the governing in her hands when he led offenses at sea or abroad. I could see why my brother had fallen in love with her. She exuded a rare mix of delicateness and strength.

"Queen Meera, what happened to Nala was a tragedy. To see my daughter in her widow's attire crushes my heart." She blinked her misty eyes.

I had switched to wearing white too in solidarity with her. But I had been a widow for over seventeen years. I'd been older than Kayal when my husband died. And I had Rish by my side to help me.

"Kayal has the grit of her mother and the nobility of her father. And she is secure in Nala's love for her," I said to console her mother.

"Nala's love is a double-edged sword, my queen. As much as she cherishes it, it does make the loneliness unbearable," she answered. That it did.

She continued, "If she heads back to Padi, everything will remind her of the time she spent with Nala. I wanted to see if she can stay here in Malla till she gives birth." She reached and touched my arm gently.

A queen has to be a mother to her kingdom as well as her children. I sighed and shook my head. "Aranya, my son has died, and I am still alive. So I understand your anguish. But she is carrying the heir to

Padi. That is where she belongs. Once Rish and Jay settle this dispute with Kanishka, I will travel back with her. Giving birth in Padi will only strengthen the claim of her child."

Tears shone in her eyes, and she gripped the arm of the chair.

"You are welcome to join us in Padi, Aranya," I added and squeezed her hand. With Jay's marriage to Ratnavali, I guessed she would welcome a chance to be away from them. I was lucky. My husband had never married another woman. Only I had not cherished him enough while he lived.

"You are a fountain of strength, my lady," she added with a slight tremor in her voice. "I hope Kayal learns how to overcome her obstacles from you." My source of strength, Rish, had just left me, and he might never return. I could not blame him for I had treated him poorly.

"She can learn from both of us. And we can pamper her and our impending grandchild," I said.

Her lips curled up a grain. "Yamini sang a song to me. She must have learned it from you," she added with pride in her granddaughter's ability. My face brightened. Yamini reminded me of Nala at that age. The two grandmothers then spent the rest of our time extolling the virtues of our grandchild.

In a few days, I invited Atul to join me for my mid-day meal. He countered my invitation by asking me to join him and his cousin. Since I wore no jewels or make-up, it took me no time to get ready. The boy appeared at my threshold promptly to escort me. His smile slipped when he saw me.

"I hate to see you like this, Mother," he said.

"Like what, Son?"

"No jewels. No color," Atul said with a grimace.

I took his hand, and we made our way to Vikram's chambers. "When I lost—" I paused. His father was still alive. "When I lost my husband, I lived for you, my children. Now, with Nala dead, a part of me wants to cease."

"Mother, you are frightening me. I still need you. Amar needs you. He is lost in self-pity, and only your love can pull him out." He stopped and gazed at me, seeking assurance in my face. I reached up and pushed his hair back. He bent his head slightly to make it easier for me. While the boy resembled me, he took after his father in height. And his long hair reminded me of Rish's flowing locks before he cut it short.

"I am still here, Son," I added, and we resumed our steps.

"Mother, Vikram agonizes about hurting Nala. He was not himself when it happened. Please don't hold it against him," my son pleaded.

I had avoided my nephew till now, worrying about my reaction. He took my beautiful child away. I pressed my lips together, and Atul tensed beside me.

"Don't worry, Son. I carry no weapons, and my gaze will not burn him," I said. His brows furrowed.

When we arrived, Vikram prostrated on the ground, his forehead touching my feet and hands gripping my ankles.

"Aunt Meera, forgive me for my heinous act," he cried, tears dripping onto my toes. My anger melted away at the sight of his contrition.

"My child, rise," I said, tapping his shoulder. He stood up, sniffling as his hair curled around his ears. I hugged him tightly, rubbing his back while he mumbled his apology over and over again.

Soon, the three of us sat down to eat. Jay's servant Muthu brought us our food. Seeing me, he murmured his condolences. I accepted with a dip of my head, not wanting to upset my nephew by mentioning Nala. I noticed that only Jay's loyal men guarded and served us today. My brother had ensured Vikram's condition remained hidden.

I observed my nephew's fingers twitch as he moved the food around, barely eating any. Atul, on the other hand, relished the meal.

After Muthu cleared our plates away, I sat beside my nephew and took his hand in mine. I asked, "What happened that stormy night?"

Across us, Atul opened and closed his mouth a few times. But he remained quiet.

Vikram tensed at my question, and I squeezed his palm. And waited patiently.

"I held Uday from behind while keeping us both afloat. He had lied. He could not swim. And he panicked as the waves grew in height. When a large wave hit us, he grabbed my throat. Choking me," he said, touching his neck. In his vulnerability, he looked more like his mother. And less like my brother.

"I tried to escape his grip. To prevent him from drowning us both," he cried, looking at Atul and me. I reached the back of his neck and stroked it gently.

Atul moved to his other side and put his arm around his shoulder. Atul's touch calmed him, and his breathing eased into a steady rhythm. Jay had raised them both, and they had grown closer than most brothers.

"He must have struck me because I lost awareness for a while. When I awoke, I was clinging to a wooden plank, and our ships were nowhere in sight. Thirsty and tired, I removed my heavy sword and sheath and dropped them into the sea. Then I swam toward Malla. When the sun came overhead, my arms grew limp, and I just let the current carry me." He paused here and stared out the window.

"Night and another day passed. The next thing I remember was a man hovering over me. He gave me some water to drink. From the rocking of his vessel, I surmised I was on a boat. He brought us ashore. I could not tell where."

Another long pause. Neither Atul nor I spoke. "I did not reveal my true identity to the fisherman. I told him I was a distant Vindhya cousin. I paid him one of my gold earrings and promised another at the end of the journey, and he took me on a cart to Akash."

"Akash?" Atul asked. We had found him south of Akash.

"Yes. On the way, we encountered some Buddhist monks traveling to Akash. They spoke in a strange accent like they were visiting Malla. One of the elderly monks was a skilled healer, and he treated my injuries. The man who rescued me left me in their care and departed. He had not anticipated the journey to Akash to take so long, and he wanted to return to his family."

"Some monks from Kashgar are seeking refuge in Akash," Atul said. "You could have met them on their journey."

Vikram shrugged his shoulders. "I told them the same tale I told the fisherman, and we traveled west." I felt a tremor in his hand as he drew a breath. Atul and I barely moved.

"One of the monks gave me a potion. After I drank it, I felt like I was floating in the air. I lost my awareness. Then slowly, nightmares plagued me, and I could not wake up from them." Sweat glistened on his forehead. Like I would do with my sons, I wiped his face with the end of my sari. Atul fetched him some water, and Vikram took some sips.

"I don't remember much. I remember the strange man in saffron robes with his bald head and mad eyes. His face hovered near mine whenever my eyes opened." He rubbed his face as if trying to erase him from memory.

"He must have taken care of me because I don't remember eating or drinking. My dreams became worse. Waves pounded my body, and the cold water drowned my breath. I could not breathe or call for help," he gasped.

I leaned forward, forgetting to breathe.

"Then, one day, I woke up among two men. Strangers. They said the royal family was near, and they would take me to them. But to be wary of a man named Nala. By then, I barely recalled my own name and followed them in a haze. Each step caused my head to break into pieces. One of them gave me tiny sips of the potion, and it let me stay alive by keeping the pain away." Atul and I exchanged glances. Poppy milk. And whatever else mixed in to cause him his nightmares.

"Then, after a day of walking, I started perceiving things around me. We were near a stream when one of them started screaming. Vasant and—" he paused and buried his face in his hand.

"It is okay, Son. We know what happened next," I whispered. Nala rescued him, only to plunge into his death.

He lifted his head. "When I saw Nala, something in my head screamed at me. To kill him. Before he kills me," he whispered with a strange glint in his eyes, and a blind terror choked me.

21

JAY

"Jay," called Meera as she entered my chambers. I rose from behind my table to greet her.

"What brings you here, Meera? I would have come to you if you sent for me."

"There was no time for that. I am coming from Vikram's room. Someone gave him mind-altering herbs," she answered, her words flowing like a river rapid.

"Mind-altering? How do you know?" I asked, rubbing my chin.

"I asked my nephew to narrate what happened to him since the storm," she said.

I gasped. "How could you, Meera? The boy is still recovering." The physician had advised against bringing up any traumatic subject with him.

"How could I?" she shot back. "Why didn't you ask him earlier? He has kept it all to himself, and it corroded his mind. Talking about it has unburdened him."

Did I make a mistake by not talking to him about his actions? Irritation flared in my chest. "I am his father and king. And you knew I have not asked him these questions—"

She snapped at me, "Do I need your blessing to talk to my nephew?"

"Yes, in this matter," I growled.

"Are you speaking as my brother or as the king of Malla?" she asked in a cold voice.

"As if that matters," I muttered.

"I might listen to my brother. But if you are ordering me around as a king, I want to remind you that you hid behind my skirt during your first council meeting." She looked at me like she used to in our youth. When I had done something inappropriate for a crown prince, I knew that look meant a long lecture when we were alone.

"I was five, and our mother—" I started and then stopped. I was acting like a fool. With everyone else, I had to be king. Always. With her, I was her little brother first. She remembered all my stumbles along the way and had helped me remedy them.

"Did you realize you sounded like an imbecile?" Her eyes lit up briefly like a cloud moving to reveal the sun.

"Yes," I agreed and laughed. I had missed my sister. I could reveal to her my doubts and mistakes without the worry of being judged as a poor king.

"What did my son reveal?" I asked her, and she narrated a strange tale.

"Monks? If they traveled to Akash, why would they abandon him south of here?"

Her brows furrowed. "They brought Vikram to us after planting a seed of doubt in his mind. A seed that grew roots and stabbed Nala."

I gaped at her with my mouth open.

"They turned my nephew into a deadly weapon against my son," she said with a tremor in her voice.

I put my arm around her back and guided her to a bench. My mind spun like the wheel of a chariot. "You are right. I should have talked to my son about this earlier. I was worried about hurting him further."

"I know how that feels. I avoid conversations with Amar and Atul frequently these days. Fearing I would smack them," she winced.

"I hit Vikram a few days ago," I mumbled, heat rising in my cheeks.

She stared at me. "Was it about Ratnavali?" she asked perceptively.

I nodded.

"Jay, you cannot let him disparage her or your marriage. She is your wife. There is no going back, whatever you wish. She is blameless and deserves to be treated with respect, especially by your family. Any disrespect to her reflects poorly on you."

I rubbed my forehead. Just thinking about this mess hurt my head. "What do you suggest I do?"

She sat gazing at the foot of the bench. Our father had designed it. The sculptors had carved each leg to resemble a tiger paw. "Your son has returned. A temple visit with your wives and him would be in order."

"I feel like I am moving a boulder uphill. I think I am making progress, and then the boulder rolls down."

She laughed at my analogy bitterly. "That aptly describes what I am feeling."

I brought us back to her reason for visiting. "Monks from Kashgar are here in Akash seeking shelter. I will ask Kapil to fetch the head monk. I will get to the bottom of this."

When Kapil arrived, I told him a summary of what I had learned from my sister. He listened without interrupting me.

"My Majesty, my spies have been watching these monks in Akash. I have had no reports of any suspicious activity. They seem to be pious Buddhists like they claim."

"Do we have any confirmation that he truly has the Kashgar prince with him?" I asked.

"There is a young boy who lives with them. But no confirmation that he is the rightful prince, my Majesty. I have sent two men to Kashgar. With the chaos there, it will take months for me to ascertain the news."

I rubbed my forehead. It would not be prudent to make them suspicious before we had evidence. "While I cannot imagine Head Monk Yonten being behind any nefarious activity, they are already meddling in the royal affairs of one state. Nothing stops them from meddling in ours. Bring him back to discuss the safety of the prince in his custody. I want to see the boy too."

Kapil inclined his head. As he shifted to leave, I said, "Kapil, one more thing."

He glanced at me, waiting. I clenched my fist. It was time. "Resume Prince Vikram's training. Ask Prince Atul to be his sparring partner. Get my son back on a horse. Tell them it is an order from me."

"I am glad Prince Vikram is back," he replied softly and departed.

The next day, a boy of about thirteen or fourteen stood in front of me. "This is Prince Aggabodhi," said Yonten.

The boy wore saffron robes and no jewels. He bowed his shaved head. "I thank you for your hospitality, King Jay," he spoke clearly with only a trace of an accent.

"Do all of Kashgar speak our language so well?" I asked, bowing to him in return.

"They barely speak it at all. My father hired a tutor for me when things worsened," he said. Only a slight downward curve of his lips indicated any displeasure in his present state.

"I hope I can be of help in reuniting you with him," I said.

"He might be gone," Prince Aggabodhi said with trembling lips.

I cursed myself. With the turmoil in Kashgar, I had no reliable news from there. I glanced at Yonten to see if he knew more than me.

"I have no new messages from King Rajasuriya," he said. He then handed me a ring. "We feared for our safety, so we did not bring any letters from the king. But I carried the royal ring on my person."

I inspected the gold ring closely. It bore their royal crest, a banyan tree. I handed it to Kapil. While he checked it, I guided the visitors to my table.

As the servants served our food, I talked to them about their living quarters.

"Thanks to your generosity and Buddha's grace, we found a small house in Akash. We have a place to pray and sleep. And Chief Guard Kapil sent a cart with food supplies so we can cook our meals."

Soon the servants departed.

Coconut rice, spicy pumpkin stew with lentils, stuffed small purple eggplants, banana flower fritters, and a ripe banana coated with honey crowded my banana leaf. Using my fingers, I scooped up a mix of the eggplant with the rice. The hot peppers in the vegetables balanced the sweet coconut rice.

The growing prince finished all the food on his leaf.

"Should I ask them to bring more?" I asked with the corners of my mouth turned up.

"Just the fritters, King Jay. I like their crunch," the boy said with a grin.

After the meal, we moved to the sitting room.

"Kapil, why don't you take the prince to the training yard and our stables?" I asked.

He nodded while Yonten added, "Away from prying eyes. Remember you are pretending to be a monk now."

After they departed, I asked, "Who is training the prince?"

"I have been teaching him history and language, King Jay."

"Warfare?" I pried.

"We, as monks, cannot train him in the use of weapons."

I rubbed my forehead. "He is young. It is important to continue his training. I can make arrangements with Kapil to train him in secrecy."

The monk hesitated. "I promised his father to keep him safe."

"Then it is even more important for him to learn to wield a weapon properly," I persisted. "To protect himself and others."

He inclined his head. "I place him in your custody during his training."

"Monk Yonten, are any of your disciples missing?"

His brows raised, he asked, "How did you know, King Jay? One of the older healers who escaped with us to Malla had gone east to get some supplies. He should have returned to us by now. But neither he nor the man who accompanied him is back."

My heart raced as it did before a battle. I leaned forward. "Tell me more about them."

"The healer has been with me for decades. He was devoted to helping the sick heal. He lost his herb supplies at sea. So he wanted to replenish them. The man who went with him is a newcomer. For the past three years, he worked in the monastery, cooking and cleaning. He is originally from Magadha, so when he offered to come with us, I accepted. He was invaluable in guiding us once we landed on your shores."

"When did they leave?" I asked, my mind leaping ahead.

"About two months ago. May I ask why these questions? Did you find them? Or know what happened to them?"

I shook my head and spoke carefully so I did not reveal too much about Vikram. "Unfortunately, I have little of value to tell. One of my men encountered a monk east of here. But he lost him on his way to Akash. I will have my men look for them."

He did not seem satisfied with my explanation, but he did not press me.

A few days later, I walked to my son's chambers. The afternoon sun filtered through the trees onto the hallway. Men and women scurried about like ants.

Vikram rose on my entry. He was alone and dressed in a white dhoti lined with golden threads for our temple visit. I shut the door and approached him.

A muscle twitching in his jaw betrayed his emotion in an otherwise calm face.

I adjusted the simple crown resting on his head. "When I thought I had lost you at sea, I nearly went mad," I said, a lump forming in my throat at the memory.

He stepped closer. "Father."

I put one arm around his shoulders, wiping my eyes with the other.

"I apologize for the other day," he murmured.

I gazed at his face. "Your anger was not without merit, Son." His eyes widened. "But Ratnavali is guileless." His face reddened at the mention of her name. "Don't hurt her for my actions."

"I-I don't intend to hurt her," he stammered.

I patted his back. "Let us not keep them waiting," I said, and we strode out of the room. My son would have chatted constantly before his drowning. Now, he appeared contemplative. I also noticed that his frequent twitching had reduced—a sign of his healing.

"How is your training?" I asked.

His face brightened. "Atul and I fought with spears today. The first day, even when he held back, he defeated me within moments. This morning I fought toe to toe with him. It took him longer to knock me. Uncle Kapil said I have improved vastly in the last few days."

I grinned at him. "I will come and watch you soon."

We reached the stables. Aranya, Sudha, and Ratnavali were already seated inside a chariot. Two gentle mares stood nearby. Vikram bowed to the women, and we mounted our rides. Sudha beamed at her son, her pleasure in his recovery evident on her face.

On our way, Vikram smiled and greeted the passersby. My eyes lit up at this sign of normalcy.

We dismounted at the temple entrance. Vikram walked to the chariot to help my wives.

Aranya took his outstretched hand and descended. "Son, you are almost taller than your father. It is time to find you a bride," she said. The boy had turned sixteen a few months ago. I should start looking for matches for him.

Faint color rose in his cheeks as he said, "That is for you and father to decide."

Sudha hugged her son as he helped her.

As I watched them, Aranya stopped next to me. "When he went missing, you haunted the palace like a ghost."

I glanced at her. Her few gray hairs along her ears shone in the light. "Accompany Ratnavali inside," I said. Her eyes searched my face. She was my queen. She knew that these appearances mattered. She dipped her head in assent.

Vikram held out his hand to the lone chariot occupant.

"I am glad to see you, Prince Vikram," Ratnavali said as she grasped his hand.

"I am sorry I could not save your brother, Princess—Moth—," he stuttered. Watching them stand awkwardly reminded me of their closeness in age. If we had known Vikram was alive, her father would have wanted him to be the groom. Not me. The thought struck me like a whip on my back.

"Don't worry, Jay," whispered Aranya in my ears. "He is merely a boy. No girl is going to prefer him over you. Not for a few more years." Her words rubbed me like salt on a raw wound. I pressed my lips together. I was not jealous of my son.

"Ratnavali," Aranya called before I could respond, and Ratnavali hurried toward us. They strolled inside.

Sudha clasped her son's arm, and they entered the courtyard together.

I stood for a moment to calm the turbulence in my head. Then I followed them slowly, pausing to talk to the temple visitors.

As I walked past granite pillars sculpted with scenes from the Mahabharata war, a voice reached me. "Danger awaits the prophesied prince."

I searched the hall and found a grandmother holding her grandson. She pointed out some carvings to the young boy. As I was about to move, she turned to me. With strange unfocused eyes, she said, "Keep him safe."

Unnerved by her voice, my legs froze to the ground. Was she addressing me? The boy shrieked loudly, breaking my spell. In my current state, even stories told to a child infused fear. I reined in my ludicrous thoughts and joined my family.

* * *

A MESSENGER ARRIVED from Giri Thari that night. Kapil brought the man to me.

"We found a dead man wearing saffron robes two miles from the campsite," he said.

My eyes widened. "How old was he?"

"Past his middle age, King Jay." Could he be the healer who went missing?

"Anyone else with him?"

"One or two villagers claimed to have seen two monks in that area.

122

But no word about the other man." My heart thudded. Who was the other man? Had he killed the monk and abducted my son? Or betrayed his partner? What did he want? No answers came to me.

"Kapil, talk to Yonten. Ask him to send a man who can identify the healer." I turned to the messenger. "The monks are missing one of their disciples. Their healer left two months ago to collect some supplies. Let one of them come with you to see if they can recognize the dead man. I will write a note for Giri."

As I dipped the feather tip in ink, my mind raced. I could defeat an enemy on the battlefield with conventional methods. But I would need bait to capture one who played hide and seek.

22

MEERA

I arrived in Heera's chambers as the maids lit the brass and silver lamps. The delicate fragrance from the scented oil diffused in the air as the wicker burned brightly.

Heera approached me in a sandalwood-colored sari that glowed in the light. "Aunt Meera," she called with extended arms. I grasped them and hugged her. Among the many things spreading darkness in my life, she shone like a bright star.

Amar entered the room and squinted in my direction. I strolled toward him.

"Mother," he called. I reached up to cup his face with tenderness. He leaned into my palm, relaxing for a moment, letting go of the pain surrounding him.

"Gramma," a high-pitched voice called my name. I bent down and scooped up my grandchild in my arms. Jay had gone to the temple with his Malla family. Since we still mourned Nala, the Padi clan stayed behind. Kayal followed Yamini, her tiny bump visible underneath her white sari.

When Atul entered the room, Yamini leaped into his arms. "Horsey!" she exclaimed loudly.

He tugged her ear. "Not tonight. We can go riding tomorrow morning. Maybe Uncle Amar will join us."

Before Amar could find a reason to refuse, Kayal answered, "Great idea." She took the child to feed her while the rest gathered in Heera's sitting room.

"I have not been on a horse since—" Amar pointed his index finger at his scarred face.

"I saw your mare in the stables today. She is itching for a ride. You hold on to her reins, and she will take care of everything else," Atul answered.

Amar swallowed. "It will be lovely to get some fresh air," he muttered.

Atul stepped closer to his brother. "And I can blindfold myself. I am sure I can control my horse better than my older brother."

Amar straightened his shoulders and scoffed. "You can try." I realized I had held my breath as this conversation happened. I slowly released it. When had Atul become so perceptive to say the right thing to nudge people to action?

Later that evening, as we sat down to eat, Amar said, "Uncle Rish must have reached Padi a few days ago. We should hear from him soon."

I glanced at Atul at the mention of Rish's name. A momentary shadow crossed his face, but he rearranged it quickly. He made a ball containing tamarind rice and fried plantain in the center and tossed it into his mouth.

"Will Kanishka agree to drop his claim?" asked Kayal.

"If he wants to live," Amar said.

I wondered about it. Why did he stake a claim on the Padi throne? Did he have an alliance that we knew nothing of? Who had an army formidable enough to fight us? My nephew ruled Saral, and my brother ruled Malla. Both would back Amar. Kanishka's actions made no sense to me.

Kayal touched her brother-in-law's shoulder. "Nala trusted you to lead Padi. You know how much the kingdom meant to him. He did not make this choice lightly."

Amar flushed at her words. "Queen Kayal, I hope you are carrying the next heir to Padi. And I will serve—" he paused to wet his lips. "I will serve as his regent till he comes of age." It gladdened me to see the gradual shift in my son.

"If I give birth to a princess, the queen's crown will look good on my sister," Kayal said, smiling at Heera.

Amar's face darkened. "Regent is one thing. Sitting on the throne? How can a blind man lead a kingdom?"

Heera clasped his arm. "You will not be blind. You will have many eyes, including mine."

A pensive look settled on his face. Deciding to give him space, I asked, "Has Vikram gone to the temple?"

"I assume so, Mother. I helped him get ready," Atul answered.

Kayal tensed at the mention of her brother's name. He'd murdered her husband, so I did not blame her for her reaction. But my nephew seemed to have been a mere arrow in someone's quiver. The man who fired the arrow deserved our scorn. Not the poor boy.

That night, as I got ready for bed, a knock sounded on my door.

"Meera," Jay called. I opened the door, surprised to see him at this hour. Had my idea for the temple visit turned sour?

He came in and paced. I shut the door and stood still.

He stopped suddenly and spun to face me. "Meera, I think these events are connected."

"What events?" I asked, puzzled.

"Amar's fire, Vikram's kidnapping, and Kanishka's bold claim to the Padi throne. They must be linked," he said, his words tumbling like a waterfall.

I furrowed my brows. "Are you saying Kanishka deliberately murdered my son to usurp the throne?" He almost murdered Amar as well. Heat coated my words as I followed his thread.

Jay shook his head. "Not Kanishka himself. That boy is not clever enough for this. But someone set this in motion on his behalf. They likely wanted to hurt Nala on his journey south. Instead, Amar was injured. They waited patiently for another opportunity. When Vikram fell into their trap, they used him to murder the king of Padi. Their target appears to be the Padi throne. There is only one man I know who is devious enough to set a plan like this in motion." He stared at me.

Fear clutched my chest. "Parth!" I gasped. "B-But he is dead." My brother-in-law Parth poisoned my husband. As punishment, we had banished him to Kashgar. And Jay had him killed.

"Kapil had hired a sellsword to execute him. We had received credible information confirming his demise. But that slippery snake must have faked his death and escaped. And he then changed his identity and joined the monks, marking his time to come back to Magadha."

I stared at Jay with my mouth hanging open. Parth had killed his kind and generous brother. He would show no mercy to his nephews. I staggered, and Jay caught my elbow.

"Meera, he has the upper hand now. And he is operating in the shadows. I ordered Kapil and Giri to fish him out."

His words did not penetrate the terror that gripped me. Parth would not stop till he destroyed my family. I had to protect Kayal, Amar, Heera, and Atul. My breath came in short gasps.

"Meera," Jay grabbed my shoulders and squeezed them gently. My awareness came flooding back, and sweat broke out on my forehead.

"Whoever it is, they are no match for you and me," Jay said, holding my gaze.

His calm assurance chased away some of my despair. "What if he remains invisible and pulls the strings of the puppets under his control?" I asked.

Jay rubbed his nose. "I assume that will be his plan. He is not a conventional enemy to kill on the battlefield. He is not going to follow the rules of warfare. Poison, treason, backstabbing, all repugnant to us, will be his weapons of choice."

I followed along. "We have to pretend to fall for his tactics. Make him believe his strategy is working." Would we be able to defeat this vile man? We had no other choice. I suddenly remembered my daughter, Priya. Queen of Saral. I'd received a message from her recently. Chandra and the child growing inside her made her tired, and she wished for me to be with her. My wish matched hers, but Padi needed me more than she did. "Jay, Vasant cannot be in the dark about this. Neither can Amar."

He nodded. "And Kapil and Rish. I will send a trusted messenger to Vasant. Parth has murdered twice. We cannot let him strike again." Our eyes reflected our worry and determination.

The next day, we gathered in Jay's chambers. We had decided to conceal Parth's name from everyone but Kapil. With no evidence beyond our suspicion, it felt prudent to keep that notion to ourselves.

"We have reason to believe someone poisoned Vikram's mind to attack Nala. The people behind this odious act may also be supporting Kanishka's claim to the throne," Jay said. He stood tall in the middle with no fear or hesitancy on his face.

"Vikram's drowning was an accident. No one could have anticipated that," Atul mused.

"That is true. But when an injured prince arrived on the scene, this person or group used it to their advantage," I said. Jay nodded.

"This is someone very dangerous then," Kayal stated.

Vicious, I thought.

"Dangerous and cunning. A small crack is all that is needed to collapse a kingdom," Jay said ominously. Silence reigned after his words.

"How do we protect ourselves?" Amar asked.

Jay glanced at Kapil, his spymaster.

"We are using two messengers instead of one. Harder to attack or corrupt two men. We are requesting King Vasant to do the same. We check all our food, and I am personally interrogating any new servants we have hired. My spies are on alert and spreading their web to catch our prey," Kapil said. I wished our suspicions about Parth were proved wrong. But who else would target the Padi royalty and rally to Kanishka's side. With Kashgar in turmoil, Kapil will have difficulty tracing the sellsword. We had to rely on catching the culprit here in Malla.

"This is not an enemy that will follow our laws. Be vigilant. Talk to Kapil or me if you have any suspicions," Jay stated as he dismissed us.

In a few days, a guard arrived at my door.

"A messenger has arrived from Commander Rish, my lady. King Jay asked me to fetch you to the small council room." At the mention of Rish's name, my heart skipped a few beats.

I hurried after him. When I arrived, slightly out of breath, I surveyed the room. My brother and my sons stood around the teak table while mother and daughter, Queen Aranya and Queen Kayal, sat beside each other. A man with many battle scars on his arms and chest stood in front of them, twisting his long beard. He bowed upon seeing me.

"We were waiting for you, Meera," Jay said. "Give us the news from Rish," he commanded the newcomer.

"Prince Kanishka denied any interest in usurping the throne, my Majesty," the soldier said.

Jay threw his head back and laughed deeply, and it echoed off the walls.

23
JAY

eera scowled at my laughter. *I have not gone mad yet, Sister.* Of course, Kanishka would deny everything. His father had taught him well.

"What about General Gambhir?" Meera asked.

"General Gambhir and Prince Naren have pledged their fealty to Queen Kayal and Prince Amar, my lady. They expressed their eagerness to welcome Princess Heera to Padi." Till the traitors were rooted out, I would not be sending my daughters to Padi.

He continued, "Commander Rish spoke with the Padi council as well. He requested a small delegation to meet him at our northern command post, near the Padi border." He wanted to see us on Malla lands. That was a message in itself.

"Did he want us to gather on the Malla side of the border?" Meera asked. Her thoughts likely ran along the same path as mine.

"Yes, my lady. He mentioned our northern command post under General Darsh Vindhya."

I dismissed him shortly after. A quiet settled over the room, allowing the sound of birds from outside to float in.

"Rish does not trust them," Meera stated, her lips pressed together. Her eyes sought me, and I inclined my head in agreement.

"I will take some men with me and meet Uncle Rish," Amar said, drumming his fingers on the table.

"No," Meera and I said in unison. She waved at me to continue.

"Amar, you are next in line to the throne. Until we know who our enemies are, I want us to be cautious," I added.

He squinted at me. "If it is dangerous for me to go, it is more dangerous for Queen Kayal."

Meera wound the end of her sari around her finger and took a breath in. "I will go meet him," she said.

I nodded. "Yes, that would be wise. You are still the beloved queen of Padi."

Her eyes gleamed. "Beloved or not, I have been the queen mother for a long while."

I rubbed my chin. "You cannot go alone. I will come with you, Meera."

Kayal shook her head. "Father, you are the king of Malla, ruler of Magadha. If Kanishka is sowing discord, your presence will aid it." I frowned at my daughter. My presence would put an end to this masquerade that Kanishka had any chance to grab the throne.

"I agree, Jay. This needs to be a Padi delegate," Meera said, looking at me. "It will be better to converge away from the Malla command post as well. But still on this side."

I understood her desire to act as a Padi queen. But I could not let Meera go alone. Or send my daughters with her. "Take Atul with you. He is a Padi prince." At least in name, if not in blood.

At the mention of his name, Atul's head swiveled side to side between his mother and me. He was not a member of the Padi royal family. But that knowledge remained a secret known only to a few of us. Anyone else who suspected the truth would be too afraid of my wrath to mention it.

Meera opened and closed her mouth a couple of times. "Yes, he can speak for his brother," she said. The boy remained silent.

I started making arrangements for their travel. Amar, Atul, Kapil, and I discussed the plans. Most of the Padi men who arrived with Nala stayed in Akash, and they would be the primary escort with key Malla men embedded within them for safety.

The night before their departure, we gathered around the rosewood table in my room to eat our evening meal. The sun had set, and stars glittered in the sky. A gentle breeze rustled the trees outside.

"If Rish thinks it is safe for me to go to Daya, I am planning to head there, Jay," Meera said.

I clenched the hilt of my sword. "They will not harm you publicly. You are akin to the mother of Padi." I lowered my voice and leaned toward her. "But, with the company you are keeping, they are bound to spread rumors." I would have to speak to Atul to prevent him from undermining Rish's authority.

A tightness appeared around her eyes. The last few months had aged my sister. Cracks emerged in her normally regal appearance. "I know the traps he sets," she whispered as she glanced at Atul.

Amar and Atul conversed about the trip, their heads almost touching.

"Why do you keep looking at me like that?" Vikram suddenly asked in a trembling voice.

I startled and followed his gaze as Kayal shrank back from him.

"I didn't mean to hurt him," he wailed at his sister as Sudha clasped his arm. He pulled away from his mother and stood up. Atul and I rose from our chairs. My heart hammered in my chest as I inspected my son to make sure he had no weapons.

"Vikram," I gently called as I approached him.

"If Aunt Meera can accept my apology, why can't you do the same?" he yelled in a shrill voice. Tears welled up in Kayal's eyes as she gaped at her brother. I did not know what it would take for her to forgive him. Vikram had murdered Nala, her husband, and cursed her to a life of loneliness. Aranya put a hand on her daughter.

I grasped my son's shoulders. He tensed at my touch and spun to face me.

"Give her time," I whispered.

Suddenly, he buried his face in my shoulder and broke into sobs. My heart squeezed tightly at his emotions. I wrapped my arms around my son, rubbing his back. That confident young prince who had traveled to Sunda was gone. In his place stood this broken boy. I did not know how to put him back together.

Kayal moved to the door with her mother with an apologetic backward glance. I sighed at the pain reflected in her misty eyes and waved her away. My children were hurting, and I had no means to help them.

Everyone else dispersed except for Sudha. We guided our son to a seat and sat on either side of him.

"I am going to miss Atul," he hiccupped. "His steady breathing helped me fall asleep."

Sudha glanced at me, deep lines on her forehead.

"You can sleep with me tonight," I said, squeezing his shoulder. "Both of you," I added. "My bed is large enough for the three of us."

"What? You want me to sleep with you like I am four?" Vikram asked with raised eyebrows.

I remembered the four-year-old boy who ruled the palace. He must be still in there somewhere.

Sudha tousled his hair. "I miss those days," she said with yearning.

"It is settled. Get the servants to bring what you need from your rooms. I have some work to do, but I will join you soon."

I rose and kissed his forehead. On impulse, I bent to kiss his mother's forehead as well. She did not push me away. Her arm wound around my waist instead.

I stayed in her embrace for a few moments, and then I left them alone and went to find Atul.

My nephew was throwing garments into an open trunk when I arrived in his room. Darkness shrouded his face with a lone lamp emitting a faint light. I needed to see his face for my conversation.

"Get someone to light some lamps," I said.

"I can do it, Uncle Jay. How is Vikram?" he asked, lighting several brass and silver floor lamps. A gentle glow spread around the room, dispelling the shadows.

I rubbed my forehead. "His mother is with him, and he will stay with us tonight."

"Uncle Jay, I can stay—"

I gazed at my nephew. I had raised him as my own for close to seventeen years now. "Your aunt and I will take care of Vikram. Your mother needs you more than I. You go with her."

He gulped and nodded.

"Atul, my sister entrusted you to my care when you were just a few days old. In the meantime, she ruled a kingdom and raised your brothers and sister with the help of Commander Rish. It was the wish of King Atul, after whom you are named, that Rish served as Nala's regent. He has been a loyal sword serving your mother and me for decades. He deserves your respect, not scorn," I said, scrutinizing him.

He stared at the floor with his mouth set in a hard line.

"He is on a mission at my command. Make sure you don't jeopardize it," I added, more harshly than intended.

Jaw clenched, he glanced at me. He looked like he would burst into a flame. But slowly, he brought himself under control and dipped his head.

More softly, I said, "My sister has lost her oldest son, and her middle son has lost his vision. Be a comfort to her." *Not a thorn in her side.*

He flushed at my remark, embarrassed. "I will not disappoint you, Uncle Jay."

With a pat on his back, I departed. I strode the halls of the palace toward my daughter's chamber. Smoke from the mounted flaming torches hovered in the air, obscuring the ceiling.

I knocked on her door, and a young maid let me in. My daughter sat in front of her mirror, braiding her hair for the night.

"I will finish the rest myself," Kayal said, dismissing the girl. She exited the room, leaving us alone.

I wandered to her window. A half-moon hung in the sky, painting the towers silver.

"I don't hate my brother," Kayal said, squeezing her eyes shut.

I approached her and touched her head. I understood how she felt more than she knew. I remembered my rage when I gazed at Atul or Ratnavali while Vikram was still missing.

She hugged my waist and buried her face in my stomach. "My child, what you are feeling is normal. I don't blame you," I said, rubbing her arm.

She glanced up, fighting back her tears. "Father, I see Nala stabbed and bleeding whenever I gaze at Vikram." Her voice shook with emotion.

I bent down to press my lips to her head. "Time heals most wounds, even one this deep," I said. At least I hoped it did. "You are carrying a child. Stay away from your brother if his sight upsets you. He will eventually understand why you feel this way."

As the moon rose overhead, I entered my bedroom with a lamp in my hand.

"Jay," called Sudha from the middle of the bed. Vikram slept to her right, his chest rising and falling slowly. I noticed he held his mother's sari in his fist.

"Do you need help?" she asked, pointing at my crown.

I smiled at her question. "I can manage," I said and set the lamp on a table. I took the crown off my head and held it in my hand for a moment. Even this simple crown I wore daily weighed me down. I took off my sword and jewels and rinsed my face.

I blew the lamp and walked toward my wife. Except for the few nights I spent with my new wife, I rarely shared my bed with anyone these days, and it had been years since Sudha and I shared ours. I had abstained from our marriage bed after Vikram was born to protect her health. That had become a lasting habit. I adjusted the pillows and settled on them.

"Where did we go wrong?" she whispered, sliding closer to me.

"You have done nothing wrong," I said, turning to face her. *Whereas I have committed too many blunders.* Tears welled in her eyes, and I wiped them away. "I will find whoever did this to him." *And kill them.*

I shifted near her, and she nestled against my chest. She started to say something, but our son muttered in his sleep. She stayed silent and slowly drifted off to sleep in my arms. I stared at the ceiling for a long time, worries plaguing me.

Early the next morning, I stood on the steps, watching Meera and

Atul head to our northern border. A man on a horse galloped in the opposite direction toward me and dismounted in front of the palace.

My guards inspected him and let him through. He ran up to me.

"A message from General Giri Thari, my Majesty."

"Let us go inside," I said and took him to the small council room.

"We identified the dead monk as the healer from Kashgar," he said.

Though this confirmed my suspicion, my head still spun on hearing the news. I had banished Parth to Kashgar and ordered his execution. Could he be back to haunt me? He almost outwitted me last time. Was I ready for him now?

24
MEERA

wo men hauled my trunks away as I surveyed my room. My maid, Kantha, would remain in Akash. At her age, she detested frequent trips, and I had planned to leave her here anyway while I traveled to Saral with my daughter. Nala's death halted those travel plans. I put thoughts of my mother's land away. I might never visit her home, and pining after it brought me no comfort. A younger maid accompanying me on this journey was traveling with the supply cart.

I heard footsteps and glanced up to see my son.

"Mother, are you ready?" Atul asked, entering the chamber. He wore a bright smile on his face that masked the strain of the last few days. I nodded and took his extended hand. He escorted me outside.

A mist hung in the morning air, and a lone rooster crowed a feeble welcome to the dawn. Jay waited for us near the stables. The tightness around his eyes spoke of the burden he carried on his shoulders. My brother had several last-minute questions and suggestions for us. When he started repeating himself, I stopped him.

"Jay, take care of Kayal and Amar. We'll be fine."

He gave me a tired smile and hugged me. "Darsh Vindhya and his men are ready for any attacks," he said as he guided me into the chariot.

"They will not attempt anything in the open," I answered. "But I will still be cautious," I added to reassure him. And myself. I had no idea what plots had hatched in Parth's twisted mind if he was behind this. We had only vague suspicions.

Atul touched his uncle's feet to seek his blessing. Jay pulled him into an embrace. "You are a Malla prince as much as a Padi prince. Don't forget that."

Atul climbed in beside me. I gazed at him, surprised.

"Are you not riding?"

"No, Mother. Today, I want to sit with you," he said sheepishly.

"Send me a message when you reach Rish," Jay called as he moved away.

Atul signaled to the charioteer, and our horses took off. A cloud of dust rose in the air as our small procession of horses, chariots, and carts started down the road. The sun rose in the sky, and the mist slowly burned away. I watched the receding city when a horse came galloping toward us. Without stopping, it crossed us and headed to the palace. A messenger. Atul strained his neck to glance back at him.

"Your uncle will send us any important news," I told him.

The charioteer would not hear our conversation over the sound of the rattling wheels. Should I use this time to ask him about the rumors he'd heard? What if he asked me direct questions? I did not want to lie to him, but the truth would hurt him.

He drew figures on his right thigh with his index finger. "I am sorry for causing you anguish, Mother. With my words and actions." He lifted his head and gazed at me, his eyes burning with emotions.

I touched his cheek. While I had raised my other three children, I had sent my youngest to be fostered by my brother because I had worried the boy might resemble his birth father. Jay had given him plenty of love and affection. Still, guilt surged in me for keeping Rish and Atul apart while he was growing up.

"I was betrothed to Prince Amar, the older Padi prince. A vile man who would have made my life miserable. To protect me from my future husband, Jay appointed Rish Vindhya as head of my guard," I said, my eyes drifting to watch the fields pass by. Memories I had kept locked tightly leaked out.

"Mother—"

"You don't want to hear the story?" I asked, turning toward him.

Color crept up his face. Was he embarrassed? "I have heard this tale from others. Not from you." He swallowed and then said, "I want to hear it from you."

"Prince Amar died suspiciously and freed me from my nightmares. I married his brother, Prince Atul. Commander Rish still came to Padi along with my new husband and me." I remembered the early days of my marriage with Atul. I did not feel the passion I felt with Rish, but Atul was warmhearted and adored me. Slowly, like a winter snowfall piling up, my love for my husband built upon his constant affection. I had learned to live without desperate and wild love.

Except for that one fateful day with Rish.

"King Atul was just like your brother, Nala. Generous and strong-willed. A rare combination," I said with a smile.

My son's face brightened. Then it clouded. My smile vanished too. We both remembered Nala's short life.

"He was taken away too soon from me, just like Nala. Before Atul died, he named Rish Vindhya as the regent to your then nine-year-old brother. Atul could not make me the regent. Instead, he allowed me to rule through Rish," I said. I had leaned heavily on Rish to help me raise Nala and Amar. And he had supported me unconditionally. In return, I had hurt him over and over again.

Tears filled my eyes. "Mother," Atul said gently and put his arm around my shoulder. "I have brought back your bad memories."

I rubbed my nose. "Not all of them were bad. I had many years of happiness with your father." That was true. I had watched Rish train Nala and Amar. He had immense patience with their antics. The boys had adored him in return. And would be full of tales of all they had learned. Loneliness filled a widow's life. I drew comfort from Rish even if our shadows did not touch. A simple activity like watching the snowfall on the mountains with Rish had given me a moment's pleasure. We would barely say a word to each other, but his mere presence by my side sharing my joy kept me sane. I could not share these tales with my son.

"I wielded no sword, Son. Rish Vindhya was my sword. He helped me rule Padi till your brother came of age. As a widow, I could not have done it without his might. Whatever rumors—" I choked on these words.

He flushed deeply. "M-mother," he stammered. He stared at his fingers for some moments. "I was a fool to listen to rumors. I will not make the same mistake again."

The urge to tell him the truth bubbled up like a pot of boiling milk. I poured cold water over it.

Our journey over the next few days proceeded without any obstacles. After that first day, Atul rode his horse, and I sat alone in my chariot. With plenty of time to dwell on all my mistakes. A futile act that I quickly abandoned.

The day before we reached our destination, one of our supply carts overturned, hurting the two oxen and the driver.

I sat on a rock under a tree, watching the men straighten the cart. Atul conversed with them and marched toward me.

"We need to find replacement oxen, Mother. Ours are injured. The driver broke his hip. Our healer is treating him. He will remain in the nearby village to recover," he said.

"Are we camping here tonight then?" I asked, letting him make the decision. He was almost a grown man, and I needed to treat him like one.

He rubbed his forehead. "It will be dark by the time we repair the cart. Yes, I will ask the men to set up camp here."

As the sun sank beneath the horizon, tents rose alongside the fields. Around the cook fire, the men gathered, regaling each other with their stories. I sat in a corner eating the simple rice. Atul moved among the soldiers, talking to each cluster. There was an ease in the way he chatted. Younger than most of them, he still managed to command their respect. My brother had taught him well.

The next day, we rose with the sun and dismantled the tents.

Around midday, a dust cloud approached us from the north. A tiger flag fluttered in the wind. Malla men.

I peeked outside the chariot. Rish Vindhya arrived at the head, and his face brightened on seeing me. Then his glance fell on Atul riding his stallion, and immediately a mask shadowed his expression. I viewed my son for his reaction. His face remained neutral, but the fist clenched around the reins betrayed his anxiety.

Darsh Vindhya, Jay's brother-in-law, appeared alongside Rish. We stopped to greet the newcomers. Atul dismounted and helped me out of my chariot.

"Queen Meera, Prince Atul," said Darsh with a bow. Rish mimicked his action.

After we exchanged greetings, Rish said, "My lady, we can eat our evening meal with Darsh. Then, we will proceed further north to camp a mile from our command post."

Soon we arrived in front of a modest mansion. Rish ushered me to a small room.

"Hot water baths are hard to come by once we reach our campsite. Do you want me to ask someone to bring you one here?" Rish asked while his eyes regarded my dusty sari.

My bones ached from the clattering chariot, and a soak in hot water sounded agreeable. But watching his unreadable expression, all intelligent thought fled my mind. "Do I reek of horses?" I asked. Then, I felt my face glow. Why had I asked him that?

Rish looked at me strangely. "You smell—" he paused with his lips parted slightly. What did I smell like to him? He shook his head as if clearing stray thoughts. "It's not that. I remembered how much you relished a bath."

"I don't want to keep everyone waiting," I said.

"Not at all, my lady. I will ask Darsh to give Prince Atul a tour of the command post before we gather to eat. That should give you plenty of time."

His gaze lingered on my face. I waited for him to say something more. Rish was usually direct with his words. One of the many ways he'd aided me. But he left soon without divulging his views. I mourned the chasm that seemed to have erupted between us.

Later, Atul, Rish, and I gathered in a hall to eat our evening meal with General Darsh and a few of his Lieutenants. Atul had explored the training facilities and posed many questions to the men.

"With a friendly king in Padi, most of the soldiers have been traveling with King Jay or serving in other parts of Malla. How soon can you summon all the troops here, if needed?" asked Atul.

Darsh said, "Most of them can arrive in a week. In a fortnight, we can muster all of them."

Rish added, "I have already requested General Darsh to bring men back from non-critical missions. Do we have seven thousand men stationed here?"

"Yes, Uncle Rish. Another two thousand are on their way," Darsh said.

"We have sufficient men to defend against any attack," Rish said, glancing at me. I noticed he avoided looking at my son, even while answering his question. His tense shoulders suggested a man waiting for a different kind of attack.

Atul nodded courteously. "While I hope it does not come to that, it is good to be prepared." He gazed at Rish as he spoke. Rish caught his eyes and seemed surprised at the lack of hostility. As the meal progressed, Rish visibly relaxed. The knot in my stomach slowly dissolved.

We took leave of Darsh at the command post and continued north to an open meadow beside a lake. A flock of cranes took flight when the horses arrived. Servants took the horses and other animals to the lake to water them. Rows of tents greeted me, and the aroma from large pots of stew cooked over wooden fires filled the air.

I retired to my tent. Atul arrived shortly after and paced the floor restlessly. We waited for Rish to join us. He did not keep us waiting long.

"My lady, my lord," he said in greeting as he entered the tent.

My skin prickled at his formal address.

"Commander Rish," Atul answered, halting his march.

"What news from Padi?" I asked.

"My queen, Prince Kanishka pledged his loyalty to Prince Amar and denied any interest in the throne."

"Were you convinced of his innocence?" Atul asked. Still no sign of bitterness visible on his face. Either he had overcome it based on our earlier conversation or hid it well. I welcomed it regardless.

"No, Prince Atul. I heard from reliable sources that Prince Kanishka, Prince Naren, and General Gambhir met in secret, without the knowledge of the small council. Many times. They have been plotting and did not take care to hide it. Even though they deny it vehemently now."

"Is anyone else aiding them?" I asked.

"There have been several messages to one of the three men in question. They claim the messengers were from Padi, but our spies suspect they came from Malla," said Rish.

I wound my sari around my finger.

"Have we taken any steps to find where the messages originated?" Atul asked.

"Yes, my lord. Kapil Biha is leading that effort." I thought *I* had mastered hiding my feelings. Rish surpassed me in how he addressed his son.

Though we pretended otherwise, all three of us looked uncomfortable, like we arrived wearing the wrong outfit for a special occasion.

Suddenly, a movement caught my eye, and I scanned the tent. A guard stood outside, and a torch illuminated his profile through the tent cloth. Nothing else was out of place. It must have been the wind.

I turned to Rish. "What do you recommend we do?"

A glint caught my eye. From the corner of my sight, I saw a hand appear alongside the tent wall. There were no openings there. Then the next moment, it disappeared. Had I imagined it?

A scream caught in my throat as something flew toward my son. I stood paralyzed, watching in horror. With his back to the flying object, he continued asking questions.

"Atul," I yelled, finally getting my mouth to work.

Rish saw the terror playing on my face. In the blink of an eye, he pushed Atul to the ground. Relief flooded my mind. I ran toward my son to make sure he was unhurt. The boy caught himself and rolled onto his side. I kneeled beside him, my hand on his chest, my breath coming in gasps.

"I am fine, Mother," he said, sitting up.

A grunt sounded from above.

Both of us looked up to see Rish fall to the ground with a dagger protruding from his chest. A cry escaped me as I jumped to catch the falling man. My heart fled my body at the sight of the blood pooling on his. *Please, gods. Don't let Rish die! I cannot live without him.*

2 5
JAY

letter from King Kanva arrived. A flash of irritation surged through me at his words, like stepping on a sharp rock.

"I am glad Prince Vikram has returned safely. If we had found him earlier, he could have married Ratnavali."

Did he regret offering his daughter's hand to me in marriage? *Too old.* My son's mocking words burst into my memory. I nearly crushed the palm leaf scroll I held. My daughter had married the blind groom Kanva had rejected. He'd had his choice, and he'd chosen me. Too late to wish otherwise.

Before I could dwell on this further, Kapil entered my chamber holding a long walking stick that could also be yielded as a club. He had injured his left hip and thigh in a skirmish a few years ago. He had made a remarkable recovery since then. His limp was hardly noticeable these days.

I raised my eyebrows at the stick. "Since when do you need that support?"

"When I have to find you urgently, King Jay," he said with an upturn of his lips.

I frowned at him. "Kapil, you know I would be happy to come to you."

"Yes, my Majesty. Not many kings would have made me Chief Guard after my injury. You have made many accommodations for me."

I scoffed, then joked, "What? You think I will not replace you in a moment if I find someone better than you? It is your misfortune that you are stuck with me." A loyal friend like him was rarer than snow in Malla.

His face brightened.

"What is the grave matter?" I prodded.

"Monk Yonten is here seeking your audience. He refused to tell me any details. Only that it is urgent he sees you today."

"Is this about the dead healer?"

Kapil shrugged.

"Let us go to him," I said.

I matched his strides as we walked to a room I used for private audiences. The typically calm monk stood tapping his fingers together, his shadow falling on the west wall across from him.

When the door shut, the man almost leaped toward me.

"King Jay, Prince Aggabodhi is missing," he said, grabbing my hands. Even with his injury, Kapil pulled out his dagger in an instant. With a tiny shake of my head, I stopped him from advancing. I doubted the monk was a threat to me. Kapil sheathed the blade. Still, I could see him holding his cane in both hands, ready to wield it as a weapon. The monk noticed this and moved further away from me.

"Missing?" I asked, glancing at Kapil. He seemed surprised as well.

"He was with us last night. He ate his meal and prayed with us before going to bed. This morning, we cannot find him," he said, his words tumbling over each other. He locked and unlocked his fingers, betraying his nervousness.

"Monk Yonten, did the boy have any friends? Could he have gone with them?" Kapil asked.

"Not really. I forced him to keep to himself. It is difficult to trust strangers in this regard, though I preach compassion," he said.

"Did he sleep alone?"

"No, King Jay. Two older monks slept in the same room. Neither saw or heard anything last night."

I rubbed my nose. "Does it look like he left willingly?"

"Yes, it appears so." He paused for a moment with his head cast down. "First, my healer turns up dead. Then the prince goes missing. What do I do now? I promised the king I would keep him safe." He gazed up at me with a mute appeal.

I realized I had neglected the matter with Aggabodhi. "Monk Yonten, don't tell anyone about the missing prince. Let my men investigate this matter. I will send for you when I have any information. Until then, please function normally."

After I assured him we would act on this immediately, he left.

"Did we have one of our men watching the prince?" I asked.

Kapil nodded. "Yes, unobtrusively. I will find out if they saw anything."

"The prince is of value only to Kashgar nobles. Or their rivals. I hope no harm has come to him. Mount a search for him discreetly."

The monks had sought my shelter. So far, I had been incapable of protecting them. I felt like a leaky roof that offered no protection from a storm.

"My lord?" A voice interrupted my chain of thoughts as I walked back to my chamber. Ratnavali stood a few feet away in the bright hall to my room. She had put her hair up in a bun that resembled a crown. Carefully placed pearls gleamed against her dark tresses.

She waited till I neared her and then fell in step with me. Her anklets made a pleasing sound with each step, like raindrops falling on a pot.

When I entered my room, she immediately started her tale. "My father wrote to me. All is well in Sunda. My brothers miss me." She paused and bit her lips. "When can I go visit them?" she asked. She'd lined her eyes with kajal, making them appear like two fishes.

"There are mysterious happenings in Malla. Till I figure out who is behind them, it is not safe for you to travel," I said.

She blinked and nodded, the disappointment evident in her eyes. She was lonely, I realized. My wives, Aranya and Sudha, had little time or patience for my young wife. My daughter, Kayal, mourned her husband. And Heera detested my marriage. I could not blame any of them. I had neglected Ratnavali too.

I stretched my arm, and she grasped it timidly. I pulled her closer to me and put my arm around her waist.

"When the time comes, I will take you myself. With a little prince or princess."

Color crept along her cheeks like a sky painted pink as the sun descended. "My f-flow is late," she stuttered.

I lifted her chin and kissed her softly. It had not yet been two months since our wedding. I did not want to get her hopes up or mine. "It is too early to reveal this to others," I said.

She bit her lips again. "I don't know much about—" she said, spreading her arms wide.

"My sister's maid Kantha is here. Meera claims she is a miracle worker. I will have her talk to you about taking care of yourself."

She placed her head on my chest and sighed. A knock sounded on my door. "Come in," I said without releasing my wife. She squirmed for a moment, trying to move away from me. A smile erupted on my face at her discomfort. Usually, one of my guards would open the door. It was hard to keep secrets from someone who shadowed you day and night. She gazed up at me, and her face blossomed like a bud blooming when the light touched it.

Kapil entered the room and paused. His alert eyes took in the scene in front of him, and he shut the door. His face betrayed no emotions. He had stood guard outside my door for decades and had witnessed my fear and ferocity.

"What is it?" I asked, glancing at him. He bowed to the princess and said, "It is about the monks, my Majesty."

I released my wife. "I will come and see you soon," I said to her, and she departed with a smile on her lips.

Once the door closed behind her, Kapil said, "My guard saw a young boy leave with an older man around midnight last night. The prince seemed acquainted with the man."

I clenched my fist. "Could he be the man who went missing with the dead healer?"

"I suspect so," Kapil said.

Like a spider, he had woven an intricate web. Was it a trap for me? Or had he caught me already?

26

MEERA

efore I caught Rish, Atul rolled on the ground to land
under him. He stretched his arms to halt his father's fall
and lowered Rish's head gently to the ground.

"Mother, I will go fetch the physician," he said and ran outside.

I gazed at the man I loved with tears flowing down my cheek.

"Meera," Rish gasped and shut his eyes.

Tradition and duty forbade me from doing what my heart wanted
to do—hold him in my arms. I made a decision. *If he dies tonight, let
him perish on my lap.* I lifted his head and placed it on my thigh. I had
never felt so helpless in my life, watching the blood ooze out of his
chest.

His eyes opened, and they sought my face. "Meera," he moaned.

"I am here," I whispered.

"I never regretted loving you," he whispered, eyes devouring my
face like parched earth gulping water. A sob escaped me.

I heard voices outside the tent. A moment later, Atul stepped in
with the physician and his assistant.

"Mother," he hissed, his tone a warning for me, as he scanned my
tears and the man on my lap.

The physician knelt beside me. "My lady, I need to pull the dagger out. It is best if we let the commander rest on the floor."

Atul helped me stand, his frown expressing his displeasure. "Why don't you stay in my tent for the night, Mother?" he asked, holding my elbow.

I shook my head as I wiped my eyes with my sari. I had abandoned Rish many times in the past. But not tonight.

A feeble cry escaped from the injured man as the physician pulled the weapon out. I felt like someone had set my skin on fire. I grasped my son's arm and averted my gaze, unable to view the gory scene.

Atul turned to look at the physician. "That knife was meant for me."

A tremor ran through me as I remembered my terror from earlier. Rish had saved our son's life and mine. My heart could not have tolerated losing another child. I drew Atul into a tight hug and wept.

Atul put his arms around me and echoed, "He saved my life."

After a few moments, he released me. "I am going to see if they caught the culprit, Mother," he said and left me alone.

The physician cleaned the wound and applied boiled turmeric roots to it. He then wrapped it with banana leaf and tied a clean cloth over it. Rish moaned as the hot wrap touched his skin.

As he rose, the healer wiped his hands on a rag. "My lady, he has lost a lot of blood. Moving him is not prudent. It is best to leave him here for now. I have given him some potion to help him sleep. I will check on him soon. If his skin is hot, wiping it with cold water will cool him down."

"Will he survive this wound?" I asked, trying hard to mask my grief.

"The dagger pierced his left side, so it spared his heart. He is not young, but there is a chance he may recover," he said.

I thanked him, and he departed. I sat beside Rish, my hands folded in prayer.

"Rish, don't leave me alone. I need you. Come back to me," I murmured, hoping he heard my desperate plea. Usually, I would visit a temple and fall at the deity's feet to save his life. Since I mourned my son's death, I could not visit a temple for a year. Instead, I imagined God Krishna's feet and bowed my head. *Please don't take him from me.*

"Mother," Atul whispered, and I opened my eyes to view my son. He dropped beside me. "The attacker tried to escape, but our soldiers caught him. He is the new driver we hired when our cart rolled. It looks like that accident was the result of deliberate sabotage."

My eyes widened. "Sabotage? For what purpose?"

"This is where it made no sense to me. He claims a foreign man paid him gold coins to hurt me."

"Foreign?"

Atul shrugged.

The only foreign men we have are from Kashgar seeking refuge in Malla. Why would they want to hurt my son?

"Did you check his coins?"

"Yes. Malla coins," he said. If someone wanted to claim the Padi throne, it made sense for them to kill Nala and Atul. Then a blind Amar could be set aside for Kanishka. Parth was banished to Kashgar and could pretend to be from there. Was he behind this plot to place his son on the throne? Or was there another unknown enemy?

Rish groaned softly. I noticed his parched mouth and rose to wet a cloth. I squeezed it lightly between his lips, allowing a few drops to descend his throat. I did not need hope or happiness in my life. All I asked for was the strength I derived from the man on the ground. *Please don't take that from me.*

Atul observed me, fidgeting his fingers. Like a dam breaking, emotions flooded my body. "I love your father," I whispered, pushing the hair away from Rish's forehead. I had hurt them both by keeping them apart.

He froze, and all color drained from his face. After a long pause, he said in a strange voice, "The rumors were true."

With blazing eyes, I glanced at him. "Rumors?" How dare he mention them now while Rish was hurt?

He did not notice my anger. Instead, he asked, "Who else knows?"

"Uncle Jay, your f-father," I stammered. I meant as his father, both the man who claimed him as his son and the man who could never claim it.

"How could you, Mother?" he said and hauled himself up.

"How could I? Rish is dying, and I want you to know the truth." I desperately wished I was not too late.

"Truth? I preferred the lie. Am I even a prince?" Atul cried in anguish and stormed out.

27

JAY

"The man who arrived from Kashgar with the monks left only a meager set of belongings behind. Some old rags. Nothing that reveals any story," said Kapil.

I had expected this, but the news still disappointed me.

"I have spies looking for a man traveling with a boy," Kapil continued. The gray hair at his temples stood like a shield wall of soldiers.

"Kapil, if Parth is behind this, why would he kidnap the prince?" I rubbed my chin, pondering the question myself.

"Last time, Parth was in cahoots with King Nakul. He aided Nakul in seizing Malla. In return, Nakul would have placed him on the Padi throne," Kapil said, tapping his thigh. That happened over seventeen years ago, and he'd almost deceived us then.

"This time, he could have entered a similar arrangement with the men ruling Kashgar. If he kills the prince for them, in return, they may help him capture Padi."

Kapil shook his head. "The revolution is led by angry peasants. Yes, they have overthrown the king of Kashgar. But I cannot see them commanding an army."

"These men make up the army. Held together by a belief, they may be more loyal than an army I command with gold coins," I said.

"Have you heard anything from Kashgar?" I grew impatient for news.

"Not yet, my Majesty. But I expect to hear from them soon."

I nodded. If I rescued Prince Aggabodhi, I would become entangled in the fight for Kashgar. But did I have a choice?

I laughed suddenly. "Imagine us mounting an army to conquer Kashgar."

Kapil smiled. "I would follow you if not for my injury, Jay. A sword still sings in your hands." I remembered all the adventures we'd had. We'd fought off pirates at sea, fended off invaders in Sunda, and traveled all over Malla.

"You were my shield. Without you—" When I knew Kapil protected me, it was easy to risk my own life.

"Without me, the able men I've handpicked for you will still protect you," he said.

"They don't know me as you do," I said, nostalgic.

"We can always do what older kings did. Send younger men to die for us," he suggested.

I laughed. "We have earned our rest," I said. But my mind whispered a different song—*one more battle.*

Vikram strolled into my chambers as the sun began its descent.

"Son," I said, observing the boy. His skin had lost its pallid dullness. His time spent outdoors had been good for him.

He picked up an ivory-handled knife from the table and ran his fingers over the grip, which was carved like a striking cobra.

"How is your training coming along?" I asked. Kapil had mentioned he was making slow progress.

"It was better when I trained with Cousin Atul," he answered without looking at me.

"Atul will be back soon," I said, dropping the scroll I was reading.

"Father, Uncle Kapil has me riding with two guards. They don't talk to me, and a solitary ride is as boring as watching a snail move," he said.

My lips turned up at his analogy. As a young child, he had lain on his stomach to watch snails crawl.

"Why don't you ride with Amar?"

He sighed, and I gazed at him. "I stabbed his brother. He avoids me like I am the harbinger of evil."

I rose from my seat with a frown. I reached Vikram and squeezed his shoulder. "I can ride with you on some days."

"That would be nice, Father," he said politely. It did not sound like he wanted my company. I waited for him to state what was on his mind. "I was hoping Princess Ratnavali could ride with me," he asked, a faint color creeping up his cheeks.

"Ratnavali?" I asked. She might be carrying my child.

He nodded. "She must be bored," he said and then bit his lip. "I do not mean it as disrespect, Father. Forget I asked."

I touched the back of his neck. "No, nothing wrong with you riding with her. She is lonely, as you guessed. I don't always have time for her."

He looked at me hopefully, like a dog waiting for food.

"But she cannot. Not for a few months," I added.

"Why? Is she ill?"

"No, not ill. Ratnavali—it is still early—but she might be carrying a child," I said, heat rising in my face.

"Child? Yours?" he snarled and stepped away from me.

"She is my wife," I began sharply.

He interrupted me rudely. "Grandmother Charu told me how Grandfather did not want a rival tiger cub for you. That is why you have no brothers. I went missing for a few fortnights, and you already planned to replace me." He appeared young with his wounded look.

"Replace you? Vikram, that is—" I stopped, unable to finish my sentence. I had married her to beget another heir.

"Why stop with Ratnavali? Marry a few more girls, Father. Have them give you better sons than me," he said and kicked the leg of the table.

"Vikram," I warned him.

He glared at me before leaving the room.

2 8

MEERA

After Atul left, I sat in a daze, weary to my aching bones. I had told him Rish was his father. Not King Atul, his namesake. Of course, that had upset him. Why had I not thought of that? No matter the path I chose, either father or son or both would suffer.

Suddenly, I noticed a tremor run through Rish's body. Then his right arm and right leg flexed and extended in quick movements, like a tree limb hitting a wall during a storm. His head swung from one side to another, and my heart lurched with him. I ran outside.

"Guard, get the physician. Quickly," I yelled. When the man took off, I went inside. Rish's lips had turned blue, and my breathing came in gasps. *What do I do? How do I make it stop?*

As sudden as the onset, all movements ceased abruptly. I froze in place. Had I lost him? I could not breathe, and I felt like my sorrows drowned me.

The physician hurried in. "What happened, my lady?" he asked, approaching Rish.

"Is he alive?" I whispered, my life slowly draining out of me.

The healer opened one eye and then the other. "He is alive."

I opened my mouth to gulp air, and my senses started working again. "He had a seizure."

157

"That sometimes happens with stab wounds," he said, continuing his inspection. His young assistant entered the tent.

"We will be monitoring to see if he has another attack, my lady. I will ask my assistant to stay here all night."

I ambled out, wrapping my sari around my shoulders. The night air felt cold against my skin, and the stars seemed to mock my fears. A few torches fluttered in the wind, but their fight against the darkness appeared futile.

A near-full moon reflected in the lake, its shape distorted by the ripples. The water beckoned me, and I wandered toward it. I sat on the gravel shore, pulling my knees up. Like the relentless waves, misery hounded me. I leaned my head on my knees, tired.

A voice reached me as my mind struggled to awake. I stretched my arms, and they creaked like an old door. Pain shot through my legs as I sat up. I had fallen asleep in an uncomfortable posture, and my body ached from it. A faint light snaked along the horizon. A few men awake at that early hour skirted around me to reach the water.

I heard the crunch of the gravel.

"Mother," Atul called.

My heart thudded as I turned to gaze at him. I did not want to witness his disappointment and anger. Instead, worry tinged his face.

He reached my side and gently helped me to my feet. "You are cold. What are you doing here at this hour?"

I stumbled, and his arm tightened around my waist. I leaned on him, letting him support me. "Rish had a seizure last night, and the healer's apprentice stayed with him. I came to get some fresh air, but I appear to have fallen asleep." Was he still alive? I did not have any strength left to face his death.

I stumbled again, and Atul caught me. "Mother—" he started.

"Son, about last night—" I said at the same time.

I stopped and cupped his face. He blinked rapidly and took a breath in. "I am still your mother. Jay is still your uncle. Nala, Priya, and Amar are still your siblings."

His jaw tightened under my fingers. "But I cannot sit on the Padi throne."

I pressed my lips together and dropped my hand. "No," I whispered. I could not repeat my father's mistake with Nakul. As a Padi queen, I had to follow the traditional lineage. "Did you dream of wearing the crown?" He had two older brothers. Such a dream would have meant their deaths.

"N-no," he stammered. After a pause, he said, "No, I never dreamt of that."

"Then, nothing has changed," I whispered.

"Except, I am not a prince."

"You are my son—"

"And that makes me prince of what?" His lips trembled with emotion.

"To the world, you are still a Padi prince," I said, knowing this answer would not satisfy him.

He grunted in response. It hurt me that my son valued a title more than my love. For all my royal birth, I could not bestow titles to my children.

We resumed walking in silence. I halted outside my tent, my stomach twisted into knots with worry. Atul proceeded ahead of me and stepped inside. After a moment, his head peeked out.

"He is awake."

I released the breath I held and walked in. Rish stayed hidden behind the healer. I moved around till he came into view. Slowly, his face turned toward me.

"Queen Meera," he said hoarsely. His eyes pierced my heart.

"Commander Rish," I mumbled and moved closer.

"How is he?" asked Atul.

"He is not out of danger yet," said the physician. "But today looks better than last night. My apprentice cleaned him and gave him some broth mixed with herbs. I will check on him soon."

He departed, leaving us alone. An awkward silence filled the air. Then, slowly Atul moved toward him. He knelt beside his father and clasped his arm. Rish did not know I had revealed the truth to my son. He glanced at the boy, puzzled.

"You shielded me from an attacker's dagger yesterday," Atul said with a tremor in his voice.

"I only did my duty as your mother's guard," Rish whispered.

Atul gazed at me, and Rish followed his line of sight.

"My mother told me you had a greater duty than guard."

Rish's eyes searched my face, and I nodded, my emotions threatening to overcome me. Rish looked at his son and the hand he held. A lone tear ran down his cheek.

"Mother, please use my tent this morning to freshen up. I will have my servant shift my belongings here and take yours to my tent. I will stay with the commander. We have a lot of catching up to do." His eyes returned to his father's face. Like a seed from the previous summer sprouting after a rain, a tiny ray of hope took root in my heart.

In a few days, I hurried to Atul's tent. As I opened the flap, I heard voices and paused.

"Commander, when I broke my fast this morning with some of the soldiers, I regaled them with the story of how you saved my life. An elderly man uttered the words 'like father like son.'"

My heart stopped for a moment. Which father and son?

"He said your father saved my grandfather's life. Can you please tell me the details?" Atul asked. Veera Vindhya had died for my father, King Vikram. One of Atul's grandfathers had saved the life of the other.

I peeked into the tent. Rish rested on a bed, and Atul sat beside him on a wooden stool.

"My father served as the commander of King Vikram's guards. The king had fallen off his horse during a battle. My father picked him up from the ground and rode away. Arrows chased them, and two found their mark on my father's back, but he did not halt till he brought his king to safety. Then, he collapsed and died."

"I met your mother when she came to offer her sympathies," he said.

I clanged my bangles to announce my presence and entered the room.

"Mother," Atul said, rising from his seat.

Rish's eyes followed me as I approached him. I came to a halt beside my son. Our son. Rish's face appeared younger and more relaxed without the unease of the past weighing upon him. "I thought I heard someone mention me," I said with a smile.

"Commander was narrating the story of how his father saved King Vikram," Atul said. "I am learning about my grandfather," he added with a slight upturn of his lips. Which grandfather? The boy was learning to speak in riddles.

I tousled his hair. "Where did I come to be in this story?"

"I was telling him about meeting you in Akash after my father's death, my queen," Rish said, his eyes wrapping me in a warm cocoon.

Atul cleared his throat, his face flushed. "I have matters to take care of." He squeezed his father's wrist and left.

I sat on the stool he had vacated.

"Prince Atul has your eyes, Meera. Though his actions remind me of young Prince Jay," Rish said reverently. I could sense the pride bursting forth from him.

"Jay raised him, so that is not a surprise," I said. "How are you?"

"Under your care, I am thriving, my queen," he said, his eyes twinkling like stars in a moonless sky. "If you can give me a sip of water from your hands, that will bless this servant."

My face brightened as I fetched some water. Instead of handing Rish the tumbler, I brought the tip to his mouth. He raised himself on his elbows and drank thirstily. Some spilled down his chin, and I almost wiped them with my sari. I caught myself in time. Instead, I handed him a clean rag. He wiped his chin with a sigh.

His sigh bothered me. Tradition chained me in its bonds. I still could not act so informally. Even though Atul knew the truth, no one else could.

"I asked Atul to send word to your daughter," I said. "And your wife," I added. I hoped he sensed my rebuke. He was bound by his duty too.

He frowned. "I do not want them to worry. Rima has her hands full with two young children and my wife—" He paused and glanced at me. "She is content to spend her days with her grandchildren."

"I told them you are healing well." A few years ago, Rish's wife came to Malla to stay with her stepdaughter. My brother had forced him to marry her when Atul was born to avoid the spread of rumors about us. Rima, his daughter from Rish's first marriage, had given birth to her child then. Apart from a few visits, Rish had shown little interest in bringing his wife back to stay. "If you want her to come here to take care of you, I will welcome her." *Will I, though?* I wanted the man for myself.

He laughed bitterly. "I married her at the command of my king. If you order your men to bring her, they will. My wants notwithstanding."

"Rish," I said sharply.

He rubbed his eyes. "I cannot do this anymore," he whispered. "To pretend all is well—to deny my feelings."

"Do you think it has been easy for me? I have spent seventeen years alone each night, crying myself to sleep. Even the tears have dried up now." My words came out as an accusation though none of it was his fault.

"Meera," he said my name as if his life were twined with it. "I stood guard outside your door on many of those nights. Helpless to do anything. Unable to offer any solace." Bitterness crept into his voice again.

I sat down, not trusting my legs to hold me. "I lived because of you," I murmured and covered his hand with mine. "You were the moon that lit my path on the dark nights; you helped chase my despair away."

Rish gazed at our hands—touching—spreading warmth—binding us. "You told Atul," he whispered.

"You almost died. I could not deny him the truth," I quivered.

He flipped my palm and gently rubbed my wrist with his thumb. "I need to nearly die more often," he said, eyes crinkling in a smile.

"Don't," I warned him. I could not bear to lose him.

His eyes sought mine, and waves of emotion emanated from him to pound at my shores.

"My lady, can you grant me a wish?"

My heart pounded with fear. What if Rish wanted to abandon me and spend his remaining days in Malla?

"Yes," I said feebly.

He intertwined his fingers in mine. "Marry me."

29
JAY

My opponent was on his stomach, and I held his ankle. I twisted it lightly as he tried to wriggle out of my grip. Sweat dripped from both our bodies as we wrestled.

"My Majesty," one of my guards called. The usually calm man fidgeted like my opponent on the floor. I dropped the ankle and rose. Wiping my face, I asked, "What is it?"

"Chief Guard Kapil urged me to bring you," he answered.

Kapil? "Lead me," I said and followed him. Night descended around us, and two men lit the torches along our path. They bowed to me as I headed to the palace. Inside the castle, a mellow light spread from the lamps.

"Where is Kapil?"

"In Princess Ratnavali's chamber, my Majesty," he said, causing me to stumble.

Regaining my steps, I asked, "Ratnavali?"

"Yes, King Jay."

What was Kapil doing in her chamber? Shadows growing from the dark halls matched the darkness spreading in my mind. We arrived outside her door, and I could hear noises inside. I entered the room as my heart raced like a deer running away from a tiger. The door shut behind me.

My eyes scanned the area, and I noticed the overturned table and stool. The voices murmured from the bedroom.

"Kapil," I called and made my way there.

He leaned on his cane and turned to face me. His pale face gleamed eerily in the light from a floor lamp. Then he glanced down, and I followed his gaze. As two feet came into view, my heart nearly stopped. *Ratnavali?* A silk sari covered the legs. The royal physician hid the rest of her from me.

I struggled to breathe as I approached them. A knife protruded from her stomach, and blood trickled out of it. I had seen half-maimed bodies on a battlefield countless times. But the sight of her blood nearly caused me to scream. I clenched my fist to control my emotions. I glimpsed her face, drained of color, but she was conscious. *Ratnavali!*

"What happened?" I asked.

"Kantha found her. She had come to give her some sweet balls," Kapil said, a shadow passing through his face. I glanced back at my new wife. My gaze slid down to her abdomen, and I noticed the weapon sticking out of it. Something familiar about it. Ivory handle. My chest squeezed tightly. It was mine.

"Who was here before Kantha?" I asked though I knew the answer.

He came closer and whispered, "Prince Vikram," in my ear. I remembered Vikram picking up the knife on my table a few days ago. Had he kept it? Fear crept along my skin, smothering me. Had he *stabbed* her?

"Find him and bring him to me," I ordered.

Kapil left me with the physician and his two disciples.

"How is she?"

The physician did not answer immediately. "Hard to tell, my Majesty. That knife pierced her womb."

Thoughts raced through my mind. *Womb? Her child! My child! Did I lose the child? Did my son try to kill his sibling? What kind of monster had I raised?*

Kantha entered with another maid.

"Did you bring the hot water?"

"Yes," said the maid and handed the healer a pot.

"King Jay," Kantha said as she came closer. "The princess was healthy when I left her this evening." Her lips trembled in fear.

"Kantha, we will find the culprit. Stay here and help her. I will come back," I said and departed.

My feet took me to Vikram's chambers. Kapil stood inside with his men.

"He is missing."

"Missing?"

He nodded. "He went into his room and shut himself in. His guards stood outside. However, he is not here anymore."

"Tunnels? There is an entry from his chamber," I said and walked to his bedroom. The tunnel door was open, and two men peeked into it.

"King Jay," they greeted me.

Another voice could be heard from the hole. "Prince—" he halted when he saw my face.

"Continue," I commanded.

"My Majesty, it appears Prince Vikram left through the tunnel." The tunnels ran like a maze, and a new person could easily get lost in them. Not Vikram. He knew the way.

"No one stopped him?" I asked foolishly. Of course, no one had.

"He is the prince of Malla. Unless you order him stopped, our guards will obey his commands," Kapil said. I knew this. I was once the crown prince of this land. I had not named him my heir yet, but everyone treated him as such.

"Drop into the tunnel and search for him. If you find him, restrain him till I get there," I commanded, and three guards vanished into the tunnel.

"Kapil, let us look for him in the forest," I said and started toward the door.

"King Jay, I am not sure it is wise for you to join the search. I have plenty of men for this," he hesitated.

"You just told me you needed my orders to overrule his."

Kapil pressed his lips together but did not argue further.

Our horses were ready when we reached the stables. We rode to the forest where the tunnel exited. One of my men tracked not only my son's footprints but other signs like crushed grass along the path, which led us into the woods. The moonlight washed everything gray, and the tree trunks stood bathed in shadows. An owl hooted and flew into the night to hunt. Was Vikram the hunter or the prey? I remembered the boy sleeping in my bed a few days ago, afraid of being alone. I imagined him huddled somewhere, lonely and frightened. Tears stung my eyes, and I blinked them back.

We made slow progress, stopping every few yards to look at a bent stem or a flattened leaf. The crisp night air wound around us, bringing the smell of dampness. In one spot, an entire shrub appeared squashed. Maybe my son had crouched in it. Crossing the path felt like a dance with Vikram. His presence touched my skin even in his absence.

Two miles away, signs of a cart showed up. His footprints disappeared.

"This cart was waiting for him, my Majesty. See the dung droppings?"

I observed the large brown clumps. The animals must have waited for a while in this spot. The boy had an accomplice. Where had he gone?

"Kapil, did his guards ever see him with a stranger?"

He beckoned one of his guards forward. "My Majesty, a man stood in the fields yesterday as we rode past him. On the way back, the prince approached and spoke to him. He had asked us to remain out of earshot."

"How old was he?" I asked, a coldness spreading throughout my limbs.

"In the fourth or fifth decade of his life," he answered.

"Did Vikram act as if he knew him?"

"He did, King Jay. The prince neared him and asked the man what he wanted. I did not hear anything else. The stranger handed Prince

Vikram something in a leaf wrapping at the end of their conversation." I exchanged looks with Kapil. Our missing monk?

"They cannot have gone far. Kapil, set up roadblocks and search all carriages leaving Akash. Send men on foot to scour our neighborhoods. Find my son."

*P*ure joy erupted in me, even though his wish was ridiculous. Marry him? Had he lost his wit?

He gazed at me with those eyes that sought to read my mind. Could he sense my love for him?

"I am a widow. Have you forgotten that?" My existence consisted of long, lonely nights. Dreaming of the near-impossible would only result in more grief.

"Do you know the story of Nala and Damayanti?" The warmth from his fingers spread into mine.

Nala and Damayanti? What did that have to do with marrying him? "Yes, I have heard the tale of the pious Damayanti who stood by her husband even when he lost everything."

A smile played on Rish's lips upon hearing how I chose to present her. "She chooses to wed Nala in a swayamvara, the groom-choosing ceremony. The unworthy man gambled his fortunes away and left his wife in the middle of the forest. Then her father arranges another marriage for her."

I frowned. "In which she puts the garland around Nala's neck again."

"Love makes you do foolish things. I cannot blame Damayanti. But women marrying again was allowed back then," he beseeched me.

"Rish, that is an ancient story." I pulled my fingers out of his grip.

"My lady, no one needs to know. You can remain a widow to the world. Just wed me in a secret ceremony," he said. With the wrap around his chest, he looked oddly vulnerable. I experienced an urge to take him in my arms. I sat still until the moment passed.

"What will a secret ceremony achieve, Rish?" I asked, puzzled by this sudden request from him.

He remained quiet for a few moments. The noises from the day's activities reached us from outside. The stomping of the horses, clanging of swords, and indistinguishable voices filled the silence.

"It will give me a claim where I have none," Rish said. The vulnerability I saw earlier disappeared. Instead, a determination appeared upon his chin. "A claim that will allow me to remain by your side when you try to send me away."

"Rish, I don't—" I started and then stopped. I had sent him away when my feelings threatened to overpower my sanity. Even his recent trip to Sunda was a result of my despondency almost driving me into his arms.

"What if my answer is no? Will you leave me?" My voice trembled at my question, and I did not try to mask it. Like an endless sand desert, loneliness stretched in front of me.

"Meera, I have never left your side voluntarily." His eyes caressed my face. "Is that what worries you?"

I twisted the end of my sari. "I take you for granted. And I worry that I will push you to your limit."

He put his palm face-up, inviting me to grasp it. I gently placed my palm on top of his. "I worry that you will push me away," he said and folded his fingers over my hand. Somehow, that touch expressed all his love, affection, and respect for me. The desire to hold him surged in me. "Our worries stem from the same place. I have a way to solve it. A simple garland exchange will suffice."

We beamed at each other, my body relaxing in his grip.

"My answer is still n—"

"Before you answer, know this. I never fought for us before. I accepted your decision to place your duty to the kingdom above our love. But after thirty years, we deserve some happiness. I am ready to fight now."

A grin appeared on my face, and it reflected on his.

Atul walked in, and immediately Rish released his grip on my hand, and I slid it toward me. I flushed like I was a maiden secretly meeting her lover. Rish smirked at my discomfort, and I shot daggers at him.

Atul's perceptive eyes swept from his father to me. If he noticed anything, he kept his composure, except for the faint color rising in his neck.

"Mother, we cannot let Kanishka get away with sending this attacker."

I sat up. "Do we have new evidence linking him to the attack?"

"No, but nothing else makes sense. I don't like being hunted, especially by a coward who cannot wage a war in the open. I will go to Padi and make Kanishka see that he will not succeed." He skipped from foot to foot, bubbling with youthful energy.

I glanced at Rish.

He gazed at his son.

"Mother, Commander," Atul prompted.

"There is risk in the mission," Rish said.

"I am planning to take some of Darsh Vindhya's men with me. Kanishka fired the first arrow. He attacked me. He started the fire, and he needs to know the flames will devour him. The might of Malla is behind us. And I am willing to use them against my enemies," Atul said fiercely. For a moment, I pictured Jay saying the same words.

Rish stared at him with his mouth open. Slowly, he said, "Prince Atul, though Kanishka is resorting to cowardly ways, he is a dangerous opponent. My advice would be to take your mother with you. She will keep you from making any—" He left the rest unsaid.

"Good idea," Atul grinned.

"I don't want to leave—yet," I changed what I wanted to say. But they understood my hesitation to leave Rish while he remained bedridden.

"I will be fine, my lady. It will give you time to ponder my earlier question." Warmth spread on my face as his gaze lingered on mine.

Atul raised his eyebrows at Rish's words but did not prod.

A guard arrived outside. "Prince Atul."

"Come in," he said.

"A message from Malla," the guard said and handed my son a scroll.

Atul ripped open the seal and read the letter. "Vikram is missing. I need to go help Uncle Jay," he cried out.

He handed the letter to me. It was in Jay's handwriting. "Vikram left the palace, and we are searching for him. I suspect the same culprit is behind this. Don't let it jeopardize your Padi mission. All the more important to settle affairs there. Take extra precautions and appoint guards for Atul."

Poor Jay. How was he dealing with this? I hoped they would find my nephew soon, for my brother's sake. I agreed with him, though. Not much we could do to help if the search was already underway. "Atul, I know you want to help find your cousin. But your aid is not needed. Your uncle has able men to track him."

Atul shook his head. "Mother, no one knows Vikram as I do. I should have never left Akash. Then, Vikram would not have run away. Please let me go back and help."

I sought Rish's guidance. He stretched his hand, and I placed the letter in it. "Prince Atul, King Jay's orders are clear. He wants us to focus on our Padi mission," he said after he perused it.

Atul bit his lip. I approached him and touched his shoulder. "Son, you are not to blame for Vikram's disappearance."

He drew in a breath and nodded. "I will make arrangements for us to travel to Padi."

"King Jay is right. Atul—," Rish paused with a frown, realizing his error in uttering his son's name. The more time we spent together, the harder it would be to keep these walls intact. "Prince Atul needs his own guards to keep him safe. We can find a mix of Padi and Malla men for it," he said.

"I will leave that in your hands, Commander. I will trust you to find the right men for the duty," Atul replied. He drew patterns on his hip with his finger. "And it is okay to address me by my name. I am much younger than you."

Before Rish could respond, Atul stammered, "Not that you need my p-permission." Then our son looked at me in confusion. Now that he knew the truth of his birth, I could imagine his discomfiture.

"My lord, I am humbled by your esteem. Your brothers treated me with the same respect and kindness. It will be my honor to pick your guards," Rish said, a gentle reminder in his tone to continue our charade. Rish and I had years of practice.

Atul's bewilderment cleared, and he inclined his head.

It had been three months since I'd left Padi. During that time, someone murdered my oldest son while failing in their attempt to kill my other sons. Would we be safe in Padi? An unease spread within my stomach at the lack of an answer.

31

JAY

I peeked into Ratnavali's chambers. A maid watching my wife rose on seeing me. I approached the bed and stared at the girl resting on it. No jewels adorned her pallid skin, and she appeared like a child. I lifted the thin blanket covering her. Blood-stained cotton wraps covered her abdomen. My chest constricted at this sight, and I tucked the sheet back around her.

"Has she awakened yet?" I asked the maid.

"No, King Jay."

"Send for me when she does. No matter the hour."

I headed to see Sudha with a heaviness in my heart. Over the years, I had consoled several mothers and fathers about the demise of their sons on a battlefield. While it was never easy, this conversation with Sudha would highlight all my failures as a father and husband.

She sat frozen on her seat, gazing out the window when I entered her room. The moon hid behind a cloud, afraid of witnessing the scene about to unfold. A single oil lamp failed to fully dispel the darkness.

"Did you find him?" she asked, her back to me.

"No," I said.

174

"You drove him away, Jay," she accused, still facing away as if looking at me would be unbearable.

I had no answer.

"How is Ratnavali? she asked, not trying to keep her contempt for me masked.

I rubbed my forehead. "Unconscious."

She spun to face me then, her eyes swollen and nose dark. The moon peeked out to wash her in a ghostly pale light.

"I cannot bear to think of him alone somewhere." Her voice wobbled as tears pooled in her eyes.

I walked toward her and kneeled in front of her.

"I cannot—" She broke into a sob, and I touched her shoulder. She stiffened initially and then slumped slowly onto my chest. I folded her in my arms and tucked her under my chin.

"I will bring him back," I promised.

She pulled away from me and sniffed. "Don't make empty promises, Jay. I have never asked for glory or honor as your queen. All I wanted was a child. And when he is on the threshold of adulthood, first you lost him, and now you've chased him away." She turned away from me, her back bracing as if she prepared for my failure.

I left, then wandered the palace halls, putting off returning to my bedroom, Sudha's voice haunting me. Dev, my guard commander, found me on a terrace, lying on my back and observing the stars. "My Majesty, Queen Aranya is waiting for you in your chamber." He had rescued us nearly three decades ago from the clutches of her father. "Your daughters are with her, along with Prince Amar," he added.

A family reunion. They must have heard the news about Vikram.

I walked in, and my daughters surrounded me.

"Have you found him?"

"Did he stab Ratnavali?"

"Let your father sit," Aranya admonished them. She pointed to an empty spot next to her on a bench. I took it and stretched my legs in front of me.

Kayal and Heera sat across from us on adjacent chairs, and Amar perched on a stool beside his wife.

"Vikram seems to have left the palace grounds on a cart. Kapil is searching for him," I said, gazing at my queen.

"He had an accomplice?" Amar asked.

I nodded. Then I realized my nephew could not see me. "Yes, it appears so."

"Why did he hurt Ratnavali?" asked Heera.

"Don't address her by her name. She is married to your father," Aranya scolded her child.

Before Heera could quarrel with her, I said, "Ratnavali was pregnant, and I shared the news with your brother. It upset him."

Kayal gasped. "So he decided to hurt his stepmother and run away?" She had apparently still not forgiven him for murdering her husband.

"The guards reported that he'd met a stranger yesterday. I suspect he received some drugs from his contact. That may have caused him to act in this savage manner," I said, trying to excuse his brutal behavior. I could not imagine him committing this deed while sane.

"Father, I know it is hard to believe my little brother is capable of such violence. But this is not his first time. He has already killed an innocent man. His brother-in-law." Kayal looked tired, and her arm rested on her swollen stomach.

"Kayal, I have seen what your brother is capable of. When we find him, we can decide the right punishment for both acts. There is nothing we can do tonight, though. Get some rest."

With a wave, I dismissed them. Aranya remained behind. "Did Kapil look for the source of these potions and poisons?"

"He did. The murdered Buddhist healer purchased several herbs. Our suspect is using that stash. He has not made any new purchases himself."

She slid closer to me, and her fingers combed my hair. "Jay, you are allowed to make mistakes."

"Not when the consequences are deadly," I said. I could smell the coconut oil in my wife's hair, which was still mostly black, with a few stray gray hairs enhancing her beauty.

"Do you regret marrying me?" I asked, suddenly in need of solace and reassurance. The moon came out from behind the cloud and illuminated the room. She had cared for me in Saral when I was wounded. I fell in love with her then, and that love had only deepened in the years since. Was that enough for her?

The thick lashes framing her eyes fluttered as she gazed at me tenderly. "I married the boy I loved, and we rule the kingdom together. We have two beautiful daughters. Not many queens have such good fortune," she said, rubbing my ears. Her touch melted my insides, and I yearned for more.

"There is one mistake we can fix today. It has been too long since you kissed your queen," she said as her lips parted invitingly.

Despite all the dreariness, a warmth spread in my heart. I pulled Aranya onto my lap as my restless mouth touched her soft lips, gently at first. Then the kiss grew with familiarity and passion.

The next day, Kapil's voice woke me from my slumber.

"Come in," I said, rubbing my eyes. I noticed Aranya nestled against my shoulder, her chest rising and falling in a steady rhythm. Resisting the urge to kiss her, I pulled the blanket up to cover her bare shoulders.

"A message from Prince Atul," Kapil said as he walked in. His alert eyes scanned the room, taking in everything.

"What is it?"

"A man tried to kill Prince Atul. Commander Rish saved his life. But the dagger plunged into him instead."

"Is Rish alive?" I asked. Meera loved him more than I had realized before. My sister would be devastated if he perished.

"He is critically hurt. We may not know his condition for a few days."

Aranya stirred in her sleep, her arm winding around my neck. "Wait for me in front. I will be with you shortly," I said and untangled myself from my wife's grasp.

I stood up and stretched while my mind awakened before my body and ran over the events of the past few days. This enemy had patience and perseverance. It would be foolish to underestimate him. I tied my dhoti around my waist and washed my face in the basin.

I entered the sitting room and found Kapil leaning against the table. He straightened when he saw me. Yesterday was a long day, and he looked like he had not seen his bed. I pushed the stool toward him.

"Sit," I ordered. Kapil lowered himself with his lips curved up.

"Amar, Nala, and now Atul. These are Padi princes. My suspicion against Parth strengthens with this latest attack."

Kapil nodded. "If he has Prince Vikram in his custody, I suspect he will use him as a hostage to negotiate with you. To neutralize your might."

"Kapil, we need to be on alert. Our fake monk has weaved an intricate trap for us." I might be caught in it already. If someone threatened Vikram's life, would I relinquish the Padi throne?

"Would you like to send a message back to Prince Atul?"

"Yes, let me write it," I said and sat at my table. I picked up a scroll and dipped a feather tip into the ink. Atul would want to come back to Akash when he heard about Vikram. I needed him to wrap up the mission in Padi first. I held back news about the attack on my wife to avoid smearing my son's name.

I finished writing and then handed the scroll to Kapil. "Find a fresh horse and man to take this."

Later that day, I tried to do my kingly duties while Kapil kept me updated about the search. Somehow, even with the vast number of men at my disposal, we could not find my son. By the next day, my patience was gone.

"Kapil, I cannot sit idly while Vikram is missing," I said. I had led from the front on battlefields.

"My Majesty, our enemy will anticipate your move. I don't want to put your life in jeopardy."

An idea came to me. "I can wear a disguise and search on foot."

Kapil stared at me. "I need a way for your guards to be with you."

I gave him a crooked smile, glad he had not refused my plan. Another crazy scheme bubbled up. "Traveling music troupe," I suggested.

The next day, our ten-member music troupe stood outside a temple. Dressed in colorful clothes and turbans, we attracted attention. A few young children followed us as we marched through the street. The large windpipes concealed our swords and daggers. The drums concealed axes and arrows.

A guard played a few notes on a bamboo flute as we strolled, our eyes scanning the street. Another drummed an earthen clay pot, following a simple beat.

"Come watch us tonight," Dev shouted to a few passersby to keep up our pretense.

At the end of the street, a young girl watched us for a few moments. She then disappeared around the corner. Something about her caught my attention.

"Let us follow that girl," I whispered. If they found my command strange, they kept the thought to themselves. I was looking for Prince Aggabodhi or Vikram. Why was I following a girl instead?

We turned the corner and found the child in front of a fruit vendor.

"Her hair," Dev whispered.

I observed her closely. Her forehead seemed unusually large, and her hair appeared like it had slipped back an inch. "It is not hers." That was what caught my attention before. Why did a young child need artificial hair? Had she fallen ill and lost her hair?

As we crossed her, the child gazed at us in wonder. There was something familiar about her face.

"Let us rest under the banyan tree at the end of the street," I said. A pair of monkeys parted the leaves to watch us settle down. The men arranged themselves around me, each one facing a different direction. A keen eye could discern their alertness.

One of the guards started narrating a story, and many *oohs* and *aahs* followed.

After finishing her shopping, the girl walked past us toward the fields. She still had the body of a child and walked stiffly in her cotton skirt and blouse.

"You can come to watch us after dark at the market," Dev shouted at her. Her eyes widened in wonder, and she hurried away.

Dev signaled to two of my men dressed as vegetable hawkers, and they followed her at a distance.

After a while, one of them came back to report. "She entered a hut at the start of the forest. When night falls, we will approach it from the forest and watch the occupants."

We strode through a few side streets with no other leads. As the sky darkened, we dispersed, and I made my way back to the palace. The actual musicians headed to the market to perform that night while I sat in darkness in my room, despairing for my son.

I heard hurried footsteps, and a maid entered. "Princess Ratnavali is awake, my Majesty."

As I rose to follow her, Dev entered. "It is a boy. The child we followed this morning was male."

"Prince Aggabodhi," I cried out, remembering the prince with his shaved head.

32

MEERA

tul invited the Malla northern commander, Darsh Vindhya, to the campsite. The men spent their days together, plotting the trip to Padi. With Rish's aid, Atul carefully chose men to accompany us on the journey and dispatched scouts ahead of us. One thousand Malla soldiers assembled to travel with us to Padi, a powerful show of Malla might.

The day arrived, bright and crisp, mocking my fears. I stood beside Rish, listening to his last-minute advice to Atul. "Don't underestimate Kanishka. Be on the alert. I have already asked your guards to check your food for poison." The two had grown closer since the attack.

Atul nodded diligently. "I remember all your words, Commander." He then bent his head toward Rish and whispered, "Do I have your blessings?"

Rish appeared stunned. A son would usually seek his father's blessing before embarking on a journey of this length. Realization dawned on me of what I had deprived them both. Blinking his eyes, Rish touched his son's head. "Your brother made his wishes known. Either his unborn son or his brother, Amar, sits on the throne. Fight to make his wish come true."

Atul hauled himself straight and squeezed Rish's hand. "Mother, I will wait by the chariot," he said and departed.

A long silence ensued. "My brother raised him well," I murmured.

Rish gazed at me with misty eyes.

I sighed. "Rish, I apologize—"

"No need for an apology, my lady. These tears are for King Nala," he said, rubbing his eyes.

"Nala?" I asked, puzzled.

"Yes, my lady. The then boy-king would lean toward me in council meetings and say the same words uttered by Prince Atul before taking any actions. Do I have your blessings, Uncle Rish?"

Tears pooled in my eyes. Rish had served as regent to Nala and had raised him to be king.

"Nala came to me the night before his wedding. 'Uncle Rish, what advice would my father give me,' he asked." Rish paused here and stared at the low tent ceiling.

"What did you tell him?" I asked, my heart aching for my son.

Rish gazed at me. "'I don't know what your father would tell you about marriage. But I saw how he was with your mother. He cherished her. He sought her advice publicly and trusted her. Be like your father.' That is what I told him."

"Nala followed your counsel and treated his wife like a queen of his kingdom and heart," I said as a lump formed in my throat.

"He was his father's son," Rish responded. "King Atul was a rare king. And a rarer man. He understood your true worth. If you had married a lesser man, I might have fought for you earlier."

I remembered my husband's arms around me as tears dripped down my chin. "If this is your way to get me to say yes, it is not working."

He laughed with his eyes crinkling. "In some ways, he loved you better. I don't deny it," he whispered. "I have loved you longer." His words cocooned me in warmth like a coal fire.

I wiped my tears as gratitude surged in my chest at my fortune to have found such ardor. "Stay alive, Rish."

"I will be waiting for your answer, my queen."

Outside, Atul helped me into the chariot. "Join me, Son," I said.

He looked surprised at my request, but he heeded it. The men traveling by foot had left yesterday. Horses, carts, and carriages slowly progressed through the winding roads to Padi. Fields of wheat with tender green stalks swayed in the gentle wind on either side.

I wanted to apologize to my son for depriving him of his father's love. Before I could say anything, he spoke.

"Mother, I know what the commander is to me. But I cannot think of him in that role. Someone else occupies it," he said, his eyes cast down.

"Who?" I asked. He had never known my husband.

"Uncle Jay, Mother," he said, looking up. "He raised me from birth."

Jay. Of course. I smiled at my son and pushed his hair away from his forehead. "Jay promised to raise you as his own. He has kept his promise then."

Atul relaxed his shoulders. "I had a happy childhood in Akash. Uncle taught me alongside Vasant and Vikram. The two of them were destined to be kings, but he treated me as an equal. I learned warfare and history lessons along with sword-fighting and archery. He invited us to council meetings. I swam in the Champak River with my cousins, who were more like my brothers. Kayal and Heera treated me like a little brother too."

I thought I had run out of tears, but they glistened at my son's eager words. I had been a fool. Rish had raised Nala and Amar and saw them as his sons. Meanwhile, Atul saw Jay as his father figure. Whatever other mistakes I had committed, I had not deprived these two of love.

"Who did you see as your mother then, Aranya or Sudha?" I teased him.

He laughed. "You, Mother. I saw you frequently in Malla or Padi. You would never let me out of your sight during those visits." He would have grown since the last visit, and I would hold him tightly and shower him with kisses.

I tugged his ear now.

He put his arm around my shoulder. "And Uncle Jay would talk about your childhood in Malla often, so even in your absence, you were always with me."

"I have to thank Jay for all he did." I worried about my brother. Vikram's absence must torment him.

"You were right, Mother. The news you shared changed very little in reality." Atul surprised me with his maturity.

We sat in silence as I watched the lush fields glistening in the morning sun.

"I never meant to hurt you, my child," I said as a distant temple bell tolled.

"You did not, Mother. And the commander is a good man who appears devoted to you," he said, flushing like the boy he was. Having seen me as a widow all his life, I could guess why he would be embarrassed to discuss his father's affection for me.

Our journey was uneventful, and in a few days, the forts of Daya stood before me. In the previous years, Nala would have arranged for us to spend summer amidst the mountains in Nanga. With his untimely death, the royal family remained here in Daya. As the chariot entered the city, people gathered on either side of the street. I sat alone while Atul rode on his mare in front.

Women reached out to me with their hands stretched. As the crowds thronged, the carriage slowed down. "Our queen," someone called. An older woman stood with her palms touching as if saying a prayer on my behalf.

"Where is King Nala?" a voice yelled.

"Queen Meera," a chorus went up, drowning out any lone yells.

At the palace entrance, I dismounted. Prince Kanishka and others stood at the top of the stairs. General Gambhir ran down to greet us.

"Let us get you inside, Queen Meera," he said.

"In a moment, General. Let me address the people first," I said. As the carriage moved, people crowded around me. With Atul's help, I climbed a few steps and faced them.

"I bring grievous news with me. King Nala perished at the hands of an invisible enemy." A solemn cry went up for Nala, and my stomach twisted into knots. "Before he died, he tasked me with seeing his unborn son or his brother Amar crowned as the next king of Padi."

I turned to Atul. He stood tall and clasped the hilt of his sword. "My brother, King Nala, died as he lived—thinking about the welfare of Padi. My mother and I will continue that tradition. We will hold audiences with you to hear your grievances." A murmur of condolences spread.

"We heard Prince Amar is hurt," someone stated.

"We suspect the same enemy that killed Nala caused the fire that burned Amar. Fortunately, there is no risk to his life or limbs. He recently married Princess Heera of Malla. They will be traveling to Padi soon," Atul answered.

The crowd dispersed shortly, and we headed inside.

"You must be tired after the journey. I will call for a council meeting tomorrow," General Gambhir said.

"General, the day is young. I am ready to meet with the council now," Atul said. With his boyish looks, he looked young next to the general.

"I will gather the others," Gambhir said.

Atul inclined his head. "I will take Mother to the council room."

As I walked the halls of the palace, memories of Nala came flooding back. He had ruled Padi for seventeen years, most of it as still a boy. Atul led me inside the warm room, and I sat at the table, remembering the countless times I had been here with my husband or son. Atul stood behind me, his foot's tapping sound muted by the colorful rugs on the floor.

Prince Naren, Prince Kanishka, and General Gambhir walked in with others. *They outnumber us,* I thought. The hair on my arms stood up.

"Please be seated," I waved at them, hiding my anxiety.

Atul moved to the center of the room. "Elders, a few days ago, someone tried to kill me. Not in combat like a warrior. A hired assassin's dagger flew through the shadows, aimed for my throat. Only Commander Rish's alertness saved my life." Atul paused and scanned the room.

I watched Kanishka closely. He gazed at his folded hands with his lips pressed together.

"General Gambhir, I want you to help me investigate this matter with the utmost immediacy."

"Yes, my lord," Gambhir answered.

"I want all messages sent or received from this palace to be checked by my guards," Atul added quietly.

Bodies shifted in their seats, signaling an unease. Kanishka erupted. "Who are you to come in and order us?"

"I am Prince Atul of Padi, Cousin Kanishka," Atul said with no trace of anger.

"You are no prince of Padi," Kanishka hissed, directing his gaze toward me. I breathed in deeply to calm the storm brewing in my stomach. And I observed Naren and Gambhir. Neither rose to defend my honor.

Atul's eyes swept the room. "Are you insulting my mother?" Only a slight tightening of his jaw betrayed his emotions.

Kanishka pushed his chair back. "I don't care about Queen Meera's personal affairs. I do care about polluting the Padi line with imposters," he snarled.

Atul appeared young and vulnerable in this gathering of adults. "Cousin Kanishka, you can apologize to my mother or spend a few days in our dungeon," Atul commanded, with a touch of uncertainty coating his voice.

Kanishka stared defiantly, with his hand poised near his sword. I saw glances pass between Naren and Gambhir. If the Padi men were in cohorts, there were more of them than us inside the room. My heart lurched with sudden worry.

33
JAY

My heart pounded like thunder on a stormy night. "Who else is with him?" I longed to find my son.

"Our men spotted a man with the boy," Dev said.

"Anyone else?" My hands went cold with anticipation.

He shook his head. "That is all I have heard so far. I will investigate the house."

Where is Vikram? "Dev, ask our men not to let them out of sight. And wait for me. Let me see Ratnavali first, and then I will join you," I ordered.

I strode to see my wife with my mind caught in a swift current of conflicting emotions.

I remembered chasing after my son as he hid behind pillars and thrones, screaming with delight, "I'll catch you!" The memory brought tears into my eyes. These past few months, I had been helpless with grief.

I slowed my pace as I neared her room and shut my eyes for a moment to suppress the other worries. Then I entered her chamber with anxiety creeping up my spine. Kantha sat beside her on the bed, feeding her some liquid.

As I approached them, Kantha rose. "Finish feeding her," I said.

Ratnavali looked at me then with sunken eyes, like a wilted flower past its bloom. My throat tightened at this sight.

"I am done, my Majesty," Kantha replied and withdrew.

I took the spot vacated by her and sat on the bed.

"Do you remember what happened that day?" I asked, gently clasping Ratnavali's hand.

Her eyes glittered with tears. "Prince Vikram—" she said, and a sob escaped her, wrenching my heart.

"It is okay. You are safe now," I whispered, kissing her knuckles softly.

"I lost my baby," she wailed, her voice shrill with panic.

I held both her hands against my heart. "Ratnavali," I said softly, drenched in her grief.

Her sobs subsided gradually. I wiped her tears with my thumb.

"Due to my injury, I may never bear another child, King Jay. I will fail in the one duty I have."

Duty. I'd tied this chain to her neck. "My dear Ratnavali, the failure is mine in not safeguarding you and the child. I will not make the same mistake again. You have not failed me." I kissed her forehead. Guilt rose in me like smoke from fire for binding her to my fate.

"Will you send me back to Sunda if I am barren?" she asked. Did she want to return to Sunda?

"You are my wife. Your place is by my side. You can visit your father if you want after you recover."

She closed her eyes in exhaustion and drifted off to sleep. I watched her for a few more moments. I had committed one blunder after another recently, with my marriage to her at the top of that list. I shut my feelings of guilt in a box and locked it. Then I departed, leaving her in the hands of a maid.

Dev waited for me. I changed out of my silk dhoti into one of faded white cotton. I removed all my royal jewels and set out with him. We rode our horses under the moonlight, racing past the fort. We dismounted at the edge of the forest and left the animals with a guard. I glanced around. In the distance, my palace loomed black against the deep blue of the sky. In front, the trees rose over my head, swaying lightly in the wind. We entered the woods on foot, making our way slowly through the undergrowth.

A sudden noise erupted, Dev pushed me behind him, and my guards surrounded me. Shields emerged in their hands. Frozen like statues, we scanned the dark. Nothing. Then snorting loudly, a mother boar darted in front of us with her babies. We remained motionless. After nothing else surfaced, Dev relaxed, and we moved forward.

One of my guards hooted like an owl. I heard an answering call. A man jumped softly from his hiding spot up in the trees a few yards away and came toward us.

"Are they in there?" I asked.

"Yes, my Majesty. The boy is in a hut with another man. Earlier, when I crawled closer, I could hear a low moan from inside. There might be another person."

In the clear night air, I could not easily breathe. I opened my mouth to gulp air. Time stood still as I remembered the day my son was born. I had felt an elation that I had never experienced before when I first held him. To imagine him a prisoner of a twisted man sent spears into my chest. I shook my head to bring myself to the present.

"Send a man to peek in the hut and confirm the occupants," I said. If Vikram was in there, I wanted him rescued, not killed.

Dev dispatched a man to scout the house while we waited. I sat hidden behind a tree trunk with two guards concealed among its branches. A mouse scurried into a hole in the ground past my leg. The vermin reminded me of Parth, hiding and scheming instead of fighting face to face like a warrior. My heart pounded with rage.

Dev approached me.

"There is a third person in the hut," he said. My son. A calmness settled in my heart. I knew what I had to do.

"Dev, surround their shelter. Get some archers who can shoot with accuracy," I ordered in hushed tones.

Dev sent word with a guard to fetch fifty men. Men from the city guard arrived and stationed themselves around the edges of the forest.

I moved stealthily among the bushes and took my place among them. A tall archer arrived at my left. With a swift nod, he lifted the bow and notched his arrow.

I scanned the horizon. "We make our move at first light."

Then as faint rays lightened the sky, the hut door opened. I stiffened for a moment, then hid. Two figures stood at the threshold, one taller than the other but neither a child. My heart jumped into my throat.

"Relieve yourself in the bushes," a voice I had not heard in nearly two decades said.

I clenched the hilt of my sword and searched the forest for Dev. Our eyes met, and he inclined his head.

My son shuffled forward in the arms of Parth, my old enemy.

34

MEERA

Kanishka glared at Atul while clutching the hilt of his sword. An ominous silence descended around us as we measured each other. My young son seemed no match for the grown men assembled.

Atul clasped his hands behind his back. "General Gambhir, were you present when my father, King Atul, proclaimed me his son?" I remembered the fateful day when my husband saved me from dishonor.

Gambhir stammered, "Y-yes." He then glanced at Naren.

"Hmm. Then that makes me Prince Atul of Padi."

Naren cleared his throat. Before he could answer, Kanishka erupted. "Enough of this nonsense. You are no prince."

"I am only a boy, but even I know treasonous words when I hear them. Don't you agree, General Gambhir?" Atul asked, his eyes pinning the man.

Gambhir fidgeted in his seat. "Prince Kanishka, Prince Atul—"

"I am not going to let this pretender get away with this," Kanishka snarled and drew his sword. Blood drained from my face. I could not let him hurt Atul. The cowards in the room sworn to the Padi king sat motionlessly. What had Kanishka promised them?

Atul straightened to his full height. "What do you intend to do?" he asked with a slight edge to his voice.

Kanishka pointed the sword at Atul, the blade glinting in the light.

"Let there be no bloodshed here," Naren muttered, still seated. I wanted to slap the idiot.

Kanishka smirked and yelled, "Guards!"

The door opened, and a stream of soldiers in Padi gear streamed in.

"Take him away," he waved at Atul. My body tensed like a deer sighting a hunter.

The men drew their weapons. I glanced at Atul. His hand hovered near his sword. I could not see another child of mine harmed. My instincts howled: Run! Run! Why had I agreed to this plan?

Kanishka grinned like a mad man. Then suddenly, he screamed, "Uncle Gambhir, Uncle Naren." The spears and swords pointed at his neck. Did the guards turn against him? I suddenly recognized the men who crowded the room. They had traveled to Malla with us. Loyal men uncorrupted by Kanishka. Did Atul station them outside? I gazed at my son in pride.

Two of Atul's newly picked guards stood protectively in front of him. His head of the guard, a tall man with an imposing mustache, said, "Sheath the sword, my lord."

Kanishka yelled, "You will regret this." Once before, I had underestimated his father and lost my husband. Worry pooled in my stomach.

Atul folded his arms across his chest. "Cousin Kanishka, I will give you another chance."

I observed Gambhir and Naren scanning the room and the hall. Several Malla soldiers stood in the shadows beyond the door. Like worms wriggling and crawling over one another in a nest, these two men were looking for an escape. Where were the councilmen loyal to Nala? Why did none of them stand up for me? Many questions poured into my mind. I set aside these thoughts.

"Don't be a fool, Kanishka. Apologize to Queen Meera and Prince Atul," Naren stated.

Kanishka slumped. "My apologies, Queen Meera," he mumbled

with his eyes cast down. He dropped his sword on the table. Red color crept along his neck.

I wanted to throw him in prison, but he was a Padi prince with loyal supporters. I had to exercise caution to weed out the rats. "Kanishka, my husband believed in the goodness of the people. Following in his footsteps, I carry no ill will toward you," I said. *Except if you harm my family again. Then, I would be ready to unleash woe upon you.*

Atul discussed a few more routine matters and dismissed the group. He walked with me to my chambers, both of us greeting passersby cordially and accepting their condolences.

Guards entered my chambers ahead of us and searched them. "All clear," one of them said, and they shut the door behind them as they departed.

I had left these quarters three months ago, looking forward to two weddings and then visiting my daughter in Saral. Instead, I had lost my firstborn to traitors. When I scanned the room, I saw my husband and firstborn everywhere I turned—young Nala rushing in with a message from Jay—my husband holding me in his arms. I sank into a chair, drained from the day's activities.

Atul paced the floor.

"A viper's pit!" he exclaimed, turning to look at me.

"I am proud of you, Son. You held your own today." He had kept his composure while Kanishka had threatened him.

His face brightened momentarily. Then he said, "I don't trust any of them. Do we arrest Kanishka now?"

"Not yet. He has built a following. Let him lead us to the disloyal men. Then, we can replace them all."

"Commander Rish told me who the faithful men are. I will eat my midday meal with some of them."

I nodded. "I will visit Princess Mala later today. Come see me tonight."

Atul dipped his head. As he reached the door, a knock sounded on it. He opened it, and his head guard walked in, closing the door behind him.

"My lord, my lady, someone tampered with the water for the horses," he said gravely.

"How many were affected?" I asked, feeling sick thinking about the animals.

"An astute stable boy noticed the first few horses acting strangely, so we knew something was wrong. Still, we will have to put those to sleep."

I gazed at Atul. "Whoever we are facing will destroy Padi to get what they want."

He frowned at me. "How do we prepare?"

"Guard our water and food supplies. Also, our granary. And weapon storage." I hoped these madmen did not burn our crops.

He bit his lip. "I need more men. I will send a message to General Darsh Vindhya." He left shortly to take care of these things.

The women of the court visited me to offer their condolences. Some had heard rumors about me wearing a white sari and wanted to see for themselves. Others had come to see how I was holding up in the face of these tragedies. A few loyal friends attended to me to offer their support.

With the steady stream of visitors, I was unable to get away to see Mala. As the evening approached, the lady herself strolled into my chambers. Her ample hips swayed in a peacock blue sari.

"Queen Meera, I did not believe my ears when I heard the news about King Nala," she said. "I told Gambhir this could not be true." I had sanctioned her union with Gambhir.

She paused and stared at me, her eyes wide. I knew I had aged with the events of the past few months.

"Nala's demise was unexpected," I said, my eyes dry. I still mourned my son, but I currently needed my wits about me.

After accepting her condolences, I steered the conversation. "A faction supporting Kanishka has emerged during my absence. Do you know anything about it?"

She shook her head vehemently.

"Of course, as the son of Prince Parth, he is fourth in line for the throne," I added, including Atul in the list, though I would not condone him occupying the Padi throne.

"My lady, we all support Queen Kayal and her unborn child. I pray it is a boy," she said faithfully. Good answer. *If the child turned out to be a girl, would you and your husband support Amar on the throne? Or champion Kanishka?* I kept the questions to myself.

After she left, I wandered to Nala's chambers. A stale smell emanated from the tidy rooms. I drifted to the dining room and gazed at the portrait of Nala on the throne. A gentle smile played on his kind face. A heaviness settled in my stomach at the knowledge that I would never hear him talk again.

"Mother," Atul cried out as he entered.

Something in his tone caused my toes to curl.

"Son?"

He appeared as if he had seen a ghost.

"Message from Amar," he said in a trembling voice. Tears pooled in his eyes, causing a surge of panic in my heart.

35

JAY

*A*rrows were notched and aimed at Parth. He stood close to Vikram. Too close for us to shoot him with accuracy.

Parth and Vikram halted in front of some bushes. I controlled the urge to run to my son.

While the sky lightened gradually, the earth remained submerged in shadows. Merging with the shade, two soldiers crawled on the soil toward the hut to rescue the boy. I wanted to ensure the safety of Prince Aggabodhi before attacking Parth.

Suddenly, Parth turned toward the hut. "Who is it?" he asked. I was sure he could hear my heart pounding like a rolling chariot wheel.

My men halted their crawl.

"I heard something," Parth said, his hand on Vikram's elbow. Vikram's head hung loose with no indication that he'd heard Parth. What had he done to my child?

One of my men standing at the edge of the trees sneezed, his feeble attempt to cover his mouth with a cloth doing little to mute the noise.

Parth's head swiveled left to right, and he uttered a vile invective. Then he dragged Vikram toward the hut. The two men on the ground rose and ran into the house.

"Stop," Parth shouted.

I stepped clear of the trees, clothed like a peasant. "Let him go," I said, trying hard to keep my voice devoid of emotions.

He spun to face me, twisting my son along with him. I clenched my fist. "King Jay," he smirked.

A dagger appeared in his hand. He held it carelessly against Vikram's throat. "Tell your men to leave my hut."

"Parth, you are surrounded. With nowhere to go. Let Vikram go, and I will spare your life." I made no move to call my men off.

He drew the sharp edge of the dagger across my son's cheek. In the rising sun, I saw a red line form. Vikram's head snapped up, and his eyes glanced at me. I saw a flicker of recognition, and my heart jumped into my throat.

"You don't control me. If you want your son alive, get your men off this field. I need a bag of gold coins and two horses. And safe passage to Padi. Once Kanishka is crowned king of Padi, I will release the boy," he said with a cruel smile. The morning sun painted his face in a gruesome light.

I nodded at Dev. "Leave the hut," he ordered his men. The two men strode out, and Prince Aggabodhi walked behind them.

"You go back in," Parth yelled at the boy. The prince scanned the trees, and his gaze fell on me. His brows furrowed, seeing me in simple clothes.

"Prince Aggabodhi, leave with my men. They will protect you," I said. A dark cloud gathered in the sky.

"King Jay?" he asked.

I inclined my head.

"I made a terrible mistake," he said, and his shoulders convulsed in a sob.

"You cannot leave," Parth howled.

The boy looked like a trapped animal. *Run*, I mouthed. My thumb pointed away from Parth. He understood and took off toward the woods. Two of my soldiers followed him as dew rose from the ground in a cloud of steam.

Parth yelped like a fox stuck by an arrow. "I will kill him, I will kill him," he threatened with the sharp blade pressed against my son's throat.

"If you hurt my son, one hundred arrows will pierce your body," I warned. My archers stood at the ready, and the tip of their arrows gleamed in the sun. "I will find Kanishka and cut him into pieces with my own hands." There. He knew his son's life was in jeopardy.

Parth glared at me across the field of grass. I held his gaze. Deep lines etched his face, and a thin wisp of gray hair covered his head. After a staring contest that lasted a few moments, Parth turned aside. I hoped he realized the futility of his position.

Darkness descended on the field, and light rain started drizzling on us. My son was startled by the rain and glanced around.

"Vikram," I called to him. I wanted nothing more than for him to be safely in my arms.

His eyes settled on me. The rain gave him a weepy appearance. "Father," he whispered.

"Enough," Parth shouted. "Give me two horses," he repeated.

I ignored him. "Son," I said, trying to reach the boy.

"Did I kill her?" Vikram asked, awareness and pain infusing his face.

"No, she will live," I said. "Come to me."

I took a step toward him.

Parth tensed and pressed the blade back into my son. "Don't move, or I will kill him." I hoped it was an empty threat. If Vikram died, Parth would not live a moment longer. Nor his son.

I continued to walk as my guards followed me with their eyes.

"Let him go and take me in his place," I said. "You can hold the blade against me." At that moment, I forgot about the kingdom. I only cared about my son. I was prepared to die to save him.

"Do you think me a fool?" Parth hissed.

I removed the shawl covering my chest and dropped it on the mud. My damp hair stuck to my head. "I carry no weapons," I said. The rain plastered the white dhoti to my body. I spun in place to show him my backside. "I will make a better hostage than him."

Parth peered at me hungrily. In his place, I would accept the switch. And then plunge the knife into me to create chaos in the kingdom. Parth would not live after that. But my death would weaken the Malla kingdom. And Kanishka could still gain the Padi throne. A tiny voice whispered that my death would put the lives of thousands of my people in danger. I squashed that voice. Meera could bear that burden. I could only think about my son now. I had to save him. Protect him.

"I will pardon Kanishka," I dangled the bait in front of Parth.

My son looked at me. "No, Father. I committed the offense. I cannot let you take the punishment," he whispered.

Tears pooled in my eyes and mingled with the rain. "It is my duty to protect you." With my life if needed. For him, I would let my kingdom go to pieces.

"Stop," Parth yelled.

I halted ten yards away.

"He will kill you, Father," Vikram said.

That was a price I was willing to pay. But I did not say it aloud. "Son, listen to me carefully. Let me swap places with you, and you go with Dev." I just wanted to hold him one more time before I died.

"Father, I am not worth saving. Not with your life." No. Why would he say that? He was young, with his whole life ahead of him.

"Vikram, I am your father and king. And this is an order. Step away from him. Parth, release him."

Parth held the knife with the sharp end pointing out, his eyes darting between us.

Vikram shook his head. "Malla needs you, Father."

He then lunged at Parth. They fell to the ground and rolled. I ran toward them, my heart dropping to my stomach. Parth emerged on top, and he pressed Vikram to the dirt.

"Shoot him," I yelled. No arrows came flying by. Idiots. They were worried about hitting me. I could hear several footsteps stomping through the puddles, rushing toward us.

Parth adjusted the knife in his hand and raised it high.

"No," I wailed and jumped.

He plunged it into my son's chest. And again. I pounced on him and pushed him away. A blade stabbed my back, but I felt nothing.

I looked at my boy on the ground, covered in mud and blood. I lifted his head and placed it on my lap. I cradled him in my arms as tears streamed down my face.

3 6

MEERA

"What message did Amar send?" I asked, worried about the answer.

"Uncle Jay and Vikram were hurt in a scuffle with Parth," Atul whispered as if saying it aloud would make their condition worse.

"Hurt? Parth? Did they catch him?" My questions spilled out in a jumble.

"They caught Parth and threw him in the dungeon. But not before he stabbed Vikram and Uncle Jay. They are both critically wounded." Critically wounded? My breath nearly stopped on hearing it. Jay! My brother had supported me unconditionally in all my foolish decisions. He'd raised Atul as his own at my request. He was the pillar bearing the weight of Magadha. I could not rule this land without Jay. I could not imagine losing him. My mind uttered a silent prayer to Goddess Durga. *Save Jay. Save Malla.*

"Does your brother say anything else?"

"Yes, Mother. Parth wanted Kanishka crowned the king. They found Kanishka's scrolls in Parth's possession. What do we do now? Leave for Malla?" he asked, his brows furrowed.

I shook my head. "Not yet. We have cleanup work to do here.

Arrest Kanishka for conspiring with Parth. Restrain Naren and Gambhir till we can ascertain their role in this."

He dipped his head. "I will gather loyal men."

A sudden noise caused us to turn. Kanishka approached us with five other men, swords drawn. Our two guards drew their weapons and took a defensive stance in front of us.

"There is nowhere to run," Kanishka snarled. "I will not hurt you if you cooperate. We will take you as prisoners and make a swap for my father."

"Mother?" Atul asked my permission to fight. His hands hovered near his sword, and he gazed at Kanishka. His stance reminded me of a tiger ready to pounce on its prey. I wanted him to run and hide. But I was raised in the warrior tradition, even if I wielded no weapons.

"Fight for your brother," I declared.

Atul drew his sword and uttered a battle cry. "For Queen Meera." Then, he spun like a dancer on stage, his blade flashing in the light from the lamps.

But there were too many of them. Two men targeted Atul, and one of them slashed my son's forehead. Blood dripped down his face. A few inches below, it would have been his eyes. A warrior mother could never show despair while sending her sons to die. But I wanted to pull him back. Desperately.

Atul grunted and stabbed the man in his chest. The sword plunged deep, and he pulled it out in one swift motion. Blood and more spilled in a violent gush. Then he kicked him aside. As the man collapsed, Atul stumbled. My son could not see. The blood was in his eyes.

I tore the edge of my sari and ran to him. The second soldier crept closer to my son. "Atul," I yelled a warning as I grabbed a tiny statue from a table. The sculpted rock fit in my palm. As I edged closer, the soldier's blade swiped my leg. I stepped back to avoid another strike. Then I threw the statue at him, and it hit his stomach. "I was the queen of Padi. Have you no shame in attacking us?"

He groaned and clutched his mid-section.

"Mother! Stay behind me," Atul cried as he crouched with his sword at the ready.

"Let me tie this around your forehead," I said. Atul shook his head and wiped his eyes. Blood dripped onto his dhoti and covered it with crimson spots.

The soldier I had hit came back. My admonishment meant nothing to him. I stared at him. Maybe he was not from Padi. Atul pushed me back gently and blocked his attack with the flat side of his blade. The movement of his sword was not in rhythm with his steps, confusing his opponent. A hoarse roar tore through my son's clenched teeth. I scuttled back further and scanned the room for more objects to throw.

Atul plunged his sword into the man and drew his innards out. His opponent muttered feebly, his fingers trying vainly to stem the flow of blood. The red liquid pooled on the floor as he fell.

Kanishka yelled loudly, and I turned to see him slice the thigh of one of our guards. The guard went down on his knees, and Kanishka chopped his head. Blood splattered all over, and the separated head rolled on the floor. I bit my lip to suppress an urge to throw up the contents of my last meal.

Our remaining guard had moved into the hallway fighting with his opponent. That left three men in the room. One of them hobbled on his feet. Though he appeared hurt, he still looked formidable. All of them formed a semicircle around my son.

"You are disposable, Atul. If you want to remain alive, drop your sword now. Otherwise, you can join your brother, Nala," Kanishka hissed, wiping his mouth with the back of his hand. At the mention of my firstborn, anger surged in me. I needed to help my son.

Atul once again assumed a defensive position. The men attacked, and Atul weaved in and out of their blades. One nicked his arm, and a red gash emerged. Another cut a hole in his dhoti. Fear hammered my heart. They moved too fast for me to hit them with the clay pot I held.

Holding his sword with both hands, Atul leaped onto the injured man and stabbed his throat. He pushed the falling man into others, and they stumbled back.

Two against one. Suddenly, the guard fighting outside marched in.

"I will take him," Atul said, pointing the sharp edge at Kanishka.

Kanishka cowered at the change in fortune. Then he ran outside the room. Atul chased him. I panicked because it was unworthy to kill a fleeing man.

I darted around the still fighting pair and peeked outside. Atul climbed onto the parapet and spun in front of Kanishka, slicing through the air with his sword. Without losing his balance, he attacked anew, mid-spin.

"I will not stab you in the back like a coward," Atul said and held his sword at the ready. Kanishka recoiled from the weapon. Then he lunged in desperation.

A loud crash sounded at the end of the hallway, and the door broke open. A stream of soldiers rushed in. Sweat broke out on my forehead. Whose guards were they, ours or Kanishka's? Then I saw the head of Atul's guard run in front.

"My lord," he said as he arrived near us. "They had locked the door, and it took us time to break our way through."

"Arrest him," Atul waved at Kanishka. Two men surrounded the traitor and bound his arms behind him. He cursed us as they dragged him away.

I rushed to Atul and hugged him tightly. "You fought valiantly, Son. Your uncle would be proud of you." During the fight, he'd ignored Kanishka's taunts. A feat even grown men found difficult.

He gave me a crooked smile.

"Get the physician," I ordered a man nearby as I tied the piece from my sari around Atul's forehead. The white cloth turned red.

"I am fine, Mother," he said. Then he gasped. "You are hurt."

I followed his gaze and looked at my leg. My sari had a tear near my right thigh, and blood seeped out. As I looked at it, a dull pain spread throughout the limb.

"The healer can treat us both. Have the men restrain General Gambhir and Prince Naren in their rooms," I said. I had promised Nala I would take care of his kingdom. Though the burden chafed my shoulders, I had a responsibility to clear the web spun by Parth. "They can stand trial for their crimes."

37

JAY

Soft fingers combed my hair, the touch a gentle kiss of the butterfly. Then, I tasted warm nectar, food of the gods.

"Jay," a voice pulled me out of my dream. I did not want to leave yet. I wanted to stay in my suspended state.

A firmer hand gripped my shoulder. "Jay, we don't have much time." The plea tore my heart, and I opened my eyes.

Aranya? Aranya!

Then, like a flash flood, memories surged through me. I sat up straight, and my blanket fell, exposing my bare chest. I noticed the wrap around it. I smelled of banana leaves and herbs.

"Vikram?" I asked hoarsely, afraid of the answer. What did she mean by we did not have time?

"He wants to see you," Aranya whispered, her eyes full of pity.

I stood up, and pain shot through my shoulder. It was only a tiny stream compared to the ocean of grief pounding my mind.

"You lost a lot of blood," Aranya said, clutching my elbow.

"Where is he?"

"In his chamber," she said, and we set out together. I felt like each step took me closer to doom.

When we arrived at the threshold of his bedroom, she let go of me.

205

The setting sun painted the walls in bright hues. I found my son on the bed with his mother holding his hand. The royal physician hovered nearby.

I approached them slowly. Sudha rose on seeing me, her eyes swollen and her appearance disheveled.

"Jay," she cried and sobbed on my shoulder. Sharp pain rose in my chest. From the wound or her distress, I could not tell. I squeezed her arm while gazing at my son. With his eyes shut, he seemed to be sleeping. I took the spot vacated by my wife.

I noticed the blanket covering him was stained with blood. With trembling hands, I lifted it. Though his chest was wrapped heavily, the red liquid still soaked the bandages.

"How is he?" I asked.

Before the physician could answer, my son opened his eyes slowly as if it took him a tremendous effort to do such a simple act.

"Father," he whispered.

I leaned closer to his face and stroked his cheek.

"Forgive me," he said.

As tears dripped down my nose, I said, "There is nothing to forgive."

As a lamp kindled, his eyes burned brightly. He turned to his mother. "Mother, do not weep for me. When the wind kisses your cheek, think of me."

She collapsed next to him, cradling his head. "Son, you completed my life," she whispered.

I rubbed the bridge of his nose gently. His eyes darted between his parents, his face at peace. Then, he shut his eyes and drifted off to eternal sleep. Nevermore.

The physician hurried over and checked him. "The prince is no more." He confirmed our fears.

As darkness swept into the room, Sudha and I sat there next to his cold body. She leaned against my chest, and I wrapped an arm around her. The world around us ceased to exist. Only our sorrow seemed real.

"Remember the day he was born," she asked.

"Like yesterday." I remembered the undiluted joy which had filled me when I'd first held him.

Vikram's death had taken a part of us with him. The part that delighted in seeing stars appear in a night sky. The part that knew how to laugh.

"Mother," Heera said and pulled us out of our nightmare. She reached out to Sudha. My wife startled at the word. She sat up, then took the hand held out to her. Heera led her out of the room.

"Father," Kayal said, her voice choking with emotion. I gazed at her in the light from the lamp she held. Kayal sniffed.

I stood up and kissed Vikram's forehead. Kayal put her arm through mine and pulled me along. I let her guide me. When we reached my room, I slumped onto my bed. She covered me with a blanket like I was a child of four.

No sleep claimed me that night as I stared at the ceiling.

The next day, someone helped me dress, and I let them. Amar arrived in my room to take me to the cremation site.

From a distance, the stacked wood for the pyre drew my eye. I stared at Vikram's corpse resting on top of the sandalwood. As my son, it was his responsibility to light my pyre. But here I stood instead, against the natural order.

Someone handed me a burning stick. With trembling hands, I lit the wood in a few places. With numbness cloaking me, I watched as my son was reduced to ashes. A part of me burned with him as I pondered his unfinished life. At sixteen, had he even kissed a girl? I knew he had never been to a battle except for the scuffle with Parth. I had dreamed of him wearing the crown that I wore. That dream had gone up in smoke along with him. And my life unraveled. If I had the strength, I would have tossed my crown into the fire.

The rest of the day passed in a fog. Somehow, I made it back to my room that night. And I did not leave it for days.

38

MEERA

A golden crown embedded with sapphires sparkled from the king's throne. Leaning against the throne was the Padi scepter. No king occupied the chair, though. I sat on a smaller silver chair on a lower rung, and my eyes swept those gathered.

Prince Kanishka stood slumped between two guards with no chains restraining him at my behest. He was Nala's cousin regardless of his actions. Prince Naren and General Gambhir stood a few feet apart from Kanishka as if to separate themselves from his crimes. Atul sat beside me, his index finger drawing a circle on his thigh. Other royals and council members stood on either side. Some had a somber expression, while others kept glancing at the trio of Kanishka, Naren, and Gambhir.

I nodded at Atul.

He rose from his seat and walked a few feet to stand in front of the throne. "Padi elders, we are gathered here in our time-honored tradition of serving justice. King Nala appointed my brother, Amar, as the regent to the throne. My mother and I are here on Amar's behalf. We will hold court today in his stead," he said, scanning the room. His gaze rested on our minister.

The minister moved forward and addressed the prince. "Prince

208

Kanishka, you are accused of treason against the crown and conspiring with your father, Prince Parth, to usurp the throne. You are also accused of an attempted assault against Prince Atul. And a planned attack against the prince and Queen Mother Meera here in our castle. Do you deny any of these charges?"

Kanishka's eyes darted toward Naren and Gambhir. They avoided his gaze by staring at the floor. He licked his lips nervously. "I intended no harm. I just wanted to capture them and exchange them for my father."

Meant no harm? Then why had my son, Nala, died? He had ruled Padi wisely. Parth and Kanishka had murdered him. I tried to suppress the rage that coursed in my veins at the loss of my child.

"My lord, only Queen Kayal or Prince Amar have the authority to order their capture. Queen Mother Meera and Prince Atul rank higher than you. On whose authority did you act?"

Kanishka blinked a few times but did not answer.

The minister, a man about my age, continued patiently. "Did you conspire with your father to seize the Padi kingdom?"

"Seize? It is mine by birthright!" Kanishka exclaimed.

"My lord, under our laws, the throne would pass to King Nala's unborn son, his brothers, and then to you. There are two men alive who precede your claim."

"Only one. And Amar is blind," Kanishka muttered. Then angrily, he turned to the men gathered in the room. "Do you want to be led by a sightless prince?" he sneered.

"My lord, King Nala chose his brother to rule after him. The words of the king outweigh all other claims."

"In Mahabharatha, the younger Prince Pandu ascended the throne in place of the elder Prince Dhritarashtra, who was born blind," Kanishka mentioned the epic as his defense.

"My lord, according to our laws, King Nala's choice of his heir matters the most. He selected his unborn child, if male, then his brother, Prince Amar. After that, the claim passes to his younger brother, Prince Atul, who is here," the minister explained our traditions. "Your attempt to seize the throne is an act of treason."

I could not allow Atul to claim the throne because he had no Padi blood in him. But that remained a secret between us.

Kanishka glared at Atul but did not repeat his previous accusations.

"Do you deny aiding your father, a man punished for betraying his king?" I asked. He had written to his father to plot my sons' demises.

Kanishka's shoulders sagged on hearing my words.

I spoke, "It saddens me greatly to punish Kanishka for his crimes. But punish him I must, so he serves as an example. He will meet the same fate as his father, Parth." I paused and looked around. Kanishka crumbled in front of us. Atul and I had decided that the father and son duo merited the same punishment. Jay would not banish Parth again. He would likely put him to death.

"Keep him locked in the dungeon till then," Atul ordered. Our guards dragged him away, and he went meekly, all fight gone from him.

The minister turned to Naren and Gambhir. "Prince Naren, General Gambhir, you swore an oath to serve the king of Padi faithfully. You are accused of failing to uphold that oath."

Naren and Gambhir glanced at Atul and me. "My lady, I served King Atul and King Nala faithfully," Gambhir said. I remembered he did not stand behind me when Parth poisoned my husband. Nor did he attempt to stop Parth's son now. His behavior followed a pattern of loyalty only when it was convenient.

Naren mumbled similar words. While Kanishka connived with his father, these two were guilty of lesser crimes. They failed to uphold the laws of the land. Instead, they aligned themselves with power.

"Your service to the kingdom is why your lives are spared," I said. The two men inhaled sharply. "You will be stripped of all your titles, and you will hold no office," I continued, meting out their punishment. Two guards approached them to retrieve their insignia rings and other royal artifacts.

Atul appointed a new general for the Padi army and two new members to our small council. We had only just started clearing the rot, and our work continued for the next few days.

One day as Atul and I sat in my chambers discussing our affairs, a guard announced a visitor. I glanced up to see Rish leaning against the door frame, out of breath. Warmth spread through my face on seeing him. Atul rushed to his side and held his elbow.

"Commander, have you recovered sufficiently to travel?" Atul asked with concern as he helped him to a seat.

Rish looked at me, his eyes full of sadness. The warmth from earlier fled to be replaced by coldness.

"Prince Vikram is dead," he said without a preamble. "We received the message from Prince Amar. I decided to deliver it in person."

My hand covered my mouth as I sat still in shock. Atul froze in place.

"Jay?" I whispered.

"King Jay will recover from his physical injuries. But I heard he has refused to leave his room, abandoning his duties."

My heart melted at Jay's plight. While I pitied my brother, I realized Atul had not moved yet. I rose and went to my son. When I touched his shoulder, he fell into my arms, weeping. I held him tightly, his long frame folding to fit into my grasp.

"I should have been there to protect Vikram," he cried.

"Son, we cannot always protect the ones we love," I said, remembering my husband and Nala. "But we should still try to help those who need us. Your Uncle Jay is hurting deeply. Go to him. Help him heal."

He straightened and wiped his eyes. "What about you, Mother?"

"I will stay here till Amar arrives," I said, glancing at Rish.

Atul looked at his father too. "Will you remain here with my mother?" he asked.

Rish nodded, his eyes lingering on me. I knew he would. He had predicted I would send Atul away and had come to be at my side, so I would not be alone. Gratitude surged in my heart.

Satisfied, Atul said, "I will leave immediately."

39

JAY

y chair faced the window, and I watched the clouds sail past. I did not remember seeking this spot; my memory had deserted me.

"We have united Prince Aggabodhi with the monks, and I have embedded two of my guards with them," Kapil said.

One cloud that looked like a cotton flower transformed into a tiger. And before my eyes, it dispersed into thin strips, just like Malla under my rule.

Kapil mentioned more things, but my mind did not comprehend his words. There was something important I had to ask him, but I could not recollect it.

The same day or maybe the next day, Sudha stood beside my chair. "Jay, I am going to the Vindhya palace. Every sight here reminds me of Vikram, and I cannot take it anymore."

I wanted to say something, but a flock of ducks flew in the sky. I watched the duck in the center leading the other birds. It was an able leader to guide others for miles across lands. Unlike me.

Then I realized I was alone. Sudha had left. Had I talked to her? Darkness descended around me.

My hands were tied to a tree, unable to move. My son collapsed to

212

his knees a few feet from me. "Father," he pleaded as knives plunged into his heart.

I struggled against my bindings, screaming, "Son."

I woke up in a sweat.

"It is okay, Jay," a voice murmured. In the faint light of the predawn sky, I saw Aranya next to me, her arm around my waist. When had she gotten into my bed? I scanned the room to make sure it was my room. Then I moved her hand and rose. I went to the basin and splashed some water on my face. The cold water did little to disperse my nightmare. I wandered to my door and opened it.

"King Jay," Dev said, his eyes wide.

"Take me to the stables," I ordered. I did not remember the way.

My stallion remembered me and nuzzled my neck. I rubbed his forehead gently before mounting. I let him lead the way and sat holding the reins, my mind many miles away. The sharp wind tingled my skin, and tears flowed from my eyes. As the sun rose, morning mist rose with it.

When I returned to my room, Aranya had gathered Kayal, Heera, and Amar for a morning meal. She guided me to a chair and placed a plate of steamed rice cakes in front of me. I stared at the white round mounds. Vikram had loved to dip them in the spicy stew.

"Uncle Jay, Parth is awaiting his trial," Amar said.

Trial? Something stirred in my memory. I had promised Kayal to punish the man who had murdered her husband. "Cut his head off," I said, still staring at the food.

Aranya tore a piece from my plate, dipped it into the pumpkin stew, and brought it to my mouth. "Eat, Jay. You cannot starve like this," she said, her tone grave with concern. Then she started feeding me. "Amar, Parth murdered the king of Padi. You can hold court during his trial," she told my nephew.

Voices floated around me, and I felt as if I was falling from the sky. Suddenly I choked on the food and started coughing. Heera jumped up and rubbed my back. The food went down, but not the anguish stuck in my throat.

I rose, still coughing. Aranya handed me a silver cup with water. I took a sip and placed the tumbler back on the table. I wandered to my bedroom and collapsed on the bed.

"I wished I had died when your mother did," a voice said. I opened my eyes slowly. I could not see anything at first. A single lamp struggled to dispel the darkness. Instead, it created shadows.

The voice! Somu? Somu!

"Then you buried your face in my lap, and I transferred my love to you." He sat beside my bed, gently rubbing my arm.

"You loved my mother." It was not a question. Meera and I had known about it for many years.

"Oh, she did not return my love that way. But that did not stop me from…" He did not elaborate, but I guessed. He came with my mother to Malla and had stayed with me.

"She was a fearless girl. Your father barely kept up," he said with deep affection. "She would not want her son to mope around in grief. Especially the son who so closely matched her spirit."

"Me?" I had not known my mother well. She died when I was five.

"Yes. Of your siblings, you are the one most like her. You have tamed your spirit since you became king, but it is there. You are not afraid to ignore the frequently trodden path and pave your own way."

I sighed. "My son is no more, Somu."

"My king," he said gently and grasped my hand. "You are a ruler. You would have sent him to fight your battles in a year or two. And prepared for him to die. Just like your father did. Do you not remember how many times you put your life in danger? Without producing an heir?"

I had crisscrossed the seas fighting savages and pirates.

"Mourn him. But you are not doomed. You have daughters," he paused. I gazed at his lined face. "And nephews." He had brought the news of my brother's birth to my father. So he knew the truth about Nakul and my nephew Vasant.

Somu picked up a silver bowl from the floor. A faint smell of cardamom and ghee wafted in the air. "Are you hungry? I had this prepared especially for you."

I sat up and accepted the bowl from him. Rice cooked with jaggery and milk, garnished with cashews. I ate three morsels, more than I had eaten in days. Tears flowed down my cheeks at his kindness and care. I deserved neither.

The next day, I washed the grime and dirt off my body and wore clean clothes. I picked up my crown and inspected it. The golden crown crusted with rubies felt heavy in my hands. More than I could bear at the moment. So I left without it and made my way to Kayal's room.

I heard Kayal talking to her sister as I stood outside. I stepped in, and silence descended for a moment. Then my daughters rushed to my side and hugged me. I put my arms around them and held them tightly.

"Father," Heera cried. "We were worried about you." Heera, who radiated warmth and light, had faint lines on her forehead. But there was something more. Her face glowed and appeared more rounded.

"Are you with child?" I asked.

With a blush creeping up her cheeks, she nodded. I kissed her forehead and then her sister's. Kayal's stomach protruded as if she held a tiny pumpkin in her midsection.

"Father, when our sons are older, we are going to send them to Akash so you can train them," Kayal said, squeezing my hand.

"If your Aunt Meera allows it," I said. I had ruined my own son. I was not sure I could raise my grandsons any better. I tried to smile, but the effort was too much, so I gave up.

"Why wouldn't she?" asked Heera. "You raised her son." Atul. Did he know about Vikram? The boys were close. Would he blame me for his cousin's death? Like I blamed myself?

"Father, Heera, and I are planning to go to Padi soon. With Amar. I want this child to be born on Padi soil."

Tears welled in my eyes. I sniffed and nodded. "I will ask Kapil to send guards with you."

"Amar has already made all the arrangements," Heera said.

I stared at her with my mouth open.

Kayal laughed at my expression. "Amar is a changed man now. I watched the trial from the balcony. He was fair and just. He gave

Parth ample opportunities to speak. But in the end, he ordered him to be executed. Aunt Meera would have been proud."

"That is good news then," I said. With Meera's wisdom, Kayal's strength, and Heera's warmth guiding him, Amar would make a good ruler.

"Parth threatened vengeance through Kashgar. Uncle Kapil has found more information about that land," Kayal added. I had no interest in Kashgar, so I asked her no further questions.

That evening I sat in my favorite chair facing the window. The sun disappeared behind clouds, and darkness arrived early along with Amar and Kapil.

"Uncle Jay, Parth's execution is set for tomorrow."

"I will be there to make sure he stays dead this time," I said.

"During the trial, he warned us of an impending threat from Kashgar. We are harboring Prince Aggabodhi," he added. *Threat?* Bigger than the ones of my making?

"My Majesty, we should send a trade delegation to Kashgar—"

"Amar, take care of it." I waved them away. Kashgar was the last thing on my mind.

My nephew hesitated. "Uncle Jay, I suggested sending a representative from each of the three Magadha kingdoms."

"Hmm," I said absently. A sliver of a moon appeared in the sky. I heard a murmur behind my back.

Then, Kapil said, "We will come back another time."

"Father," Vikram cried weakly, trying to keep his head above water.

I swam toward him, but the currents kept pushing me back. "Son," I shouted. Only his eyes remained above water, reflecting his fear of drowning. I kicked furiously, fighting the giant waves. When I reached the spot I'd last seen him, he'd vanished. "Vikram," I cried.

"Jay," a voice called my name.

I woke up drenched in sweat. I rubbed my eyes and gazed up at my wife.

Aranya was used to my nightmares. "Are you sure you want to witness Parth's punishment?"

I nodded. I had to do this for my daughter and son. I dressed in my silk clothes and gold jewelry. Kapil arrived to escort me.

"I had failed you, Jay. Twice," he murmured.

I raised my eyebrows.

"I had failed to kill Parth in Kashgar. And I failed to stop him from committing his atrocities in Malla." His limp seemed more pronounced than before.

He was right, though. He and I had lost our spellbinding abilities. But I could not set my crown down. Neither did I want him to abandon his duties.

"I had ignored Kashgar for long. Let us put your plan into action. Let us find out what is happening there."

We arrived in the courtyard, and I noticed a small crowd. I spotted Amar among them and strode to him.

"Amar," I called his name to announce my presence.

"Uncle Jay," he said and squinted in my direction. "They are fetching Parth."

As he uttered those words, I heard the rattling of chains. I glanced in the direction of the sound. Parth trudged forward between two guards through a dark passage.

The men guided him to the center of the yard and removed his chains. Blinking in the sun, Parth rubbed his wrists as his neck swiveled side to side. His glance rested on Amar briefly.

"Blind prince. I had planned to kill your brother, but you were caught in the fire. A win for me, nonetheless," he gloated. Amar turned pale.

"Enough," I ordered.

Parth turned to face me. "King Jay, I did not expect to see you. I thought you would be mourning that boy. Did you miss me?"

I wanted to choke him with my bare hands. I clenched my fists tightly to suppress my rage.

His eyes landed on my curled fingers, and a cruel smile broke out on his face. "Jay, what I have started will not stop with my death. Magadha will burn like your son's pyre. And you will go up in flames," he said gleefully.

I signaled to my men. They grabbed Parth and pushed him to his knees. A man recited all Parth's crimes, a list that had grown in the last few months. The executioner swung his sword and severed his head in one sweep. He did not deserve to die so painlessly.

* * *

I STARED at the ceiling as the sun streamed in through the windows. The sounds of the morning reached me, but I felt no desire to leave my bed.

"Jay," Aranya called.

I raised my head and gazed at her. She looked like she had been awake for a few hours.

"Kayal, Heera, and Amar are here. They have come to get your blessing."

"They are leaving today?" I asked, swinging my legs down.

"Yes, they are departing this morning," she said patiently. I washed my face and looked in the mirror. A face with dark shadows under its eyes stared back. More gray hair had sprouted along my forehead and on my chin. I fixed my clothes and went to the sitting room.

Amar and Heera touched my feet together. "I wish you both happiness," I said, tears welling in my eyes. I tapped Amar on the shoulder and embraced my daughter.

"Come visit us, Father," she urged.

Kayal bent to touch my feet, but I pulled her into a hug. "I wish you a healthy son," I said. "Take care of yourself."

"Yamini, come and get your grandpa's blessings," she called. The child hid behind a chair and giggled. I sneaked to her slowly and scooped her up in my arms. I kissed both her cheeks. She pinched my nose.

"Why are you so sad?" she asked.

My breath caught in my throat. "I am sad to see you leave," I said.

"We will come back, grampa," she said and put her tiny hands around my neck. I held her close to my chest before handing her to her mother.

Suddenly I remembered Aranya had planned to go to Padi with them. If she left, I would be alone in this palace. My stomach coiled at that thought. I gazed at her and asked, "Are you going with them?"

She shook her head. "I am staying with you."

I let out the breath I had held. It was selfish of me to want my wife to stay here in Akash, but I needed her. And she knew it.

While Aranya went to the palace courtyard to send them off, I stayed behind and watched the procession from my window, sadness overwhelming me. My daughters had gone, and I had no son.

After they left, the palace lost all liveliness. I stayed in my room most days, rarely venturing outside.

Like many days recently, I lingered in bed that morning, watching the light playing on my ceiling.

"My lord," Ratnavali said. *Ratnavali!* I had married that poor girl and forgotten about her in recent days. Or rather, I'd avoided her since I could only handle so much pain and guilt.

I got up on my elbows and looked at her. She still looked pale from her injury.

She hesitated at the threshold. I dropped back onto my pillow and patted a spot next to me. She walked in slowly and sat.

"How are you?" I asked.

She tried to control her sobs, but they escaped nevertheless. I pulled her onto my chest and rubbed her back. "I may never bear a child," she cried. I had brought this curse on her.

"Ratna, if it matters to you, we can adopt a girl," I said to console her. I did not want to raise another child because I failed miserably in my last venture. But I would do it for her.

Her sobs subsided, and she straightened, wiping her eyes with her sari. "Does it matter to you?" she asked.

I laughed bitterly. "No, I would rather not raise more children only to lose them."

She bit her lip. "I am sorry about Prince Vikram."

She left me shortly after, and I rose to gaze out the window.

"Uncle Jay," a chorus echoed in the room, and I turned toward the sound. My nephews, Atul and Vasant, stood in front of me.

"We came as soon as we heard the news," Vasant said.

"I am sorry I was not here to protect Vikram," Atul cried out.

I extended my arms to pull them into a hug and wept with them. My children! They stayed in my room reminiscing about their childhood. I kept quiet initially, but their conversation drew me in. I slowly joined them, opening up about the antics and mischiefs the three of them had gotten into.

"How are my sister and nephew?" Atul asked.

"Priya has gotten big and bad-tempered. The hot Saral weather does not help," Vasant said, his lips curling up. "Chandra is a handful. Uncle Jay, I don't know how you managed to raise the five of us. I can barely keep up with one child."

"Remember when you decided you were ready to fight with a real sword?" Atul asked with a grin. "Vikram and I hid in terror while you chased us."

I remembered finding nine-year-old Vasant running after the four-year-old boys with a blade that glistened like molten gold. I'd had a near panic attack.

"I was a fool. Thankfully, Uncle Jay took my weapon away before I hurt anyone." I had hugged the three of them afterward, with my heart thudding.

Before I knew it, night sneaked up on us. A servant arrived to light the lamps. Another fetched our evening meal. I sat at the table with Vasant and Atul like I had done many times in the past. I nibbled at my food while watching Atul eat with relish. Vikram had a hearty appetite too.

"Uncle Jay, neither Atul nor I knew our father. With the love and care you showered on me, you never gave me a reason to miss him. Know that you have more than one son," Vasant said, reaching out to touch my hand.

I choked on hearing his words. "King Vasant of Saral, I have been watching you with pride," I said. Suddenly, my heart seemed lighter than it had in weeks.

40

MEERA

I knocked on Rish's door, hoping to consult him on some matters. His wife opened the door. Surprised to see her, I stood frozen for a moment. She smiled at me warmly and beckoned me inside with a hand motion. A childhood illness had taken away her ability to speak and hear. I stepped in and scanned the room with trepidation. As Nala's regent, Rish lived in large quarters. No sign of Rish inside, and I let my breath out. In her presence, I felt guilty about my love for her husband. I knew I had no reason for the guilt. I had not trespassed on their marriage bed. And I had known him far longer than her. But guilt cloaked me anyway.

Using signs, I asked her to let Rish know about my visit. She nodded. Then she grabbed my hands and pressed them to her eyes in a gesture of gratitude. I did not understand the cause for her appreciation, and I struggled to accept it graciously. She did not seem to notice my turmoil.

As I made my way back to my chambers, a slight irritation bubbled up in me like a thorn pricking my finger. And I did not want to examine the impetus for it.

Rish came to see me soon after. "My lady, I heard you were looking for me."

"From your wife?" I asked sharply. I sounded like a hurt child.

"Are you jealous, my queen?" His lips curled up slightly, and that made me angrier.

"I'm not jealous." I sounded unconvincing because I did want him all to myself. But I could not admit that.

He smiled, and tiny lines appeared around the corners of his eyes like rays of sunshine. "It does make me happy thinking that you may be. It is nice to be wanted like that."

I wanted to kiss him passionately to stake my claim. This sudden madness would do me no good, so I spun away from him to control my emotions.

He stepped close to me. Too close. I could lean back into his broad shoulders. Instead, I stood tall.

"She came to take care of me after receiving your letter," he said as if it was my fault. I had informed her of his injury.

"I cannot hurt her too," I said and moved away from him.

"Hurt her? Why would you hurt her?" he asked, puzzled.

I turned to face him. "Rish, have you forgotten what you asked of me?"

"It is etched in my memory," he said with a sigh.

His sigh bothered me. "You must know it will hurt her." While it was common for a man to take on a second wife if the first one failed to produce a son, the woman nevertheless resented this tradition.

"How about me? You don't mind wounding me?"

A lump formed in my throat at his question.

"Don't answer that," he said gently, his intense gaze penetrating my heart. "I know you don't want to injure me either. The only person you don't mind injuring is yourself. Since I have tied my fate to yours, I am along with you on this painful journey, watching you deny yourself any happiness."

I stood still for a moment. "I have a duty—" What was my duty anymore?

He waited for me to tell him why I could not choose him. Again. Why did I deny my heart? I had loved him for a long time, and the love had endured three marriages. But when it came to Rish, what I wanted to do remained the opposite of what I had to do.

"Is the door locked?" I asked as I stepped toward him.

"No," he said, his brows furrowed.

"Can you lock it? I don't want us interrupted." My passion was not one of youthful exuberance that flowed like a flash flood. Mine was a deep ocean current.

He opened his mouth to say something. Then he shook his head as if clearing his thoughts and went to latch the door.

He came back to stand where he stood before, his eyes watching me without judgment.

No man had held me in seventeen years. And I yearned to rest my head, even if only for a few heartbeats, on his chest. I approached him and stopped a foot from him. I placed my hand on his chest, and I could sense his heart beating swiftly. I settled my cheek on his heart, my head fitting under his chin.

He exhaled sharply. "Meera?"

"Hold me, Rish. We are not hurting anyone if we embrace, are we?"

His hands folded around me, tentatively at first. Then he squeezed me around my mid-back and drew me against him, almost pulling me off the ground. I could feel my chest flattening against his, our hearts beating wildly. I did not remember ever being held by him before. I wrapped my arms around his waist and burrowed my face into the base of his throat, and breathed him in. A warm scent floated from him as he rested his chin on my head. Then, he pulled away slightly, his hands sliding to my waist. "Only me, because of the restraint I have to show," he said softly, regarding me.

I knew no one with better control of their feelings. Rish was the king of restraint. "You must be used to it by now," I said, breathing deeply.

"I have never been able to rein in my thoughts," he said, his mouth twisting into a tiny smile.

"You think of me often?" He occupied a significant portion of mine.

"You are always in my thoughts, awake or asleep. I dream of

sharing my bed and waking up next to you." Instead of crying myself to sleep, I wanted to live in his dreams.

I sunk deeper into his arms, a riot of emotions flooding my body. As I unwound, tears flowed down my cheeks, wetting his skin. Life without him would be unbearable.

He lifted my chin and wiped them away with his finger. My lips parted under his touch. Slowly, his thumb traced my mouth, and I gasped. His eyes caressed my face. Then, he kissed me gently like I was a fragile flower that bloomed once in a decade. My body melted under his touch, and my fingers grabbed his short hair.

"Queen Meera," a knock sounded on the door.

I jumped away from him. "Hide," I whispered in panic.

He raised his eyebrow. "Hide? Atul and King Jay know the truth. Who else are we hiding from?"

"Rish," I admonished him.

"My lady, I am still your guard. There is no need for me to hide. But you might want to fix your hair and sari," he grinned.

A matching smile appeared on my face as I combed his hair with my fingers. Then, I went into my bedroom to re-tie my sari.

Rish opened the door. "What is it?" he asked, no hesitation in his voice.

"A message from Prince Amar," a man replied. My heart thudded, worried that he would sense something was wrong. But I did not hear any shock in his tone at seeing Rish.

I heard the door close and footsteps approaching me. "What does Amar say?" I asked.

"Queen Kayal, Prince Amar, and Princess Heera are on their way to Padi," Rish said and handed me a scroll.

"Amar executed Parth. I will let him come and mete out the same punishment to his son."

"Wise decision, my lady. I will go make arrangements for their arrival," he said. Then, he reached and took my hand in his.

"W-we—I," I stammered. What were we doing?

He brought my hand up and kissed my knuckles. "I can survive on stolen kisses. I have lived on less," he said. Warmth overflowed from his eyes.

On impulse, I pulled him into another hug. I wanted to remember the pleasure of his arms around my waist and store it away for the lonely nights.

My son, nieces, and granddaughter arrived in the city soon after. I stood on the steps of the palace to welcome them.

"Mother!" Amar exclaimed when I touched his cheek. He hugged me tightly. "I met Atul on the way here. He told me about the attacks on you. Where is Kanishka? He cannot go unpunished for his treasonous act."

"There will be time for punishment," Kayal said as she approached us. She handed her sleeping daughter to my son.

Then, Kayal and Heera touched my feet. I gathered them in my arms with tears glistening in my eyes.

As we entered the castle, I whispered in Kayal's ears. "I am sure you will see Nala in each stone of this palace. It is okay to miss him, my child." I had Rish to help me survive. What would Kayal do?

"I will remember our love, Aunt Meera. That will ease some of the pain," Kayal answered. I squeezed her arm.

Later that day, my family gathered around me for our meal.

"Where is Uncle Rish?" Amar asked. "Is he here?" he asked, peering around the room.

"I did not invite him," I said. I feared they would sense a change in us. We had not done anything beyond share some quiet moments with Rish's arms around me, simple acts that brought me a mountain of comfort. Yet, I felt guilty about it now in front of my children.

"Do you mind if I ask Uncle Rish to join us, Mother? I have many things to discuss with him."

I nodded, and he sent for him. When Rish entered the room, I kept my gaze on the child I held on my lap. I fed Yamini from my plate while telling her a story about a lion.

"Prince Amar," Rish said warmly, and they embraced each other.

"Uncle Rish, I want to discuss with you the matter of Kashgar. Parth alluded that he had sought their help to fight for Padi. Just because Parth is dead, the threat from Kashgar has not ceased," Amar said.

Rish observed this and asked, "What does King Jay think?"

Kayal responded. "Father is lost in grief."

Heera added, "Amar wants to send an envoy from Magadha, at least one messenger from each kingdom. He sent a message to Cousin Vasant."

As the conversation progressed, peace claimed my mind. Padi was in safe hands with these three at the helm.

Amar ordered his executioner to decapitate Kanishka for treason. A week later, in a public square, a man read Kanishka's crimes against Padi. Then the executioner's sword descended on his neck.

Kayal ruled as the queen of Padi with Amar's help. She joined Amar in the small council meetings and placed trustworthy and loyal men in various positions of power. Brief moments of hope interspersed with Kayal's long periods of grief at her husband's death. With Heera's radiant warmth, these hopeful moments grew brighter. Some days felt almost normal. And these normal days stretched into weeks.

Amar had transformed since his accident. The doubts that had plagued him receded to be replaced by a purpose. Kayal consulted with him on all matters, and Heera's warmth evaporated his misgivings.

The cook prepared special food for my pregnant nieces at my order, and I looked on with contentment as the sisters grew closer together. Kayal was into the seventh month of her pregnancy, and I hoped the arrival of her child would break Padi out of its vicious cycle of losing its kings.

One day a message arrived from Malla. Penned by my brother, it simply said, "Come to Akash to discuss Atul's future." It gladdened my heart to see the note in my brother's handwriting. Did it mean he had overcome his grief?

I shared the contents with Amar, Kayal, Heera, and Rish.

"We have two months till the baby arrives, Aunt Meera. That is plenty of time for you to visit Akash and return," Kayal said.

Amar agreed. "Winter is months away as well, so the journey will not be treacherous."

I gazed at Rish. Atul's future concerned him as well. "Will you accompany me to Akash?" I asked.

Before he could reply, Amar said, "Mother, take him with you. You are miserable without him. And Uncle Rish pines for you during your absence." Kayal and Heera giggled at this remark.

I nearly choked at my son's words. I stood and turned away from them to hide the tears welling in my eyes. "Forgive me," I said softly. It did not matter whether they were wronged. As a queen, I should have been more reticent about my feelings.

Amar sounded flustered. "I meant no disrespect, Mother."

"You have not done anything wrong, Aunt Meera," Heera stated. Shame filled me still.

"Mother," Amar put his arm on my shoulder. "Nala would have handled this more elegantly than me. Father has been dead for seventeen years. You have led a life without blemish. That you care for Uncle Rish has been apparent to Nala and me for some time now. From all the stories you shared, we had surmised that you had met each other before your wedding to Father. Is it so wrong that you still consider him a friend?"

If only Rish had remained a friend. He was more than that. Was it wrong to continue to love him? Would I ever stop? Shame governed my actions, but I had derived so much happiness from just being held by him. Was that so wrong? I stole a glance at Rish, and our eyes met. There was no reproach in his gaze, just acceptance. He could have left me any time in the last three decades. But he had stayed, even though I had offered him very little in return. A feeling of calm surrounded me. I kissed Amar's forehead.

"I never meant to hurt you or Nala," I whispered. I had loved their father in my own way.

"You did not, Mother," Amar said, hugging me.

After the others left, Rish lingered. "Atul's future? Do you know what it is about?"

I shook my head. "I don't know. But if Jay is thinking about Atul, then it is a good sign of him controlling his despair."

He pressed his lips together. "It is not easy to overcome the loss of a child."

I swallowed. Nala's loss still sometimes overwhelmed me. We stayed quiet in our thoughts.

Then, I wound my sari end. I felt the urge to explain myself. "Rish, about earlier, I wish I did not feel ashamed of my emotions. But I worry about my actions tainting my children. I know I don't make it easy for you."

"Meera, nothing about us is easy. And I want you to forgive yourself."

"Forgive myself?"

"Yes. You asked others to forgive you. But that is not what is burning a hole in you. You have punished yourself for years. You deserve happiness too."

Tears welled in my eyes. Forgiveness would allow me to start anew. "I w-will try," I stammered. "Are you coming with me to Akash then?"

Rish smiled and stepped forward. "Unless you have changed your mind," he said, his face close to mine.

"No. Life without you is unimaginable," I whispered.

"Then don't imagine it, my lady. I am with you. Always," he said, bending to kiss my brow.

41

JAY

"We are sending messengers from each of the Magadha kingdoms. Their mission will be to further trade with Kashgar. Merchants from each of our regions will display their wares. About fifty soldiers disguised as servants will accompany them," Kapil said. As the sun moved across the sky, the light shifted in the small council room, throwing shadows onto our table.

I had already chosen my envoy, and Vasant brought his own men with him. "When is the Padi envoy arriving?" I asked.

"I expect them to arrive within the week," Kapil answered. Amar had said he would send his men once he arrived in Padi. He must have reached there by now.

"Giri, is a ship ready to take them to Kashgar?" I asked.

General Giri, my southern commander, answered in the affirmative. "We have three ships, ready to take them across the Nira sea. We will fly flags from all three kingdoms."

"How about the monks who sought refuge here? Are any of them joining our men on this journey?" Atul asked.

I shook my head. "I want this to remain a Magadha mission."

"The king of Kashgar has sought your help to recover his kingdom. How far are we willing to go to help Prince Aggabodhi, Uncle Jay?" Vasant asked.

I glanced at my nephews and my small council. "I don't want to risk Magadha blood in a futile war. I also want to know if the king has any support from the other noble houses and the common folk. If the people rebelled against him, I will withhold my support."

Vasant nodded his agreement. "We can continue to offer shelter and protection to the prince here on Magadha soil."

"My men will gauge the rebels' military strength while they are in Kashgar," Giri answered.

"I am sending a couple of spies who know the local language," Kapil said.

"Let us wait to find out more before deciding how to help Prince Aggabodhi. Atul, are you training with him?"

"Every day, Uncle Jay."

"Good. We will prepare him to rule a nation if the need arises."

We discussed other matters, then dispersed.

My nephews joined Aranya and me for our midday meal.

"Uncle Jay, Aunt Aranya, I wish I could stay longer with you. But Priya is pregnant, and I don't want to burden her with affairs of the court for long. Nor do I want to miss the arrival of my child. I will be leaving for Saral in a few days," Vasant said.

My hands felt cold. I knew this day was coming, but I thought I had more time. If my nephews left, would I descend back into gloom? Aranya glanced at me, and I could sense the same worry in her.

"I am not leaving yet, Uncle Jay," Atul said as if he recognized my concern.

My breathing settled into a regular rhythm as I looked at my nephew. Since my daughters had joined my sister in Padi, I hoped Meera could spare him.

After my nephews left, Aranya turned to me. "Are you going to crown him your heir before he departs?"

"Vasant?"

"Yes. Our grandsons will be Padi princes first. If you don't decide, the vultures will start circling us soon."

I rubbed my forehead. "Malla might gain an heir, but Saral will lose its king. Vasant is an able ruler, well-liked by the common folk. If I make him my heir, I have to reveal the reason for it. That would cause an uproar in Saral. If I don't reveal the cause, Malla chiefs will revolt."

"Our physician told me Ratnavali is unlikely to bear another child," Aranya said, her brows furrowed. I clenched my fist, guilt pouring out of me at Ratnavali's fate. "Giri Thari has a daughter. You can marry—"

"No," I shouted. I took a breath in to control my emotions. This was not Aranya's fault. "I have no desire to take another wife. Three is plenty."

She started laughing.

"What is causing you amusement?" I asked, my lips curling up too.

She wiped her eyes with her sari. "You have faced enemies on the battlefield with more ease than your wives."

I grinned. "And you want poor Vasant to suffer the same fate? If I make him my heir, I have to wed him to at least two of my chiefs' daughters."

"Queen Meera will not approve of Vasant taking another wife. Not with her daughter sitting on the throne," Aranya said, pushing my hair back.

I caught her hand and held it against my chest. "No, my sister will not. I dare not go against her wishes. Are you sure you are unable to carry another child?"

She laughed again. "Too old. I have not had a flow in a year. And I never was able to become pregnant again, even when I was younger. Not after Heera." She turned somber.

I raised her knuckles to my lips. "The fault lies with me. I was away from home for long periods."

"What do we do now?"

"Adopt a son. In the Mahabharata epic, King Bharata eschewed his sons and set another on the throne." As I uttered the words, I dreaded raising another child from birth. Where would I find a boy?

"From one of your chiefs?" Aranya asked.

I shrugged as no answers came to me.

"Jay, we cannot put this off for long."

"I know, but I cannot decide now, Aranya. I will think about this, though." I reassured her. "How is Ratnavali?" I asked.

"She has recovered from the stab wound. I took her with me to visit some families with sick children."

I stared at her. "How did she—?"

"She is a princess and familiar with the duties. She has returned today to see the children. She is going to be very useful. Since Heera has gone to Padi, Ratnavali can help me with many tasks."

I had committed several errors in my past, but marrying Aranya was not one of them. "I don't thank you enough for all you do," I said. I approached her and placed my arm over her shoulder.

She wrapped hers around my waist and buried her head in my stomach. "Come back to me, Jay. That is all I need." I imagined being lost in the dark woods and walking toward the light and finding her. I bent to kiss her head for illuminating my path.

A few days later, Vasant departed for Saral. Atul and I stood on the palace steps, watching the procession. "I hope you don't have to leave me soon," I said to my nephew.

He looked at me strangely.

"What is it, Atul?"

"Can we talk, Uncle Jay? Somewhere quiet?" He drew a map on his leg with his finger.

My heart raced, fearing he would decide to join his mother. But I nodded. "Let us walk."

We walked to the palace gardens, and the scent of fresh blooming flowers surrounded me. A myna bird sang close to us, and a leaf landed on my nephew's hair. I reached to pick the golden leaf and gazed at him. He looked like my father in the portrait hanging in my room.

"What is on your mind?"

"I know about—my mother told me when Commander Rish saved my life," he said, staring at the ground.

"About your father?" I imagined learning I was not the son of King Vikram. It took me months to adapt to the news that I was not the firstborn son. My stomach twisted into knots at my nephew's plight.

He nodded, avoiding my gaze.

"You are still my nephew," I said and touched his shoulder.

He glanced at me with moist eyes. "I am no prince," he said with trembling lips.

"Not of Padi. But you can be a prince of Malla," I said, squeezing his arm. Was he a prince? Riya, Vasant's mother, was never called a princess of Malla though her mother was one.

He did not look convinced of it. "Can I stay here in Akash, Uncle Jay?" he pleaded.

"Nephew, this is your home. I will never ask you to leave," I said, hugging him with one arm. As I dropped my arm, he rubbed his eyes. Atul became my shadow over the next few days. He sat in the council meetings and then discussed his views with me at mealtimes. I learned the boy had a keen head for court affairs. I watched him train Prince Aggabodhi in the yard. He combined gentleness and firmness to help the young prince learn.

One day, Atul and I sat in my room discussing Kashgar. A cool breeze floated in, bringing with it the smell of rain clouds.

"Bandits, my Majesty. In Malla," Kapil said as he entered the room.

"They see me and glimpse an aging tiger," I surmised.

"Still with sharp claws that can rip them apart," he said. "With your permission, I will send some men to capture them."

"I will go, Uncle Jay," Atul said immediately.

"To capture bandits?" A sudden panic seized me at the thought of losing him.

"Yes, Uncle Jay."

I shook my head. "No, it is too dangerous."

Kapil and Atul stared at me with their mouths open. While I had done far more dangerous things, this felt different.

"I will be careful, Uncle Jay. Please allow me," Atul begged.

I could not keep him tied to me. Not in fear. "Kapil, appoint two guards for him. Have them swear an oath to protect him."

Kapil nodded and left.

Atul gazed at me. "I had guards to protect me before. But none that swore an oath to me. Is that needed? I am nobody."

"You are my beloved sister's son. And my father's grandson. You have Malla blood flowing through you." When I said it aloud, I realized it myself. Son of a queen and grandson of a king, why couldn't he be a prince?

His face brightened at my remark. "I will not disappoint you."

The next day, he touched my feet to seek my blessing. "Come back victorious," I said. I watched him ride off along with a dozen other soldiers.

That night, I listened to Aranya's steady breathing while staring at the ceiling. Fear settled in my stomach and climbed its way up into my throat.

Atul ran away from the bandits while they chased him with drawn knives. Then he slipped and fell. The menacing men advanced on him.

"Uncle Jay," he screamed, and I woke up in a sweat.

Aranya yawned next to me. "Go back to sleep, Jay. Atul will be fine."

The moon peeked inside our bedroom, painting my wife in a silvery glow. "Are you awake?" I asked.

"I am now," she said and turned toward me.

"I should have gone with Atul. He is barely seventeen. I will leave at dawn and join them." The thought of losing my nephew twisted my stomach.

Aranya touched my cheek with her palm. "Jay, you were sixteen when we met. And you defeated my father in a battle. Let the boy prove himself without his uncle coming to his rescue."

I remembered our journey through Saral. She had rescued me. Maybe my nephew would meet a girl. I would be a hindrance during that encounter. I smiled at that thought and put my arm around Aranya.

The Padi envoy, along with light rains, arrived shortly after Atul's departure. I gathered Prince Aggabodhi, Monk Yonten, the envoys, and my council.

"Monk Yonten, my men will be sailing to Kashgar under a peace flag. Will the rebels treat them as messengers and provide them safe passage?" As the wind shifted, raindrops sprayed the windowsill. The sound outside muted the sound inside.

The monk nodded. "Denying entry would be paramount to declaring war. It is not in their interest to start a war, so they will allow you passage and even give your men an audience. But the current ruling faction is treacherous and ambitious. If they find any weakness, they will exploit it."

We pored over the Kashgar map and decided where to land the ships. Giri and Kapil took swift actions to get the men ready.

The next few days stretched like a frayed rope. I longed for news of my nephew.

One afternoon, I was training in the yard with Dev, my old sparring partner, when Kapil walked in.

"They are back," he said.

"Atul?"

He nodded.

I ran outside and saw the horses. Atul sat on a brown mare in front. Seeing me, he jumped off his saddle with a wide grin. A heavy load melted in my chest. I realized I didn't even care what had happened to the bandits. I was glad to see him. As he bent to touch my feet, I pulled him into a hug. Then I held him at arm's length to check him. I saw no visible injuries.

"Uncle Jay, we have captured most of the bandits. We killed a few who tried to escape," he said triumphantly.

I patted his back. "Let us go to my chambers. You can tell me all about it there."

"We rode in carts, disguised as a wedding party. Some of the men had draped saris to look authentic." Atul grinned as he narrated his tale. We sat across from each other at my table carved with a tiger family.

"We wanted to catch them in action. Just as the eastern sky lightened, the bandits attacked us. Instead of a cartful of silk saris and jewels, soldiers with weapons burst out. A young boy about my age attacked me." His face clouded for a moment.

"Did you kill him?" I remembered the first time I had finished off a man in battle. I had nightmares for days afterward.

"No, I could not kill him. I wounded him instead," Atul said, biting his lip.

"Bravery is not in killing others, Atul." He gazed at me. "It lies in your willingness to lay your life to protect others."

His tense shoulders relaxed slightly.

I continued. "I killed my first man at your age. It was the right thing to do, but I was haunted for days." I remembered my yearning to talk to my father about my misgivings. But he was in Akash while I toiled in Saral.

"This boy looked like Vikram and me. I could not bring myself to —" Atul said. "But I captured him. I hope to talk to him and see if I can help him."

"You did the right thing, Son," I said as pride coated my words.

Warmth spread over my nephew's face. "I was worried I would disappoint you, Uncle Jay. You always do the right thing."

I laughed. "Atul, I wish I chose the correct path about half the time. Even that is beyond my reach."

He stared at me with his mouth open.

I reached across and squeezed his arm with a knot of pride caught in my throat. "You have not disappointed me. You have made me proud."

He smiled shyly. "It is all your teachings."

"Finish your tale," I said with a strange joy filling my chest.

"I disarmed a few others. The bandits were no match for our troops, and we rounded them up. Then I gathered the village elders and shared the news with them. The bandits had terrorized them and disrupted their daily lives. They expressed their gratitude to you, Uncle Jay."

When he left my chambers, I sat at my desk to pen a letter to Meera.

Aranya strolled in.

I looked up and said, "I have found my heir. You mentioned him months ago, and my eyes are opening to the possibility only now."

42

MEERA

I felt like I had barely arrived in Padi while my maid and I packed my trunk for the journey to Akash.

"My lady," Rish called from my sitting room. I gave some instructions to my maid and walked toward Rish.

I stopped a few feet away and gazed at him. He appeared uneasy, pushing his hair away from his forehead.

"Queen Meera, my wife wants to visit Malla. I came to seek your consent to bring her with me." He fidgeted with a loose thread on his clothing.

My consent? I imagined for a moment denying his request. She would be sharing his tent while I stayed alone in my oversized one. I stopped myself from such uncharitable thoughts. She did not deserve my scorn.

"You don't need my permission to travel with your wife, Commander Rish," I said formally.

His eyes scanned my face, and I fought hard to keep it neutral. He inclined his head and left.

On the day of our departure, Amar and my nieces came to bid me farewell. I hugged them and prayed silently for their well-being. As I stepped into my chariot, I saw Rish watching two men load his trunks into a cart. He then helped his wife into another carriage as she beamed at him. He made some gestures with his hand and mounted his horse. My heart sank to my feet, and I turned away from them.

When we halted to eat our midday meal, I searched for Rish, dreading to find him with her. She was eating her food alone, seated on a blanket spread on the grass. I walked to her with my lotus leaf plate.

"May I join you?" I asked, then realized she could not hear me. My shadow fell on her, and she gazed up. She started to rise, and I gestured for her to stay seated. I pointed to the empty spot next to her and then at me. She understood my gesture and smoothed the blanket for me. I sank beside her.

We ate in silence as I realized I knew very few signs to converse with her. A gentle wind rustled her hair. She was about a decade younger than me, and her skin remained smooth. She wore a silk saree in the color of a mango leaf with silver thread embroidery around the border. Matching gold earrings and necklace glittered on her. Vindhya house was the wealthiest of Malla's three regions, and Rish did not lack gold coins.

She found me staring at her and smiled. She had a kind face that would age well. She waved her hand, asking me a question. I struggled to understand it.

"She is asking if you like your food," Rish said. I gazed up to see him standing a few feet away. I turned to her and nodded.

"Is everything alright, Queen Meera?" His face was inscrutable.

"It is, Commander Rish. I wanted to give your wife company." He dipped his head and moved away. I watched him join some men standing under a banyan tree.

We finished our meal in silence.

That evening as the tents rose, I went for a stroll. I felt like a leaf tossing and turning in a flowing river with nothing to anchor me. Rish did not belong to me. He belonged to someone else. That thought twisted a knife in my heart.

After washing my hands and face, I sat down to eat the evening meal my maid placed in front of me.

"My lady," Rish called from outside the tent.

Go away, I thought. But my mouth said, "Come in."

He entered the tent, and the place shrank in his presence. "May I join you, Queen Meera?" he asked.

I nodded and glanced at my maid. She left to fetch him a plate of food. He remained standing, and I stared at the table, an awkward silence stretching between us.

"Why are you here and not with your wife?" I asked. It came out as an accusation. I was tired of feeling hurt.

He appeared troubled by my question. "I wanted to make sure—"

"That I was not curled up on the floor?" I lashed out at him in anger.

"What do you expect me to do, my queen? The woman I chose rejected me. Instead, my king forced me to marry brides I would not have chosen for myself." I could sense his rage simmering.

I had no right to be jealous, but I wanted him all to myself. How had he controlled his feelings around me when I was married? "How did you bear it?" I asked.

He mistook my question. "My marriages? My first wife was miserable in Padi. I tried to make her happy, but I failed. Then she got pregnant, and her tears flowed daily. I grew tired of wading through her gloom, so I was relieved when she died. Then I felt guilty about feeling that way."

I stared at him with a lump in my throat.

He glanced at me. "My current wife—" He hesitated. "Her needs are simple. She demands very little of me. And you have sacrificed so much more than I, so I don't mind doing my little part."

"I should not have let you get tangled up in my web," I said, tears welling up in my eyes at the agony I had caused him.

"Meera, I did not have a choice because of how I felt."

Before he could elaborate, the food arrived. I hastily blinked my tears away. After my maid set his plate on the table, she departed. Rish dropped down to his seat.

Instead of eating, he twisted a band he wore on his finger. An eternity ago, I had given him a ring of mine.

"Do you still have the one I gave you?" I asked. Would he even remember?

He gazed up with a question on his face. "The ring?"

I nodded.

Like clouds departing to reveal the moon, his face lit up. He took out a drawstring pouch and opened it on the table. I spotted a ring nestled among the gold and silver coins.

"I have been tempted to wear it as a pendant. But it is safer from prying eyes in my pouch." He rubbed the band with his thumb.

I gulped some air as I watched him put the ring away. Our eyes met.

"You never asked me to return it."

"I wanted you to keep it." A token of my love that I could not reveal to the world. Like the ring hidden in his pouch.

Before he could say anything, I said, "I am sorry, Rish. For all the pain I caused you." I could not be mad at Rish for a decision forced upon him by my brother. Jay had insisted Rish marry again to protect me.

"Meera, it was my choice to remain at your side. I only wish I could have done more to comfort you."

"You did!" I exclaimed. "I could not have survived without you."

He gazed at me tenderly. "I have never loved anyone else." His declaration tingled my spine.

"Is that why she has not borne you a child?" I asked, speaking aloud the thought that flashed in my head. Then heat rose in my cheeks for uttering those words. What was the cause of this petty jealousy I felt?

He looked at me, puzzled. "The sickness that took away her speech and hearing made her barren." He had not shied away from any of his duties as a husband. When I imagined them together, a dozen knives pricked my skin. Then I remembered all the times Rish had seen me in the company of my husband. I suddenly understood how he must have felt and why he asked me to marry him.

Our food had gone cold. I pushed my plate away. "I do want to belong to you."

"Meera," he whispered, his eyes enfolding me.

"And you to me," I added, drinking in his face.

He reached for my arm under the table. "I am yours."

I shook my head and removed my hand from his. "You belong to her, even if you don't want to." Even if I did not want it.

"I don't deny that she has a claim on me. I will feed her, clothe her, protect her, and comfort her. But there is no burning passion in me for her. That part of me belongs to you, even if you don't want to accept it."

I could not have all of him, and I could not give him all of me. Would I be happy with part of him? What choice did we have?

"In ancient times, a woman could choose to marry a man in a *Gandharva* wedding ceremony. All they needed was mutual love," he said, his eyes searching my face.

"My father and mother married in such a way," I said. They had loved each other and married in secret. My mother had borne Nakul and had to pass him as her cousin's son. She had been a stronger woman than I. But my mother was a maiden when she wed my father, not a widow like me. I did not want to reject Rish again. My refusal only made us unhappy. Still, I did not see any path for us to take. Maybe one would emerge. Instead of saying no, I said, "I am not ready yet."

His eyes stayed on mine. "Waiting is not new to me."

* * *

EMPTY SKIES STRETCHED AHEAD of me after returning to our journey. The towers, palaces, and temples of Akash gleamed in the light from the warm morning sun. Rish rode alongside my chariot, and I stole a glance at him. He sat tall on his mount. He turned, and our eyes met.

"Home," he said. He meant Akash.

"Yes," I agreed. I meant us. Rish was my home.

Jay, Aranya, and Atul stood at the palace steps. As the chariot halted, Atul ran down the steps to help me. I took the hand he held out and observed my son. He appeared cheerful and brimming with vigor.

I descended, and he bent to touch my feet. I laid a hand on his head, thanking the gods for keeping him safe. As he straightened, I hugged him tightly.

"You are looking well, Son."

He smiled. "Akash has always lifted my spirits." I knew then he was home too.

I gazed past him at my brother as Jay made his way to me. He appeared thinner than before, and more gray hair had sprouted near his ears. But I sensed that the worst was behind him.

He sought my blessing, then kissed my head. "Meera, Akash feels more like home when you are here."

Behind us, Atul greeted his father. "Commander."

I heard Rish return the greeting. "Prince Atul."

Jay whispered in my ear. "So the charade continues." It did not surprise me that Atul had revealed his newly acquired knowledge to Jay.

On our way inside, Aranya said, "I have been extremely grateful for Atul's presence here, Queen Meera. He helped pull Jay out of his well of despair."

She still looked beautiful with her hair in a bun. The few gray hairs enhanced her beauty rather than marring it.

"It looks like they aided each other. Atul radiates a quiet joy."

I glanced at the backs of the three men. They marched ahead of us, all three discussing something intently, my brother, my son, and my— Sword? That described my relationship with Rish. He protected me, even though the sharp blade cut me deep sometimes. Love? He was that. He wanted to become my husband even if the union remained a secret known only to us. I was a widow. By tradition, bound to remain one all my life. Another marriage appeared a leap too wide for me.

That evening, I arrived early in Jay's chambers.

He stood on seeing me and guided me to a bench. Seated next to each other, he said, "The others will join us for our meal, but I wanted to talk to you first."

"About Atul?"

He nodded and clenched and unclenched his fist.

I waited, wondering what he had in mind. "Jay?"

He looked at me. "I have no son of my own," he said, and I saw the pain flit across his face.

I took his hand in mine.

He squeezed my hand gently. "Atul is like a son to me. I have raised him from birth. He is of Malla blood. I seek your consent to make him my crown prince," Jay said.

"Your heir?" I asked, his request flashing in my head like a lightning blaze across the sky.

He nodded.

"But..." Jay knew the truth about his birth. Atul was illegitimate, even if it pained me to think this way.

"He is your son and my nephew." Then Jay leaned in. "His father is a nobleman of Malla blood. Only Malla blood flows in Atul," he whispered.

I stared at him, stunned.

43

JAY

"Jay, this is the throne of our ancestors. How could you set Atul on it?" Meera asked, winding her sari around her finger. A sign of her agitation.

"He is trained in our history, warcraft, and our laws. I see all the good qualities of a ruler in him," I said.

Meera looked up at me. "His actions in Padi reminded me of you," she said, pride coating her words.

I smiled. "I am proud of him as well. It is my responsibility to ensure the succession of the Malla line." I hesitated and added, "He is a better choice than my son, Vikram, was." I realized that now. In temperament, Atul proved that he could learn from his mistakes.

"But—" Meera paused. Then in a voice that I could barely hear, she said, "He was born out of wedlock."

I knew how she felt, but my views had shifted. "Did you love his father?" I corrected myself. "Do you love his father?"

"Yes," she said, tears glistening in her eyes.

I put my arm around her shoulder. I knew Rish worshiped the ground she walked on. That was why I chose him to be her guard all those years ago. "My dear sister, if he was conceived in love, there can be nothing wrong with his birth. I understand not seating him on the

Padi throne. That would be a violation of our laws. But Malla blood runs through his veins. I don't see any reason to deny Malla an able ruler."

She broke into a sob at my words. "Meera," I said, pulling her into my arms. It must have broken her heart to see Rish nearly every day and not be with him. "If it upsets you, then marry him," I said lightly, in a teasing tone.

She laughed weakly and rubbed her eyes. "Rish has asked me to marry him."

That revelation startled me. "You said no," I guessed. I loved my sister, but she clung to traditions like they rooted her. We both did.

She surprised me. "I have not refused Rish yet."

I gazed at her. "In the Mahabharata epic, Draupadi married five brothers. She bore each of them a son," I said to assuage her guilt.

She smiled through her tears. "Rish mentioned the story of Damayanti."

"Damayanti?" I asked, puzzled. That was a story of a devoted wife and would not sway Meera.

"Her father thought she was a widow and arranged a swayamvara for her to choose another groom."

I did not remember that detail from the play I had watched. "Are you still able to bear a child?" I asked. Our tradition dictated that women marry only one man, so there was no confusion about the father.

Faint color rose on my sister's cheek. "Jay, I am three years older than you." I raised my brow. "I am too old. There is no risk of that," she added, winding her sari around her finger.

With the danger of a child removed, was there any reason for them not to wed? I realized I would feel better if the parents of the future king of Malla were married. So would Atul. "In place of our father, I am happy to sanction the wedding. It cannot be a public ceremony because our tradition dictates otherwise. But it will ease my mind and Atul's."

"Jay, what will the people of Padi think if they find out their queen has remarried?"

I had forgotten how we had landed in this discussion of marriages. "Meera, you are no longer the queen of Padi. Kayal is the queen, and she bears that burden now. And she has clothed herself in a widow's white. And the Parth and Kanishka of the world will scheme regardless of our conduct. People want a ruler that will let them live in peace. Atul will be a ruler of that nature." I brought the conversation back to my nephew.

"Have you told Atul?" Meera asked, gazing through the window.

"Not yet. I wanted to ask you first."

She glanced at me. "Malla is fortunate to have you as their king."

"You would not have said that a few weeks ago," I grimaced, remembering my pain.

"You are a grieving father. No one will begrudge you a few weeks to mourn," she said kindly. "I need to talk to Rish," she added.

"Rish? He will not go against my wishes," I said.

She frowned at me. "Jay, I don't want you forcing this on Rish as his king. I want to gauge his thoughts first."

I smiled. "What is the use of being the king then?"

Her lips curled up. "Jay!"

"I will not interfere in your conversation with Rish," I said with open palms. "But I am willing to fight for this," I stated.

4 4

MEERA

*A*ranya arrived first. The look she gave Jay, and the gentle shake of his head told me she was aware of Jay's desire.

Atul and Rish arrived together. In a moment of panic, I imagined a prominent likeness in their appearance that would reveal the nature of their relationship. My worry was needless. While Atul had inherited his father's height, in all other aspects, he looked more like my brother.

The conversation flowed easily. Atul narrated the story of his bandit raid. Like my brother, Atul had an elusive charm to make this story about others and not just himself. Men would follow Jay through a raging firestorm. That was one of the reasons he'd won many of his battles. But Jay grew up knowing his destiny to wear the crown. Atul did not, and I had recently shattered any dreams he held. I wondered how Atul would react to his uncle's wish.

That night I tossed and turned in bed, thinking about Jay's request. When my brother had gone missing, my father had mentioned crowning one of my sons as his heir. That was before my wedding, and I had worried that my betrothed, Prince Amar of Padi, would use it to enslave Malla. Amar had died before our wedding, and I had married his brother instead. And Jay returned to Akash victoriously,

247

so such talk perished. With Rish, there was no danger of any plot against Malla.

I decided to talk to him in the morning.

I asked him to meet me at the palace pond, and I walked to the palace garden. A cacophony of birds rose from the trees. I stopped near the pond to view the golden reflection of the morning sun on the water. Rish waited for me at the edge.

"I sense a change in Prince Atul," he said. "He seems at peace helping King Jay."

"Jay wants more from him," I said. He faced me as I gazed at the shimmering pond surface. "Will you row me across the pond?" I asked. I wanted to have this conversation away from prying ears.

He raised his eyebrows at my request but complied. He pushed a boat into the water and held the oar to me. "Please grab this to get in, my lady," he said.

I wished he had stretched his hand instead. Shaking my head at these futile thoughts, I held the wooden oar and climbed in. He hopped in and started rowing.

He had draped a white silk shawl across one of his shoulders and tied the ends at his waist. A thick golden chain glittered around his neck. Apart from these, his chest was bare, and his muscles rippled as his hands moved in unison. There was no spare flesh on his body.

"The boat does allow one to observe without any obstructions," he said with a teasing smile.

I looked at him in mock anger. "Is that what you are doing?"

He laughed. "Yes, and I have a beautiful view in front of me. I used to love our boat rides together. While you searched for lilies to pluck, I watched you."

I smiled at his memory. "Your view has changed in thirty years." That was the last time I had been on a boat with him. Before I had married the prince of Padi.

His eyes traveled from my head to my waist in slow motion. "For the better," he said. Our eyes met.

"With the gray hair and the wrinkles?" I teased.

"I have plenty of those too. They enhance your beauty, though,"

Rish answered. To be considered beautiful by him at my age spoke to his fondness of me, not to my actual physical appearance. A gentle glow spread within me.

Rish stopped rowing, and I realized we were in the middle of the pond. He waited for me, seemingly in no hurry. The golden rings on his ears gleamed dully in the sun.

"Jay asked my consent to crown Atul as his heir," I said and glanced at Rish.

"P-prince Atul?" he stammered. We were alone on the water, yet he chose to address his son using his title.

I nodded.

He opened and closed his mouth a few times. "What did you tell him, my queen?"

"I told him I had to talk to you first." I'd decided to send Atul to be fostered by my brother without consulting Rish. I had denied him all rights as a father. I hoped it was not too late to make amends.

"Me?" he hesitated. "Meera, if King Jay orders—"

"Jay will not force us, and I want us to decide jointly." I should have done this before.

His face changed slowly like a sculpture taking form. "I recognize the honor you are bestowing on me, my queen," he said.

"One due to you," I replied.

We sat quietly, listening to the gentle waves rocking the boat.

"House Vindhya is bound to serve the King of Malla," he said. "I am the second son of a second son, my lady. Even in my wildest dreams, I would not have imagined a son of mine becoming the Vindhya chief, let alone the crown prince." How could he imagine it when I could barely grasp it?

"Do you oppose it?"

He knitted his brows together. "Prince Atul was raised to serve his brothers and his cousin. Sometimes, men like that make better rulers than ones raised to rule."

I gazed at the man who had served me for decades. "Like my father. He was also a second son, who rose to the throne after his brother's death." *He had committed many mistakes, though.*

"Prince Atul will hopefully have years to learn from King Jay," Rish said as if he read my mind.

He expressed none of the doubts about his son's birth that plagued me still. "What about his unusual birth?"

A dark cloud passed overhead, matching the one that flitted across his face. "Would you have objected to Prince Vikram ascending the throne?" he asked.

"No," I said, puzzled by his question.

"You deem Prince Vikram's parents, Sudha Vindhya and King Jay, worthy then? Is it you or me that you deem unworthy?" he asked, and I felt like he had slapped me.

"R-Rish," I stuttered.

"Are you ashamed of me, Meera?" he asked in a tone that shook my heart.

Before I could answer, raindrops fell on us. He picked up the oars and rowed to the shore swiftly.

"Rish, I am not ashamed of you. Of us. I had hoped to marry you once," I said in a pleading voice.

"Before you realized marrying a prince meant your sons would inherit the throne, and your daughters would marry kings," he spat out his words.

"Rish," I said, anger rising in me.

The rain sliding down his face gave him a tearful appearance. "Did you ever give me a chance?" Rish asked. I could hear all the pent-up frustrations of the last three decades in his voice. His bitterness at my choosing duty over love at each turn echoed in my ears and reverberated in my heart.

The boat hit the land and jolted my body. He jumped out, and for a moment, I thought he would leave me alone. But he was too well-bred for that. He pressed the boat with his foot and extended the tip of the oar to me. As I held it and climbed out, I stumbled. In an instant, his hand grasped my elbow, stabilizing me.

Once I landed my feet on solid ground, he dipped his head and vanished, leaving me alone with his accusations.

45
JAY

I strolled to the training yard greeting the men I met on the way. With a few, I lingered to inquire after their health or family. When I entered the yard, I noticed Rish fighting with a thrusting spear. He held it with both hands and attacked his opponent rapidly. The younger man who faced him struggled to defend himself. A thrust from Rish pushed him to the floor, and Rish shifted his spear to one hand and raised it above his shoulder. I glanced at his knitted brows and hurried toward them. I worried Rish would plunge the tip into the other soldier. The man on the ground crawled away. "Commander Rish, stop."

Rish grunted and lowered his spear. He offered a hand to his opponent, who grabbed it and rose. Rish turned away and saw me. "My Majesty," he bowed his head.

"Walk with me," I said.

He fell in step with me, wiping his forehead.

"What is bothering you? You pummeled him instead of taking the opportunity to teach him." Rish had trained recruits and my nephews. This roughness was uncharacteristic of him.

"My apologies, King Jay," he said but did not elaborate.

I guessed. "Meera told you my wish?"

He glanced up and nodded.

"And it upset you?" I asked. We stood under a neem tree, away from others.

"On the contrary. I am honored by it, King Jay," he said.

I had guessed wrong. Something I said would not evoke such passion in him. It must be something Meera had told him. I hesitated to get involved in my sister's affairs even if it did affect my nephew Atul and my desire to crown him.

"Would your father have sanctioned our union?" he asked, pushing his hair from his face.

I stared at him. "At one time, perhaps. My father was very fond of Meera. Before I went missing in Saral, he may have given his blessing. It would have kept Meera in Akash, which was to both our liking." But I had disappeared in Saral, and my father had agreed to her betrothal to the Padi prince to avoid a conflict. I wondered why he asked this question. Had he fought with Meera? That would explain his reluctance to discuss the matter with me.

Before I could probe him, I spotted my sister walking toward us. Rish froze on the spot, and his eyes tracked her movement. As Meera approached us, I saw her red-tinted nose. A wave of sudden anger coursed through me. "Did he hurt you?" I hissed.

Meera ignored me completely. "Rish, I never thought you unworthy," she said softly.

Unworthy? That would explain his question. It was not surprising for him to be plagued by self-doubts. He loved the princess of Malla, who was superior to him in many ways. My mentioning her superiority would hardly help them, though.

I gazed at Meera, and I could see the guilt and pain reflected on her face. "She thinks *she* is unworthy," I stated. "Meera, I don't care who the father of the boy is. He is your son, and that is good enough for me to make him my heir," I said. Rish flinched at my words, but I had to set Meera right.

Meera turned toward me. "Jay!"

"I speak the truth, Meera." Then I glared at Rish. "If this idiot doubts you, he is unworthy of you. I am speaking as your brother, not as his king."

Meera's lips curled up in a smile. "Go away, Jay."

"If you want him thrown into the dungeon, you know where to find me."

They took no notice of me.

4 6

MEERA

"**W**hy would you think you are unworthy?" Rish asked, his eyes stuck to my face.

"I could ask you the same question, Rish."

"I am hardly your peer in stature, wealth, or nobility, Meera. When you married the prince of Padi, I knew I could not compete with him. He made you the queen of his land and heart. What did I have to offer?" Rish pressed his lips together.

"I would have been your wife, and that would have been sufficient for Meera as a woman," I said, sweeping his face in my gaze.

"But not sufficient for *Princess* Meera," he said, his eyes clouding.

"Princess Meera lived in a golden cage of duty and traditions. I had to set aside what I wanted and instead do what was right for Malla."

He wiped his brow. "I knew that, Meera. I admired your devotion, and it made you a great queen. But why do you think yourself unworthy?"

I sighed. "When I told Atul about his birth, he said he was not even a prince anymore. I might be a princess, but I have nothing to bestow upon my children. They only inherit the titles of their father."

He shifted toward me. "You are worthy of a dozen kings. I agree with King Jay. Prince Atul deserves the throne for being your son."

254

Warmth flooded me. "This queen has striven to become worthy of you. I have dreamt of being an ordinary girl who could marry the man of her heart."

His lips parted as he gazed at me. "I wish I could take you in my arms." He looked at me like he wanted to absorb me into him.

I laughed merrily, imagining his arms around me. After floating in the clouds, I landed back on the ground. I asked, "What about Atul?"

His eyes lit up. "I have no objections. I will lay my sword at his feet and swear my allegiance."

I frowned at his response. Rish deserved Atul's deference as his father. I had denied him that courtesy all these years. I had to remedy that. "He is your son, and he knows it. He will treat you with respect."

Rish smiled, and his eyes crinkled into tiny webs. My heart pounded as I resisted the urge to touch him. "When he is my king, I will pay him my respects too. What about you? Do you consent to King Jay's wish?"

An unknown fear still coated my mind. But I saw no reason to deny Jay's request. I nodded. "I will go tell Jay."

"He will be in the training yard, my lady. I can fetch him for you. Do you fetch a king?" He grinned.

"He might throw you in the dungeon. Don't worry. I will come and set you free. There is only one prison I want to keep you in," I said, returning his smile.

"I am happy to stay in that cell for life," he said while his eyes pierced my core.

I returned to my chambers, listening to the birds flocking to the sky. I saw two pigeons on one of the towers nuzzling against each other. I stood for a moment to watch them as my heart sang.

Jay arrived in my chamber later that day. "I saw a cheerful Rish earlier today. And you are brimming with joy. All is well?" A smile played on his lips.

"I am still a widow. Nothing has changed on that front," I said, more to tamp down my emotions.

Jay grew serious. "The same fate awaits my daughter."

I thought about the lonely nights that stretched in front of her.

"She loved Nala. She has children to raise and a kingdom to rule. And her sister will prevent her from descending into desolation."

Jay viewed me doubtfully.

I decided to change the conversation. "Jay, you have Rish's and my consent to crown Atul."

His eyes twinkled at my words. "Meera, as my heir, I will decide his future, including whom he marries."

I frowned. "With his consent."

Jay shrugged. "Yes, the same consent afforded to you and me."

Panic surged in my throat. I was unable to marry the man I had loved. "Jay, I don't want him to suffer."

"Unlike you, he can still marry a girl of his choice, as long as he weds the brides I pick as well. Meera, the crown is a burden to bear. I believe he has the strength to bear it."

I shut my eyes for a moment. My son did have the courage and the wisdom. "If Atul decides he does not want this chain around his neck, I don't want him forced into it."

Jay rubbed the bridge of his nose. "I will not force him. But I will not give up easily either."

The boy adored Jay. I could not imagine him going against his uncle's wishes. I assented slowly. Then I lifted my eyes and gazed at my brother. He was born a second son but raised as the heir. I could see the effects of carrying this heavy load on him. An avalanche of grief nearly buried him. He had finally dug his way out. "I am glad to see you coming back to life."

"You can thank your son for it," he said. "I will reveal this to him at our evening meal."

47
JAY

*a*ranya viewed me patiently as I narrated receiving my sister's support. "I will ask Atul during our meal."

My wife shook her head. "Then no one will eat. Please wait till after the meal." Then she clutched her hands on her lap. "Jay, is Rish really Atul's father?" she whispered.

I blinked, unable to share my sister's secret with her. I did not like keeping secrets from my wife, but this was not mine to admit. "He is Meera's." She noticed that I did not deny her question, and she would draw the proper conclusion from it.

Meera arrived first, and she looked like a mother tiger ready to protect her cub. I remembered her defending me fiercely when we were younger, and I smiled at my sister fondly. "I am not going to hurt my nephew."

Meera softened visibly. "No, that is not my worry."

Aranya's eyes darted between us, and I could sense her mind visiting the past seventeen years to interpret my decisions.

Meera discerned something amiss as well. She gazed at Aranya. "Has he told you?" We had resorted to talking in riddles. I surmised she wanted to know if I had divulged who Atul's father was.

Aranya shook her head. "He did not reveal anything, Queen Meera. But I guessed."

"She is my queen, Meera."

Before I could say more, she interrupted me. "I trust her," Meera said.

Aranya inclined her head as Atul strode in. "Have we heard from the men dispatched to Kashgar, Uncle Jay?" he asked.

"Yes, they have set sail on the Nira Sea," I said. As I shared the message, Rish entered the room, so I repeated the tale.

Aranya shepherded us into the dining room, and plates of hot food arrived. We talked about the men on the way to Kashgar as we ate the aromatic tamarind rice along with roasted taro root coated with spices.

"Prince Aggabodhi is curious about our culture. He asks me many questions and waits patiently for my answer. I don't remember having any patience at his age," Atul said.

"You were his age just yesterday." His developing friendship with Aggabodhi could help them both. My nephew could help the young prince reclaim his throne one day and establish a lasting tie with Kashgar.

"Uncle Jay, I am seventeen," he said in a mock hurt tone.

"Seventeen! It is time to find him a bride," Aranya chimed in.

Atul turned crimson in embarrassment and gazed down at his plate.

"Maybe he has already found someone," I said with a smile.

He looked up at my remark. "Found?"

"Is there a girl you like?" I elaborated.

"But I—There's no one," he stammered, glancing at his mother. With a pang, I wondered if Vikram had ever taken a liking to anyone.

Meera glared at me and turned to her son. "Your uncle Jay met Aunt Aranya at your age. He was lucky to fall in love with a princess." A slight hint of bitterness coated her words.

I noticed Rish wince at her choice of words. She realized it too and gazed at him. Meera was wrong about one thing. I could have fallen in love with almost any unmarried girl. If I had sought her hand, unlikely

I would have been refused. The rules were different for the royal women.

"When I met Jay, he was unconscious. I am not sure I would have liked him if he was talking," Aranya looked at me, her lips tilting up.

"That explains many things," I said, wanting to pull her onto my lap. But I settled to let our knees touch under the table.

After the meal, we gathered in the sitting room, the women seated and the men standing. The wicker lamps flickered as the gentle wind wafted in.

"I lost my son, and as a father, that hole in my heart will never close." I clenched the hilt of my sword as the raw pain still grated me like salt on a wound. "But Malla is without an heir, and as her king, I have to ensure the continuation of the line." I paused and scanned the room. Aranya gazed at me while Meera and Rish stole glances at each other and Atul. My nephew hung on to my words.

"After thinking about this for many days, I have chosen a successor. A young man capable of leading this kingdom." Atul leaned forward, eager to hear the name. "I have received consent from his mother," I said and glanced at Meera. Atul followed my gaze with a frown. As he turned back, I held his eyes. "Prince Atul, I would like to name you the Crown Prince of Malla."

The color drained from his face, and he sat with his mouth slightly open. Silence ruled the room. Meera rose from her chair and approached him. Touching the back of his head, she whispered, "Son, your uncle, and I think you will be an able ruler. But being a king is not a burden you can set down. So we will give you time to consider this."

Her touch unraveled him, and he looked at her like he was still a child. "Mother, but how could I—I am not—" His lips trembled, and tears gathered in his eyes.

Rish shifted uneasily on hearing the anguish in his voice.

Meera gathered Atul into a hug, and he hunched over to rest his head on her shoulder. "Son, I wish I could wipe away the hurt I have caused you. But I don't regret the love I feel for your father. He is a brave, generous, and loyal man." Her eyes found Rish over Atul's back.

"Being his son is something you can be proud of." Rish stood still as a statue, his eyes never leaving them.

Atul stepped back from her grasp and gazed at her in a mixture of wonder and sadness. "Mother, I'm sorry. I should not have—" He paused, struggling with his emotions and words. He spun to view his father.

I decided to shift the conversation back. "Nephew, what do you want to do?" I asked, trying to keep my voice calm. A storm raged in my heart as I feared his rejection.

"Uncle Jay, I have an older brother. If I claimed the crown, will I be judged as a usurper?" His index finger drew circles on his hip as he lowered his eyes to the ground.

"You did not answer my question," I said.

He lifted his teary eyes. "Uncle Jay, the people of Malla revere you. They don't even know I exist. How could I fulfill the enormous hopes and dreams people have?"

"Nephew, were you expecting to sit on the throne tomorrow? Because I might disappoint you there and live for another twenty years."

"Or longer," Aranya chimed in.

Atul blushed in embarrassment.

"Jay, stop teasing him," Meera chided me. She turned to her son. "You will be under your uncle's wings."

I jumped in. "You learned our history alongside your cousins. You are already well-versed in battle craft and our laws. And you will have plenty of time to introduce yourself to the people of Malla."

He regarded us thoughtfully. "Uncle Jay, you taught me everything I know already." He rubbed his chin and gazed at his mother. "As crown prince, rumors about me will flourish, and our enemies will gossip about us, Mother." His eyes reflected his concern for her.

She touched his cheek lightly. "Rumors will not hurt me."

"You will squash the rumors and threaten to chop off the tongue of anyone who speaks ill of your mother," I stated calmly. My nephew spun toward me with his eyes wide. In time, he would learn to wield his immense power. Such power could easily corrupt as well. It would be my responsibility to help guide him.

Atul swung toward Rish. "Do you—Are you—" He struggled with his question. A range of emotions played on his youthful face.

Rish helped him. "I trust King Jay's choice," he said.

"I don't want you disrespecting—" Meera started abruptly and then paused as faint color crept up her neck.

Atul started at her words and turned toward his mother.

She glanced at him. "I want you to treat your elders with respect." The elder she had in mind was most likely his father. Most kings succeeded to their throne after their father's passing. Atul would be an exception, with a non-royal lineage on his paternal side.

It was the boy's turn to color deeply. He nodded vigorously, his words failing him again. Then he stopped suddenly, a frown creasing his forehead. "Did I say or do something discourteous?"

I answered for my sister. "Not likely. Just don't expect her to follow your command. Your mother usually brings up the story of the five-year-old me hiding behind her skirt whenever she thinks I am trying to order her around. You are her son, so she possibly has more ways to embarrass you."

Atul frowned. "My command? Uncle Jay, I would never command my mother. Are you teasing me again?"

"Ignore your uncle," Aranya said. "But like him, I am eager to hear your answer to his wish."

Atul gazed at us with misty eyes. "Uncle Jay, I am honored by your request. I did not imagine such a possibility even in my dreams. So can you please give me a day to mull this over?"

I was disappointed he did not accept it immediately, but I kept my feelings masked. "Nephew, take your time."

That night, I closed my eyes to let sleep swallow me like rising river water. But a cold nightmare engulfed me that repeated the same scene over and over again. My son pleaded with me to save him, and when I reached him, he simply vanished. I woke up in a cold sweat struggling to breathe, my heart racing. Then, slowly, I heard the sound of Aranya's steady breathing. She had taken to spending her nights with me, afraid to leave me alone. I dropped back onto my bed and wrapped my arm around her waist, drawing her into my chest, inhaling in her coconut-scented hair. She shifted in her sleep until there were no spaces between us, burying her face against my neck. I slipped into a restless sleep listening to her breathe.

48

MEERA

I woke up to a cloudy sky with the wind rustling the trees in the palace gardens. Birds called out to each other in jarring notes, raising alarms. As I got ready for the day, drops of rain fell on the balcony, sounding like the anklet bells of dancers spinning on stage.

My dressing had become simpler since I wore only a white sari devoid of adornments. After my morning meal, I planned to pay a visit to Ratnavali. Kantha, my companion more than my maid, had taken care of her and brought her back to health. Afterward, I wanted to check on my son. Jay's request must have shocked him. I could invite him to join me for our midday meal. As these thoughts swirled in my head, a knock sounded on my door.

"Enter," I said and walked to the sitting room. Atul opened the door and strode in, along with Rish. My eyes darted between them in surprise. "I was just thinking about you," I told my son.

Rish shut the door and stood in the background, allowing our son to speak.

Atul stopped a few feet from me and rubbed his hands together. "I wanted to check if there was a precedent for crowning a son of a princess as King of Malla. King Jay, not my uncle, but my great-great-grandfather, was the son of a princess. His grandfather had no sons, so he fostered two or three grandsons of his daughters and then named King Jay as his heir."

A mix of emotions rolled through me as I listened. Pride surged in me at hearing my son wanting to find out if there were others like him. Also, worry pooled in my stomach at the hurt my reveal had caused him. "He was one of the greatest kings to rule Malla." I glanced at Rish, who had become a statue.

Atul nodded. "His grandfather chose the best grandson to rule. I am concerned Uncle Jay might lack similar choices and is choosing me out of necessity." He briefly squeezed his eyes shut. My feelings mirrored the storm raging outside.

"Son, I know my brother well. He cares deeply about Malla and its people. He will not have made this decision lightly. He saw the qualities of a good ruler in you. I see them too," I said. I wanted to fold him into my arms and comfort him, but I resisted. Any comfort I provided would be fleeting. This was a decision he needed to make since it could set him on an arduous path for the rest of his life.

Atul swallowed. "The lives of soldiers, farmers, and ordinary men and women will depend on me." His voice shook slightly. "A king sends men to fight."

I looked to Rish for help.

"Warriors have a duty too, just like kings. We swear to protect our lands and the people who rule these lands. We are prepared to follow our king into battle and die defending him. A good king understands that and uses us wisely," Rish said. He had lived by this code all his life, like his father before him.

Atul released a breath. "Being a king will require great sacrifices from me. Like the ones made by you and—," he paused and glanced at Rish. "And my father."

Rish reacted like the sun warmed his face on hearing himself addressed as a father. His eyes misted up, and he strolled in closer to his son.

Gazing at Rish, I said, "Yes, it does require tremendous sacrifices from you and the ones who love you. You learn to place the kingdom and her needs before your own." *Including sending one's newborn away.*

Rish's eyes caught mine and engulfed me in a tenderness that coated me like warm honey.

I added, "Initially, you might earn loyalty through tradition and heritage. To continue to enjoy that trust, you need to lay your shoulder to the wheel of the chariot and push it in the right direction to ensure our people have peace and prosperity. Though the weight of this will be hard to bear, the triumph will be glorious."

Atul straightened his shoulders at my words. "Mother, Father, you have lived your life as an example for me to follow. I am ready to walk in your footsteps with your blessings." His eyes sparkled with his determination.

He touched my feet, and I hugged him tightly. "I am willing to pour all my strength into you," I said, kissing his forehead.

Atul smiled crookedly. "I will need that, Mother." He approached Rish and bent to touch his feet. Rish gathered him in his arms and embraced him, with a lone tear trickling from his right eye. "Son, if you have inherited your mother's trait to do what is right, you will make a great king," he said, releasing him. "Strange that I helped raise your brothers but not you," Rish murmured, his voice drifting into the past. "I can share the advice I provided King Nala on his coronation day. You can never be fully prepared for your battles, on the field or in the court. What is important is that you remember who you are fighting for."

Atul glanced at us and nodded. "I had better go inform Uncle Jay. I thought he would burst into flames yesterday when I told him I needed time."

We watched him depart the room with our hearts full. Rish looked at me fondly when the door closed behind Atul. "He is your son. There is no doubt about it. I always thought you would make a great ruler. Maybe he will fulfill that destiny."

His words reminded me of a prophecy imparted to me. I stood shocked as the words came rushing into my head.

"What is it, my queen?" Rish asked, concern in his voice.

"I was told my son would rule the three kingdoms."

"Told?"

"After my wedding, when Atul and I handed out gifts, a woman uttered those words to me. I never took it seriously, but my father once claimed that a girl had predicted his coronation while his older brother still lived. Her words came true. When I was born, she had also told him my son would reign the three kingdoms." Could her words come true again?

Rish frowned. "And you think it is the same woman who came to the wedding?"

That seemed far-fetched. My father barely remembered the girl, and I had no proof that the same person had predicted both events. I shook my head. "I don't know. Jay would laugh at me if I told him this."

Rish moved closer to me. "Three kingdoms? It is best if we keep this to ourselves, Meera. It will put Atul's life in jeopardy."

My skin turned cold. "Danger?" Rish was right. Not only about Atul being in danger. My one son headed Padi, and my son-in-law ruled Saral. To rule all kingdoms, Atul would have to fight his kin. Or lose them.

"Meera," Rish said softly, raising his hand as if to touch my cheek. He dropped it instead and bound his fingers behind his back. "Forget what some strange woman said to you. We have enough real concerns."

I let out my breath. I wanted to bury my head in his chest and let him comfort me. He saw the longing in my face and stepped closer. His hand brushed my elbow lightly. "Atul grew up with King Vasant, who is also married to his sister. He is not going to pick a fight with his brother or brother-in-law."

Jay had not yet made Atul his heir. I could not let my imagination run wild. I reined in my thoughts.

"What a turn of events. Our boy will be king one day," Rish said as his lips curled up.

Our boy! My spine tingled on hearing those words. I grinned at him slowly, his joy echoing in me.

49
JAY

My patience stretched thin like a frayed rope near the end of its life. I curtailed my temptation to summon Atul and carried on with my morning duties. Rain splattered against the palace walls as I made my way to the small council. The breeze that accompanied it felt cool against my skin, soothing my mind. I lingered for a moment to watch the gray clouds passing overhead and then headed inside. My men waited for me.

"Giri, how are the river levels in Thari lands?" I asked Giri.

The southern commander straightened. "The rivers are running low, my Majesty. This rain is a welcome relief for our farmers."

"No risk of flooding?"

"There might be flash floods here and there, but we have planted trees in most of the flood-susceptible areas to prevent soil erosion. The dam across the Chambal River will help us regulate the flow of water."

Any heavy flooding before the harvest would damage our rice crops. I turned to Hasan Vindhya, who had arrived in Akash recently. "Do we have sufficient grains stocked in our granary?"

"Yes, my Majesty. We had a bountiful harvest last year." The stockpile would also come in handy if a war broke out with Kashgar.

A shadow fell across my face, and I glanced up to see Atul hovering near the door. He looked grave, and I knew he had made a decision.

"Atul and I have an important matter to discuss. We will continue the council meeting tomorrow," I said and dismissed them.

The others left, leaving me alone with my nephew.

"Uncle Jay, you placed tremendous trust upon my abilities when you asked me to be your heir. I accept this honor and seek your blessing." He bent and touched my feet.

Emotions overwhelmed me, relief at his acceptance, regret at Vikram's death, and jubilation in having fulfilled one of my key duties. I placed my hand on his head. "May you be blessed with an abundance of wisdom to rule this land."

He rose and looked at me starry-eyed. As the third son, the boy had time to dream. I felt a pang as I realized I was going to replace his fancies with a tether that tied him to the fate of the kingdom.

"What comes next, Uncle Jay?"

"I will share the news with my small council and the chiefs of the three houses of Malla." I would seek marriage alliances to gain support for his reign. "Atul, when I crown you, you will take a sacred vow to protect this land and its people, to place her needs ahead of yours, to sacrifice your happiness to ensure the happiness of others."

He pressed his lips together. "Like my mother sacrificed her happiness," he whispered. Our eyes met, and I saw his reflected determination and trepidation. Our hearts were to remain closed to temptations, but he was proof that nature often demands its own way. My sister succumbed to her urges and lived with its consequences. A rare moment of vulnerability from a woman who had seemed impervious to ordinary desires.

I nodded. "Your mother is a paragon of virtue, embodiment of the qualities needed in a queen."

"And you, Uncle Jay. Like the polar star guiding sailors, you guided Vasant and Nala with your light and set them on the right path as rulers of Saral and Padi. You are giving me a choice, but you had none."

I had a choice to walk away from it all and crown my nephew

Vasant as the king. But I could not do it. The boy was a child of five, and I would have had to reveal secrets best kept buried. Meera would not have allowed me to abandon the throne either. "My path in life was set since birth, Atul. I knew of no other path to take." I smiled at him. "I am glad you've agreed to bear this burden. It is a noble duty. Meet me in the small throne room. I will introduce my heir to the world."

* * *

I SUMMONED my men and stood waiting behind the ornate silver throne. The crown encrusted with rubies rested on my head. Aranya wore a silk saree that matched the red gems of my headdress and sat on a smaller throne beside mine. Meera and Atul arrived together, the mother somber and the son animated. Rish walked in with his brother and blended with the shadows. Once all had gathered, I moved to the front.

"Less than two months ago, I cremated my son. I thought I had burned my aspirations for this land along with him. But out of the ashes, a new wish was born. My nephew Atul, son of my beloved sister, arrived to comfort me. However, he did more than that. He allowed me to hope again." I glanced at the young man standing in front of me, and all eyes followed mine. My nephew had pulled me out of my despair and given me a new purpose. Atul stood still, his gaze traveling around the room before coming to rest on me.

"I raised Atul from birth and tutored him in the ways of kings. He is well versed in the history of this land. He is able and willing to defend her against enemies within and without." I scanned the room, and upturned faces gazed at me in anticipation. "Today, with great expectations for the future, I name Prince Atul as my heir and the crown prince of Malla." Silence filled the hall after my announcement. Then Kapil Biha cheered, "Long live, Prince Atul." Others echoed his words. Filled with hope and joy, I joined them.

Atul bowed his head as he accepted the honor. As the shouts ebbed away, I beckoned him to join me. He turned to his mother and touched her feet. She kissed his forehead while whispering something in his ear. He strode toward me with his head held high. When he arrived beside me, he stooped to touch my feet. For a fleeting moment, I imagined my own son standing next to me, a simple golden crown glittering on his head. Sudden tears blinded my eyes. I blinked them away rapidly while I patted Atul's shoulder. "You can say a few words, Atul."

He nodded and marched to the front of the throne. "Malla elders, I accept this tremendous responsibility with the knowledge that there is much for me to learn. Uncle Jay mentioned raising me since birth. I have known no other father than him." His voice trembled with emotion as he uttered those words, and I stared at him, observing the meaning of them. He thought of me as his father. Not King Atul, his namesake, who had died before he was born. Not Rish, his birth father, who had never taught him to ride a horse or wield a sword. Me! I remembered holding him and my son on my lap as I sat on the throne, narrating the stories of kings past. How did I not realize he was as much my son as Vikram was? Like a churning ocean, feelings welled up in my heart.

He continued, "I have watched my uncle rule with strength and compassion. As a young child, I would ask him many questions, and he answered them all patiently. When he appointed commanders and generals, he would tell us that a king cannot be everywhere, so it is important to pick the right men to carry on his vision. With the same foresight, he has chosen me as his heir, bestowing me with this highest honor. King Jay, I will dedicate all my life to becoming worthy of this crown." His words uttered in earnest touched us all like the brush of a warm breeze. I knew then that I had made the right decision for Malla's future.

"Long Live, Prince Atul," I said as the clouds parted and the sunlight streamed in. A chorus followed.

"Minister, please consult with the royal astrologer for a suitable date to crown him as the king-in-waiting," I said and dismissed them.

I asked Kapil and Atul to join me in my chambers. "Kapil, he needs his own guards," I said once we were inside. My mind traveled back to the day I had chosen Kapil as one of my five guards. He had served me loyally over the decades.

Kapil nodded. "I will pick some second or third sons of Vindhya, Thari, and Biha houses to join his guard along with seasoned warriors."

Guards became your shadows, and the bonds formed with them on a battlefield endured for a king's life. "Atul, you can choose one or more from among your friends as well."

My nephew inclined his head. "I had hoped to serve as part of Vikram's guard," he muttered, his eyes clouding briefly. He would have followed the path of his grandfather and father then.

"Some of the bravest Malla men served as king's guards. Veera Vindhya died for my father, and Kapil here has saved my life countless times." At the mention of Veera Vindhya, Atul blinked. Veera was Rish's father, his grandfather.

I carried on with my instructions to Kapil, allowing my nephew to collect himself. "Send messages to Naren Biha, King Vasant of Saral, and Queen Kayal of Padi." I knew Naren, my Biha Chief, had a daughter about Atul's age. "Ask Naren to bring his daughter along with him."

I waved Kapil away and turned to Atul. "As the crown prince, you need strong alliances with the three regions of Malla. Marriage is the most reliable way to secure them. Naren Biha and Giri Thari both have daughters. I will ask them to bring their daughters to your crowning ceremony. If you don't like them—"

He interrupted me with a shy smile. "I have met these two girls before, Uncle Jay. I had never imagined I would marry one of them, so I talked to them freely. I have no objections to marrying either."

I laughed as I regarded my nephew. "I reckon they are pretty girls too."

He grinned bashfully and pushed his hair away from his forehead. "My mother is the one who needs to approve these unions." Meera knew the value of these relationships, so I expected her to consent.

"We can talk about it at our midday meal," I said. Atul and I headed to my chambers. The rain had subsided, and light poured into the hallways.

Aranya waited for us there. "Crown Prince Atul, I am grateful for the smile you have brought to your uncle's face," she greeted him.

"Aunt Aranya, please bless me to continue bringing joy to you and Uncle Jay," Atul said as he touched her feet. She embraced him tightly.

Meera and Rish joined us shortly. As we ate, I discussed my plans for Atul's marriage.

"Vindhya house is the most powerful of the three. My father-in-law, Mani Vindhya, had hoped to see his grandson on the throne. With Vikram's death, that dream has perished. He will be reluctant to support Atul because he will see him as a Padi prince. And Atul cannot marry a Vindhya girl because of his blood ties," I mused. The son of Rish Vindhya would share a sibling bond with any Vindhya girl. Even if we keep Atul's identity a secret, I did not want to violate these sacred traditions.

Atul frowned. "How do we win their support, Uncle Jay?"

I turned to Rish. "Your brother, Hasan Vindhya, is visiting us. If you reveal the truth about Atul to him, then Hasan can—"

"Jay!" Meera exclaimed sharply, her eyes darting between Rish and me.

"Meera, I understand your concern. You are worried this might taint Nala's unborn child or Amar. Luckily, both of them inherited Padi traits. So rumors about them are unlikely to stick. And I will fight for my grandson's rights to the Padi throne. To do that, I need Vindhya gold. Atul's Vindhya blood is an asset," I argued.

"Hasan has known the truth for many years now," Rish said softly. Meera stared at him with her mouth open. He met her gaze. "We were in Akash for King Nala's wedding a few years back. Prince Atul fell off his horse one day, and I had rushed to his side. The prince escaped with minor scrapes, but Hasan had seen my reaction. My brother confronted me that night." Rish swallowed and glanced at Atul. "My brother said he knew a father's anguished face. I did not deny or confirm his suspicions." Rish looked at my sister. "I avoided Prince

Atul from then on, but that only strengthened my brother's belief. Hasan knows me well."

Atul observed the scene between his parents. "Mother, with your sanction, I would like to seek Uncle Hasan's blessing."

Meera caught my eyes, her doubts reflected in them. I dipped my head to signal my consent to Atul's request.

She released her breath. "Do it in Jay's presence. Hasan will not disobey his king."

I agreed. "Bring Hasan to my chambers later today," I told Rish.

My nephew stood gazing at my father's portrait as we waited for the Vindhya brothers. I observed the striking similarities between him and his grandfather. He was my heir in more ways than one.

"Would my grandfather have approved of me?" he asked in a tone filled with a subtle yearning. Atul did not know that my father left his son behind to grow up as the Saral prince and that his grandson Vasant now ruled as the King of Saral.

"Your grandfather would have been immensely proud of you. Just like me," I said. The boy looked at me with a deep hunger for acceptance. "Atul, you are Meera's son. That alone makes you eligible for the throne." My throat closed as I watched his lips curl briefly, a fleeting smile that faded away immediately. "Your father is a remarkable man. He raised your brothers to rule Padi and has stood by your mother even when there was no hope for them." Atul stood still, his eyes riveted on me. "You have nothing to be ashamed of, Son." I smiled gently. "You only have to live up to the lofty ideals set by your parents."

Before Atul could reply, a knock sounded on the door. "Enter," I said and walked to the sitting room. Hasan and Rish strode in. The brothers were of similar height. The passing years had softened Hasan's once-hard body, deepening the lines etched on his face and turning his hair gray. Rish's body still looked like a warrior's, and threads of dark hair still mingled with the silver.

They bowed to me. "King Jay."

Atul stood just inside the room, stiff and nervous.

"Prince Atul," Hasan said with a bow.

Rish held his son's gaze, perusing every contour of his face as if seeing them for the first time. Hasan's eyes darted between his brother and nephew.

Atul stepped forward, squaring his shoulders. "Uncle Hasan, please bless me," he said and touched his feet.

Hasan blinked the tears welling up in his eyes. "All these years," he whispered and touched Atul's head. "May you rule with the wisdom of your mother and the courage of your father."

Breathing hoarsely, Rish looked on tenderly.

"Hasan, I would like you to procure Vindhya support for Atul," I said. "Only revealing what is necessary," I added.

Hasan nodded slowly, his eyes still on his nephew. "Prince Atul can count on Vindhya sword and gold."

Later that night, Aranya stood in front of me. She glowed like a goddess in the light from the wicker lamps. "Jay, I have asked Ratnavali to spend the night with you."

"Ratnavali?" I had neglected her, and guilt swirled in me.

"Yes," Aranya said impatiently. "Jay, stop acting as if being married to you is a punishment."

Her words brought a smile to my face. "It isn't?"

She echoed my grin and reached to hold my hand. "In our travels through life, we have had our share of shadows over the years, but there have been far more bright places."

I raised her hand to my lips, kissing her knuckles. We were young lovers once with a newfound wonder for each other. "I am glad you agreed to run away with me all those years ago," I said huskily.

Her cheeks flushed, and she leaned in and kissed me. "My king, you had captured my heart, and I chased my dream of marrying the boy I loved. All this while, I have had a splendid time ruling beside you. Recently, I was worried that I had lost you. But with Atul's help, you found your way back to me."

I grinned at the woman I adored, knowing it was a blessing to hold her heart.

* * *

RATNAVALI and I woke up together with the sun streaming in. She smiled at me shyly as we rested amid the tangle of sheets. "I missed you," she said.

The confession stunned me. "Did you?" I asked, weaving my fingers through hers. I might have underestimated her.

She nodded in response. "Do you regret marrying me?" she asked, looking away as if afraid of my answer.

"Ratnavali," I said, cupping her face. "No. I never regretted marrying you. But I did worry that I was too old for you."

She laughed. "King Jay, many young men would be envious of your strength. I grew up hearing your legendary stories. You had helped my father vanquish our enemies, and I had dreamed of marrying someone like you." She stopped, and our eyes met.

Her words unfurled a pair of wings in my chest. I leaned over to kiss her lips. She murmured my name in a kind of reverence that caused my throat to catch. I wrapped my arm around her waist, and she closed her eyes with a sigh. Our breaths mingled warm and wet as I pulled her against me, savoring the scent of her body.

A fortnight later, on a crisp morning, while I dressed in my royal clothes for Atul's crowning ceremony, a knock sounded on my door.

"Come in," I said absently, expecting Kapil. Instead, Sudha entered.

I stared at her, loss and pain rushing at me, leaving me vulnerable. She looked at me as if lightning had struck her.

"What are you doing here?" I asked, my voice breaking. Images of my son broken and bleeding flooded my mind.

"Queen Aranya sent for me," she said, still hovering near the door.

I remembered she had lost her only child. "I am sorry," I mumbled and walked toward her. "About our son," I said and reached for her hand. When she did not resist, I pulled her into a hug.

She breathed against my chest. "I am sorry too for leaving you. I was bitter and in pain."

A lump formed in my throat. "Sudha, I understand if you never want to see me again. But I want you to stay."

Her eyes pooled with tears as she looked up at me. "Our son is gone," she whispered.

"We will never get him back," I said, a sudden ache stabbing me. His departure had made us into different people with deep scars. "But I need you, Sudha. To share my grief. To fill my empty years."

Her eyes clouded. "I made a mistake in leaving you. I found no comfort at my father's."

I pressed my lips to her forehead. "His face still haunts me every night."

"I have not slept since—" she choked, and I tightened my arms around her. We stood together in sorrow.

"My Majesty," Kapil said from the door, pulling me back to the present. "It is time."

"I will be there," I said, still gazing at my wife. "Will you join me?" I asked her.

Sudha stepped back from my grasp, wiping her eyes. "You chose Atul as your heir," she stated simply.

I nodded. "My dreams were hollowed out, but the kingdom still needed a crown prince."

She looked somber. "Atul is a good boy. He kept my Vikram safe."

"Better than me," I agreed.

"Please give me a few moments. I will see you there," Sudha said. We needed time to heal, but I was glad she was here.

I squeezed her arm and marched out.

Atul stood in front of me, magnificent in his youth. As the auspicious nadaswaram played, I placed a simple gold crown on his head. Chants of "Victory to Malla, Victory to Prince Atul" rang throughout the room.

Aranya had arranged for a modest feast in his honor. I stood next to Meera as we both observed her son mingling with his guests.

"Jay, you have raised him well. The boy had a happy childhood in Akash," she said.

"I am proud of him. He has the makings of a great king in him," I answered.

She turned to me. "Atul will learn from one of the greatest kings of Malla. You," she said. We both had suffered immense losses in the past few months. She had handled the death of her son with far more grace than I possessed.

I wrapped my arm around her shoulder. "Meera, while I teach your son, please prepare my daughter Kayal for the hard life ahead of her." It astounded me that my sister had managed to survive her hardships without turning bitter.

"Jay, I will care for Kayal and Heera like they are my own daughters. Kayal has the strength of her father and the candidness of her mother. She will persevere, and with her sister's contagious warmth, she might find joy as well."

I looked down at her. "How about you, Meera? You deserve some happiness too."

She did not answer my question, but her eyes scanned the room. The man she sought spun around and caught her eyes. A gentle bliss covered her face as Rish approached her. I squeezed her arm and went to find my wife.

Aranya stood at the center of the room, ensuring the event went flawlessly. I let my fingertips touch hers.

"Walk with me," I said, and we moved to a quiet corner away from others.

"Jay, the ceremony earlier was impeccable. I had to fight my tears," she said, smiling at me warmly.

"You sent for Sudha," I stated.

She nodded. "Her place is beside you. In her anger, she left the one man who could comfort and heal her. And you muttered her name a few times in your sleep."

"I said her name?" I asked stupidly, a rush of embarrassment flooding my face.

"Jay, she is your wife. And you felt guilty about the hurt and pain she suffered though there was nothing you could have done to prevent it. She is here now. Console her. It will help both of you recover."

"How can I ever repay you?" I asked as my heart jumped into my throat.

She gazed at me tenderly. "You chose me as your wife and queen for this very reason. I am just doing my duty. Your father ignored your stepmother. I am glad you are not repeating his mistakes. And you've mumbled my name fervently too. Many times."

My lips curled up. "I am not surprised by that. You are ever-present in my thoughts."

Her face brightened as she continued. "I have a selfish motive for fetching Sudha. Sudha and Ratnavali will take care of you while I go to Padi with Queen Meera. Our daughters are pregnant, and I would like to be present when our grandchildren are born."

I nodded. "Send for me when the babies are born. I will visit you in Padi. It will give Atul a chance to play king."

She grinned at me. "Maybe you and I can go on a trip to Nanga. I have always wanted to see those snow-covered mountains."

I remembered our journey through Saral when I'd fallen in love with her. "I can arrange that, my queen," I said, my heart filled with elation.

5 0

MEERA

"My queen, the crown suits Prince Atul very well," Rish said, beaming at me. His eyes appeared like a calm sea, warm and inviting.

Careful as ever, Rish still addressed our son by his title. My lips curled up at the sight of the man I loved. "Atul does wear his crown well."

The boy himself materialized before us, bursting with energy. "Mother," he said, running his eyes over his father and me. "I cannot tell you how happy I am that you attended this ceremony." His gaze lingered on his father, and I sensed Atul's words were specifically meant for him. Rish gleamed with pride as he glanced at our son. I could feel Atul's ripple of excitement as he scanned the room. "Uncle Jay has been inviting me to all his small council meetings and asks me for my ideas. I almost feel useful."

I touched his arm lightly. "You have been an immense help already in pulling your uncle out of his quagmire of despair." Atul's eyes slid to a young girl who floated into our sight, Naren Biha's daughter and one of his betrotheds. The girl broke into a smile on seeing him, and a matching grin appeared on my son's face.

"You can go and talk to her." I sent him away with a wave. He

279

strolled to her, and then they disappeared into the crowd. It brought back memories of the clandestine moments I had shared with his father. I could feel Rish's gaze on me, and I lifted my face to his. I could tell he remembered the same stolen moments from the way his eyes took on a dreamy quality.

"My lady, I will be going to Vindhya with my brother tomorrow. King Jay wants us to gain my cousin's support for his heir. And I can visit my daughter and leave my wife with her." My eyes narrowed in panic as if I might lose him forever. Sensing my distress, he said soothingly, "I will be back for Prince Atul's weddings."

The next few days passed in a whirlwind of activity, getting ready for Atul's dual nuptials to the Biha and Thari daughters. Two days before the ceremony, Atul entered my chamber.

He looked nervous, almost guilty and a sudden worry crawled through me. "Are you having second thoughts about marrying one of these girls?" I asked.

He frowned in confusion. "My marriage?"

I nodded.

His face lightened. "No, Mother. I like them both," he added with a shy smile.

I waited for him to tell me what was on his mind. He cleared his throat. "Mother, Uncle Jay showed me all the secret passages and tunnels into the palace. I just learned that this room has a secret passage."

It was my turn to be bewildered. Why did he bring this matter up now? I raised my brows slightly at his remark.

He drew shapes on his thigh. What was causing him to be this nervous? "These rooms are meant for visiting royalty. A secret passage allows the Malla king to spy on them or, if need be, let them escape," I said.

"This passage ends in an empty room that is locked," he said, blushing now.

Baffled at his behavior, I asked, "Why are you telling me this? Is my brother spying on me?" That seemed unlikely. Jay had no need for that. If he had a question, he would ask me directly.

He shook his head vehemently. "Uncle Jay would never stoop to that. He reveres you." And then words tumbled out of him in a whisper. "If you consent, I can arrange for Father to stay in the now vacant room that leads here. He is arriving today."

I drew in my breath sharply as I imagined Rish's arms folded around me.

"Mother," he implored me. "Uncle Jay told me it is my duty to make people happy. I want to start with my parents."

"You think my happiness lies in Rish sneaking into my room?" I asked, my voice harsher than I intended because of the emotions churning in me. I felt guilty about wanting Rish. I was raised to put my duty above my needs. I had strayed from that path once, and the consequence of that act stood in front of me. However, I did not regret my son. Nor did I regret my love. What was this barrier holding me back? Was it my reluctance to savor the warmth of the sun while I wore the widow's white? If my daughter-in-law, Kayal, found solace in a man's arms, I would not begrudge her that.

Unaware of my turmoil, Atul turned red. "I did not—I thought—" He paused and let out his breath. "Mother, you clearly miss him. And there is no doubt of father's regard for you. I apologize for the furtive nature of this, but at least for a few days while you remain in Akash, you will be able to spend some time alone with him."

Color crept up his forehead; the boy was embarrassed, and my gaze softened. I reached up to ruffle his hair. Seeing me stand almost on my toes to touch his head, he bent down slightly. "That was thoughtful of you," I said. "But what happens when I am back in Padi? I cannot get used to this," I added with a trembling voice. Tears pooled in my eyes as I imagined long, lonely nights. I was worn and alone.

"Mother, I will ask my brother to build a secret passage between your rooms in Padi," he said almost in anger. I lifted my eyes to his face. His eyes narrowed, and he said, "I know there are traditions to follow. But no good can come from keeping you apart. Amar will do anything for you and Father."

Strange guilt still reared its head as if I had betrayed my marriage vows by considering this.

Watching me closely, Atul said, "Mother, I am sorry for causing you this pain. I rashly thought we could surprise Father. Forget it."

A lump caught in my throat. Surprise Rish? Would he want this? A brief time together, even if it did not last? I remembered what I had told Jay about his wife, Aranya. She was someone who did what she set her mind to without waiting for others' opinions.

I made an impulsive decision. "Put Rish in that room and show him the secret passage."

* * *

KANTHA VISITED ME SOON AFTER. "Prince Atul looked regal in his crown, my lady."

I smiled at her warmly. "Yes, I cannot believe my youngest is heir to the Malla throne."

She smiled back. "If he has your sense of duty and wisdom, Malla is in good hands."

I had left her behind when I'd traveled to Padi earlier. Akash was her home, though she had accompanied me to Padi many years ago. I wanted to give her a choice to stay. "Kantha, I will leave for Padi soon. If you want to remain in Akash, Jay will provide for all your needs."

She shook her head. "My lady, I don't have any family of my own. You are mine." Tears brimmed in her eyes.

I embraced her gently with a knot in my stomach unfurling. "I am glad you are coming with me."

That night, I paced my room nervously like a new bride waiting for her husband. I had moved the rug that covered the trapdoor. A brass lamp illuminated the iron door, and I glanced at it from time to time. A sliver of a moon continued to rise in the sky, and there was no sign of Rish. Sudden doubt took hold of me. Had Rish rejected this offer of Atul's? Emptiness in my life stretched like the shadows around me.

A knock sounded on the trapdoor, and I froze in place. It lifted slowly, and a figure emerged in the darkness.

"Atul?" What was he doing here?

He climbed into the room. "He insisted I come with him," he said with a faint trace of annoyance.

I observed the second person who appeared behind him with a pounding heart. With his hands on the edge of the floor, Rish met my eyes.

"My queen, the prince said you had agreed to use this tunnel," he said with a frown.

I swallowed, unable to answer him. But he read the answer on my face.

"You did," he said softly and pulled himself up.

I twisted the end of my sari around my index finger, watching him straighten.

Atul stood awkwardly for a moment. He then cleared his throat. "I will leave the same way," he said and vanished into the hole, shutting the door behind him.

Rish continued to gaze at me. "Atul had learned about the hidden passages from my brother," I said, my stomach in knots.

"Prince Atul has just been crowned. Is this wise?" he asked me.

His question angered me. "Is what wise?" I asked, pretending ignorance.

"Us sneaking around like two young lovers," Rish said, looking at me strangely.

As he echoed the words I had uttered to my son, I felt like someone squeezed my heart. I pressed my lips together, determined to stave off any tears.

But I did not fool him. His face an unreadable mask, he approached me. "Tell me what you want, my lady."

"What I want?" I asked, swallowing my tears. "I want to wake up in your arms," I said as a throbbing pain lodged in my chest.

His breath came out as a gasp. "I want that too, Meera. Is that why you asked me to come here tonight? Did you expect us to share your bed, though nothing binds us together?" Rish asked while his eyes searched the depths of my heart.

I struggled with his question. Even our fleeting kisses felt like a betrayal. "I don't know," I said. While I yearned for his touch, I had learned to suppress my longings. But what about his needs?

Also, something did bind us together—our love. "I do love you," I said, fighting a sob that threatened to erupt. I had imagined finding a man to love would have been hard. Instead, being with him turned out to be nearly unattainable.

His eyes caressed my face tenderly. "I know," he whispered. "But that has never been enough. I crave more than you are willing to give."

His gaze dipped to my lips. "I am yours, heart and mind. But you have never been mine. If we are wed, then by the laws of this land, you can rightfully wake up next to me. Even the king cannot interfere in it. But, when I asked you to marry me, you refused." His actions revealed his affections, while my actions hid my love for him. I saw that now.

Also, I had not refused him yet. Had I hurt him by my lack of acceptance? "Rish—" I started, but he interrupted me.

"You have always done what is right, Meera. Except for that one fateful day when you saved my life. My marriage proposal did not feel right to you. I have come to accept that. But I am a man who has loved you for nearly three decades. I cannot kiss you for one night and then pretend you don't mean anything for a lifetime. I don't have that kind of strength anymore." Suddenly all the hurt and pain he carried were visible to me like scars on his body.

"Even a marriage would not solve everything, Rish. Do you expect to hold my hand while riding on a chariot? That is impossible. You know it as well as I do," I said as a fresh stab of pain erupted in my stomach.

"No, our relationship will remain shrouded in fog," he said patiently, like explaining things to a child. "But you are the mother of my son. Marrying you is the right thing to do." I was a widow of the king of Padi. I still could not imagine remarrying. Why did I allow these customs to chain me? If our actions did not hurt anyone else, it made little sense for me to cling to them.

He paused, and his eyes beseeched me. "Marriage will give me some rights in this relationship. As a queen and mother of kings, all the prerogative in this relation rests with you. I am the man who cannot even address his son by his name. I have no power in this connection. Prince Atul pointed out the hidden passage to me, expecting me to open the trapdoor and emerge in your room." His eyes narrowed in pain, and he cast them down while pushing the hair away from his face. When he raised his sight back to me, my heart nearly stopped at his misery. "That is not how it works between us. It is one thing to knock on your door and be turned away. However, I cannot just surface in your room through a tunnel without your explicit consent. I am bound by my vows to you and the king of Malla. There are rules I cannot break."

"You do have the power to hurt me," I mumbled, struggling with the pain pooling in my chest, causing me difficulties breathing.

"Do you believe I would do anything that hurts you or Prince Atul?" he whispered.

"No," I shook my head. I had never worried about him hurting me. I trusted him completely. As that thought emerged, I realized my mistake.

"Rish, any bond with you feels like a betrayal of my wedding vows to my husband," I said, trying to explain my feelings.

He nodded in understanding. "I know I cannot compete with the king of Padi for your affections."

"You have it wrong. Loving you came easily. I married him for duty. Caring about him took time. It happened only because of his generosity and fidelity. That is why I am filled with guilt. Because my feelings for you always outshone my feelings for him."

He gazed at me with his eyes wide open.

I continued. "But my guilt and doubts for a man who has been dead for seventeen years are hurting the man I have loved for nearly three decades." I made a decision then, one that followed my heart rather than tradition.

I stepped closer to him, imagining my life as his wife. "When we are married, are you planning to emerge in my room unannounced?"

He looked like a treasure seeker led to a door hiding what he sought. "If I say I was not planning on leaving your side, will that make it more or less likely for you to marry me?"

I smiled. "How does one get married in a *Gandharva* wedding ceremony?"

His breathing came rapidly. "The couple declare their love for each other."

"I have loved you since I gave you my ring," I said, my eyes fixed on his.

His lips parted slightly. "I love you more now than I ever have."

"What comes next?"

"They consent to marry."

I moved close to him and could feel his warm breath on my face. "I want to be your wife if you will still have me," I said breathlessly.

He cupped my face, and it felt like the most natural act. "Meera, nothing could be more agreeable to me."

"Is that it? Are we married now?"

Rish smiled mischievously. "There is one last step." He pulled me against him tightly, his hands clasped in the small of my back, my body molding against his. He then bent to kiss me slowly, as if he wanted to extend this moment forever. I weaved my fingers through his hair and savored his smell and taste. I could live in his arms for the rest of my life.

Trailing kisses on my neck and throat with a warmth that melted my skin, he said, "We consummate our relationship."

The next morning, I sighed contently, snuggling closer to Rish, letting him warm my body. As my eyes opened, I felt Rish's intent gaze on my face. When our eyes met, he smiled tenderly like a cloud parting to reveal the sun. Butterflies fluttered in my stomach, and an unsuppressed smile broke out on my face. He looked almost like the boy I had fallen in love with as if the past years had melted away overnight. It had been a long time since I had awakened to another's touch. This is how it should have been for us all these years, sharing a bed and our bodies, rising together at dawn.

"Seventeen years wasted. We will never get those years back, Rish," I said about our lost years.

His fingers combed my hair. "Those years are not returning. But they were not completely hopeless. Every morning, I would wake up and think about you. I had hope, however feeble." He paused and leaned in to kiss me with a dreamy look in his eyes. "I will spend the rest of my life filling our remaining days with bliss."

I felt a wave of satisfaction wash over me at the love written upon his face.

"What new right does this marriage bestow upon you?" I teased him, my finger tracing the contours of his ribs.

"I need only one. To stay with you forever," Rish answered, drawing me against him.

My spine tingled on hearing him. *Together forever.* "Is that a promise?"

"One I intend to keep with my last breath," he answered.

EPILOGUE – A YEAR LATER

MEERA

A breeze blew in from the Pune Sea, offering some relief from the sweltering heat. I stood in front of my mother's portrait, gazing at her luxurious curls.

"You did not inherit her looks, but you have inherited her voice," my uncle said from a bench behind me.

I turned toward him and smiled. He pointed to the spot next to him. "It is hard for me to gaze up at you. Come and sit next to me," he said. I dropped down beside him. "Some of our life lights flicker and splutter for a long time. Her light burned for a brief time, but she brought warmth to all who knew her."

I remembered her singing while holding my brother on her lap, her voice wrapping us in comfort. My father had never recovered from her death and instead went through the remainder of his life as if he had lost a part of him.

"Thank you for sharing your childhood stories with me, Uncle Kandan," I said. It had brought me closer to my mother and her land.

"Meera, what better way to spend time in my old age than reminiscing about the days gone past? The young people around me have no patience for my tales," he said with a grin.

"My lady," Rish called as he stood at the entrance to the room.

"Come in and see my mother."

He strolled in and viewed the picture. "She left a lot of her on King Jay," he said.

"My brother inherited her curls," I agreed.

"My sister was never one to follow the rules, especially when it concerned two hearts meant to be together," my uncle muttered, his eyes darting between Rish and me.

A swell of panic pounded me, and my old fears returned. It had been a mistake for us to travel together if we were so transparent. I sensed Rish registered at least some of my uncle's words. His back stiffened initially, and then he turned toward us. His eyes swept my face affectionately, and I drew strength from my husband. The panic subsided, and heat coated my face instead. Rish had insisted on accompanying me on this journey and would not accept no for an answer. One of the only privileges he'd fought for in our marriage. Not that I resisted him for long. I yearned for his company too.

"Don't look so stricken, my child," my uncle continued gently. "You keep your feelings well guarded. So does he, for the most part. In a couple of unguarded moments, I have seen the way he regards you like you are the most precious woman in the whole universe."

Rish regarded me that way now, and my heart raced.

"Is it time?" I asked him to get away from here.

Rish nodded.

"We are riding to the forest where my parents met, Uncle Kandan," I said.

"Your mother followed her heart," Uncle Kandan replied meaningfully.

After bidding him farewell, Rish and I strolled through the palace halls to the stables. The sea glistened beyond the sandy shores and a few coconut trees swayed in the wind. We rode our horses into the forest, the trees sheltering us from the sun. At a small clearing, we halted, and I scanned my surroundings. A gentle wind rustled the leaves, bringing the fragrance of hundreds of flowers with it. I inhaled deeply. "This is where he fell in love with her," I said of my parents.

"With my father as their witness," Rish said, and I turned to him in surprise. I had forgotten his father's role in their tale. Veera Vindhya had accompanied my father on his maiden journey to Saral. He had also returned with the newly-crowned king to rescue my mother. Veera had known all their secrets.

"My father married my mother in a *Gandharva* ceremony in this forest," I said. *Like us.*

"Your father was a wise man," Rish answered as he dismounted. His fingers did not linger on my waist as he helped me down, though I wished for it. Slowly we strolled into the forest, letting the sounds of nature fill our silence.

"What would *your* father say if he knew his grandson was heir to the throne?" I asked.

"He had dedicated his life to serving his king and kingdom. I can only imagine him being pleased that his grandson would serve his kingdom in a way only a king can—as Malla's foremost guardian."

"Atul has a son now. We will have to stop in Akash to see the baby." This was not my first grandchild, but his birth gave me a strange pleasure as this was our first grandchild together.

"I had never imagined this possibility," Rish whispered with awe in his voice. Our eyes met, and his affection for me spread to all corners of my body. "Of a life together with you."

A lump formed in my throat. Our relationship still had to be cloaked in secrecy, but even with these hurdles, life with him brought immense satisfaction.

He continued to gaze at me like I held the answers to his questions. I remembered my uncle's words earlier.

"You should not be staring at me like that," I chided him, unable to contain the joy spreading in my heart.

He grinned at me. "Like what?" he teased, knowing full well what I meant. He knew me better than I did.

"Like I am the center of your world."

"You are my sun, my lady." His eyes caressed my face, and I imagined his calloused palm touching it instead.

"It is not good to stare at the sun," I said in mock anger.

He laughed. "I have never been good at concealing my feelings. I am overflowing with love, and it is hard to hide the spills."

A wide smile broke out on my face.

We halted near a large tree whose trunk spread four feet wide. With no words exchanged, we found a secluded spot behind it. A leaf had lodged in his hair, and I stepped closer to pluck it out. He scanned the area around us like a predator on a hunt. After making sure of our solitude, he placed his hand on the small of my back and pulled me into him. My soft body yielded against his firm frame. He kissed my brow as the sound of insects swept around us. I leaned my head on his shoulder.

His eyes twinkled wickedly. "If there is no hurry, we can stay in Akash for a few weeks. The hidden tunnel to your room came in handy last time."

It had felt magical to cuddle to sleep with his arms around me and to wake up to his sprawled body next to me. I remembered my uncle's words to me. My mother did leave some of her wild side in me. It took many years and a persistent love to bring it out. "I have a surprise for you in Padi," I said, the warmth pooling in my chest. Atul knew about our wedding and had suggested I move to new quarters with a secret passage for his father to visit me. I had agreed to his suggestion. Atul set the plan in motion with his brother Amar, even if Atul had kept him in the dark about the reason. Rish and I could not have everything others took for granted in their marriage. We accepted that. But we could have something.

"Surprise?"

"A path for you to find your way home to me," I murmured against his chest.

"Meera," Rish whispered my name with intense passion as he bent down to kiss me.

He was my home, wherever we went.

* * *

JAY

Aranya skimmed the letter from our daughter Heera. "Both our grandsons are doing well." She looked up at me. "I miss them. The baby has not been crowned as king yet. I wonder if she mentions anything about it." Then she continued to peruse the message. Amar would rule the kingdom as regent till his nephew came of age. "Here it is. When the baby turns one, Kayal is planning the coronation. Heera wants us to come for the ceremony and stay with them for a few months."

"One year? What is the hurry? They should wait for him to turn five," I said, holding my hand out.

She placed the letter in it. "One or five, what difference does it make? Amar and Kayal are going to govern till he turns sixteen. If it is held sooner, I can go visit them."

I raised my head from the scroll and smiled at my wife. "You can visit your daughters anytime. You don't need to wait for your grandson's coronation. Meera is traveling through Saral currently. They have to wait for her to return to Padi anyway."

She grinned at me. "I am still the queen of this land. I cannot abandon you or Malla just to visit them."

Then she eyed the door. "Hope all is going well with the delivery. I should go check on them."

As she finished uttering these words, Sudha appeared at our threshold, exhausted and exalted. "It is a boy," she said. My great-nephew and Prince Atul's first child had arrived.

I beckoned a servant. "Ring bells all over Akash to usher in his arrival," I ordered. Then, I walked with my wives to meet our future king's son.

I found Ratnavali fussing over the new mother. My young bride had become close to Atul's wives, girls closer to her age. As someone raised to be a princess, she was helping them learn the court manners and intricacies.

Atul stood next to the sleeping child with a look of wonder on his face.

"Have you held him yet?" asked Aranya as she approached them.

"Held him?" Atul shook his head nervously. "He is so small."

Aranya picked up the baby and brought him to me. As I gazed at his full head of hair, he yawned with his small fists clenched near his ears and puckered his tiny mouth. "Seems like yesterday when I held your father in my palms," I said softly to the newborn before glancing at my nephew. "Come here and hold your son," I ordered.

The young father came forward hesitantly. I helped Atul position his hands, and Aranya placed the baby in his palms. Tears welling in his eyes, Atul beamed at his son while the bells tolled in the city, welcoming our newest prince.

* * *

"My Majesty," Kapil called from the threshold.

Still smiling, I approached him.

"One of the ships we sent to Kashgar has returned to a port on Nira Sea." Sweat glistened on his forehead, and he blinked a few times. My usually confident guard seemed to struggle with an odd emotion. A strange foreboding took hold in my stomach as I viewed him, and my smile vanished.

"A few days ago, our men spotted the ship several yards from the shore, floating on the waves. By nightfall, no one had left the boat. So the next day, a few of our men rowed to it." He gazed at me with wide eyes. "They found the vessel filled with men from Magadha. All slain. Corpses in various stages of decay. Except for one boy."

I imagined bodies piled on top of each other. Anger coursed my veins. "How did the ship travel from Kashgar with lifeless men?"

"Something dark at work here," Kapil whispered. Then, he handed me a scroll. "The lone survivor handed this to our men. He is in shock and frightened. He kept saying the men were killed by magic."

"Magic?" Magic only existed in old legends.

I read the letter with ever-growing dread. "Return Prince Aggabodhi or Magadha will suffer a similar fate." It was addressed to me and signed by Ori.

"Who is Ori?"

"He claims to be a seer, my Majesty."

"Seer? Why is he threatening me? Ori murdered my men, Kapil. This is an act of war."

Atul joined us with a puzzled look. "Uncle Jay, what is the matter?"

I gazed at my nephew. "A new threat looms on the horizon," I said and passed the scroll to him. He and Aggabodhi had become good friends in the last year.

"Return Aggabodhi? We cannot do that, Uncle. I pledged to support him."

"Then we need a plan to infiltrate Kashgar, ambush our enemy and return the rightful ruler to the throne."

"Allow me the honor to lead this quest, King Jay," Prince Atul requested. I nodded. He was ready for his own adventures.

ALSO BY ANNA BUSHI

I am working on two series next. Sign-up for my Newsletter at AnnaBushi.com to get my new release notifications.

One is a historical romance series with a draft title of Svayamvara weddings. Svayamvara is an ancient Indian tradition that allowed the bride to choose her groom. The tales will portray a princess whose heart is in conflict, set in medieval India with a healthy serving of royal political intrigue. Who will she garland and choose for her husband?

The other series is a historical fantasy spin-off with Prince Atul and Prince Aggabodhi - Draft series title Prophesied Prince

"Queen she will be one day, her name will be celebrated, near and far. Her son will rule the three kingdoms and beyond."

ACKNOWLEDGMENTS

When Meera lost her husband in book two, I knew how I wanted her tale to end. But widows rarely remarried in medieval India. To stay true to the historical customs and practices, I made Meera and Rish wed in secrecy. It also happened after Meera's childbearing years, another nod to the life of women in medieval times. While with a few words, I can give my characters a happy ending, even today, many women face hurdles to getting an education, choosing their partners, or leading the life they want. Through the medieval lens, I hope my book allows us to glimpse the plight of such women and do our part to break the barriers.

Prince Atul and Prince Aggabodhi's story does not end here. Their adventures require a historical fantasy spin-off series because Kashgar is a magical realm.

Special thanks to Priya Nagarajan and Mary Logue for reading the chapters as I wrote them and providing me invaluable feedback.

Thanks to Christa Yelich-Koth for helping refine this book and the beautiful cover art. Thanks to Toni Cox for proofreading and R.J. Van Wart for the map.

Sarah Faxon, Theresa Halvorsen, Dennis Crosby, and others in my local writing community, thanks for your support as I journey on this mostly solitary pursuit.

On the personal side, thanks to my parents for nurturing my love of reading and supplying me with used books to read. I thank my husband for the many ways he helps me pursue this dream and my daughters for inspiring me with their kindness and compassion. To my brother, cousins, and extended family, thanks for believing in me.

Many friends supported my journey, and I would like to thank them all. I am thinking of Melina, Devina, Devi, Uma, Smita, Ranga, Neesa, Sushma, Kalpana, Seetha, Priya, Nanda, Brian, JR Jean, Meera, and many others. Your support has meant a lot to me.

To all my dear readers, I thank you from the bottom of my heart.

ABOUT THE AUTHOR

The stories I read growing up inspired me to write. I am interested in medieval India and within that society, examining the human heart in conflict. I like to place my female characters in difficult situations and see how they learn to survive with no actual power. And watch my male characters fall in love while fighting for king and land. I love exploring the struggle between love and duty.

I live in California with my family. Visit me at annabushi.com to learn about upcoming books.

Reviews are priceless to authors like me. Your reviews would introduce my book to other readers. Thank you for supporting me by posting a review.

facebook.com/annabushibook
instagram.com/anna.bushi.book
amazon.com/author/annabushi